D0707227

Incident at Lukla

The Actors

Dr. Elsie Hornbein – *CIA's senior officer on Tibetan issues working under diplomatic cover as the U.S. Cultural Attaché in New Delhi. Buddhist scholar, anthropologist and Kama Sutra student.*

Dr. Harry Ripp – *CIA's Singapore station head, a specialist on Maoist guerrillas and operating under non-official cover as an economic journalist and lecturer on 'microlending'.*

"Chandra" – *Nom de guerre of Maoist guerrilla commander, labor leader, Central Committee member, yoga aspirant, now seeking retirement.*

Annie Wendover – *Home-schooled former Peace Corps Volunteer from Wyoming working temporarily in Nepal as a trekking guide and contemplating her future.*

Pemba Lodrup – *Former novice monk at Tengboche monastery. Sherpa mountaineering guide, airport constable, potato farmer.*

Thondup Gaomei – *Arms trader, Colonel in China's Border Command in charge of the Nepal sector. Famous mountaineer and son of a Tibetan martyr.*

Gyalpo Rinpoche – *Abbot of Tengboche Monastery.*

General Tu – *Head of China's Border Command and dealer in exotic commodities.*

Dipankara Macleod – *Academic dropout, gay anthropologist, salon host, scholar of erotic metaphysics.*

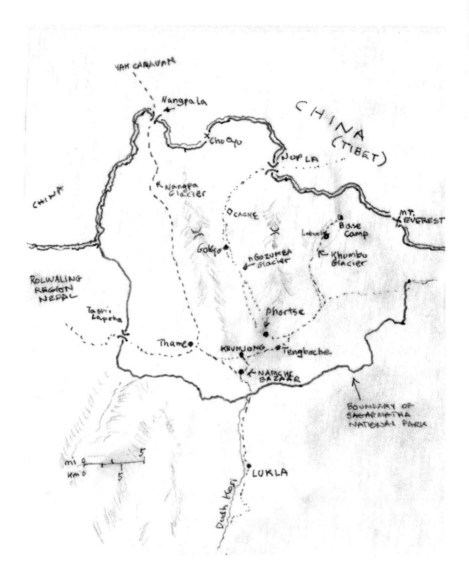

Wurlitzer's Sketch Map

INCIDENT at
LUKLA

A Novel by
DAVID PADWA

A partial version of this title was printed as a limited edition in Kathmandu, Nepal in 2012 by Vajra Publications. The first complete edition of this book was published by Hapax Press in 2013 and printed in the United States of America.

INCIDENT AT LUKLA

Copyright © 2012, 2013 by David Padwa

All rights reserved.

ISBN 978-9937-506-94-6 (Nepal)

ISBN 978-0-9895908-0-8 (USA)

No part of this book may be reproduced or transmitted in any form or by any means whatsoever without express written permission from the author, except in the case of brief quotations embodied in critical articles and reviews.

Subject classification categories

1. Political espionage – China – Fiction

2. Mountaineering adventure– Himalayas – Fiction

3. Buddhist culture – Tibet – Fiction

Incident at Lukla is a work of fiction. All situations and dialogue and all characters are products of the author's imagination and are not to be construed as depicting actual events and any resemblance to persons living or dead is entirely coincidental.

Text design by Image Ratio. Typeface: Adobe Caslon

For information on this title contact the publisher: incident@hapax.org

HAPAX PRESS, P.O. Box 1988, Santa Fe, NM 87504

für Bettina

George W., Sir:

This turn has become the way: wait when acting; add one further turn. Hidden by time there lives this extra-advantage, coiled and elegant. Our choices now disguise, wait for what the world wants — old courtesy, new strategy. We follow by going ahead of what we know is coming.

By hand — *Thomas Jefferson*

EVERYTHING AFFECTS EVERYTHING

Three teen-aged novices from the Sherpa monastery of Thubten Choling were returning from errands at the market-town of Junbesi. They were carrying boxes of glass chimneys for the monastery's kerosene lamps, and it being the first warm day at winter's end they perspired from hilarity on the steep trail. One of them had taken a small orchid from a tree branch and had it behind his ear, mimicking a lewd secular entertainment as they howled with laughter, a sound mixed with forest birdsongs.

Nearby, as they approached a little tea house, they paused to watch a swift rivulet turn a prayer-wheel in a roofed box. They counted one hundred and eight rotations. The mud walled tea house, a clay two-hole stove at the entrance, sat at the crook of a switchback in a steep-sided forest ablaze with rhododendrons. The maroon robed teen-agers chose to spend their rupee allowance on fried potatoes with chilies. Having the place to themselves they spooned slices in the hot sauce and laughed when, without any warning, a home-made grenade was hurled in through a window at the rear. The explosion did deadly work, killing two of the novices, blinding and scarring the third. The aged proprietor who had been cutting fire-wood a furlong away, was uninjured. All the glass lamp-chimneys were destroyed.

Some people said they were poorly behaved, publicly indifferent to the endless hardship that oppressed working people around them endured; as if there wasn't a revolution going on in Nepal, and people giving their lives. Was this how clergy conducted themselves? Didn't they know what had happened to monasteries in Tibet in Mao's time? Sour voices said monks lived on the generosity of others, did nothing in return, and were tolerated only on the sufferance of the Party.

At the bar of the Bangkok Intercontinental two American intelligence professionals were analyzing the meaning of this event and speculating about

1

its consequences. The woman is solid looking with a sturdy frame, somewhere in her fifties, confident in her manner. He is slightly older, faintly Slavic looking, a salesman who has learned to listen carefully. It is very late and they've been sipping rum tonics for hours. But their body language has a touch of formality. They had been talking mostly about terrorism and Buddhism. They were also attempting to know more of one another.

Deep in her cups she was explaining that an ancient teaching called 'interdependent co-origination' described how humans were created by sex, to suffer birth and death, and to be bound into the world of causality. She scribed a wide circle in the air with her right arm. We were tied to a wheel of existence, because of sex. It didn't matter that she was childless. She had been born. Taking human existence. Because of sex somewhere in the past.

He agreed, there was no telling where it would lead, and ordered another round, their last. "Where would we be without sex?" he asked, rhetorically. "It may turn your wheel of time but tell that to the monks who got killed. And their families. Terror. Can't blame it on sex."

"I'm not too sure. We just can't see the wheel turn," she drawled after a hiccup. "We're like insects. The Lamas say that deaths and births occur by events whose deep origins remain unknown. Everything gets connected in a web, going to infinity in all directions through time. Remote lives totally changed because those monks died. Everything that is, is because other things are. Everything affects everything. There are no unsupported thoughts." She said it affirmatively, pretending to bang a desk, and swallowed what remained of her drink. "They were born and they died. Feel compassion. What else?"

"You're basically saying it's biological. A tool serving nature's reproduction of itself. It really is uncanny. Sex, I mean."

"Darwinian. Everything's impermanent, in a flux, conditioned on something else," she slurred her words. "This knowledge, difficult for ordinary minds, like ours. Too hard to slow the passage of mental time, enough to see into the outer reaches of causality itself. You'll see, that grenade attack on the monks will spin a web of fate for all time. Missing horse shoe nails really cause kingdoms to fall. Think about it. What should we do? Who benefits from that little terrorism? Anyone on earth? Why should we be interested in small-time evil?"

She let the question hang in the air. They were drunk. Bar Buddhism. And the bar was shutting down. The weekend Southeast Asia Review meeting was over. They had flights out in the morning. As they rose he nodded in contemplative agreement. "Good thing we're too old," he said as they walked half steadily to the lift. They swayed and grinned at one another, sensing an invisible joke. That seemed to be the joke.

"Good night, Elsie," he said as she exited on the 9th floor. We follow by going ahead of what we know is coming, he remembered.

"Good night Ripp. Nice seeing you," he was on 14.

Months passed. Harry Ripp, the Singapore station-chief, was surprised at how often he thought about her. Even the night before, while making perfunctory love to his new Malaysian girlfriend. So he felt a touch of happiness when Elsie phoned from the Embassy in New Delhi. Strictly business. There were three matters. Could he clear his calendar for a couple of days, she asked.

"The Indians are pressing for a meeting and they want you there. The Deputy Home Secretary and a Lt. General Vidya Kumar – their new counter-intelligence *primo* – want to discuss the guerrilla situation in Nepal. There's been a strategic shift in the Cabinet's thinking and they want to touch base with us before they fly off to Washington."

Singapore offered daily non-stops to New Delhi and they made a date in the following week, blocking out two days for meetings at the Embassy That disposed of, Elsie came to her second matter, the Maoists and the Buddhists. Despite the grenade incident one of her informants thought there was some sort of back and forth going on – improbable as it seemed – between the Nepalese Maoist guerrillas and the Tibetan Government-in-Exile in India. A meeting of some kind was being discussed. Had he heard anything about this?

"Well, it's far out" Ripp said, "it'll freak the Chinese, but I hadn't heard of it. One of the Nepalese zone-commanders on the Central Committee, *nom de guerre* "Chandra", visits the Buddhist monasteries in the Sherpa regions. He might have something when I get to him in a couple of weeks. But that's small change. What's the third item?"

"A potential diplomatic bombshell if we finally figure out who's moving weapons from China to the Nepalese guerrillas. And who's funding it? Well, Berrigan called me this morning from Langley. Remember General Tu?"

"Chinese Border Command. Top unofficial connection to the Maoists."

"Berrigan says they've connected him to a Chinese Colonel in Lhasa named Thondup Gaomei. Ever heard of him?"

"Yeah, runs security on the Nepal border. Smuggling too. What's the connection to General Tu?"

"That's what I want to know. Anyway, see you when you get here next week. It's been months. Got to go. Keep cheerful."

She sounded upbeat and in a rush as he tried to visualize her. The last time he saw her was at a principals' meeting in Bangkok, when she got metaphysical at a bar on a Sunday night. An off day and the meeting group scattered around the large kidney-shaped pool at the hotel. Elsie half-reclining on a lounge chair ostensibly reading a book behind large dark sunglasses, as large as his own. Their angle was slightly off but Ripp couldn't stop thinking she was looking at him. She filled her one piece swimsuit, perhaps a size too small, and was glistening with perspiration. There was meat on her, he thought, unlike his wiry Singaporean beauties. All those years of looking at one another, devoid of action.

Ripp had an erection that night thinking of her, and he eased to sleep fantasizing about her cleavages. Her plummy voice on the phone line had produced a subtle sensation in his groin. An erotic mental picture of her in an excited state, of her pink freckled torso heaving, accomplished its evolutionary trick and the result amused him as it came and went. There had to be a master switch hidden in the brain somewhere, he thought, made by the root program. Still, the plumbing wasn't so bad for a man in his early sixties in bed by himself. She had to be near his age. He wondered and hoped she might be capable of desirous arousal. By him.

The luring images of Elsie strengthened an attraction that had floated into awareness recently. Ever since the *cordyceps* matter she had started making appearances in his night thoughts. He was pleased at the thought of seeing her again, even if only on company business. Who knew who she's on the hook with? Yet what if it clicked? To run something together.

Possibly, for the first time after nearly twenty-five years working in the same trade for the same employer, they might be doing an operation together. Probably the last before retirement. It would be a good chance to explore things, to test the chemistry. They had always liked one another professionally but had never been close. Just formal meetings of one kind or another. She might contemplate the retirement angle just like him, since they both faced it at year's end. Back to the States with a nice pension after twenty-five years of tenured service in Asia with the Agency. Amazing. They started in the same intake, the same cadet class and were at the Farm together. As a grand career finale, a joint operation promised to look like a priapic affair.

Elsie

She was glad it was the end of the week. The day-to-day bureaucratic life was getting to her and she disliked her weight and facial wrinkles and sagging skin and mousey hair turning grey. Childless, unmated, it was time for a new direction in life. Finish the year, and back to the States with pension and health benefits. Going home. The end of all these years living in India, determined not to work at the old business any longer.

Elsie Hornbein held CIA's unofficial Tibet portfolio. She was the final authority at the American Embassy in New Delhi, where all things Tibetan were examined. No thing that touched on Tibet failed to cross her desk. As long as anyone could remember, even after the Nixon trip, Tibet watching was always conducted from New Delhi and not from Beijing. No tidbit of gossip was too small. They knew it in Washington, they knew it in New Delhi, they even knew it in Beijing. Anything or anyone that was colored by Tibet belonged to Dr. Hornbein. Over thirty years of Tibet specialization for a girl from Virginia. She was no longer sure how it had happened. It just did.

She inherited the tired and dispirited old networks and learned where the actual bodies were buried. These days State Department had little interest in Tibetans, officially just another Chinese minority like the Mongols, like the Manchu. Like the Sioux or the Comanche not that long ago. Kennedy's Ambassador Galbraith definitely didn't like them. These days less troublesome than Uighurs or Kurds. Elsie had the portfolio though there was less worth watching as the years passed. The position wouldn't have a successor.

Birding and gardening wouldn't be bad, she thought. And a good library nearby. Finish this year and just loaf. Pick up water colors again. The family trust had come to an end, and she had the big house and the acreage. There had never been the right man to stimulate the desire for family life, not even the brief marriage when she was in graduate school. Marvelous male friends and quite a few lovers perhaps, but not family material. But it was nice to be held frequently, and there was less and less of that.

It would be so much simpler if Tibetan polyandry was adopted in America. A few guys, they don't really have to be genetic brothers, who just get along with one another, and they all share a single household and she rules while they take monthly turns to share her bed. What peace. What happiness there would be. But who knows? In this late-life stage the most interesting autumnal bird was Harry Ripp. She could sense him thinking about her. She thought about him too for that matter. They were once hard-bodied youths, trained enthusiastic acolytes of an idealistic Agency. Twenty four years later she thought they were becoming shriveled and pickled. She wondered if there were spores of tenderness remaining in the frozen vacuum of Agency practice? Had they wrecked their lives or not?

She did admire him. They were in the same intake, the cohort recruited following a change of administrations. European assignments were becoming passé and the central focus of United States foreign policy was shifting to Asia. Since the end of the Cold War trans-Atlantic postings were for tea-sippers. Ripp had Singapore and was productive as hell. An elderly James Bond. He could go from white shoe banking with the Chinese upper crust at the Jockey Club, to disappearing into the forests of *Bangla* for weeks at a time as he made rounds under cover, deciphering the weird worlds of jungle Leninism, guns-for-drugs narco-terrorism, or an emerging hookup between Marx and Mohammed. She found herself counting the days till he came to Delhi.

Cordyceps

At his desk in the luxurious Singapore station Ripp was shuffling through the low priority reports that came in overnight. A small item from Kathmandu carried a note that it was a copy of an original left on the desk of a trade ministry employee. The head-note showed the source document to be a series of tables on Nepal's external trade. The subsection in hand was devoted to Nepal's trade with China.

He was generally familiar with the gross numbers, but a table estimating the values of smuggled untaxed trade caught his eye. Like the French historians, lists fascinated him. From China: thermos flasks, blankets, shoes, crockery, flashlight batteries, feathers, antiques, velvet, cigarettes, *pashmina*, silk, animal skins, yak tails, yak hair, salt, borax, szaibelyite, – a mineral of some sort? – clay, and buttons.

And counter-trade from Nepal: agricultural tools, clothes, pharmaceuticals, copper-ware, gemstones, coffee, tea, barley, rice, flour, dry fruits, vegetable oils, *misri* – crystallized sugar lumps, as he recalled – tobacco, snuff, canned food, agricultural chemicals, *cordyceps sinensis*, dyes, spices, watches, shoes, kerosene, kitchen utensils. What was that item, *cordyceps sinensis*? He didn't have a clue. A Linnaean classification. Sounded like a plant.

But what attracted his interest were the numbers alongside. The civil-servant author of the paper estimated that nearly 5 tons of *cordyceps sinensis* failed to pay

Nepalese excise taxes and were exported to China without license — some to overseas markets down through Calcutta, some overland through Tibet. In the paper's bureaucratic hedging language the untaxed annual trade was estimated at 25 billion Nepalese rupees, or approximately 20 million dollars. Ripp sat up straight. No one had ever told him about something called *cordyceps sinensis*. 20 million smackers! Untaxed smuggled goods to China worth over $2000 a pound! There had to be networks. This warranted looking into. Importing 10,000 pounds of a smuggled commodity with a funny name was something the Chinese weren't exactly trying to stop. They were the importers. Who were the other players? What do they do with it?

He reached for the Agency's hot desk and got to Meryl, his favorite sleuth who came from Google before the public offering, and he asked for a core dump. A day later she called back.

"Fascinating" she related. "*Cordyceps sinensis*, the scientific name for an edible high-altitude mushroom with written references dating back over a thousand years. Sogdian accounting ledgers show that Tibetans traded it to Persia in exchange for lapis in the eighth century. The popular name in Sherpa-Tibetan is *yartsa gumba*. Chinese encyclopedias call it *dong chungcxiao*" — she sounded it out for him — "which translates as 'summer-plant, winter-worm', but most Chinese know it as the 'caterpillar fungus', *chungcxiao*."

"And why do they call it that?" she asked in the voice of an impatient schoolteacher, "because the parasitic fungus infects the caterpillar stage of a moth. This moth, *thidarodes hepialus*, lays eggs in the short grass yak pastures above tree line which hatch into caterpillars and they feed on the fungal mycelia in the soil. Once in the alimentary tract the fungus actually begins to digest the guts of the caterpillar until it finally takes over its entire body. After a while a small plant starts sprouting out of the caterpillar's head and keeps growing until the empty husk of what was once a caterpillar simply becomes the root of an individual mushroom."

"Weird. What's it good for?"

"Erectile dysfunction."

"Ah?"

"The market is almost entirely Chinese men on the mainland and overseas. You can probably find the stuff in Singapore pharmacies. It's called a 'tonic' but gets used mostly as a preparation against impotence; considered much better than ginseng, and a lot more expensive. Try some, and tell me if it works" she said coyly. As Ripp had never heard of it he told her he would, and in fact he was certain he would try it. The women in his floating world of Singapore sex had never said a word.

"Say more", he said.

"Like what?"

"Like production."

"Harvesting and trading *gumba* used to be a traditional source of income for people living in China's mountains but these days few people collect it so China imports as much as it can find, mostly from Nepal. There's a lot of variability in quantity because of weather and over-harvesting; and there's also an interesting Lotka-Volterra cycle at work in the biological dynamics. Does that interest you by any chance?" Ripp knew she was amusing herself.

"The stuff gets harvested over a week or so sometime in June and July. The collectors work on their knees searching for the little plants in the rough ground, as they're fairly small. They use a trowel or a little hoe to lift the plant together with its divot, and supposedly an experienced collector can find 20 or more mushrooms a day. Separating each plant from its soil gets done in the evenings, and afterwards they're all put out into the sun to dry. There's a lot of variability in price depending on whether the mushroom is whole. Just like pecans."

"Why's that?"

"Well, sympathetic magic. You see, the upright fruiting body of the fungus, the *stroma*, is particularly prized when intact. They even craft special ornamental boxes in which intact single dried *gumba* mushrooms are sold. They call it a treasure of the earth spirits. The reason being obvious – I'll send you a few images – the tiny mushroom looks almost exactly like an erect, slightly curved penis. Therefore, sympathetic magic. The *stroma* is delicate when fresh but becomes almost wooden when fully dried which is why careful handling brings a premium. They claim drying just concentrates whatever does the work, the potency remaining stable. It's probably a vasodilator of some sort because even small broken pieces are sold for good value."

"Marketing?"

"Ah. After the *gumba* is cleaned, dried and weighed locally it gets priced in the Fall, which is when it's traded. During the 'cultural revolution' private collecting in China was punished and attempts to socialize *gumba* collection in the name of the people didn't get very far. Add urbanization to that and the whole skill of domestic collecting got lost for generations so China started importing the stuff as soon as they could afford it. A domestic market of half a billion horny men can't be under-estimated. What's that old Victorian saw – if every Chinaman wore his shirt one inch longer then the cotton mills of Manchester would run forever."

"Distribution?"

"A lot moves through India to Calcutta, for Chinese coastal destinations, but because it's collected in the mountains maybe half goes directly into China overland through a few high passes between Bhutan on the east and Ladakh on the west. Some *gumba* gets smuggled out of Nepal by road. Hidden in door panels on the one highway to Tibet, just like Mexican dope runners. The Chinese are happy to let the stuff come in. In eastern Nepal the harvest goes into Tibet by the local pre-industrial transport system, yak caravans over the Nangpa-La in the Khumbu. I wouldn't be surprised if your General Tu had his hand in it."

"Tu's an arms dealer, what ties him to the *gumba* trade?"

"We're just guessing. He's at the hub of these weird syndicates. Exotic animals, pearls, traditional Chinese medicines, that kind of thing. In the case of *gumba*, once across the border the stuff reaches the main wholesale market for medicinal plants in Chengdu, from where it is distributed throughout the mainland, and overseas. Five tons would be a fortune. Last known prices were north of $5 a gram. A "dose" would range between 3 and 9 grams. That would make an ounce around $150. Come to think of it, I'm not sure if that's the broken penis price or the intact price. I'll look into it. If you happen to remember, tell me what they sell it for in the Singapore pharmacies. Mind, they'll tell you to use it daily because it's supposedly cumulative, so it can be an expensive habit."

"Especially if it doesn't work" he said.

"What's your angle with this stuff" she asked. "Planning an April Fool's joke?"

"I don't know what it is, but I smell something. Keep beating the bushes for me. It's interesting news if General Tu is involved. Anyway, I've got to go to New Delhi for a few days and put my head together with Hornbein. I've asked Bob Wurlitzer in Kathmandu to dig around as well."

Wurlitzer called two days later. It was just before ten at night. Ripp was in bed, reading.

"Am I calling too late?"

"No, what's up?"

"I have something for you. I thought you'd like to know."

"Go on."

"I asked around town about this mushroom thing and one of my sources with a family member on the Central Committee, came back to me. It turns out that three years ago the Maoist leadership started taxing *gumba* collectors. Then two years ago they started taxing wholesalers at the central markets. Last year the cadres raised the tax on individual collectors to equal half the harvest. And for this year, guess what?"

Ripp replied dryly. "Completely socialize the harvest, prohibit private collecting, and deal with Chinese buyers directly themselves. They'll call it an emergency measure. For the revolution. You know, *vinceremos*."

"Hats off, Ripp. You're ahead of me."

"It's the logical next step. The collectors get collectivized. Orwellian Marxism. But what's the big deal?"

"Well, here's why I'm calling. My informant says that the Standing Committee picked the guy responsible for moving most of this year's *gumba* harvest from eastern Nepal into Tibet."

"Who?"

"The guerrilla honcho you're planning to make a pass at. Zone Commander Chandra."

Ripp

Ripp had long decided to avoid any responsibility for bringing a child into a mad overpopulated world, and therefore granted himself a worry-free social life as an English speaking professional with a rewarding expatriate career in a modern tropical island state. Splendid housing, beautiful women, fine wines and art, a small ketch at the yacht club, good health, interesting work.

He had a dual assignment. The first was to gather confidential information from agent and sub-agent networks at executive levels in the financial services industries of Southeast Asia. In this role he enjoyed a solid cover identity, having worked for years as a professional consultant in the Asian banking sector, who published a private newsletter and served on the adjunct faculty at the University of Singapore. He was thought of as the op-ed writer, the lecturer, consultant to banks and accounting firms, the serious journalist who covered economic stories in the lesser world of non-governmental organizations and micro-finance.

The second assignment was more challenging, devoted to monitoring left-wing guerrilla movements. Naxalites, Maoists, and the Assam Liberation Front were the main actors in an arc of low-level asymmetric warfare through eastern India, lowland Nepal, lower Bhutan, and parts of Bangladesh. As an authority on micro-lending Ripp traveled innocently under cover by bus through the small towns and cities of the Himalayan piedmont, ostensibly conducting research on some topic, offering seminars at local colleges, preaching the gospel of micro-finance, writing articles, doing interviews, and improving credit analysis techniques for local bank managers.

Beneath this robust cover Ripp ran networks of agents recruited personally over the years, and through them penetrated the Maoist and Naxalite guerrilla movements, charted their organizational structures, identified guerrilla commanders, disrupted weapon supply chains, and learned of contacts with revolutionaries in other countries, as in Latin America. He produced detailed and quality intelligence product on transnational guerrilla movements along India's porous border with Nepal. While America wasn't a player in that corner of Asia – the long-standing operation was of secondary interest to Washington – the Indians were fanatically hungry for Ripp's yield and happy to trade their own exceptional intelligence product from Iran. They wanted to give him a medal and promised to hold it until he retired.

Perhaps the meeting in New Delhi was about this, he thought. Nepal jurisdictions overlapped. Elsie had the Buddhist mountain regions along the border with China and Ripp had the lowlands along the border with India; and Wurlitzer had Kathmandu, a valley as if an island. If it had to do with Maoist revolutionaries, Ripp got it; if it had to do with Buddhists it was Elsie's. That's what made the rumor of a Maoist – Buddhist meeting so interesting. It would bring them together operationally.

Berrigan, his boss, called. "About this Chandra guy. You say he's smuggling weird aphrodisiacs to China. Who's the buyer? What's the *quid pro quo*? Don't tell me they hand over cash on delivery."

"I don't have a clue," said Ripp.

"You're the head-hunter. Make a successful pass at him and the Indians will owe us big time."

"Lots of casting, few bone-fish."

"There's another thing about that guy. State's asking about the likelihood of a porters strike up in the Everest region. Your Zone Commander's the man in charge up there, isn't he? "

"A strike could wreck mountain tourism, and start a hard-currency crisis for whatever's left of the economy. Trekking and climbing groups provide most foreign exchange."

"When do you see him?"

"Next week."

"Find out why they've started killing monks."

"It doesn't really make sense. The Maoists usually leave Buddhist regions alone. Labor unrest in the Khumbu is very mild, Sherpas don't abuse porters."

They went on for a while and then Berrigan summed it up.

"White House thinks the only way to make sense of the Nepal situation is to know the stakes for the neighbors, India and China. The Chinese are sympathetic to the revolutionaries but they're certain the Nepalese government is so rotten that it'll collapse on its own without any need for interference. What do you think?"

"They're right. It's Mao's main strategy: protracted asymmetric warfare. Shopkeepers, bureaucrats, absentee landlords, the army just can't withstand protracted low-level guerrilla campaigns. Staying power's the whole thing. The length of the war more dangerous than armed incidents. As the theory says, the bombs are more symbolic than instrumental."

The Great Perfection

Elsie sat in her corner Embassy office and finished clearing a backlog of paperwork and memorandum writing. The door of her small suite bore the plaque: 'Attaché for Cultural Affairs', carrying the diplomatic rank of First Secretary. Elsie was one of two deputy station chiefs of Central Intelligence Agency in New Delhi, the one with the Tibet portfolio. As she prepared to end the day the late afternoon sun streamed into the room through the branches of the large *ficus* and she made herself calm, stopping the mental chatter in her head. Across the slant of a late afternoon beam of light the dancing motes were signaling something she couldn't see, and she let herself pass into what her Tibetans called the *dZog-Chen* mind, the Great Perfection mind.

Nowadays there were books, in English no less, on *dZog-Chen*. It boggled her imagination. Years earlier, in graduate school when she began language and textual studies with high Buddhist Lamas, the very phrase *dZog-Chen* was uttered in an actual whisper. A secret teaching. Innermost holy of holies. No pearls before any swine hereabout. No adulteration by popularizers, twisters, seducers, or worse. Say those two Tibetan words out loud and wash your mouth with soap. Profaning great teaching by speaking of it.

She had gotten used to it. She called herself an ex-Buddhist, as if such a thing existed. She could see the evolution. The cultural concern for social justice became too difficult in execution, and the energy got redirected inward where it turns into a narcissistic preoccupation with personal spiritual development. Me, me, me. My enlightenment. *Pratyeka*, private, rhinoceros-Buddhahood. What was to be done? The modern master Dudjom once said kindly to his disciples "don't go around claiming to be some successful *dZog-Chen* meditator when in fact you are nothing but farting louts, stinking of alcohol and rank with lust!"

She let go of it and returned to her slow deep breathing, dropping boundaries, vanishing to herself and becoming like old smoke in space. After a while the sun went behind a wall of the chancery and the crossing of a shadow brought her consciousness back to the room where the first thing she noticed was the hum, the *om* of air conditioning. She tidied up her desk.

It was an enjoyable and sociable job, she had to admit, but it definitely put on weight. It was the food and she determined to make her diet more *sattvic*, purer, and to play more tennis. The Queen's Club pro remarked how scarce she had been on the courts. It was just too hot. Monsoon and soaked courts wouldn't help either. Chair-bound office life in the Embassy had taken a small toll. Despite a daily fitness workout her weight was more than she liked, although Indian men loved her that way. It was all the butter. In any case she would be in Washington over the summer. There eat fresh salads and lobster, lose five pounds and practice portion control. And though there was the gym at headquarters she planned to find a fitness club near a rental in Georgetown. Time to shape up. There was a whole life ahead. She had a *yoga* mat for stretching and did twenty quiet minutes of slow deep breathing using the prolongation method taught to her by a Nun in Pangboche.

She did think she was keeping it together. Sit-ups, push-ups, dumbbells, elastic bands, and if one thought about it, the world itself was a gym. Push hard against a wall, use the stairs, stuff like that. And right food. That was the weak spot. Less butter with the rice and vegetables. Fewer cashews. Menopause hadn't been all that bad, ages ago. Hot flashes were weirdly attenuated in India's intense heat. Just step outside. It was osteoporosis to which she planned to pay attention. More physical activity for the body; the 'temple' as her *yoga* teachers called it. She liked working out with the marines in the embassy gym despite their penchant for forming a small knot around her when she stepped on the scale. The several lovers she had taken in India were dotty about bodywork and *ayurvedic* healing. They turned her on to Indian clubs, the kind you swing. And that *Kama Sutra* madness! There had been a civil servant, a business executive, a *yoga* teacher, a painter, a Maharaja, a member of Parliament, and the last, two years ago, a management consultant who had a heart attack during sex. They all knew what they liked though, the kind of intimate detail never described on the obligatory security tell-alls concerning sexual partners. And now a long dry patch. It would impress the lie-detector when asked, as usual, who she had been fucking.

She was about to switch off the light when Ripp called and went to business.

"Remember that kidnapped Peace Corps kid, over a year ago, Annie something, what was her name?"

"Wendover."

"She around? In country, or has she gone home?"

"I saw her about six months ago at an Embassy Thanksgiving party. She finished her enlistment but I think she's still in Nepal. She told someone she was going mountain climbing in the Rolwaling region. Why?"

"I want to talk with her. I just remembered that she spent a whole day with our Zone Commander Chandra. I'd like her impressions before I see the guy."

"I'll see if we can locate her."

Ripp understood how his youthful infatuation with Elsie had faded over the years, but that now something had been re-awakened. After that drunken night of philosophy. A possible end to being mere colleagues? They had both always played it by the book. All sexual liaisons were to be reported, it was understood. It was the sovereign's right to know. Period.

He reckoned that she too had probably spent over half her career in Asia and couldn't have much in the way of social networks back in the States. The big change was coming for both of them at year end. He was unattached, in good health, had a splendid pension, more than adequate private savings accumulated over the years, plus the soon to be developed waterfront lot in the Virgin Islands which he used as his legal American residence.

He once asked about her retirement plans, the time they had been together at Jogbani, in the fiasco of waiting for the kidnapped Peace Corps Volunteer. Elsie had shrugged her shoulders and turned her palms to the sky. It reawakened something. Now she came in his thoughts a lot. That very day, listening to an audiobook on his iPod while on the elliptical trainer, an entire chapter read by a skilled narrator entered a tunnel in his brain and disappeared from meaning. He didn't hear a word in the stream of sound as he thought about her and wondered if a life together could possibly work – and then with a start realized he had to scroll back to where his brain did the trick of semantically vanishing the words in his ear.

A Pharmacy

Ripp went to the Chinese market off Mountbatten Road and found a likely looking pharmacy. The stooped and elderly man at the counter put on his glasses as Ripp entered and asked to purchase some *chungcxlao*.

"*Chungcxiao?*" said the proprietor.

They went back and forth a few times as Ripp tried slightly different pronunciations and inflections. Finally, he pointed at his groin.

"Ah, hah, *chungcxiao*," said the man. "Capsules?"

Ripp nodded and the man opened a jar of capsules and asked how many were wanted. Ripp examined one of the transparent items. It was filled with a tan powder.

"*Chungcxiao?*" asked Ripp, pointing. The proprietor assured him, yes, that was it, and named the price. Ripp asked for twenty. Worth a try he thought. It was put in an envelope and after he paid and was about to leave he turned to the proprietor and held up the packet.

"Powder, yes?" The man nodded. "Pieces?" asked Ripp.

"Ah, ah, hah," said the man, beckoning him back, saying, "powdah, verr chip. This bettah," and he pulled out a shallow drawer filled with Petri dishes containing what appeared to be small dried mushroom fragments on cotton bedding. "Smahl pieces" he said.

Ripp held his thumb and forefinger an inch or more apart.

"Ah, ah, ah, hah," said the man and took out another drawer. "Indayvidyual."

In this drawer the Petri dishes had beds of yellow silk and each contained a single intact slim mushroom more or less in the shape of an erect penis. Each bore a slight variation but the resemblance was unmistakable, almost uncanny. Each had a tiny price tag attached. The man opened one of the dishes and handed him the sample. Nearly weightless, the dried mushroom was stiff and leathery, almost like a wood twig. In this desiccated condition there was little likelihood of breakage.

The man showed him the price. It was up there with caviar and saffron. Ripp shook his head. The proprietor smiled with enthusiasm and turned to the glass cabinet behind him to extract the *piece de resistance*. It was in a carved miniature cask of cinnabar. When opened it revealed a mimicry, perfect down to the details, of the erect male organ, almost two inches long. It was held against a cushion of crimson velvet by a single yellow thread. The man held it out for inspection, urging Ripp to touch it. Hard.

Careers

After Bryn Mawr College Elsie took a graduation holiday to India where a series of unplanned encounters led her to an impoverished Tibetan refugee colony where she experienced a spiritual rebirth of a kind. Not being cut out for a settled life she stayed on in India past her visa expiration, practiced meditation with various Lamas and commenced studying Tibetan Buddhism. Encouraged by her teachers, she returned to America deciding to master the language and the religion on an academic track, which ultimately led to a PhD in Tibetan studies from the University of California, Berkeley. Her doctoral dissertation was a translation and commentary to a 13th century meditation manual called "The Unchanging Aspect of Mind." It took her four years, two of which were spent among Tibetan Lamas living in exile in India. During the time in California she had been married and divorced from a young lawyer in San Francisco. Then, after receiving her doctorate, she obtained a job as Assistant Professor at the University of Maryland, in the Department of Asian Studies. There was always a bit of sex now and again, but no one of particular interest. It didn't bother her.

A person from the Agency noted a poster announcing her public talk and slide show on a weekday evening at the university auditorium. "The Political Plight of the Tibetan People." A staffer on the China desk with responsibility for monitoring matters relating to China's ethnic minorities attended her talk. He sat in the second row to get a good look at her and when the introducer recited Elsie's *curriculum vita* he took a card from his pocket and made notes. Three days later she received a call from a woman with a pleasant voice who inquired if she might be interested in a new line of employment. Congress had recently appropriated funds for staff expansion.

Ripp and Elsie were in the same cadet class at CIA where, by hazard of the draw, they hardly ever shared small group exercises, and following graduation they were each assigned to Asia from different directions. Ripp started in Hong Kong and Elsie's first posting was Second Secretary at the Embassy in Kathmandu, the position now held by Wurlitzer. In those years escapees from Tibet were still treated decently by the Nepalese Government. But during her tenure she saw how Chinese diplomats, using bribes and threats, had caused Nepal's government to adopt an extremely harsh policy toward refugees. This originated entirely from Beijing's incredibly fantastic fear of the psychological power of the Dalai Lama. A psychological power which seemed not very well understood by war strategists.

After her first multi-year posting in Nepal, and a six-month intensive course in spoken Mandarin, she was posted as Vice-Consul in Chengdu, an important city in Szechwan at the foot of the great Tibetan plateau, a splendid place from which to run agents, and where she had an affair with the British Consul. Then a year in Beijing so that she had a feel for China's capitol and finally assigned the Tibet watching portfolio in New Delhi. The permanent mission.

While she and Ripp saw one another at area conferences, class re-unions, and tangential operational meetings, circumstances never permitted much more than eye-contacts which germinated into thoughts for a few days, and which then vanished into the folds of eclipsed memories. They had a drink together once or twice when they were both in Washington but they were each dating someone. There was a bus ride in Malaysia involving thigh pressing which they both remembered. And getting smashed together in Bangkok months ago. Now Ripp was to arrive shortly and they had made a date for dinner. She expected things might open up a little. It had been in the background for so many years. They both knew it.

Harald Ripp, né Ribczak, was Chicago born of immigrant parents who had escaped Nazis and Soviets, and brought up to love America from an early age. A boy with a Jesuit education and the Latin prize at St. Ignatius. An accounting major, *cum laude*, from Roosevelt College where he captained the water polo team. Dated Catholic girls who prized their virginity and hired to an auditing firm for four years. Bored but ambitious. The guys at the Polish-American Club told him he should get an MBA.

At Northwestern toward the end of his first year a visiting CIA recruiter made a pitch. Ripp put in the paperwork, interviewed, polygraphed, waited, and accepted. The vetting would take six months. They told him to finish his degree and to report for work the following summer. So began a twenty-five career where he opted for the Clandestine Service, where he and a Ms. Elsie Hornbein were in the same junior officer class.

After the standard tradecraft curriculum at the Farm they sent him to learn Cantonese at the Naval Languages School in Monterey, California. Finally, he was a licensed Case Officer and his first station was Hong Kong, under non-official cover as a PhD candidate in the economics department of the university. His job was to identify potential agents and informants in Chinese banking and finance sectors.

Within a year he had a good address book and was moved to a small office overlooking Hong Kong harbor, working as a private financial consultant. As a young Case Officer he ran agents in the Bank of China and the trading houses. After a third year they moved him to Dacca, Bangladesh, where a friendly grant was made available for him to be a visiting lecturer at Bangla University on the subject of financial reporting standards. He studied Bengali and over five years made a name for himself at the Dacca station for sweaty and soiled visits to small towns and rural villages in the interior.

They brought him back to headquarters for a year. He studied the Chinese Army's ownership of private businesses; the counterfeit CDs of pirated media, the factories for falsely branded consumer items, the feather industry, and army unit ownership of real-estate and hotels at tourist locations. Putting generals into business, that was the ticket of new diplomacy. It worked in China. Cuba would likely follow that template too.

Finally, higher powers decided to make a long-term base for him in Singapore, a financial center and aviation hub. They bought a house and redid the interior. Within a year he had a decent client list of banks and trading houses who thought he was onto something with his research on banking opportunity in the overlooked market of micro-finance. The solidity of his cover earned him a stream of consulting income. He enjoyed his work and he was easily spoiled by the glamor. Singapore was sexually sophisticated, offering tasteful and friendly intimate *affaires*, typically lasting some months, each duly reported; mostly fine-boned Chinese women of independent means whose unique views on the meaning of life never failed to make him think. And now he thought of life with Elsie.

It was said of Ripp that Singapore was the most enviable station in the system, as any income from his banking cover above the Agency salary level and pension contribution could be put into five star expenses and lavish capital improvements to the station, and there was fine inventory of high Asian art without any pleading with the Government Accounting Office.

He worked as a singleton out of a fashionable, architecturally sleek, narrow house overlooking part of the harbor, with high tech security and a communications vault in the basement and a triplex apartment above a staff area. The cover was real, the PhD was real, the consulting work was real, his journalism by-lines were real, his course at the Lee School of Business was real, his reputation as a champion of small loans was real. He had earned the useful protection of an intelligence cover; he was frequently around and usually ignored. The mega-deal investment bankers owned the spotlight and micro-lending didn't generate big fees, though he thought the consulting income was quite nice. It was a very sophisticated operation.

Seasonally on the road, and away from Singapore for weeks at a time, he shuttled from five star suites at top hotels in Tokyo to battling mosquitoes in sooty candle-lit huts near the Bangladesh frontier with India. He liked the back-country and once undertook special forces jungle-training in Panama. The forest zone was the venue of his job, and long accustomed to the heat, he was comfortable in it. He intended to retire in the tropics.

A Hah!

One day a call came on his secure line. It was Berrigan, his boss, Assistant to the Deputy Director for Operations.

"Glad I got you Ripp. Analysis Directorate concluded same as you. The case is strong that the key back-channel guy handling weapons to the Maoists is General Tu. Our bios have him as an old timer in the Chinese Army, not very ideological, but very rich. Did a few years in Tibet before his current job. Now the top man in the Border Forces, headquartered in Beijing but moves around down on the old Nan Yang borders, Burma, Cambodia, Vietnam. He lives extremely well and our Defense Attaché got interested in learning how he got so rich. Turns out, he's the hub of a couple of old boy syndicates and cuts himself and confederates in on all sorts of cross border trade. The guy owns a snake farm in Burma, and over the years he's accumulated a fleet of personal trucks. Cast-off military vehicles that somehow come into his ownership. They're never inspected, but it's apparently innocent stuff. We've got some watchers among the drivers. No sign of drugs and obviously, nobody's running guns into China."

"What's innocent stuff?" asked Ripp.

"I got a list – nutmeg, hand worked gold jewelry, spices, horn products, mahogany, rough cut rubies, herbs, caged birds, minerals, stuff like that. Just a no-tariff tax-free business on the Burma frontier for a fleet of trucks owned by a company no one has heard of. General Tu is the big man."

"What ties him to the Maoist guerrillas?"

"Stay with me. So far so good. Now, here's what interests us. We had an older voice signature we couldn't identify but three days ago our big ears and some slick software caught the voice on a sat-phone talking to a Burmese warlord about an arms shipment to none other than your Zone Commander. There's more than enough to give us positive ID it's General Tu's voice. We thought of you right away. Okay. So far it confirms what you were saying. But here's what's new, and why I'm calling. They're talking about getting paid for the weapons, and Tu makes a passing remark that one of his officers, in Tibet he says, is going to get payment in October from Zone Commander Chandra. In Tibet."

"Chandra and a Chinese army guy in Tibet?" Ripp asked. He saw Elsie enter the picture.

"That's what he said."

"A payment in Tibet for Burmese weapons?" There was a long pause. "Holy shit, I got it! Bingo! It's the *cordyceps*! He's paying for them with this weird mushroom from the border regions. The Maoists are trading herbal erectile enhancers for weapons!"

Preparing an Interview

Ripp stepped out of the shower, dried before the long mirror and turned profile in a routine search for signs of a belly and passed inspection. A lifetime of morning sit-ups and fitness awareness had done its work and he was pleased that at his age he was still proportioned like a sprinter. Singapore beauties liked to be seen with him. Grey headed, of medium height, tan enough to pass for a lighter hued native if he wore certain clothes and was in motion. It was the face that he didn't like. Too round, nose too big, eyebrows too bushy, and the blue eyes too deep in their sockets. An acceptable jaw-line. He brushed remaining hairs, incongruously long and silky, from an islet of tuft in front, straight back over a bald patch. He planned to buzz cut it next year, grow a trim beard and wear a Chicago Cubs baseball cap.

He wondered if Elsie would like the Caribbean. He tried to imagine her on a boat. There was something about her eyes. They sometimes held a gaze disconcertingly longer than normal. Tiny signifying pauses when she looked right into him. Especially when answering questions leading to ambiguity. There was something physical beneath it. He imagined them sailing the Drake Passage together on a small boat. They'd be pensioned out in less than a year.

Retirement daydreams were interrupted by Meryl's call from Langley to offer a potted bio on Chandra.

"This is mostly from a file passed on from Indian counter-intelligence; press clippings, police notes, and hearsay from people in Kathmandu. Here we go. Born in Bhutan, moved to Calcutta. Early career as a street fighter, then labor organizer, then to Nepal in Communist Party work. Elected to the Politburo. One of the first Party members to argue that parliamentary tactics were doomed; and one of the most influential voices for choosing the path of armed struggle, even if it meant civil war. Served in parliament a few months just before armed revolution against the monarchy began. Few westerners have ever encountered him."

She paused for a sip of water and continued. "Once the insurrection started he more or less vanished from view but the Indians ID'd him as Zone 3 Commander. He surfaced a year or more back when he financed a big arms acquisition with the proceeds of a bank robbery. Kidnapped an American Peace Corps volunteer to cover his getaway. I guess you know that story."

"You bet. The Vice-President went into overdrive. Annie Wendover, the hostage who spent a day with our Zone Commander. I was trying to locate her but she's not available. Hornbein says she's climbing in the big hills and my meeting is next week."

"Let me ask something. Why on earth do you think this Chandra can be bought with an annuity?"

"He's tired, he's broke, and he's becoming very philosophical."

"So?"

"That's low hanging fruit."

"How do you know this?"

"Experience. And there are informants."

The Zone Commander visits the Lama

In the pre-monsoon Spring season the guerrilla Commander of Zone 3 and his body guards passed unnoticed among international mountain trekkers and climbers, mixed in among porter castes and native Sherpas. His destination, Tengboche Monastery, at nearly 13,000 feet, was set magnificently on a gentle ridge surrounded on all sides by the world's highest peaks. Sitting in his reception room Gyalpo Rinpoche, the Abbot and the most influential spiritual personage among the Sherpa people was expecting his political visitor. The high Lama's relationship with the Maoist soldier went back some years and had gone far beyond political matters. What once commenced as a courtesy visit had ripened into something confessional, allowing Chandra to bare his heart.

They sat together on a carpeted platform as attendants swarmed around them serving tea and biscuits. Gyalpo Rinpoche was nearly seven feet tall with a chest and stomach to match. A grey pigtail grew from the back of an otherwise nearly bald head. He rocked slowly and fingered his beads as he listened to his dark-skinned visitor, a slight and small man with grizzled white hair on head and face who spoke in soft but agitated tones.

"I'm sick of it," said Chandra. "If it goes on this way it will become like Pol Pot in Cambodia. It's insane. The responsibility for this kind of thing – on top of that gruesome bus incident – is becoming more than I can bear. I've told the Central Committee that I'm stepping down. Officially I'm here to express the sympathy of the Party. The person who threw the grenade hasn't been found and so far has escaped punishment."

"Is that person against religion?" asked the Lama.

"It's probably some young idiot taught by the Party to despise religion. Why should a desire for inner peace be compared to opium anyway?"

"Where will you go?" asked the Lama.

"South. Kerala perhaps. Never been down there. Full of fellow atheistic Hindus, contemplative Marxists who drink coffee. Another destiny."

The Rinpoche said nothing and they sat in silence for a time. The Sherpa regions along the frontier with Tibetan China stood outside the revolutionary turbulence of the lowlands. There were no landless agricultural laborers at the edge of starvation in the Khumbu region and the Maoist leadership had a clear–eyed view of Buddhism's popularity in the western world, which was another reason to avoid adverse propaganda about killings in Sherpa lands.

An attendant brought in yak meat *momos* and more tea. The conversation turned to mundane matters. They talked about the gradual disappearance of the dwarf rhododendrons, the new Swiss hydro station, the timing of potato plantings, wooden bridges in need of repair, staffing at the clinic at Kunde, illegal cutting of wood, the advent of tourist flights around Mt. Everest, and finally came to the porter's strike.

"It may not be necessary," said Chandra, "and if it happens it would only be for a day or two in the Fall. We have to carry the entire *gumba* crop up to Khumjung village. That Chinese Colonel is coming with a yak caravan to pick it up. They've already rented some fallow potato fields for a loading area."

They sat in silence again. Attendants lit incense and brushed away ash with a feather. Chanting began in another quarter of the monastery. A kerosene lamp was brought in.

"What will become of the boy who was blinded?" Chandra asked, his voice despondent.

"He'll be taken care of. He'll find useful work" the Lama replied matter-of-factly.

"Tell me one thing. How is Buddhist emptiness different from nihilism with nice paint? Why do you say it's the womb of compassion?"

"It just is. It works. There isn't nice paint in emptiness. There is no nihilism in emptiness. There is only compassion."

"I'm suffering, I tell you. There is more killing than I ever intended. This soldier's mind is suffering and this war is long."

"Start with kindness," said the Lama. "Stop the killing."

"Killing is part of humanity. Tibetans didn't kill and they got the Chinese occupation. Sri Lankan and Burmese Buddhists are killing people right now. Japanese Buddhists killed millions. And you eat the meat of dead yaks."

"The Buddha didn't live in a cold climate," said the Lama.

"Well, you'll be glad," Chandra said with finality as he stood up. "We're starting a ceasefire next week."

Attendants helped Gyalpo Rinpoche to his feet and he clasped his visitor's hands and held them warmly. Chandra turned to leave.

"*Namaste,*" he said. "I'll see you in the Fall, when the caravan comes to Khumjung."

Targets

Gossip is a known social vice of Sherpa clergy, and having heard every word, the monastery's attendant monks spread the minor pieces of news. A trader's caravan of yaks from Tibet would be crossing the Nangpa-la into the Khumbu in the Fall. Elsie's listener network had it quickly, and Ripp was electrified when he heard the news. It meant he and Elsie had a chance to have a close-up look at Colonel Thondup Gaomei. If a Chinese military officer was found spying in Nepal it would be explosive. The man would be compromised. In Ripp's experience such things always presented recruitment possibilities. He watched a fantasy pass through his mind. In some future he had recruited both the Chinese Colonel and the Zone Commander in a bravura career finale. In any case, the Colonel was Chandra's counter-party on the weapons deal brokered by General Tu. Ripp could smell a political intelligence coup on the horizon. State Department might even go along with a good plan.

Elsie's Lhasa network identified the officer by his name and rank. She called Ripp to fill him in.

"The Joint Biography Unit tracked his career and they had a file on him ever since he graduated Staff College. He's half-Tibetan, half-Han, a protégé of our man General Tu, and certainly the officer Tu mentioned on that phone call. Combat decorated; a bloody bastard it seems. Commanded mountain troops in Xinjiang. At the moment he runs the intelligence branch of the border forces on the Nepal frontier sector from his field base near Tingri. Seems he climbed Everest in his teens. There's other stuff, domestic affairs."

"Plenty to talk about" he said. "I'll see you next week. I suspect we might finally get to do something together."

There it was, as plain as day. Glorious! He was elated. They'd plan it in New Delhi and get to know one another at a new level. What was her basic temperament? Hourly he thought of her. Should he woo her? Could he? What a good opportunity to talk with her about retirement! To place his palms on her skin one day. Elsie.

At the Embassy in New Delhi Elsie darkened the office desk lamp and the harsh fluorescent lights in the corridor and walked to her Range Rover in the Embassy yard for the short drive home. The place was on a broad leafy street behind a high wall. Her *chowkidar*, Ravi, was on duty, but dozing as usual. The lights of the car brought him to attention and he swung open the gate to the small Indo-Palladian house with a giant mango tree in the forecourt.

She planned to look her best. Lose a pound or two. How would it be to work with him? Would he be bossy, hogging the action? No, she thought, he was a sly one, a foxy character, which always attracted her. He'd give her all the slack she wanted, the dog.

A Green Light

Days before catching his flight to New Delhi Ripp was on the line with Berrigan going over the case that the Zone Commander was approachable. His instincts for human psychology had yielded many recruitment gems for the Agency and they knew they had to try the idea. It started months earlier with a casual comment to Berrigan.

"I think we might be able to roll him. I can smell it," said Ripp. "I'm on to him. He's not even Nepalese you know, his legal nationality is Bhutanese. And he's a pale echo of the burning idealist he was nearly forty years ago. The fire's going out. Hornbein says Indian counter-intelligence thinks there's a split going on, the guys who wanted to turn up the heat were being held back by Chandra and others concerned with civilian casualties. Wurlitzer says there's talk of the Central Committee reassigning him later in the year. Head of the International Bureau in the political department someone said. That's new. That's what I'm hearing. They say he's getting soft."

"And what makes you think so?"

"He even told the Tengboche Abbot he was going to step down. Not exactly a young guy, and full of regrets. I'm telling you, shit, he's ripe to do a one-eighty and take a quiet exit. The Indians would treat him decently. We'll negotiate it. Make him a contract consultant. Good for his ego. He doesn't have a family which makes things easier. Put a woman in his life and the past is over."

"So?"

"I've been tracking the guy for years. My nose tells me that he just wants to retire, to get out of the game, to get out of it all. He just needs a way to do it. He's paid his dues. Now he's in crisis. He promised the Lamas there would never be bombings in the Khumbu and then somebody tossed a grenade into a tea house and killed two monks. I think he's just waiting for the right opportunity as he thinks it through."

"And you're going to create the opportunity he's been dreaming of?"

"Something like that. It's worth a shot. Let's invest."

"Does he stay in place?"

"Not a chance. He wants out but he's a hero of the revolution and they don't want him to disappear, which is what I think he wants. Another life."

"Like what?"

"Smell the flowers for the years left. We hear he's not well, maybe hepatitis. And it's not about money either. All he wants is to sit in the sun and read books on *yoga* philosophy. Those are his own words by the way. The Indians would even help him if he was willing to dance with them. Very low key."

"How you going to hook him?"

"I'm going to buy his memoirs."

"That's a lot of overhead for such slim pickings."

"Look, if we play him right," he then spoke slowly for emphasis, "we might bust security at the next RIM meeting. And that's a sensational roundup, don't you think?"

Berrigan paused. "Well, *that* could be a prize. It's your call. And, here's a pat on the back for you. The Indian Prime Minister has a state visit to Washington in October and we're warming to the Indians big-time. They want support dealing with the embarrassing fact that a low grade communist guerrilla war's going on in nearly half their country, the part that tourists don't visit, which has been going on for near forty years. It's like a running sore that won't heal. And now comes your favorite irritating subject: what happens if *jihadi* extremists from India's 150 million Muslims decide to join arms with the Maoists? The right people are beginning to ask. That's why the Director says to tell you he appreciates the good work you've been doing. It's paying real dividends with the Indian Government. Anyway, I'm out your way. I might come see you guys in Delhi."

New Delhi

Fatigued by the late flight, Ripp lay on the hotel's king-sized bed with a whiskey from the mini-bar and found himself once again imagining the possibility of having sex with Elsie. Opportunities had always been few and far between. Just years of ambiguous flirting along the outer edges of sexual magnetism. If they did it they'd be obliged to report it. Undignified for people of their station, but that was the rule. The thought of reporting to a staff bureaucrat, even if it had an MD in psychiatry, about a liaison with Elsie, was just absurd. Bloody voyeurs. But he wasn't in a rush. A slow tempo was the best strategy.

She reminded him of Meryl Streep. He could almost visualize her half-clothed. A generous bosom in a lacy white brassier which he unclasps in his mind and touches the swell of her erectile nipples and looks down her solid torso, his thumb hooking and pulling gently on an elastic waistband to show a belly and a light brown mound of curls where her legs begin. He could feel his own erectile tissues swell in synchrony.

So he rose and showered and though it was the hottest time of year he turned the air-conditioner off and opened the windows to their limit. The dry night heat flowed in. Monsoon rains would come soon and cool things. Maoist cadres would hold classes, do desk work, make banners, repair equipment. Following an interview with the Zone Commander Ripp would return to Washington for an American Summer. It had been a useful season. Networks of informants, built carefully over the years, had provided high-value information which unraveled several intelligence puzzles. Ripp now had tables of organization for a number of regional branches of Naxalite movements in North-East India and the adjacent areas of Nepal, with names to put in boxes. The names in the boxes would probably become names in prison cells. Which was usually better than being names on graves. It was very usable material and the Indians were happy to trade their Iran jewels for it. They even wanted to give him a decoration.

He dried himself, found a music channel on the bedside speaker offering evening ragas, dimmed the lights and laid himself out on the taut sheet. His mind defaulted to Elsie again but this time he fell to sleep.

And several hundred yards away, in the distinguished leafy neighborhood near the hotel, a naked Elsie was stretched out at home preparing for sleep. Her belly and her thoughts were damp under the ceiling fan's hypnotic rotation. Relaxed after an evening out she was thinking of him again. Of how she wanted to look when she met him at the Embassy gate in the morning. Her hair. They certainly went back a long time. She liked his steadiness and how the semi-academic cover suited him. Now an old goat with an interesting face. Well, not a goat. In fact not bad looking if you looked carefully. Like a fit Anthony Hopkins she thought, he must be over sixty. No kids and never married, he once said. Single in Singapore. Hard to compete against a harem of fashionable young Asian women, so he's probably spoiled, but still. She recalled being in an elevator with him and holding an eye contact and giggling. More than flirtatious. That stuff was still sexy. She imagined being held by him as she began fading to sleep.

The Embassy

At the Embassy gate Elsie and Ripp exchanged cheek-kisses and he signed in with the Marine guard who handed over a laminated identification badge.

"Good trip?" she asked.

"Got in near midnight. Dust storms. The airport's impossible, way too many people."

"You're at the Oberoi? You could've stayed at my place. There's a guest cottage and a staff."

"Another time perhaps?" – the eyes touched for an instant – "No, I'm embedded with laundry, the fitness, sauna, chambermaids, breakfast in bed with the Herald Tribune and the BBC."

"Like at home?"

"Come and see for yourself."

She gave him an arch look with the hint of a smile and brought him to a side door in the Chancery where she had booked the corner conference room down the corridor from her office. She was hosting two days of separate meetings; the deputy-level Indian visitors today, preliminary operations approval tomorrow. But her thoughts strayed to dinner with Ripp that evening. They were about to work together. She would give him her beautiful idea for the operation tonight.

"There will be five of us today," she said. "Six if the Ambassador wants to look in. He gets embarrassed when operations are discussed so he'll probably split."

"Who's the fifth?"

"Wurlitzer, down from Kathmandu, came on his own."

"Enterprising. What about tomorrow?"

"Berrigan's decided to join us. Coming tomorrow with one of his body guys. Wants to look us in the eye and join the plotting."

"Oh, he'll go for it."

She tilted the blinds to give the room a soft beige tone. An urn of tea sat on the sideboard, above which a large scale map of India was projected. Lt. General Kumar leaned back, expressionless. Lal Prakash, the Deputy Home Secretary used a laser pointer as he gave voice to the meeting in a delicious Anglo-Indian accent. He presented the heap of evidence which ultimately led to the Cabinet's recent decision to reframe the Maoist problem facing India.

"Look chaps, previously India believed that the Maoist revolution in Nepal was simply aimed at the monarchy, but Government has now concluded that the Maoist revolution is actually aimed at India, as the more important target beyond Nepal's monarchy. There's considerable collaboration and logistical support between India's Naxal guerrillas and Nepal's Maoists. Some of our people, and your people, suggest an *internationale* is at work. Foreign hands have been seen on a few occasions. Perhaps it was the latest form of the RIM." He looked at Ripp and there was a long pause to let the words hang in the air.

Lt. General Kumar spoke from his chair. "Government is in a quandary. By international law India is required to recognize the legal establishment of Nepal, a corrupt and mentally deranged family monarchy in control of an army officered by royal cousins. And India simply can not support the Maoist revolutionaries because the implications for India's own guerrilla situation are too disturbing. Government is very grateful for information received from the United States, which clearly has its own sources." Elsie touched Ripp's ankle with the tip of her foot.

The question of outside non-indigenous support of Maoist revolutionaries dominated the rest of the day. There were a series of examples. The shadowy Revolutionary International Movement, the RIM, seemed to be involved.

"Angolans and South Americans working as trainers with our home-grown Naxals," said Prakash. "Small-fry compared to foreign sovereigns. We've neutralized Pakistani support for left-revolutionaries, but the question of China's support for the Maoists, is of considerable interest."

Ripp avoided any mention of the *gumba*-for-arms trade.

After a leisurely lunch in the Embassy mess Elsie and Ripp thanked them for the briefing and they adjourned near three o'clock. Contact information was updated. Cut the Hydra's heads one at a time, offered Ripp, and don't be in too much of a rush. It's all about the gradual attrition of social networks. Patience. A generation or more. Elsie and Ripp suggested a list of people to call on when the visitors were in Washington. Real warmth in Indo-American relations was long overdue, they all agreed, and the American people were strongly in favor of such a friendship.

Bhoti Mahal's

The two of them had dinner at Bhoti Mahal's that evening. A rare time seriously alone. The loud *ghazal* trio masked eavesdropping but they naturally sat close at the semi-circular *banquette*, their faces barely a foot apart. Personal agendas were held in the background as they talked business over dinner and wine, examining joint undertakings. Ripp got right to it.

"Look, if we document the *gumba* for weapons trade this Fall it'll be diplomatically explosive. The Indians will accuse China of arming the Naxal guerrillas too since they're just overlapping trans-border networks. They'll go to the Security Council."

"Unless Washington keeps it quiet, of course. Are you planning to pitch the Zone Commander before he makes delivery?"

"Next week. They've told me to wear good shoes. Lots of walking before I get to him. How about the Colonel?"

"Would you like to try for two recruitments?" she asked. "I've got an idea. But let's hear you first."

"Okay. We set up video and audio in that Sherpa village, document the deal and expose the Chinese. Trading sex mushrooms for weapons is just too savory a story. A wild tale every news editor in the world will go for. A front-page lead for a slow weekend, a spicy tale that happens to be true. Reuters will syndicate it in a flash and the evidence and story would embarrass the Chinese military for years. A standing joke at diplomatic soirées. The Indians would make a noisy row. And, of course, the Colonel's career would be over, dead-ended at best, a court-martial probable, and if China really wants to make a case against corruption in the Border Forces maybe an execution. And the charge of self-dealing runs all the way back to Beijing. That's a plausible blackmail don't you think? All we're asking is that the guy talks to us once in a while. I've had worse levers to work with. Super if we hooked the both of them. One for the books. What's your idea?"

She suddenly nearly choked on a swallow of wine and had a coughing fit that combined with uncontrolled laughter at the same time. She had to stand and turn away from the table for a moment, before sitting down with eyes red from laughing. It took over a minute to restore her breath and she waved her palms up and down reassuringly, the hands saying wait, wait. She tried to calm herself but burst out laughing and coughing again, recycling the fits until they became milder and she was able to speak in a tight whisper. Tears ran down her cheeks. An alarmed looking waiter approached but she waved him away, dipped her napkin in a water glass and dabbed at the wine stains and she took a small sip of water. She turned to look at Ripp and as she started to speak a small burst of laughter seized her again. Finally she collared it back, swallowed the rest of the water and spoke in a choked voice.

"You've overlooked something."

"What?" Instinct told him a light was coming.

"Viagra," she said. There was a very long pause before he replied.

"You are a fucking genius."

"The hell with a stick. Let's put him in business with quality Indian counterfeits. Make him head of black-market distribution for a better product for the same market he now reaches. It's the carrot."

"We'd own him." He shook his head admiringly. "I'm losing it, I tell you. How did I miss it?"

"Plausible, you agree?"

"It's a beautiful wild idea. It'll be legend if it works." Spontaneously he turned to kiss her cheek, where the momentary touch of skin on his lips put a full stop to operational thoughts. Just the corner of her mouth.

They started a second bottle of wine as they examined the psychological details of their twin targets. Elsie would arrange the pills. The video set-up would be challenging, but they had funds and six months to prepare technicians and equipment. The specific overture to the Chinese Colonel would be important, but that was for Ripp, based on considerable first-hand experience.

Finally they settled their professional business, and after an awkward silence it was just the two of them, ready for the business of becoming personal. They ordered a ball of pistachio ice cream with two spoons and sat there smiling at one another, sharing the unarticulated joke.

"Have you tried the stuff?" she asked coyly.

"The *gumba*? A few pinches once after I heard about it. Couldn't tell anything. But don't need it yet, I just think of you and the *Kama Sutra*."

"Ha ha."

Then he said it, out of the blue. "I suppose we'd have to report it if we ever got intimate."

She shifted her gaze slowly from a napkin on the table to his eyes as she rotated her head slightly to look at him squarely. An amused expression came in slow motion across her face. "Well, that just wouldn't work, would it? Have you always reported everyone you've slept with?"

"Yup. Always. How about you?"

"Me too. Live by the book, die by the book. They know it all."

"It's insulting."

"The King's privilege. Like *droit de seigneur.*"

"Well, we're retiring soon, aren't we?"

"Seven months." She winked at him.

They sat mute in the rear of the taxi, in boozy post-prandial satisfaction as it moved smoothly down Aurangzeb Road. As they passed Windermere Gardens he took her hand, held it in the air like a boxer's, and gave it a collegial squeeze.

"We'll probably share a mustering out ceremony at headquarters. Did you know we get meritorious service medals? And by the way, if I'm not being too nosey, have you firmed up your retirement plans?" he asked, turning in the seat.

"Still vague. What about you?"

"I've got a waterfront lot in the Caribbean where I'm intending to build a house. Like to do some more sailing. Get to know Europe better. Never spent much time there."

"Alone?"

"Could I interest you?" There was a long pause.

"I'll take an option." She smiled appreciatively and scrunched up her eyes in a way that gave him hope.

The Oberoi doorman provided a snappy salute as Ripp stepped out of the car and turned to look at her. "See you tomorrow," she said. He blew an air kiss. She returned it.

Berrigan arrived the following day and they used the same conference room. He was professionally intrigued by the idea. The Zone Commander, the *cordyceps* cargo-master, was a recruitment target. Was Colonel Thondup Gaomei, the cargo consignee, also to be a recruitment target?

"Let me understand. You want approval, support, and funds to document the mushroom handover in order trap the guy in a sensational public embarrassment?"

"It's better than that," said Ripp, "we also keep him as agent in place."

"It's minor league blackmail, why should he go for it?"

"Because we also got the carrot. Elsie's brainstorm. Viagra. The guy's already wholesaling herbal sex medicines for General Tu's syndicates. We know he's in the business. Say we put him at the top of a Chinese distribution network for a modern pharmaceutical to the identical market. He'll make a fortune. If he goes for the deal, and we think he will, then we have a long term relationship. We got a carrot and we got a stick."

Berrigan took a moment to think about this as a pleased look crossed his face. "Are you guys shitting me? Elsie, I always knew you had a filthy mind. You know this takes the cake. Innovation. The President wants us to be creative, we'll give them creative. Done, I'll support it. You better have it detailed out before the operations board this summer. That's the real approval. What kind of budget do we need?"

Elsie took it to a close. "Not much. Just a few techies and fancy equipment. I'll get the Viagra from an old boyfriend. The family owns KKPharma. They manufacture generics all over Asia and Africa. And counterfeit branded products too. Copyright and trademark ignored. It's just chemistry, the molecule is identical to Pfizer's. We can have as much as we want. The family will think of it as market development. Make love not war."

The day ended. Ripp caught the late flight to Singapore. He had the picture. Make a pass at Chandra. Make a pass at the Colonel. Make a pass at Elsie.

Cease Fire

Zone Commander Chandra awoke in the middle of the night and looked at his glow-watch. 0215 hours. He had to urinate. Where was a toilet? For a moment he tried to recall where he was. He had been on the move so much recently and then he remembered; he was in the restful village of Aruna. The annoying sensation happened every night now and frequently twice a night. He shuffled barefooted to the latrine shack near the back of the hut and squatted, swaying, in half-sleep, waiting for the feeble urine stream to start. It felt blocked.

A small dog came by, curious, keeping a distance but looking at him closely. He hoped the flow would be prolonged so his bladder would actually empty. The stiffness of his joints was something he hid from others. There was a pain in his lower back if he leaned forward too far. Cataracts were forming in his left eye. And recently there was a dull throbbing hurt on his right side, just beneath his ribs where his liver would be. He felt old. Fatigue touched him every day.

Inchoate waves of guilt and anxiety followed his nightly bladder challenges which made it difficult to return to sleep. His mind turned in the darkness, restless and without hope. Questions, serious questions. Had he wasted his life? Because of a youthful dream? What had he accomplished in over thirty years of class struggle? Tens of thousands dead. Endless warfare. Warfare with the illusion one could actually know what victory could be like.

There were too many incidents. A month before Dadu's group near Salleri had set off a roadside bomb under a bus. They thought it was full of goons. 28 schoolchildren killed on an outing. A monstrous blunder. He made a rare public appearance, speaking to journalists he expressed personal apologies for the "grave mistake," and he issued a statement: "We offer serious self-criticism to the public for the civilian casualties." This was unprecedented and caused a stir in Kathmandu. Officially, over twelve thousand had been killed since armed struggle began. The real numbers were greater, he knew. And now this, two young monks, boys really, killed by a grenade near Thupten Choling. The search to find the perpetrator had been futile. How could he return to sleep?

He tried, unsuccessfully, to avoid thinking of comrades led to their doom while he remained alive and accomplished little more than harming innocent victims. The guilt was dark and fatigue was constant. And meanwhile, the monopolists of the world were ever more securely in control. The global capitalist system reached down to the smallest seed in the meanest farmer's furrow. What would it mean to overthrow the monarchy if the same forces remained at work? Human nature was too stubborn. Greed never ending. He saw it even among the most dedicated comrades. Human vanity would excuse any lie. How can a revolutionary communist leader ask such questions, he asked himself. He must be getting soft.

Why can't a man return to sleep? When he was younger he would fantasize sexual acts with the female comrades. It would usually lull him to sleep. The last time a woman had touched him was when his young Peace Corp hostage gave him a neck and shoulder massage and talked to him about America. It was almost impossible for him to imagine a sexual act. He was as celibate as an austere monk. It had once appealed to him as a principle. Now he was less sure. The Great Sage of the Himalayas performed years of austerities before abandoning them to gain realization of the middle path. Where was his own middle path?

He had asked the Central Committee to consider his relief at the end of the year. They felt it as well. His time was over. Everyone became sentimental when he first raised it, and they committed to managing the transition with dignity. He could have the foreign information bureau and be the party's liaison to the RIM. Until then the main thing was to get the *gumba* crop organized so he could hand it over to the yak traders in October and detail the weapons manifest with the Chinese Colonel. This success would match his audacious bank robbery for imaginative revolutionary action.

Before actually falling asleep again, he reviewed his plan to reach privately for the Dalai Lama's people in Dharamsala. He determined to compose a letter to his old friend Pasang Dorje which might then reach the Great Lama himself. He took this upon himself without special authorization. It was the only remaining act he could imagine. The revolution's symbolic reaching out toward Buddhist minorities might expiate many terrible events. It could be culturally significant. Every Hindu child knew that Lord Buddha was simply the ninth *avatar* of Vishnu. The revolution needed a symbolic gesture. A human face.

The remainder of the night passed somehow and Chandra rose from his string cot at first light. He parted the mosquito netting, patiently urinated again, had a stool, washed, cleaned his teeth with a *neem* twig, stretched, and performed a few self-invented calisthenics, the last of which involved leaning forward while standing with hands on knees and churning his abdominal muscles. He dressed, pulled the thin cotton curtain aside and looked into the empty village square. It would be buzzing in an hour. The fresh milk in pails, still warm from the cows, were being brought to the dairy stalls where the *lhassi* vendors were starting to heat their flattened pans. The imminent arrival of a foreign visitor called for his attention. Perhaps he could find something suitable when the journalist professor arrived. From Singapore. Preparing an article they said. *"Economic Issues in a Rural Guerrilla Zone."* Old comrades on the Central Committee considered it a propaganda opportunity and had recommended an interview. It was agreed to happen after the start of a unilateral countrywide cease fire.

What on earth could he have to say to an economist? He was a military man. Nevertheless, he informed the friends he would give Professor Ripp a full day.

The man wrote that he was working on a book and presently writing an article on the Maoist view of micro-credit and rural property rights, his academic subject. Chandra's view was short and simple. Following the monarchy's overthrow the government would nationalize all lending institutions and micro-credit would be a government function. All the rest was plumbing. In any case, it was not his area. Bank robberies were more of a specialty.

The 'red flag' village came to life. A wide trestle table beneath a thatch awning served as Chandra's office. An aide brought him morning tea. There were papers to approve. He had a meeting with three of his officers concerning the rudimentary curriculum for villagers of Marxist-Leninist-Maoist thought with which all recruits were to be familiar. It was to be the summer assignment. Officers and officer candidates should be familiar with Mao's *Talks at the Yenan Forum*.

When several small matters were dealt with he sent for a pad of notepaper, and asked not to be disturbed as he prepared himself to write a letter to Pasang Dorje, in Dharamsala, India.

Pasang Dorje

Chandra had attempted to explain the concept to the Standing Committee. They heard it with sympathetic attention and his proposal to test the views of the Dalai Lama's people in India was approved by a voice vote. The faction opposed argued that Beijing should be consulted, but Chandra got what he wanted. Though he and Pasang Dorje had exchanged letters and postal cards on several occasions, it had been over thirty years since they had last seen one another, yet Chandra could picture him vividly, memorably.

In those years Chandra was a young labor organizer among the tea plantation workers and a recruiter of Party members. Dibla, his seasonal base was in the northeast corner of India, near the part of Assam called Pemako, where the jungle meets the mountains and where the Tsang-Po river of Tibet makes a great swerve, cuts through the Himalayas, and pours down into India as the Brahmaputra. Many Tibetan escapees seeking refuge in India descended through the mountains at Tawang and then down all the way to Tezpur where a 22 hour train ride could reach Siliguri. And from there to Varanasi, Delhi, and Dharamsala.

One day a pitiful group of Tibetan religious refugees arrived in Dibla by foot. Destitute, ill, starving, frostbitten, clothed in rags and shreds, with blackened skins. They had barely escaped with their lives over the border fleeing from a

Chinese military unit which had pursued them for days. One of their company, Pasang Dorje, was so ill and weak that to all he appeared to be near death. He forcefully urged on his companions, promising to meet them in India if he recovered. Chandra and his communist comrades, moved by pity, took him into their care as an unintended guest in their household, prepared to see to his cremation if necessary. They spoon-fed him rice gruel for many days until he gained a touch of weight and could eat on his own. A medical doctor came once and diagnosed a form of tuberculosis and he was given a prescription for a medicine to take daily. It took almost a full year to nurse him back to a steady if frail health. The Nepalese communists understood he was a refugee from Chinese communists but nevertheless treated him with friendly courtesy, impressed at how he could sit motionless for so long. Finally, Pasang Dorje had recovered sufficiently to join the refugee exile community in Dharamsala which had formed around the Dalai Lama. He promised Chandra he would never forget him for the year of friendship, healing and generosity, which had saved his life.

Other than a postal card saying that he had arrived safely in Dharamsala, several years passed before Chandra had word again from Pasang Dorje. The card had taken months to reach him and was dated on Losar, the Tibetan New Year by the lunar calendar. Pasang Dorje sent his greetings and wrote that Chandra was always in his thoughts and that his gratitude was inexhaustible. There were periodic attacks of his old illness but he usually recovered and had found employment working in the Dalai Lama's household administration. Afterwards they exchanged occasional holiday greetings.

When Chandra first raised the idea it was thought facetious and dismissed quickly, but it was teased up in conversations during several toilet-cum-tea-breaks and it lingered overnight in the imagination of a few comrades. It had a certain attraction. Finally, the propaganda committee thought it ought to be tested. It seemed risk free. They thought it could have a positive and helpful resonance. An expression of Buddhist compassion towards the struggle of Nepal's oppressed classes – a statement of some resonant kind - might soften a few more hearts in the revolution's favor. The kind of message with a subtext that the Pope in Rome offers. It would play well in America and Europe. It would play well throughout Nepal; the Buddha was born in Nepal, after all. And there was one more thing. It would send a special message to China. Nepal's Maoists might conceivably revise the Chinese caricature of the Dalai Lama one day. That was to say that if the Maoist movement threatened to engross itself in the halo of a Nobel Peace Prize, the Chinese might be induced thereby to increase the quality and quantity of clandestine weapons. Was it not so? it was asked. They liked it.

Chandra sent a handwritten letter to Pasang Dorje proposing they meet to renew their friendship and exchange frank views concerning the situation in Nepal at present and in the future. He had been moved to do so by the tragic deaths of two monks. Chandra felt certain his friend would be in a position to pass on the invitation to hold an exploratory meeting directly to the grand Lama himself. He sent the letter to Dharamsala by a female courier, a Party member, a university student from a Sherpa family who was told to wait for a reply. She waited three days until she received a handwritten letter in a plain envelope. This was the envelope Chandra was fanning himself with as he sat at the table in Aruna awaiting the American journalist.

Pasang Dorje had agreed to meet and replied in a personal vein. He was happy to have an opportunity of seeing his old friend again and remarked that since the day he had left Tibet for India he had never been to Nepal, just like the Dalai Lama himself. Pasang Dorje hoped sincerely that a future Maoist government of Nepal might permit His Holiness to visit sacred Buddhist places. The prospect of discussing such matters was indeed interesting. Would it be agreeable to meet at Tengboche monastery in October? If his health permitted, Pasang Dorje was thinking of visiting Thubten Choling monastery in the lower valleys as well.

Chandra fanned a fly away from his face with the folded letter. The proposed date was ideal, as he would be in Khumjung at that time to handover the *gumba* to the yak caravan. Tengboche monastery was not much more than a three hour walk from there. The Tibetan Government in Exile was certainly aware of his standing in the guerrilla hierarchy and the idea of having an exploratory dialogue had not been dismissed immediately. If the Nobel Prize winner in Dharamsala made a suitable gesture towards the Maoist undertaking in Nepal, what might not ensue? It would be a message to China itself, would it not? A message to the whole world.

He liked it. Meeting at Gyalpo Rinpoche's monastery would ensure privacy and the Abbot's views would be helpful. Cross-border links between Tengboche and Dharamsala had been shrouded by timid inactivity and Chandra urged Pasang Dorje to see life in the red zones for himself. Chandra would provide him with an escort for the entire journey and have his bags carried. He sent him a *laissez-passer* under his authority to allow every courtesy and comfort. The weather would be agreeable in October. If his health permitted he could walk to Tengboche by way of Thubten Choling, instead of flying directly to Lukla. He could keep the air ticket in case he felt the walk was too strenuous.

An "Interview"

In Singapore Ripp lived in tailored suits, blazers, white flannels, regimental ties, with a closet shelf of Italian shoes, and his cottons laundered daily. But in the field it would be easy to miss him. He took on a more crumpled and perspired look, slightly seedy and academic; an apparent mildness in contrast to his native ironic pugnacity. A soiled canvas bag hanging from one shoulder, he looked like an agricultural equipment salesman.

The instructions they provided were clear. Make an early morning rendezvous with a man at the Biratnagar bus station who would provide him with a ticket to Phaplu where a waiting motorcyclist would bring him to his escort for two days of walking.

So it was in the late afternoon when Chandra saw the point-man from the escort squad emerge from the forest path into the central clearing of the village. He thought the long walk in would be off-putting, but the American had actually undertaken it and didn't seem tired as he came over. Chandra stood to wait for him and held out his hand, personally pleased at the novelty of having a foreign visitor.

Ripp had expected a stand-offish person but found Chandra to be a welcoming spirit. They joined and shook their four hands vigorously, and looked one another over. Then Chandra took Ripp's arm and led him to the guest dwelling. He had expected someone younger.

The greeting was warm. "Call me Chandra," he said. "Take a rest. I'll send a thermos of water and a wash bowl. It's a bit bare, but clean, and the cot should be comfortable. I'll come by in an hour and we can take food together and become better acquainted, though we retire early here. Tomorrow we can have the full day, but if you need anything just ask anyone in sight. Our 'strike hard' campaign is over and we're in a new cease-fire as you must know, and with the beginning of the rains shortly I've sent many of our youngsters home to help with the rice plantings. So I have little to do for the next few days. After that, too many meetings, so many places. Busy, busy."

Ripp was grateful for the brief rest. The quarters were spacious though there was a hint of an unpleasant odor which came and went. A three sided mud wall at waist height to which was fixed a bamboo A-frame. Clean, neat, minimal, even aesthetic. The swept earthen floor held a string cot with a mattress of folded blankets. There was a small table and stool, a towel, a bowl, and a pitcher. There was a *Yoga* journal called *The Mountain Path* on the table, which seemed out of place. Ripp thanked his host for allowing the visit and told him he looked forward to their meal together. Chandra gestured to the periodical, "We're not entirely narrow-minded brutes."

Sometimes the decisive moment in a recruitment approach would take place at the final instant, at a farewell. Ripp intended to go slowly and start at low key. Bringing Chandra over could yield valuable insights as to what the Party leadership would settle for. Chandra's outgoing personality would make things easier and there didn't seem to be a need for ice-breaking. Truly, life's second best answer was a fast 'no.' After a while he put on a fresh shirt. Having a full day tomorrow was a plus. He sat up and stretched. It was time for food. He could see Chandra coming for him.

They ate in the fading light while sitting on wooden benches at a rough table to one side of the clearing. A faint hint of the unpleasant odor came and went again. Three teenagers, two girls and a boy wearing caps with red stars, served them the rice and lentil staple of the region, with a side mixture of peanuts and onions, accompanied by hot sweet tea. They came in a procession carrying three trays and aluminum forks and spoons in honor of the guest, though fingers were the usual work.

The conversation was light as they casually summarized their careers to one another as they ate, in the off-handed way that elders of roughly equal rank enact their self-descriptions as an opportunity to display modesty. They found places they had shared at one time or another and sentimentalized over Ganguli's coffee house in Calcutta and its chess-playing habitués. A boy came over to light a kerosene lamp and pour more tea. They pulled over two string cots with thin cotton mattresses and stretched out at ease.

"And why are you doing this?" Chandra asked. "Isn't it a bit of a hardship for someone like yourself? To come all this way? I can't imagine I have that much to tell you that you don't already know."

"Oh, but I visit small banks in rural towns all over south Asia and I like getting out of offices, out of hotels, out of cities, out of airports and taxis. Getting here was a long hike, that's all. In Singapore I exercise in gyms, but I prefer hiking on trails."

Chandra laughed. "But you could go to Angkor, or Chiang-Mai if you want to hike in nice safe forests, or a guided trip to Bhutan if you want to get out of the city. Why come to miserable and troubled little Nepal? It took some doing to arrange to see me here for an interview, and I know nothing of banks except to have robbed one or two. And I'm afraid I know nothing about the subject of small loans since I'm only a soldier, not an economist. Perhaps you're coming to deliver a message of some sort?"

Ripp stayed matter–of-fact straightforward. "Look, my line of work is the pleasure I get in developing good sources for interesting story ideas. That's my career. Stories. I've been around so long that my networks have grandchildren. I'm sure you all have checked me out and know America doesn't have a dog in this fight. I share your view of the monarchy by the way, in case that needs saying. But a chance to talk with a guerrilla leader is worth something, don't you know? In addition to my article I'll be interviewed on television. Allowing me this access is quite helpful professionally, and I'm grateful. If you let me have a photo of us it will do even more for me. I promise, I'll put in print anything you want to say. The thing is I got here."

"Will you offer me a share?" said Chandra, surprised by a passing expression on Ripp's face said quickly, "I'm only joking."

Ripp went in directly "Well, there's another aspect of my work, more serious, with more at stake."

"Please tell me."

Ripp went through an old song and dance of his cover, hoping to get Chandra's head swimming with the vastness and complexity of it all, to soften him up. They were relaxed and friendly. He was coming to the end of the tea.

"I have several clients, large Asian banks, whom I advise on matters of risk analysis. Evaluating political risk is what I do. Should they put hundreds of millions of dollars at risk in Nepal? Truly, hundreds of millions. Maybe more. Many people want to know if it will be safe to invest in this country after the revolution succeeds in its aims. You saw what happened in Cuba. These days it's all about thirty or forty year credit mechanisms, you see. Infrastructure projects. Schools. Reforestation. National power grids. Mines. Rural clinics. Road building. That kind of thing. Stability and sustainability are the big issues. Armed struggle can be self-defeating at times, do you agree?"

Chandra demurred. He wasn't sure where this was going. He was a soldier who believed in the wisdom of the Party leadership. Questions about investments and interest rates were not within his competence. The important thing was to achieve victory first. "Well, we can discuss that tomorrow," Chandra said as they got up from the table.

41

Ripp started to say something but sniffed the air and asked, "what is that smell by the way?"

"Oh dear, let me show you." Despite a near full moon Chandra found a torch and took him to a grassy area behind one of the other huts, and put the beam on a grotesque sight. The scent was strong. Two carcasses with monstrous heads were fixed on spits a few inches above an ant mound. Looking more closely Ripp saw thousands of ants and several species of beetles working hard and much of the musculature was gone. The carcasses, not entirely dried out, were held together by the drying tendons.

"What am I looking at?" asked Ripp, who was staring at the gaping jaws.

"A great deal of money. We shall sell them."

"I don't understand."

"Those are tiger carcasses. The Chinese brew a liquor from unboiled bones, they say it makes men irresistible to women. Can you believe it? Millions do. Honestly."

Ripp said nothing for a moment as he let the connections settle in his brain. Tiger bones would obviously accompany the *gumba* to the same market. He played the card. "It trades with the *gumba*, doesn't it? Kathmandu newspapers say the crop's been nationalized and that you're in charge. It's the same buyer, isn't it? And who is the buyer if I may ask?"

Chandra smiled. "The buyer? Anxious Chinese men. Very observant, connecting these carcasses to the *gumba* crop. But nothing special. You can get government statistics. These kinds of commodities are part of Nepal's historic trade with China and the buyers are part of a cartel for these things. Millions of anxious Chinese men."

"With a shortage of girls, that's a recipe for trouble. Chandra, if you don't mind my pleading, there's a rare piece of journalism here. Could I get a possibly get a photo of these things tomorrow?"

"No faces, no names, no places. No clues."

"Perfectly understood. Thank you very much. I mean it's worth the whole trip. It's called a photo scoop."

Ripp was elated. He didn't want to sleep and lose the pleasure of it. Of course he would get the photo to the World Wildlife Fund and the State Department, perfect allies for what he had in mind for Colonel Thondup. *Treaty violation.* They had the carrot of Viagra and catching him trading endangered species flagrantly across international borders would be more than a stick; it would be a whip and a half. Ripp felt grateful to Chandra for the new development. Tiger carcasses.

The Next Day

They spent much of the following morning talking about micro-credit. Ripp laid out the panorama of credit systems intending to make Chandra feel naïve and appreciative of how little he knew of these matters. He had never seen other parts of the world, not even large parts of India. Chandra waved his hands and said he knew about labor unions, newspapers, recruiting cadres, ideological pamphlets, and military activity. But the descriptions of the banking sector, the plumbing, and the role of the rupee confirmed perfectly his own pre-suppositions: the ruling classes were clever bastards. And Chandra was not without questions of his own, and not particularly impressed with an academician's micro-credit story, saying it did not really offer a way out of poverty.

"Fifty workers at a textile plant were going to be more productive than 50 micro-entrepreneur weavers each working by themselves."

"Why would you be against loans to shopkeepers?" Ripp asked. "Primitive accumulation had to be private according to Marx."

"Not in Nepal," said Chandra, "nor in China. You can't keep us a nation of small proprietors, a petit bourgeoisie. Shops are just a primitive capitalist form which leads to class war. Yes, sometimes it's useful to have a pharmacist or a shoemaker. As long as it was small."

It was an interview of sorts and they enjoyed it. Ripp made notes. There were anecdotes. Finally Chandra protested that civil administration was over his head and went far beyond his skills. In the world ahead his knowledge would be useless. He was just a soldier, nearing the end of a long campaign and would retire soon. He was past his time. Younger people were taking over.

"Why don't you help us win instead of fighting us?" asked Chandra."

"You've met our Peace Corps volunteers, I know you have. They're helping you." They both thought of Annie Wendover.

"I met one not too long ago," said Chandra. "She made a positive impression."

"The one you kidnapped."

"You heard of it?"

"Made you famous for a day. Picture of her in the Herald-Tribune."

"We each had a tutorial. She explained America to me. An inspiring country in many ways, I'll admit."

"She's still in Nepal. Leading treks in the Khumbu for a commercial agency. Just imagine if someone just like her was the victim of a bomb." Ripp intended to hit him and push the theme, as he sensed Chandra's soft spot.

Chandra, at loss for words, turned the conversation to the imminent arrival of monsoon, and suggested they stroll up a local hill with a fine viewpoint. They walked in silent single file for nearly twenty minutes until reaching a broad top with a natural space to sit. The view looked up the main canyon of the Arun drainage. Great parapets of rock walls ascended to the sky and jagged little teeth of snowy mountain peaks topped a low point on the northernmost horizon. They sat in silence for a while sharing the experience that loomed far above politics. Humans seemed mere mad microbes. Ripp was encouraged by the peacefulness of the situation. It seemed like a good time to push him harder.

"Chandra, may I ask you something? It's got nothing to do with what we've been talking about so far. It's just to get a better understanding of the Party's mentality."

"You can try."

"Remember Guzman? Abimael Guzman? *Sendero Luminoso*, the Shining Path Maoist guerrilla war in Peru? Mountain country too. Used to be a philosophy professor. At least 60,000 dead. $30 billion in damage. Twelve years. They killed 17 provincial mayors, 120 judges. No one would run for office. The government had to offer life insurance to civil servants. They robbed banks, bombed embassies, police academies, churches, businesses. Shining Path killed anyone doing relief or development work. Said it was tampering with revolutionary consciousness. So they had a long struggle. A protracted struggle. Twenty years. Is that protracted? They were finally busted in 1992. Take the United Liberation front of Assam, right next door. Wants to secede from India. Thirty years of fighting. What's to show? More than 15,000 dead. Well, they say, Ireland did it."

"Some revolutions are successful, some aren't," said Chandra, not conceding anything.

"I'm trying to understand what happens to moderates because of the mad narcissisms of small differences. The centrists, the Cuban democrats, the human rights workers, the Mensheviks, the middle-of-the roaders, the indifferent, the undecided, the hesitant Party members, the Girondists of the French

Revolution. The Jacobins always put them up against the wall, curse them and shoot them. Velvet revolutions are feared as if they were worse than the bloodbath alternative. There's something inhuman going on, don't you think? Lord Shiva perhaps?"

He could see Chandra's head nodding slightly, a grim and sad expression on his face.

Ripp pushed on. "I was in India a few weeks ago. Gave a lecture to Indian economists in Poona. It was in the papers. While I was there, out in the countryside Naxal rebels kidnapped 47 people from a government relief camp for displaced villagers. Police found the bodies of 12 of the hostages with their throats slit and their corpses booby-trapped. Last week, in Biratnagar, on the way here, I heard stories that local commanders have acted with exceptional cruelty. Recently, near Salleri, 28 schoolchildren on a bus were killed in a bomb blast. Can you explain to me what's going on? What makes it worth it?"

There was an enduring silence. Their gaze tilted to the distant horizon. Chandra sighed and said softly, "I don't know the circumstances. People make mistakes. Do stupid things. Someone said revolutions aren't tea parties."

"Oh, I know, I know. But it's the mentality I'm interested in." Ripp knew he was fishing with a long pole. "I mean at the human level isn't it just impermanence, suffering, emptiness, ignorance, just like those Buddhists say?" He saw the fly drop on the surface of a dark swirling pool.

Chandra replied "What if it is?" Followed by another long silence as they sat and stared in the distance. This interview was becoming too personal for Chandra. It was time to change the subject. "Let's go down and have a rest. You have a long day tomorrow and should have a good rest tonight. We're not getting younger, you know."

"Ever thought of stepping down?" asked Ripp.

"Ha! Every single day."

"Made any plans? I'm always looking for research collaborators. Thinking about a book about life in the revolutionary arc. I've got the economic side covered but I need someone to help me develop story ideas about the mentalities at work. Get me good anecdotes. You're not without assets; you could probably get a book contract on your own, you know. Your memoirs might be just the thing. Experts tell us to plan for the years ahead, Chandra, after stepping down. I could find you a publisher."

"How much would someone pay if I just vanished?" It was a cryptic remark.

"I might be able to help you move on," said Ripp. He felt he was making progress. Let it ripen, let suspicions ferment. A crack had been mauled open, and a seed lodged down within. The whole point of the interview, plant the seed. The beginning of a recruitment. They would both be in the Khumbu in October. If Chandra was ready to come over, it would be then.

Ripp asked, "How about the rumor that your leadership is negotiating with the Dalai Lama's people?"

"Rumor?" said Chandra. "I hadn't heard of it. Why would we do that?" And he was pleased that there was such a rumor. That in itself might be enough to stir the Chinese into more liberal quantities in the weapons transaction.

Ripp went on, as if advising a poker player. "Look, you know that the Chinese manipulate you, sometimes even betray you. You must be sick of their attitude of superiority by now, not so? Talking to Dharamsala is a big tool for you people in your relation with China, don't you think?"

Chandra was shocked at the blunt truth of the statement and replied "What exactly are we supposed to be talking about?"

"Whatever. Just that you're talking. And I'll tell you something else. The Indians would be a lot less hostile if they didn't think you were the cat's-paws of China."

"Point taken. But we don't forget they have betrayed their own revolution."

They shook hands before retiring and exchanged a few final pleasantries. Ripp was permitted several photos of the tiger carcasses and then, with the help of an aide, a few of himself standing with Chandra, who then wished Ripp a good night and a safe journey saying he looked forward to reading his article. A squad would escort him all the way down to the paved road. A taxi would meet him there. And so good night and a safe journey.

Ripp sat by candlelight with his notebook evaluating the odds of recruiting the Zone Commander. The man seemed ready to cut the rope, almost eager for something totally new in his life. He had little idea of his value to the right people, like General Vidya Kumar, whose seductive debriefings would find treasure. Pick him up after he quits. Give him six months. He could take the bait. *Memoirs*. Then he snuffed the candle and turned on his side. He caught the odor of the tiger carcasses again. What a world he thought, and pointed his imagination to Elsie's lips and fell to sleep.

46

A Dream

In the middle of the night Ripp had a vivid dream. The head of the Peace Corps had written to the Agency's Director concerning Ripp's failure to rescue a kidnapped Volunteer. The White House had become involved and he was being reprimanded. Suddenly, he woke up, disoriented, saying to himself – no, that's not what happened. What happened? The Wendover girl, Miss American Pie, was at the heart of something. Chandra had seen it too.

The Director's voice had been unmistakable. "Ripp? Can you hear us? I'm here with the Vice-President."

"We're counting on you Ripp," said the Vice-President.

The Director sketched it out for him. "An American Peace Corps volunteer in Nepal was kidnapped some six hours earlier during a bank robbery by a Maoist gang. The police captured one of them, a woman trying to escape. The guerrillas are proposing an exchange for our gal Annie Wendover."

The Vice-President jumped in, "We're concerned about Miss Wendover's welfare. Damn it, I was in the first generation of Volunteers, in Nigeria, before going to law school and politics. This damn kidnapping is on the verge of turning into an international news story and has to be handled quickly. Whatever it takes. I mean it, special forces, air-support, whatever. Just give us a location, the GPS co-ordinates of where she's being held."

The Director added that Miss Wendover's father was a college roommate of one of Wyoming's senators and a cousin of the other. It was obvious. They wanted action. "What's my mission exactly?" Ripp asked. "Arranging the swap?"

"Yes. With one exception. No swap if we can rescue the Wendover girl quickly and safely," said the Vice-President. "I don't give a rat's ass for the Nepali woman." The Director agreed and said, "The gal's somewhere in your turf, Ripp, and no one knows the ground better. Let's locate her and set up a hostage rescue team. Whatever you need. You're in charge."

Ripp took a breath. He needed to control the tempo or they might end up blowing off entire agent networks as a result of a rescue attempt, successful or not. The day was hot and the buzzing of cicadas was infernal. "Mr. Vice-President, a negotiated swap could yield a better outcome all around and could be done diplomatically, let's keep it at a low level. We know the players and can do it quickly. I share your feelings about having no obligations to a captured bank robber, but I think we should let the two sides work it out. Our best shot is to facilitate the swap."

"I don't see why we have to care about commie thugs if we can safely snatch our girl. Let's put our efforts on locating her first," said the Vice-President.

"I'll do what I can," said Ripp, "but we need a parallel track. I suggest we ask the Indians to facilitate a trade for the woman Nepali police are holding, and do it now, really fast, before they bring her to Kathmandu and pray the authorities haven't roughed her up too much. Believe me, Sir, the Maoists really don't want an American hostage on their hands. The Wendover kid was just an accident. The sooner they get the Nepali woman the sooner they'll release her."

"What are you thinking?" asked the Director.

"Get Elsie Hornbein on it right now. She'll go straight to the top in Indian Counter-Intelligence and they can talk to the Government in Kathmandu within minutes to facilitate. Neither the Palace or the Maoists want our girl on their hands, believe me. Ideally, she gets exchanged for the woman grabbed by the police. Do it at Jogbani, the Indian border crossing down the road from Biratnagar. Let's push for speed, do the swap tomorrow morning, while everything's fluid and everyone's close by. A simple low-key transaction."

"They left Dhankuta on a Royal Enfield a few hours ago. Where do you think they took her?" said the Director.

"They'd go to Biratnagar, it's a city with a strong Maoist presence and plenty of sympathetic safe houses where they can stay hidden until they see what happens. They'd love to release our volunteer, but they want their comrade. Get Elsie to meet me in Jogbani tomorrow morning accompanied by a ranking Indian official. And tell Wurlitzer to inform the politburo crowd in Kathmandu, he knows who they are, that we're prepared for an exchange tomorrow. Tomorrow morning at the Jogbani crossing."

"What about you, where are you?"

"Near Cooch Behar. I'll get the Indians to fly me to Jogbani. It's a short hop. They owe me." Beyond that, the only remaining angle was to contact his agent, Joshi, and hope his network in Biratnagar finds a trace.

The Indian Air Force was ready with a single engine artillery-spotter and had Ripp at Jogbani's landing strip, not a proper airport, before dark. He changed SIM cards on his phone and found a message from Joshi. He was just across the border using the same cell tower and talking in an excited voice. He had hired a gang of street urchins to peek into garages and back-yards in search of Enfields. Some covered with spider webs and layers of grime, others immaculately shined and elevated on blocks and a few with the look of a machine in daily use. Some were out on the street, some in the front court or drive of a family dwelling.

But one with panniers was parked at the back of a house, whose entrance showed two men sitting on the steps before the front door. There was a blanket over something at their sides. They sat there until they were relieved by another pair. Neighbors said the house was rarely occupied, but lights had been turned on inside. It could be a Maoist safe-house. Half the population were sympathizers. All they had was an Enfield motorcycle and pairs of men in shifts sitting on steps while the blanket stays untouched.

Ripp had misgivings about the trigger-puller types but dutifully relayed Joshi's report to the operations center. It could be nothing. But the machos might want a rescue situation. Far more dangerous than a swap. Quicker and more spectacular. And the old-story: hurry up and wait. Waiting for Elsie to show. And the Vice-President had the Pentagon put a Special Forces team on standby. They had the GPS coordinates of a house with a Royal Enfield and two men on the front steps. Occupancy unknown. If the Indians green-lighted it they could have a hostage-rescue team at Jogbani landing strip in about three hours. From there, Biratnagar, across the border in Nepal, could be reached by road in twenty minutes.

The Vice-President made it clear again that he didn't give a damn about the Nepalese woman. "She was a bank-robber caught in the act of stealing the savings of hard working people and they could put her away for life as far as I'm concerned. But you're the man on the spot Ripp, I don't want to second-guess you. The situation is a matter of concern, real concern. The President is also concerned. The United States has to show action, and since we can pinpoint her location the people who do these things assure me they will rescue her unharmed. Anyway, discuss it with the Director, you know how I feel."

Jogbani Junction

Ripp recalled it quite well. They ended up sleeping next to one another. Elsie had arrived at Jogbani with a Major from the Indian Army. The news was encouraging; sometimes the machinery worked. The Indians were more than cooperative and had gone straight to the top in Kathmandu. The palace ordered the district police to bring the guerrilla – "she's hardly 16, by the way" – to the frontier and expel her from Nepal into India on the American commitment she would not return to Nepal. On the other side, the key people in the Party's

Standing Committee agreed immediately to bring the Peace Corps Volunteer to the border control post not later than noon.

The Major from the Indian Army was to be the official witness and diarist. There were fifteen hours to go and they settled in and were eating a simple dinner of *dal bhaat* and curry by candlelight when Ripp interrupted something he was saying, stared up at the sky wide-eyed, and slapped his forehead.

"Son of a bitch," he said "they're going to try it! They want to snatch her. They're going to go around me. I gave them the GPS coordinates of the house, damn it. I've got to move now. They've got people in motion, I can smell it."

They shared the satellite phone. Elsie called friends at the State Department who lobbied the operations directorate to hold off on a rescue. Ripp got back to the Director who affirmed there was a hostage rescue team under a Captain on its way to Jogbani as they spoke.

"You're still in charge, Ripp. It's just back-up."

"I'm going to be at the airstrip to meet them and if the officer refuses my authority I'm prepared to take early retirement."

The Director assured him he would remain in charge no matter what. He had gone to the National Security Advisor for a commitment on this. A hostage rescue scenario could present unforeseen dangers to the Wendover girl. The odds of something going wrong were too high. They were there just in case she wasn't handed over.

At the airstrip the Captain was deferential. He was at Ripp's service. As an officer and a gentleman. He rigged foam pads on the steel cabin floor and taped mosquito netting to the door frame. They all slept in their clothes. Ripp listened to her breathing.

In the morning, after a breakfast of C-rations, Elsie, the Indian major, the American Captain, and Ripp together with several aides and attendants walked to the border check-post, about a mile away. The weather was sunny between groups of towering clouds, there was a hum of insects as the group waited for action. At half past ten a three jeep convoy was seen coming down the road. Royal Nepal Army vehicles with color standards flying, the young girl prisoner in the middle one. She was escorted to the gate. Her escorts snapped to attention. The officer read a decree banning her from Nepal pursuant to an understanding with the American government. The barrier was lifted. The Indian major gazetted Elsie's receipt of the prisoner. The girl weighed less than ninety pounds. Pretty, self-confident, delighted to be at liberty, she would be sixteen next month. They fed her field rations and gave her tea. She couldn't stop smiling.

Then they waited. Noon came and went and there was no sign of Annie Wendover. There was no sign at all. At ten past the hour annoyance turned to irritation; in another five minutes to anger, and shortly after that to alarm. There was nothing. Nothing at all. Just the buzzing of insects. The American Captain turned to Ripp. Well? He gave them a nod and they sent a special forces undercover team to a house in Biratnagar and found an empty residence, with unwashed curry dishes in the sink.

"There'll be a simple explanation," said Elsie, confidently. "Don't worry yet."

Ripp wondered what he would tell the Director and the Vice-President about the girl.

The Girl

A girl needs a boy, and he is yet to come. A girl has night thoughts as a last fragment of dark chocolate dissolves slowly at the back of her tongue. At the moment, like many of her friends, she had sex in and on her mind, the childhood discovery that it displaced all other thought or woe and made for a gentle drift into sleep's protective disappearance of self. In the darkness 29-year-old Annie Wendover lay on her left side, knees curled. She pressed her palms between her thighs and let her thoughts flow in a spiraled kaleidoscope of fragmented recollections, in a fantasy-land, secular or sexual, the ancient knowledge which gets one warm.

A lifetime of sexual experience had been disappointing. A series of one or two minutes of thrusting. Like an auto ad. 'Our vehicle can go from a standing start to 60 miles an hour in five seconds flat, how's that for power?' And her latest taste of the phenomenon with Urs was equally disappointing. Why don't they get it? What's the rush? Just go slow and tender. Find the plateau, ride the wave.

Annie worried she wasn't pretty. A horsey facial appearance, a small bosom, big muscular thighs and irregular teeth. At least she was strong for her age. And mirrors being scarce in the mountains she wasn't even sure what she looked like. She thought she was sexy because she certainly felt that way. But to date her partners had been unappreciative of what a good time they were missing. She had a pang of envy for media glamour, but let it go. Who would envy her?

Only the Sherpa girls. She was too tall, with mouse-colored hair and big hands, and aside from her mother's home-schooling and college courses in English Literature and the autodidact bit, she was just plain unsophisticated. But she was athletic and erotic. Her parents doing. She tried to picture them. She'd been away two years.

Thoughts circled around former lovers. Boyfriends, not lovers, she corrected herself. Urs, the only non-American. She had never really had a lover she decided, just eleven male penetrators. Not such marvelous penetrators either. A few times with her college roommate, Linda, but that was more out of friendship than arousal. And in Nepal it was largely about bringing herself to climax. How did anyone have a long-term relation with anyone?

All from these weirdly connected mammalian body parts. The evolutionary art of wiring anatomies. She recalled her mother revealing the male and female flower parts with a magnifying lens. She held a manicure scissor, tweezers, and a camel hair brush with which she moved pollen grains, "this is the semen sweetie," from the male part of one flower to the female part of another. How deep in nature went the thrill? "The force that through the green fuse drives the flower" said Dylan Thomas, she recalled from her English poetry course. What was it all about? Biology 101? Urs from *Mitteleuropa*? A quick ejaculator with bad breath? And Darwin explains him, right? She envisioned the old boyfriends, trying to picture them one-by-one. None worth a proper fantasy. Eleven, in nine years. Four of them one-nighters. Two for a full weekend. Four, including Urs, for a full season. And one for a year. She suddenly felt sad. She wanted to be married in erotic monogamy.

Neither she nor Urs had bathed in a week, and then only in icy water. And then, to top it all there was something going on down there. A yeast or bladder infection – one or the other. A five minute scene, a week earlier. Stupid. Finally the relationship was over. Common sense at last.

Then she remembered there were twelve. One more one-night stand after climbing Pachyderm's Crack at Vedauwoo. Her first 5.10 lead. So many years ago. Bob something. Four of them just a horny bunch of state college kids. Geology majors and Aggies. Wham-bam thank-you ma'am. Frat-boy fools, egomaniacal brutes, and hopeless cases. Animals. Foreplay meant thirty seconds of harsh fingering. Where was Mr. Right? Life was short.

There was the American Vice-Consul who came through Dhankuta. And the following year a good-looking friend of his from St. Louis was passing through Nepal and came for a visit. And a Peace Corps chum up near Annapurna, with whom she started serious Himalayan climbing. Then he left for graduate school and Urs somehow replaced him.

At sleep's very border, the world shutting down, she pressed her hands deeper against her groin and the over-sized lump on her wrist pressed uncomfortably against her thigh. Have a look. She found the head-lamp and in the glow of the LED the readout on her wrist altimeter showed 18,630 feet. The Schneider map showed her true altitude at 500+ feet lower but the less dense air of a low pressure front elevated her barometric altitude. The weather had ambushed her. She was still alone more than a mile above the valley floor as the monsoon's leading edges approached the Himalayas. Alone and happy to be alive.

She was just south of the Tibetan border, in Nepal's Lumding range, where a line of peaks over 19,000 feet towered above a modest glacier and the narrow valley it created. The range lay at the westernmost edge of the vast frozen drainage-basin in the region surrounding the south-western side of Mt. Everest, the Khumbu. In the middle of the lesser range was a 21,257 foot chisel-shaped peak called Trangdak-Ri. Its north facing aspect was dominated by two enormous spines which ascended from a single buttressed prow. The first British explorers of the region had referred to a wishbone formation, but as a German team made the first ascent by the right hand rib they named the route *Stimmgabel West*, 'Tuning Fork (West)' in the British climbing journals. Described as a larger version of the Dru in Chamonix, it required sustained climbing with high commitment, presented tricky protection placements for climbers, and finished in an 80° ice field. Long, serious, remote, and fairly technical. A bold classic, it was climbed annually. An Argentinean team was attempting it this year.

The more dangerous and neglected tine of the fork, *Stimmgabel Ost*, consisted of a lizard's back series of plates and slabs, turrets and towers, separated by shallow shoulders of snow, all draped with icy veils, snowy chutes, and overhanging in places. A Polish team, the Jagiellonian Alpine Club, had sieged it years earlier with fixed lines but it had not been climbed since. Urs had planned to put in a high base camp about a third the way up the rib, and from there solo the long upper part of the arête – graded 5.12+ – all the way to the summit. She had been persuaded to carry a load for him up to his bivouac site at the base of the first serious wall.

The prior night at base camp before their dawn start had been uncomfortable. Urs's dry cough interrupted her sleep. Old Tashi, who had climbed Everest decades earlier was oblivious and snoring away. Annie had been irritated at herself. Why was she even doing this? It was far above her grade and comfort level. Her long-term interest in climbing was waning. And she liked warm rock rather than this alpine stuff. Did she want to get hurt, maybe killed one day? For what? Carrying a load for Urs? Because he was world famous? But he kept reassuring her.

At first light the two of them had swallowed the last of Tashi's tea, put on their harnesses, roped in, and started up under full loads. Tashi had them stand still for a minute while he muttered a prayer for their protection. With Annie's auxiliary load Urs had enough food and fuel and gear to support him if he had to back off and retry, or wait through a spell of poor weather.

Their first task had been to climb the great lower prow, the buttress which formed the handle of the tuning fork. Straightforward simul-climbing on hard rock for three hours, the kind of thing she liked to do. They stopped for an energy bar and a drink at the top of the buttress where the routes split, a flat triangular space the size of a small room. An Argentine cache had been tucked into a niche at the extreme corner where the wall formed an overhang and sheltered the groin between the ribs from falling debris. It was an excellent bivouac site but too close to the base area to be useful.

The climbing became more serious and had involved frequent belaying by Urs who stayed at the serious end of the rope and held her under tension through several passages. Still, the beauty and the rhythm of the climb had taken over her senses and Annie enjoyed herself. The morning had been clear and calm as they moved far above the thick cloud layer carpeting the valley floors below. To the north they could see the Nangpa-La, the Khumbu's only good pass into Tibet, and to its east the massive shape of Cho-Oyu one of the fourteen 8,000 meter peaks. Further east were the other giants of the border, Gyachung Kang, Pumori, the mother goddess Everest, and then remote Makalu, and furthest away, the tiny grey battleship silhouette of Kangchenjunga.

The east rib of the *Stimmgabel*, owing to overall steepness averaging above 70°, was relatively free of avalanche danger but required mixed rock and ice climbing at a high standard. The main challenge was to find on which side to turn past the gendarmes, the granite spires which were stepped in a series of towers surrounded by guardian pinnacles, separated occasionally by little rounded shoulders of low angle snow. The exposure on either side was extreme and the big air felt thrilling. She knew that seconding Urs was at the very edge of her capabilities. She couldn't possibly lead it. Furthermore, she had never liked dry-tooling, the style of climbing on rock passages with metal tools and crampon points. She liked using chalky fingers and having sticky rubber on her feet.

54

Urs had moved smoothly, leading and route finding. She needed tension on the crux-like pitches, but had consoled herself that they would all be simple to rappel past on descent. As they climbed up through the comb of pinnacles she looked across to the distant west rib. The Argentinean expedition had started the route a day earlier and a light wind brought over the ringing sound of hammering on anchor pegs. They were nailing in a bivouac site of their own. Annie could see them clearly. Five. Four in blue one in red. At arms' length they were the size of big ants. She could see the forms of their arms and legs and a slack rope in the wind flying in and out of visibility. The one in red waved.

As they ascended Annie studied features of the route to mark anchor points for her *abseil*, remembering how Urs nagged her to use the German instead of 'rappel.' Occasionally he banged a piton into a horizontal crack or left a Kevlar loop on a rock horn for her to use on descent, and on her own she placed runners over sturdy projections and used little chunks of granite to make small marking cairns. There were abundant natural anchors and they had estimated she would need less than four hours to reach base camp if she left Urs around midday. Descending unloaded by a series of rappels with occasional self-belayed down-climbing promised to be rapid and thrilling. It would be her first time alone at this altitude.

By early afternoon they had finished chopping out a bivouac ledge on a snow shoulder under the first wall and pegged in the final anchors for Urs' tent, stowing the load before Annie was ready to start down. The cloud deck had reached their base camp area. It was time to get moving, have a drink of water and a few last words before descending. She had done her load-carrying duty. Days earlier they agreed their brief sexual and climbing partnership was over, but she had promised to carry the load and couldn't back out – they had agreed. Fair enough. She felt clear, with a burden lifted, and Urs had been friendly and shrugged. He was focused on the climb. Friends, certainly, no hard feelings.

The season was over, monsoon was coming. Yeti Travels had a nice cash envelope waiting for her in Kathmandu and there was a plane to catch. She understood more clearly than ever, in her bones, that extreme grade mountaineering was not for her.

"So long Ursy," she said, "I'm hauling out and it's getting cloudy down there. So good luck. I'll tell the record keepers what's going on."

"You're really leaving Nepal?" he had asked.

"I'm holding unchangeable and non-refundable Cathay Pacific tickets, flying through Bangkok on the 23rd. Plus I need time to unwind, do chores and gain some weight. And stow my gear at the Yeti warehouse in Lukla. They have me leading treks this Fall. And I have to do laundry so my parents won't throw up. Anyway, you go for it. Some cloudy days below but it looks clear and stable up here. Stay safe." They embraced awkwardly for a moment. "Take care." She started down. Wyoming ahoy!

"I'll be climbing on Nuptse in the Fall," he shouted, "maybe I'll see you," and he bowed slightly with his hands together and turned to his gear as Annie started down. She passed the rope's center through the reversed karabiners, heaved both ends of the rope into the still air and clipped into the system with the friction device on her harness. She inspected and tested the anchor. Looking good. "Good luck!" she shouted as she backed over the edge, making a smooth controlled descent until she reached the next anchor point, where she tied in, pulling the rope through and setting up the system again. And so it went in a series. There were down-climbs where she had to use rock outcrops to belay herself in a weave from right and left over the mixed ground of rock, snow and ice. All she had to do was maintain a smooth and slow rate of descent in each pitch between anchors, and use her feet to balletically toe-off the rock as she rappelled down.

The weather front was stationary, unusually calm and very cold and the solo descent was a new experience at this altitude. She couldn't recall being alone on a mountain this size before. It wasn't one of the rounded trade summits like Island Peak or Mera and it sure wasn't the Tetons. She felt a touch of nervousness but the descent started smoothly, within her capabilities though it absorbed her full attention. Here and there she worked out a problem on her own. The exposure was awesome but things felt solid. The footprints of their ascent on the snow patches, the little cairns, the crampon and tool marks on rock, removed most route ambiguities, and some of the most difficult pitches that had taken an hour to climb, where Urs kept the rope under tension, were passed easily on a en rappel in minutes.

She waved at the Argentinean team on the distant west rib, framed against the sky. The red parka waved again and she continued down into the strange mixture of fear and beauty. She remembered what her father said about combat aviation: courage was the natural product of familiarity with danger. Below and about her summit ridges emerged like ships on the thick horizontal layer of the rising cloud deck. She paused to catch her breath and enjoy the awesome view before it would engulf her.

Our ape ancestors probably didn't go above tree line, she thought; people didn't really belong up here at the edge of infinity. All about lay a realm of the trans-human, a realm of gods and of emptiness. The beauty seemed utterly unreal. A glimpse of the universe without life. Blind beauty.

Benighted

And then it vanished. Conditions changed rapidly as she descended into a swiftly rising layer of cloud fueled by warm and moist valley air. At first it merely reduced visibility to a few a hundred feet, but as she descended it became an immersion into a cold thick fog, and soon after into a gentle windless snowfall. She stopped to put up her hood, tighten the collar of her shell, and chewed on half a power bar. From above the white cloud layer seemed innocent and benign, even picturesque. Now its interior was grey and menacing. Annie's need to focus on one obstacle after another aborted any other flow of thought so that it seemed hard to process her own emotions or even to think clearly.

She rested at the next anchor point and took a moment to evaluate the situation and to gather herself into calmness, to breath slowly. She knew the snow would get heavier as she went lower. In many places their footprints had vanished. If she wasn't meticulous she could easily miss the runners she had placed as anchors and the cairns erected that morning were becoming snow covered lumps. In half an hour they would be mere bulges. Then they would disappear in the immersive grey.

She came to a tower and uncertain whether to turn it on the left or right. Either way involved a near-vertical slab of rough granite. She looked it over carefully. It meant a traversing passage using her ice tools to dry hook and the front points of her crampons. Her least favorite sensation. In either case it meant going round a corner. She had looked for the scratch-marks of Urs' tools which were not to be seen. The right side looked shorter and had a more rugous surface. Until now she had used time with careful safety practices, but since entering the clouds she had to introduce more risk into the game. Getting late, time running short, and base camp still hours below.

She could taste the unique flavor of fear. Stay calm. Breathe slowly, like the old nun said; like her biathlon coach also said, breathe slowly. She toed out to the right and hooked her tools to the rock, and took five small shuffling steps when a momentary gap in the cloud revealed she was standing above thousands of feet of air. She gasped, froze for an instant, and tried to make herself weightless as she reversed course and stepped back. It was far from pleasant and required a minute or two of slow deep breathing to recover. And then, unexpectedly, the tower turned safely on the left side. At every step she issued voice commands to herself and feared it would be dark soon. How had Urs calculated four hours at most?

She once heard it somewhere: the tiger above, the abyss below, the Zen master sees the sweet berries on the cliff face. Her situation was not so exemplary. The Zen master wasn't frightened; but she was. The rib was narrow, with deceptive problems in the snow and weak light, and she was glad she couldn't see the vertiginous drop-offs because of the cloud. It would be terrifying to make out. One doesn't see the exposure so much going up and she recalled Chouinard's ironic observation that adventure only begins when something goes wrong. How had she gotten into this situation? A causal chain. Her trekking clients from Yeti Travels had cancelled and forfeited their deposit. They feared violence in Nepal after they heard that monks in the Khumbu were being killed by the Maoists. They cancelled and went to Bolivia. She was free unexpectedly and Urs persuaded her to go with him.

Visibility was down to twenty feet and the snowflakes were heavier and covering everything rapidly. The light was going, but it was still windless. It had been nearly six hours and there was no chance of reaching base camp before dark. She feared she was going to be benighted and started keeping an eye out for lee places where she could make a snow cave.

Thirty minutes later. Every movement promised hazard. So easy to be lured onto irreversible moves. What was Urs thinking? She went slowly. Her fingertips were getting numb and the tips of her toes had been so for half an hour. The light was now a serious grey without shadows. She tried her headlamp but it was disorienting in the half light and worse than useless. Damn again. She thought she could survive one night if she had to sit it out. But what then if it kept snowing? It could go on for a few days. Two nights or more without gear and she knew she would die of hypothermia. There was no choice but to keep going until she couldn't descend anymore. Maybe Urs would find her when he came down.

She swung herself left a few yards to find a stable footing before coming off the rappel rope when a puff of wind cleared the fog but redoubled the snowflakes and Annie saw the rocky rib start a long curve, which looked familiar. And then, after another down-climbing move, facing in on sliding snow with toes searching for some thing firm, she let go the handhold, and slid in self-arrest position to the top of a tilted slab. She worked her hands down to the topmost edge of the slab, and finding abundant handholds, came down to a welcome flat spot. She moved automatically, pulling the rope down, coiling it once again preparing for another toss. And at that moment Annie saw she was just above the cleavage at the fork of the two great ribs of the *Stimmgabel*. Her momentary relief turned to glee when she saw the tiny green cache tent of the Argentine expedition snugged in a niche at the deepest corner beneath the overhang where the roof jutted out from the face and sheltered the site from scouring avalanches.

A Cache

Out of danger! Tashi and base camp were only a thousand vertical feet below but too dangerous to reach under these conditions. She kept shaking her head in happy disbelief and undid her pack, took out her small foam square and kneeled before the little green tent's entrance. It was a one person single layer shelter, seven feet long by three and a half feet wide at the head, barely a yard high, with a zip-on vestibule at the foot. Dry and pegged securely to the ground.

She pulled off a glove with her teeth and tried to undo the simple bowline knot holding the zipper. But her fingers were sluggish, without sensation at the tips and it required minutes and the use of her teeth to be able to grasp the tab and pull on the big zipper to the entry vestibule. It was filled with a wire ladder, snow pickets, a long coil of 9 millimeter rope, and a snow shovel. She crouched next to the inner flap while she sucked on her fingertips. The zipper was down at ground level and she tried laboriously to place the tab between her numb forefinger and thumb. It finally opened smoothly and she crawled into the small dark interior and lay down, her hands in her armpits. It was uncomfortable but she needed the moment's rest. She slapped her hands and put fingers in her mouth and waited for the blessed sensation of pain, signifying serious frostbite had been spared. Finally, she was able to feel for the switch and turned on her headlamp. Everything in the tiny confined space was neatly arranged and without a sign of prior occupancy.

She stowed her boots and wet cagoule in the vestibule and took close to an hour to settle in and do an inventory and pass more of the tent's contents to the outer compartment. More snow stakes. Rolls of toilet paper. Dry mid-layer clothing in stuff sacks. A stove and a few bottles of gas, packets of oatmeal, and several kinds of powdered soups. One pot, one pan. A plastic tray. Three tins labeled "*Ostiones Ahumados*." A hard dry sausage. Freeze dried pasta with Spanish labels. Some sweet snacks. Chocolate! And best of all, a thick down sleeping bag and a foam pad. The Argentines had plenty of gear and were covering the possibility of a retreat. Up above it would be a climber's delight. Calm and clear.

Wearing her fleece hat she stripped down to her suit of wool underwear and crawled into the bag. The label read *"Hermanos Repeta, Buenos Aires - Grande"* and she squirmed deep into the smooth lining. Soon she stopped shivering and took time for some reflection. The tent might be home for a couple of days if it kept snowing. Beneath the roof of the nook in the deepest corner of the fork she would be safe from avalanche danger, but there was nothing to read, no MP3 player, no chess set, no boom-box, no cards. But there was food and fuel, and she was hungry after the long anxious day, admitting to herself once again that she was finished with extreme Himalayan mountaineering. Trek leader and dude guide on easy peaks was her more intelligent employment.

She half-dozed, still tasting residual chocolate at the back of her mouth. The altimeter again said pressure was falling. Now it was dark. The soft hat pulled down low over her brow, she slid deeper into the down bag and turned on her left side, knees curled, her hands warming between her thighs, thinking once again of what she would do with the rest of her life. She had pushed the envelope as far as she would go. Enough. Enchantment with danger was over. Finished. The future had to be the family ranch and a good library, the beautiful, solitary, alternative life calling for her.

Though the sleeping bag was warm she had to pee and unzipped one side, got up on her knees and unscrewed the wide cap of the pee-bottle, positioning the mouth through an opening in her long johns as she did her business. 98% successful as only a few drops escaped. Still, her underwear smelled of urine. It could go on like this for days. No radio. No iPod. A crossword puzzle book in Spanish. No music. There was nothing to do but listen to the soft sound of snowflakes and review her life. Her friend, her breath teacher, the old *yogini* who lived in the nunnery below Tengboche would be amused at her enforced meditation retreat! Alone with one's mind.

Pemba Lodrup

Annie started to doze when the sound of the outside vestibule zipper opening made her startle. A pack was being shoved into the little vestibule compartment and a man on his knees followed. She saw his headlamp's glow through the fabric and heard his breath and soft grunts. He had turned round and was searching for the zipper to the inner flap of the tent itself. Annie found her torch just as the man unzipped the flap and was about to crawl on top of her in the cramped space when she turned her light on him.

"Wahh!" he exclaimed, completely astonished, and held her in the beam of his own headlamp.

"*Namaste*," she said apologetically. And to herself 'My God, he's great looking.'He was smiling, with perfect white teeth, full of confident Sherpa cheerfulness, and unfeigned amazement.

"*Namaste*," he replied hesitantly. The expression on his face suggested he didn't know what to do, but that there was something quite funny about it all.

"I wasn't going to make it down to base," she tried, with her best apologetic face. "Started too late. There was too much snow that slowed me. I couldn't find the anchors." She said it again in Nepali but wasn't sure about the dialect.

He spoke in perfect English. "I saw you go down. You waved to me. I was helping some clients put in a high camp on the west rib."

She remembered. The ant-sized figure in the red parka with the Argentines. She was now warming their sleeping bag.

He put his palms together, bowed faintly, and extended his arm to shake her hand. "I'm Pemba," he said as he removed his fleece hat and fastened the headlamp to the loop where the tent poles crossed. "Pemba Lodrup, from Phortse."

"I'm Annie Wendover. Too slow coming down in the snow; couldn't find the rappel anchors. Maoist kids took our radios on the Rolwaling side. I feel so stupid. Is this the only bag?"

"That's okay," he said, as he raised his eyebrows and looked upward, wondering at it. "We'll have to share it. When I came in I saw the boots and the jacket and I said 'what is this?'"

"It might be days, if this keeps up."

"There's food and gas, and I get paid for days above base camp" he said as if it was alright with him. Well, hope for the best, she thought.

Their location in the nook under the overhang could not be safer or drier but as the tent was extremely cramped Pemba went to work removing boots and wet gear to the vestibule and secured the hard stuff to a peg outside the tent. They tried in an awkward way to be friendly and talked about the weather and conditions on the mountain, of climbers they knew; he had heard of Urs. There was shop talk, and estimations that it would be clear high up on the peaks. But under the cloud deck the snow was wet, abundant and unconsolidated. Too hazardous to descend the prow. They agreed they were stuck.

First Night

Annie downed her torch and watched him by the light of the hanging headlamp. He was orderly as he changed into a dry undershirt. The skin of his chest was shades lighter than his face and hands. Lanky, she thought. Urs was too muscular. What an interesting situation it was going to be. There was no way around it. They were going to spend a few days together in a small well stocked tent with a single sleeping bag.

Pemba worked back through the outer flap and filled a cooking pot with snow. He came in on his knees and said he thought it would snow through the night. He planned to dress and go out again after eating, to shovel a perimeter and make a toilet place away from the rock face with a guide line. The stove ventilation was also better now that he had relocated it. He set the snow to boil and opened two packages of Ramen noodles. Though he was nearly on top of her Annie remained in the bag watching him and wondered if he chewed garlic, thinking it was sweet that he was instinctively taking care of her.

Then they propped themselves in their down jackets like Yang and Yin around a small tray and sipped from hot mugs in the faint light of the low setting of a single LED. They talked more about climbers and Sherpas they knew. Her years in the Peace Corps and her climbs with Urs and others on lower peaks. When she asked how he hooked up with the Argentines he answered that it was through his agency, Yeti Travels. She nearly choked on a mouthful of soup.

"I don't believe it! I work through Yeti Travels too!"

He nodded, unsurprised. "So many of us. It's the oldest company for expedition and trekking support. At least 40 of us. Guides, summit climbers, icefall specialists, trek leaders from many countries, *sirdars*, porters, kitchen staff, everything. I worked through them many years and Sonam, the General Manager, I know since I was a boy. I knew climbers from my father's shop in Kathmandu. I started as a base camp kitchen boy. Then kitchen assistant at advanced base camps, high up. Kitchen on South Col. Then cooking for trekkers. Then *sirdar* for trekking groups. Then high altitude porter. Then western guides winter technique course in Khumjung. Then client support Sherpa. Then working at Concordia Hut in Switzerland. Two summers. Then climbed Cho Oyu, Latok summits. Guiding on Taweche. Lobuche, Pumori, Ama Dablam three times. Other expeditions. Once, Japanese client took me to Patagonia. Mountains, very beautiful, very dangerous."

He paused, stopping in the middle of what he was doing and spoke very softly. "My mother's two brothers, her sister's son, my cousin, and my own two brothers, five people all working on expeditions, all died in mountain misfortunes in the last ten years." He let it sink in. "Mother's brothers were killed by avalanche on Annapurna II. One of my brothers died during a rescue operation when a snow bridge collapsed under him and the other died when he was benighted on Makalu during a three day storm. And my cousin was lost on a commercial expedition to Manaslu only a few months ago. The body was never found."

Pemba now continued matter-of-factly. "A month ago my father learned he had only a few months to live and because I am his remaining male child, made me swear on all that was holy to give up the expedition mountaineering trade. When my mother died," he caught his breath, "she asked my father to stop me working in the mountains. He tried but I paid no attention. I knew many climbers who wanted me to come with them. She wanted me to be a monk, which is what I started to be as a boy. But after she died I began to live in Kathmandu with my father. Long ago he worked on some of the first European expeditions and started buying used and spare equipment from the foreigners on their way home. Then he opened a shop to sell or rent used climbing equipment and mountaineering gear in Kathmandu. I left the monastery and went to live with him. I worked in the shop after school and also part time for a British-man – I had lots of English practice because of him – and I finished school, and even went to agricultural college, one year. But I liked the mountains too much and making money and foreigners invited me. And so it went. And here I am. I could have been a monk."

Pemba's past

Pemba recalled the day his life's course changed. It was late in the afternoon on the big field below Tengboche monastery. With his lower robe held above his knees, he bumped another boy with his hips and kicked the soccer ball with a satisfying thud. The young acolytes were having at it, their once-a-day release of physical energy before evening prayers. Their heads glistened, freshly shaven at the lunar ritual. Novice monks, merely with the four preliminary vows of a first ordination, the *genyen* ceremony. Emerging from childhood, in their middle to late teens they would take on more vows, and receive the *getsul* ordination, the Buddhist clerical grade most of them would stay at for the rest of their lives. Only a few would continue their devotions to the point where they took all 363 vows of the original rules of the Buddhist faith and were ordained with the rank of *gelong*. This only was the true rank of a "monk," a *bhikku* in the original Pali and Sanskrit. A Lama was something else. A *tulku* still more different.

The soccer ball sailed above the heads of the younger boys, missed the goal markers, and avoided rolling down the sloping field only because some German trekkers fielded it. There was going to be a dazzling sunset. The orange alpenglow on the peaks surrounding the Monastery was just beginning. Pemba could close his eyes and spin round and still point a finger at any mountain that was named. Kusum Kangru, Tamserku, Kangtega, Ama Dablam, Peak 37, Baruntse, Lhotse Shar, Island Peak, Lhotse, Everest, Nuptse, Pumori, Trangdak Ri, Taweche, Kwangde. Numbur and Karyolunga in the distance. He hoped that prayers would start late enough so that they could all enjoy this clear evening.

Dawa, his best friend, shouted to him that Gyalpo Rinpoche wanted to see him. "He wants you to go to his room," he said, "not in hall." Pemba frowned. Had he done something? He rarely saw Rinpoche except at ceremonies and had hardly ever seen him alone. He raced nervously up the stone steps and around to the rear of the main temple building, the *gompa*, and was ushered into the Abbot's sitting room by the attendant.

Gyalpo Rinpoche was engulfed in an enormous brown robe and was reading from an oblong text. A few butter lamps in the small curtained alcove laid a soft light on the painted scrolls which hung along the walls. The Lama's low platform desk was crowded: various texts wrapped in yellow cloth, brass bowls holding dry grains of rice, a silver pitcher with a peacock feather in its spout, white silk scarves and orange ribbons and red threads, a brass *dorje* and bell, several photographs of Lamas, a Chinese teacup, and loops of beads, *malas*, of several sizes. The platform on which the Rinpoche sat, as well as the floor, was covered thickly with layers of colorful Tibetan rugs. Rice grains were scattered everywhere. And the complex odor of Tibetan incense.

Pemba performed three prostrations quickly. The Rinpoche gestured for him to sit alongside him on the platform rather than on the floor. Pemba was embarrassed to be sitting on the same level, so close to Rinpoche, who took his hand and studied his palm.

"Pemba-la, how long have you been here? More than seven years I think. "

"Yes, Rinpoche. Since my parents sold our house in Phortse and moved to Kathmandu."

"They gave you to religion, *chos*, and left with your brothers. And a sister too, I think." Pemba nodded. Rinpoche continued, "They came to see you a few times. And to visit old neighbors in Phortse." Pemba nodded again.

"And they have a shop in Kathmandu, in Thamel, now, I think. What kind of shop is it?"

"Yes, Rinpoche. They sell things to trekkers and climbers."

The Rinpoche sighed deeply and nodded. "Your father has sent me a letter." There was a very long pause. "Your mother is very sick. You can go to see her if you like."

They sat quietly for a while. "You can help your father and return here whenever you want." Once more they sat still, breathing together. "Here is some money" said Rinpoche, taking an envelope from within his yellow tunic. He held it out to Pemba who received it with cupped hands. "You can walk down to Jiri in a few days. From there you can take a bus to Kathmandu."

The Rinpoche selected a red protection cord from his table and tied it around Pemba's neck and then found a long white silk *khata*, the symbolic scarf, which he placed behind Pemba's neck and pulled him close with it so as to touch his own forehead to Pemba's. He held their heads pressed together for nearly a minute as he muttered a lengthy blessing.

Pemba left Gyalpo Rinpoche's presence that day with his head swirling. The sky was a dark violet above the valleys to the west. He came around to the top of the steps in front of the *gompa*, and stood alone, nervous with excitement. There was a bright moon rising and he looked out over the only world he knew. He had spent his entire life in the Khumbu's upper valleys. In the distance to the east the white wall of Nuptse was like a curtain. The sky was clear except for a long lenticular cloud streaming as a pennant from the top of *Sagarmatha*, Mount Everest. He had a sensation that his future was going to be like that, a streaming cloud of events flowing out from this very moment, here in the moonlight, in the cold, at the top of the steps. Kathmandu! He wanted to start down to Jiri at once, but decided he should wait until morning. His earthly possessions would barely fill a small cloth shoulder bag.

Kathmandu

His mother's illness was fatal. The Tibetan doctor had left a paper packet of opium pills and her passage was calm. Pemba sat the night near her lifeless body and assisted in the chants of the *bardo* ceremonies marking her way to a future re-birth.

Kathmandu was exciting with its size and the adventure of walking the city's streets. With his shaved head and maroon robes he was treated respectfully wherever he went, but especially in the vicinity of Bodhnath, where Buddhists from all the world circumambulate the great domed *stupa* surmounted by painted eyes gazing out in the four directions. At first he felt guilty that he was more interested in talking with the flirtatious Sherpa girls who worked in the surrounding circle of shops than in the religious significance of the *stupa* itself. But within a month he allowed his hair to grow out, ceased wearing robes and enjoyed rock and roll. And here he was, twenty years later, in a tent on the side of a mountain with someone called Annie Wendover.

"I told my father I would stop climbing and I started agricultural college." He shook his head, started to say something, changed his mind and put on his fleece hat. "I'll go make a latrine now."

Annie said "I'm an expert on latrines" and watched him crawl out and re-zip the outer flap. What an extraordinary situation, she thought, we'll never ever forget this.

He returned ten minutes later, mission accomplished, bright and cheerful as he undressed again. "I went to agricultural college too," she said. "In America."

"Ah. Good. Very good. I'm going to buy some land and grow potatoes. New types of potatoes. Potatoes are the future."

"Did you finish the college?"

"No. Only one year. What happened was in Kathmandu one day I met Sonam from Yeti Travels on the street and he offered me very good money to take two Japanese up Pokalde. A lot of money. You know, and very easy peak. Not dangerous. So I started working for them again. Each time I explain to my unhappy father that I am doing safe things. I promised two things, no more expedition climbing, no more summits. Then three friends from Phortse, my home village, are working as ice fall "engineers" for Everest climbers on the Khumbu Glacier, and they asked me to become their relief man. I said to my father it isn't climbing, it's just being an engineer. It was good business for us. For two years we worked Khumbu ice fall as our home. Spring and Fall. We could hear it speak to us. We knew it better than anyone. We laid out fixed lines and safe routes around *seracs*; we made aluminum bridges with hand lines across crevasses; we patrolled our work for signs of danger. We did rescues. Many commercial expeditions hired us to maintain their ropes and ladders crossing the icefall or they paid to use ours. This was our fifth season."

He shook his head. "Three weeks ago one of our team was killed when a *serac* collapsed. He was badly crushed and it was difficult and dangerous to get his body. The whole story reached the Sherpa community in Kathmandu so then my father learned I was working on the icefall steadily and became very angry with me. And then he started to cry and told me for the first time he was very sick and was going to die soon and he couldn't stop crying. He prayed that my brothers and mother's ghosts would punish me if I continued. I felt ashamed and so sad for him. He worked so hard his whole life and I love him very much. So I promised, I swore, that I would stop working in the mountains after this last job, this here, this last end-of-season job for Yeti Travels. Load carrying and support for the South Americans. Not dangerous and good money. And now, finished."

"What will you do? she asked.

It was all arranged, he explained. The *Panchayat* council at Lukla decided to support an airport constable and he had been hired. In two weeks he was on his way to Kathmandu to attend the training school over the summer and would begin work in the Fall. Lukla was getting developed and there were too many incidents of rowdiness at the airport. It was bad for tourism and there were violent fights among westerners about boarding priority. They asked him, he said, because he was bigger than most Sherpas and spoke English. He told them he would try it, while he would start searching for good potato fields. The salary was reasonable, and would add to his savings. He was finished with mountaineering.

"This is really it? The last climb?"

"Last time. That's why I'm telling you; mountains and glaciers, finished. In September I'm going to work in Lukla until the end of the season and look for a field."

"Wow."

He looked her in the eye. "Let's sleep," he said.

Sleeping Bag

While the tent had been designed for a single person Pemba had optimized the space and moved all non-essentials to the vestibule. The sleeping bag was half open with the zipper on the left. "Take the zipper side," he said, turning off the LED and crawling into the bag.

Body contact through long underwear. The necessary situation. He watched her blurred shape in the darkness as she re-entered the long bag and zipped it to the top. It was a bit tight but workable if they cooperated. A nested spoon arrangement would be best for sleeping. Their bodies would simply have to touch all the time and rotate at the same time. They would certainly be warm. With arms in the bag, Annie lay flat on her back with her head pillowed on her rolled up fleece; Pemba lay on his left side, his body straight.

"Do you snore?" she asked.

67

"I never heard about it. Do you fart?" he laughed.

She gave him an elbow. Pemba said it was her turn to tell about herself but she demurred.

"Tomorrow. I'm wiped out." She turned on her left side and Pemba settled in the same shape behind her and listened to her long breaths. She lay with knees bent slightly and Pemba lay pressing lightly along her form. His feet were still cool and she let him rest his toes against the arch of her foot.

"Good night," he said, very softly. "You can be my sister, *'Didi'*. I've taken Buddhist vows not to have uninvited sex."

So there they were. Her mind was dancing but she was determined to sleep. She forced herself to quiet by the slow breath method the old nun taught her. She went through the familiar numeration. Count during inhalations to seven, count during exhalations to eleven, repeat and repeat and maintain the count. Discursive thought of any kind is blocked by the *force majeure* of numeration. With that method she stilled herself within minutes. Becoming vegetative by breathing slowly in this way. Finally all thought and all counting stopped on its own. The nun's lesson. Simple. Stupid. Useful. Sleep came unawares.

After several hours, in unison, they turned and rolled the other way. Her face was close to the back of his neck and she smelled the faint aroma of cedar incense. Each wondered if there were signals in the body contact. The doubled feeling of attraction and self-restraint filled their minds. They turned again several times, not nearly prepared to be face to face. On one occasion an erection touched at the base of her spine and he pulled back. She also pulled away slightly. There was still an awkwardness about placing their arms to avoid an over-familiar embrace across a sleeping partner.

Pemba smiled to himself once as they turned. She was nice looking. He would like to. It was a funny situation. He would be teased if word got out. Anyway, she would say no. No is no. He had never been so close to an American woman. He imagined his hand finding her belly and touching her lower yet. Finally sleep arrived and the night passed in a pleasant awkwardness, mostly a problem of where to put one's arms, but otherwise they managed to move in unison.

First Morning

In the diffuse light it was still snowing, but less heavily, and the flakes came down at angles in a crooked wind. Free of the cramped bag, they dressed against the cold, talked about the weather, made their toilets, melted snow, and prepared oatmeal and tea. And then they settled in for the day of confinement. He made a gesture. Your turn.

"America?" he asked.

She told her story. An only child on a large and remote ranch in Wyoming; a 'Century Ranch' in the family over four generations since a deed under the original Homestead Act. The ecstasy of isolation. No brothers or sisters and very close to her parents. Father in the State legislature after six years in the air force. Home-schooled until she went to college. Father taught math, physical science, navigation, fishing, shooting, skiing, and rope-work. Mother tutored all the rest. Encyclopedias and textbooks and courses by mail for children of diplomats in hardship posts. 4H Club and the Future Ranchers of America. Never left Wyoming. Pinedale for local stuff, Laramie for the university, Jackson for sophistication, shopping, parties and dude-wrangling. The ranch took most of her father's energy and attention. He and his foreman ran the place with the assistance of seasonal labor, while her mother did the bookkeeping, read literary works, and acted as school teacher.

She wanted to see the world and applied to the Peace Corps after college. They sent her to Nepal, to Dhankuta, an agricultural hill town of about 20,000 residents, near Biratnagar at the Indian border. Further north the road-head terminated at the hinterlands of the Arun drainages and Makalu. She loved the people at first sight and studied Nepali until she was fluent and had enough hybrid Nepali-Hindi to converse easily in a sizable linguistic region. In between projects she traveled backpacker style in much of Nepal, especially along the mountain ranges. Several times she joined pick-up climbing teams who originated in a few bars in Kathmandu.

Her embossed Peace Corps card described her as a "Water and Sanitation Project Specialist." The broad assignment was to bring safe water management and waste recycling to a beat of five villages that surrounded Dhankuta. The work was pleasant and sufficiently physical and the villagers were kind to her and she always had willing recruits whenever an extra hand or two was needed. She loved the craft and imagination she could bring to each project; each taking months to realize. Water management was not that different from the ditch work back home on the ranch's irrigated pastures. Design the main and laterals to run on the best contour, keep them well formed, free of debris, and locate easy-to-operate gates. Some places had tube wells and others had springs or creeks. Build small community tanks on short towers. That kind of thing.

Her latrine projects were more ambitious. Her pride and joy. There were so many taboos about human excrement that the default situation in many villages was for people to relieve themselves outdoors, anywhere they wanted. Annie introduced low-cost toilet designs using the diagrams in her tattered Whole Earth Catalog. A pit cut into a slope. Three chambers. Cheap plastic lining. A side access from below. Piss in the middle one leading out to a drainage field. Shit in the left one for six months and once in a while throw in some straw, leaves, and a shovel-full of soil. Then six months of anaerobic composting while the right hand chamber gets used. At the end of the first year the left-hand chamber is transformed and filled with an odorless compound the texture of crumbled earth.

It took two years to make believers of the farmers and was the kind of thing that Peace Corps volunteers had on offer. Six months to convince the villagers to try her latrines and build them to plan. Six months to fill the first pit, and then cover it for six months. One crop cycle to demonstrate how the new organic fertilizer showed up in yields. In her last volunteer year the size of potatoes and radishes was the talk of the villages.

She was locally famous. And shortly afterwards she became internationally famous for her allotted fifteen minutes. And it would connect her to certain others. And Pemba to them through her. He took in every word. Everything she spoke of fascinated him. He boiled water and made tea. "Tell me," he said.

Her Adventure

During the last year of her recruitment she traveled to four of her hill villages by bus. The fifth one, Dara, she could do conveniently by bicycle as that road was almost entirely flat. It was at the end of the week and her return home had been delayed by a bad tire and she had to pedal hard to reach the Bharat Credit Bank branch in Pashpur, her neighborhood, before it closed as she wanted to replenish a pocket-full of rupees from her account. She was sweating but it felt good to push hard on the pedals and feel her heart beating from racing the clock. And if Mr. Chaterjee, the bank manager was still there she planned to urge him to extend credit to the Dara farmers who needed to replace their pump casings.

Only a minute or two after four, the heavy front doors were closed just as she reached the bank building. "*Memsahib*, don't worry. Come this way." It was old Johari, in his threadbare uniform and service cap, standing in a lane adjacent to the bank and gesturing to a narrow side door. A loaded shotgun, breech cracked open, rested over his shoulder. An immensely long and thick handlebar mustache was constantly groomed with his free hand. He had served with an Indian regiment under Montgomery at El Alamein.

"*Namaste, danjewad, Johari bhai,*" she said going straight to the single window. Das, the withdrawals teller, smiled, he hadn't yet locked his drawer. There was a sound of motorcycles and transmissions shifting into neutral. Then, as she watched Das count out her rupee notes, the fluorescent lights flickered out and a strange thing occurred. The side entrance door re-opened for an instant and a man was holding a deadly looking firearm to old Johari's head.

There were four of them, a grey-haired man, obviously the leader, and three adolescents, one of them a girl, all unmasked as if sending a message about having no concern about identification. Each with a machine-pistol and two grenades on a combat vest, and large empty backpacks. They took old Johari's shotgun and pocketed the shells. Their leader looked calmly at his hostages, which now included Mr. Chatterjee who had come out of his office.

"*Namaste,*" said the leader and spoke calmly and reassuringly in Nepali. Annie understood him as well as the others. The leader asked his hostages to sit down together in a corner. He was explaining the situation and promising they would not be harmed. He looked at her and asked the others in Nepali who she was. They all tried to protect her and went on about what a good person she was. He asked if they spoke English. "Yes, yes," was the chorus. "Good. Well, you won't be harmed," he said to her. "Just sit down there."

There were two vault areas behind a steel gate. The combination sequences to the main inner vault required two senior persons from Biratnagar who only came four times a year in an armored vehicle with an escort. The doors of the outer vault area opened to the steel trays in the teller's cash drawers on one side and a wall of private safe deposit boxes and drawers on the other. The leader made a gesture and one of the robbers swept the cash drawer notes into his backpack. The girl guarding the side door kept her weapon aimed to the floor. Her two mates extracted pry-bars and hand-sledges from their packs and went hard at assailing the private deposit boxes. There were more than a hundred of them and the leader was reciting names from a paper and calling out box numbers.

The smash-and-grab movements seemed choreographed. Foreign banknotes, bearer bonds, gold, and gems were obvious and all tossed quickly into one of the packs. They found ancient coins and seals, passports, manuscripts, stamp collections, printed papers which were held up for the leader's inspection and he said something about recognizing deeds, titles to property and contracts as the packs were being filled.

The leader looked at his wristwatch. "Four minutes," he called to the others. Then turned to the seated group and held out several lengths of nylon cord. "I apologize," he said, "but we must now tie you up. Not tight, not to hurt, just till you undo the knots in a few minutes; long enough for us. Please tell everyone this isn't a robbery by *dacoits* for personal gain; this is an appropriation by the armed wing of the Maoist Party. Long live the revolution!"

Without any resistance Chatterjee, Das, and Johari were tied individually and propped up against the steel gate, arms, hands and legs tied in thick comfortable coils and knots. The leader turned to Annie and spoke politely. "Miss, I think you will come with me. Just a brief detention, I need to borrow you for a bit. I was going to take Mr. Chaterjee, but you are even better protection. Just to have a cup of tea and a biscuit for a few hours while my people observe our rear. A tactical formality. Quite safe. It would be stupid to harm a Peace Corps volunteer. It will make a good story, no?" He waved his pistol towards the side door where the girl was still standing guard.

They heard the arrival of another motorcyclist. The leader looked at his watch, the side door opened and a young man stuck his head in and waved a signal. Time to go. In the lane there were three motorcycles in an echelon, motors idling. The proceeds of the robbery were stuffed quickly into the open panniers on a Royal Enfield, and in a moment it departed with their loot and one of the boys. The team looked relieved. There were two other motorcycles for the five of them. They hid the weapons in shopping bags and the girl fastened them to the Honda with bungee cords. The boys were in the driver's seats. The leader turned to Annie and pointed to the Suzuki. "Get on this between him and me," he said, "you'll be safe."

Actually, Annie's taste for thrills and curiosity allowed little space for fear. Her first direct contact with armed Maoists! Fantastic! A proper adventure after a week of latrine missions and a visceral sense no harm would come to her. The man was actually waiting for her. She could decline. Just walk away. She was in the alley. What could they do to her now? It opened to the broad street twenty yards ahead.

She mounted behind the driver. This will be interesting, she thought. The leader turned to the others. "Sita," he called to the young girl on the other bike, "we'll be at Nath's house," and was about to say more when they noticed a commotion at the head of the lane and someone out on the street was pointing toward them. "Go!" said the leader and jumped on the big Suzuki to press

Annie between himself and the driver. "Go!" As they rounded the corner and raced away they heard a police whistle.

Escape

Minutes later, the Suzuki dropped them at the shabby lower hillside end of Dhankuta where they pulled into the yard of a garage behind a shack consisting of a single room. An old man was tending a fire in a clay oven under a tea kettle and departed silently as they came in and sat down.

"My name is Chandra," said the leader. "And you are?"

"Annie Wendover."

"So Annie Wendover, I am pleased to meet you. I had to borrow you to wait here a while for our all clear signal. You are our insurance card, as I'm sure you realize. Much much better than Mr. Chaterjee. We have time for a cup of tea until someone will come and give you transportation to your door." He busied himself searching for cups and the tea canister. "Have a biscuit," he offered.

They had scarcely finished their cups, when the Royal Enfield arrived with empty panniers and was left idling in the courtyard. The driver spoke haltingly, sweating and nervous. He had delivered the backpacks with the proceeds, but when the others failed to make the rendezvous he parked and walked back to the bank where spectators were milling about. They all told him the same story. As Shyam's Honda came out of the lane he slowed to avoid a pedestrian and a whistle-blowing policeman ran and lunged and caught a handful of Sita's hair, pulling her off, while Shyam had to accelerate away with the weapons in the bags. The police had captured Sita.

Annie's intuition told her instantly where it would go from here. A hostage exchange. Insurance.

She heard Chandra speak to the driver and gave him crisp orders about whom to see and what to say and asked the man to repeat back what he had understood. Otherwise, Chandra said, he and "the woman" would take the motorcycle and go to Biratnagar forty miles down the road where there was a provisioned safe house and they would be hard to find. They could stay for as long as it took to get Sita back unharmed. Let people in Kathmandu arrange the details. No one wanted anything to happen to an American Peace Corps volunteer.

The driver went off and Chandra turned to her. "Will you come with me again?" he asked, "or should I say will you help us save Sita? No harm will come to you, I promise."

"Sure, let's go," she said and accepted the ticket to an adventure. She took it for granted she would be without harm.

An hour later they reached the safe house in Biratnagar, a proper small city. Several people came briefly to talk with Chandra and afterwards Annie and Chandra had the house to themselves.

"I do apologize," he said. "This is not exactly what we planned. Be a little patient and it will turn out well. We're exchanging you for Sita." He turned his palms up. What can one do?

"This is pretty interesting. I'll tell my children some day. A bank-robber kidnapped me." And she tossed her chin in the air and laughed so infectiously that Chandra joined in. Miss sunshine was at work.

"It's simple," he said. "We still suffer from operational roughness. Too much left to chance. That's why we're here. Well, we have to get Sita back, she's only a child. They just have to work out the formalities. As for now, come and let's inspect the pantry, then I will teach you some refinements of Bengali cooking."

They developed a collaboration in the kitchen. The way vegetables were handled, the yellow lentils, the rice, mustard and peanut oil, spices in dazzling variety, all the right pans and a copper pot in which they would make their curry. Water from a cistern, the clay oven stoked with kindling.

They waited for water to boil. Chandra was avuncular and Annie the attentive niece. He asked her question after question about her life, about why she came to Nepal. She overflowed her responses. The people and the mountains. She told him of her plans to go climbing at the end of her Peace Corps contract and some work ahead as a trekking guide during the Spring and Fall seasons.

"And other than Sita, was the robbery successful?" she asked.

"Probably. We had information on the owners of certain boxes, which was where we started. It wasn't just banknotes and jewelry; we mostly wanted land ownership documents, especially those from feudal titles. Do people rob banks in America?"

"I guess so."

"I admire young people like you who come to a place like Dhankuta to work on latrines. But you have a responsibility not to turn a blind eye to what is going on all around you. Willful blindness makes you an accomplice. You have been in the country nearly three years. Don't you see the corruption and theft by the so-called royal family?"

They sat into the night talking at ease as they enjoyed their food and later cleaned the dishes. He had the dimmest idea of America. He never went to the movies. Had rarely seen a television set. She was surprised at how little Chandra knew. America stood for capitalism, that was all that mattered. Annie invoked her father's view: one had to resist the tyrannizing power of the state. The state was the people, said Chandra. She searched for the booklet in her shoulder bag and retrieved *The Declaration of Independence* and *The Constitution of the United States of America*, the official edition for Volunteers. Would he like to hear some things from the American Constitution? They had time for a short history course. He agreed, with good natured tolerance. She went on for two hours. From the colonists to the Peace Corps. He wanted to know about the injustices to the native Americans. She explained that Turtle Island was for all people.

She explained the Founders feared the heated opinions of the mob and those who catered to it, and so they gave the people divided representation, a government whose power was divided, the secret of its citizens' liberties. She read the famous key phrases from the founding documents. Chandra listened skeptically but attentively, this being rather new. He found himself interested, nodded appreciatively at key moments, tapped his forefinger on the table to applaud something that caught his views. Nepal's revolution would succeed, she said, if they could maintain human freedom and human dignity. Revolutionary cruelty and the killing of innocents would produce poison. Chandra demurred.

They retired after midnight. Annie had a small room with a ceiling fan that rotated too slowly to sway a candle's flame. Excited by the situation she found it difficult to sleep but felt confident she was in no danger. In fact, she believed she had done good work. Chandra lay on the string cot in the dark. He was psychologically tired. Over forty years at the work and he could not remember, if ever, speaking with a young American. He had met westernized women a few times, but they were older and worked in NGOs or in journalism. They weren't working on latrines with a sunny disposition. She had hit home. There was an end to his denials. The revolution was eating its children, he knew it. And he searched for the technical yoga word for the profound turning about that was happening at the seat of his consciousness – *paravritti* –- and he determined to realize the psychological transformation in a practical way.

Back in the Tent

"What was Chandra like?" asked Pemba. "The government has a price on him. They don't know where he is and not many people have ever seen him. So what's he like? You spent hours with him."

75

"He's a nice man, really. A naïve communist nutcase, but a nice guy. Actually, we didn't disagree on very much. I told him about America."

"Did you ask him about bombings?"

"I did a few times, but he just sat there and stared into the floor without saying anything."

"You didn't disagree?"

"I'm not sure. And I think he's not sure either."

The tent fabric snapped in the gusting wind. But it had stopped snowing and they dressed warmly to go outside. Grey with poor visibility. They stomped the snowdrifts near the tent, made their toilets, jumped up and down and swung their arms to warm and improve their circulation. The wind blew curtains of spindrift in chaotic patterns just beyond their sheltered niche. The snow was unconsolidated and promised to bring avalanches all around them the next day. They tried unsuccessfully to detect a prevailing wind but the gusts came in all directions and the sky was too close to observe any clouds. Nothing to do but wait it out.

In the tent while looking for a hand mirror in her kit, Annie found the chit they had received from the teen aged guerrillas in the Rolwaling. It was stamped in red ink and the tips of a five pointed star had small portraits of Marx, Engels, Lenin, Stalin, and Mao. They had been asked to "donate" 5,000 rupees per person - about $150 U.S. - to the Maoists. A "receipt," was then issued which they were told must be carried at all times so that they would not be double taxed.

> "The United Revolutionary Interim People's Council for Dilup - A warm welcome to our international guests - Trekking tax bill received with thanks and [in pencil] 'benokulars and raydios2' in lu of taks - Unite All The Suppressed Communities".

"You think they're going to win?" she asked, "the Maoists?"

"For sure. A few more years. But many innocent people will die. French climbers were hit by a bomb two weeks ago on the road. One of them is in hospital, they had to amputate his leg. They were in the bed of a truck on their way to the trailhead when they were jumped. They had just arrived in Nepal. The guerrillas thought they were army because they were in an army style canvas covered truck. So many mistakes. So many innocent people. That's war. Same thing happened with a bus full of children. Yet they will win I think. But how did you escape from Chandra?" Pemba asked.

"Oh, someone came in the morning and told him that Sita had been expelled from Nepal on the word of the American government. The messenger said that I was supposed to be handed over to an American official in Jogbani, across the border in India but I didn't see the point of it. I had things to do. They were opening a latrine pit in one of the villages that afternoon and I wanted to be there. Sita was safe and I wasn't a hostage. The Zone Commander simply said I was free to go anywhere I pleased and wished me well. So I walked to the bus station and got back to Dhankuta an hour later. I planned to call the embassy to tell them I was alright. I had no idea what was going on. There was a huge to-do afterwards."

"To do?"

"I mean I got into trouble. The next day they told me to come to the Embassy in Kathmandu. The woman diplomat, Miss Hornbein, who waited for me at Jogbani, took me to lunch and explained that our government had gone to a great deal of trouble and spent a great deal of taxpayer money to arrange an exchange. So then they quizzed me for a while and asked about Chandra a whole lot."

"And what happened to Sita?"

"Great story. Miss Hornbein gave America's word that the girl wouldn't return to Nepal and took charge of her. Since she wasn't even sixteen and an orphan, they found an exception in the immigration law and in one week they had her foster-homed with a Cuban family in Miami. Unbelievable. She's in high school."

Pemba had never met anyone like Annie. The story of her life amazed him. He had met Americans, but they were usually city people. This woman came from a family of herders in a place called Wyo-Ming and she also happened to speak Nepali and understood its peoples. He could feel himself falling in love. The tent flaps rattled slightly as the wind came up and they ate slices of salami on cheese spread and soda-crackers as the tent filled with a complex chord of aromas. They were becoming chums *en route* to an unfamiliar place.

He talked about his parents again who prayed that he stop working in the mountains. In truth, he was glad it was over. He said he was granting their prayers. End of mountaineering. It was the love of his parents that made it so. Love was powerful, he added.

They were tuning the wavelengths. She said, "It's been bothering me too. I don't think I want to do this stuff very much anymore. My heart isn't strongly in it. I love the climbing game but I know my limits. I'm just not into the extreme. My parents are happy too. I'm probably finished this Fall."

"Yes. So interesting for both of us. Time to move on. I'm going to be a farmer. I'll do this airport job while I look for land I can buy. Otherwise, what can I be? What can I do? Mountain climbing and potato farming are two things I know." He paused thoughtfully. "But I'm learning to be happy and always hoping for more enlightenment." He said it with a broad smile. There it was. A code word. Enlightenment. Like a gong. What her mother said to look for, the signs of spiritual seriousness in a man, the expressed desire for self understanding. She turned to stare at him. "Where do you learn enlightenment? From the Lamas at Tengboche?"

"No, from..." he searched for a phrase, and said in a whisper "... spontaneous arising," and he was amused. He pictured his mentor in Kathmandu who had educated him and changed his life. "Actually, my teacher is a British man. Dipankara Macleod. Have you heard of him? You know, it's very difficult for ordinary Tibetans to get high teachings. Very few people even ask for such teachings. Only *tulkus* get the highest. Westerners are privileged and educated. The Lamas respect them more. They ask for and can receive high teachings. But most people here, most Buddhists, are only interested in spells and rituals."

"High teachings? On what?"

"To get a different kind of consciousness. To see your own nature."

"You'll have to show me."

"Ha ha ha. Maybe. You never know."

Second Night

As the day passed they knew that they liked one another, and even more, that there was a degree of reciprocal admiration. By dark the night sky appeared to be clearing and they could see a star or two. Wind had come up again and it was very cold. They wore their fleece hats and neck-warmers and settled in for the second night on the narrow floor space and arranged themselves again. It was far more relaxed than the previous night. She lay on her left side, knees drawn up slightly and he adjusted himself along parallel curves. They grew accustomed and then familiar with the slight pressure passing through long underwear. The narrower shape of the bag's lower end obliged their feet to entangle, though much less stiffly than the night before. Yesterday they were exhausted; today was a high calorie rest day and a considerable getting to know one another. A day of early attraction and during the night their thoughts fermented.

Pemba experienced a touch of sadness which disturbed the pleasure of resting quietly alongside her. He was so happy a moment ago. His mind was empty of everything except the sensation of their bodies. Then he realized, fatalistically, that he was going to miss the unworldly mountain experience of nights at high altitude under a fair sky. This was one of his last nights of such work. More than ten years of carrying loads, putting in fixed lines, cooking, setting up tents, short-roping clients, doing rescues, all finished. By summer's end he would be working in Lukla, down at 9,000 feet, below the clouds. A steady job with village government. A way to save a little more money and find a temporary place to live. A room with a stove and a drain was all he needed. She couldn't possibly live like that. Her family were rich cattle herders. What would she want with a crowded muddy village like Lukla?

But he wanted to hold her. It was the natural thing for a body to do. Natural. To bring his right arm across her body. Should he? Or not? She was a grown person. *Adiaw.* He was getting an erection again. And something he had eaten was giving him gas. He struggled to refrain from releasing it and it came out noiselessly. Relieved. But it stank and the gas extinguished his erection. He hoped she was asleep. They jointly turned to opposite sides several times during the night. Her nose was near the back of his shoulder. Again the smell of cedar. Sometime before dawn he reached his right arm across her upper body. It rested lightly upon her and she didn't move, as she surfaced to awareness for a moment and smiled to herself. Alright, you're a pal and it's nice.

Next Day

The next day's dawn was clear and brilliant but the roaring of avalanches began as the sun rose. They cinched up the various flaps and opened the bottom of the tent to the air and the view. From the safety of the niche the sound was like a contest of titanic drummers.

They were sipping morning tea. She asked, "So you know Gyalpo Rinpoche?"

"I lived at the monastery for seven years when I was younger," he answered. "I would see him every day but he hardly noticed me. But he knows me. I was only alone with him once, when my mother was dying and he sent me to Kathmandu."

"And you didn't go back?"

"No. I liked Kathmandu. I worked in the city for a few years and the next time I saw Rinpoche was later when I was hired as a kitchen boy to an expedition on Cholatse. It was my first time in the Khumbu since I left maybe eight years before. I went to see him, of course, to get his blessings. Then I would see him when clients wanted to get his protection cord. He always says a kind word to me."

She widened her collar and showed him a yellow cord around her neck. Pemba said "Ha! That's from Ani Palzom. She gives yellow protection cords. Gyalpo Rinpoche uses red ones. It doesn't matter, you know."

"She's from the nunnery near the river," she said. "I'm also Annie but I'm not a nun. Do you know her?"

"I know her. She's a real *yogini*," Pemba laughed. "I would see her when I was a boy. She was very beautiful when she was young. And she ran away with one of the yogis and they lived in caves and around burial grounds. Later she came back to the nunnery and shaved her head. She spins her own protection cords, and makes medical powders; and she does mental experiments and sometimes speaks in riddles. Some people say she is crazy but others say she holds high initiations and is herself a *tulku*. She gave me something wonderful once."

"I know, I met her once. We discussed what it was like to live in a cave. I kept bombarding her with questions about how to deal with fear. She told me how to fall asleep in a storm."

"Really? How?"

"We were comparing breathing practices. She was emphatic about slowing your breath. I do it lots these days. If I breath deeply and very slowly, like four or five breaths a minute, after ten minutes or so everything becomes extremely calm. It's very interesting. I think I'm changing my nervous system. Everything becomes quiet and peaceful. I can do it while reading a book or riding on a bus. Do it anytime. I'll never forget it. A valuable gift."

Something Amazing

Actually, Pemba related, he himself had also received a valuable gift, a jewel of insight from this wisdom-holding nun. It was on the day his team of French and Swiss clients had come down from a successful ascent of Ama Dablam by the standard southwest ridge. It was raining when they crossed the river and lower Pangboche was the first place where they found shelter in a lodge.

They celebrated their successful climb with considerable *chang*, and the boozy cheerfulness was infectious. Everyone in the common room stayed jolly.

Ani Palzom was seated next to him on the long platform. It was her daughter's lodge. She remembered Pemba from his boyhood years at Tengboche monastery and asked him if he remembered any of his prayers. Only the Vajrasattva *mantra*, he said, and being tipsy with *chang*, he half-seriously asked how many prayers she had memorized in the course of her life. This was not a question he would dare ask Gyalpo Rinpoche. It would be indecent. But Ani Palzom was so different, so informal. She had even been married. The rain continued. Ani Palzom said she could not remember how many she had memorized. But a great many. She gave Pemba a benign look.

Pemba swayed a moment under the alcohol and put his head close to the nun and lowered it. Supplicant. "Ani-la," he said quietly, holding his palms together in respect, "forgive me for asking such a question, but I have wanted to ask this for many years. Ani-la, you have had such high teachings and have meditated so long and everyone knows, even Gyalpo Rinpoche, you are very very wise, so I want to know one thing. If you could press and squeeze together everything you know, if you take all the prayers, all the *sutras*, all the oral teachings, and made it all into just one single word, squeezed everything you know into just one precious word, Ani-la, please, I ask you, please tell me what is that word?"

"What did she say?" Annie asked, delighted.

"She got up from where we were sitting and stood in front of me, looking closely at me, I remember that she fingered the beads of her *mala* and talked to herself as she looked at me. And she stood there a long time as if she was thinking about it. I felt stupid that I had asked such a question and embarrassed myself. Then her eyes widened, she slowly raised her finger, touched my forehead, and said the word "amazement." Then she rapped me on the head with the *mala* wrapped around her knuckles and she went off to the upper floor of the lodge."

Pemba explained to Annie that the moment he heard this word "amazement" from Ani Palzom's lips he understood he had just received a beautiful and valuable gift. In the years that followed he would think about that word constantly. His root teacher, Dipankara Macleod had seconded it. It became a key towards experiencing a magically illuminated aspect of being, the *sambhogakaya*, the all-pleasure body. At moments of great extremes in his life, of beauty and danger, when death or love or birth or pain or irreversibility were present, he would think to himself: amazing! look what's happening!! *this is really amazing!!!*

Other than Macleod, Pemba had never shared the story of the *logos* with anyone, as he had become superstitious about it. Spread the word too widely and it would cheapen, yet now he was sharing his precious gift-word with Annie. To be perched high on a mountain crag next to a strong woman, to be falling in love. There were not possibly more than a few dozen people on the planet Earth who were higher in the sky, closer to heaven, than they. That was amazing. Except for people in airplanes; but that did not count, although airplanes were also amazing. That all these things existed at once. Absolutely amazing.

Getting Closer

Sunny and clear, the day's temperature continued to rise while the little niche vibrated with the terrifying roar of millions of tons of frozen water yielding to gravity. The loudest and nearest made them flinch and hold their ears and then clasp one another instinctively; reflexively the first time or two and for comfort thereafter. And their repeated clinging and tightening brought them eye-to-eye at some point, to stare at one another through the blasts, their closeness driving out much of the fear. They began to grin at one another. At moments there was an odd sensation of mutually seeing the growth of tender feelings. Watching it move from the first awkward contact towards an alchemical transformation, to a sense of intimacy so profound that it seemed merged into a single self-aware entity of telepathic thoughts. Both were aware that something strong was happening to their minds.

By late afternoon the slopes had finished shedding and sloughing their burden for the day and the temperature fell under a clear azure sky and things became quiet. Then the wind came up, the temperature fell sharply, and snow crystals consolidated and hardened throughout the range. The night promised to be very cold and conditions seemed ideal for a start down at first light. Descent at dawn, they agreed.

They brewed tea, ate smoked oysters on wheat biscuits and went at the hard salami. They sat up wearing hats and parkas and used the sleeping bag as a shared blanket and told stories, sang children's songs they remembered and by mid-afternoon they were filling in the gaps of their exchanged biographies. Each of them wanted to know something unspoken, wanted to know but feared a wrong answer. What plans did they have for the rest of their lives?

"I'm going home for the summer" she said. "Yeti Travels expects me to lead a couple of base camp treks in the Fall. What about you? Are you married?"

Pemba laughed. No. A few Sherpa girls had proposed. But he wasn't ready. Over the years he had saved enough to buy a potato field; and then, he laughed, and only then, would he take a wife.

"Hey! What's 'tantra'?" she asked.

Pemba thought for a moment. *Secret teaching.* How could he explain if he knew so little. And even that little gained more from Macleod than from his own Lamas. "It's about how everything is connected," he said matter-of-factly. Wash my mouth, he thought.

"Say more."

This was a serious subject and he knew very well how little he knew. Ordinary monks did not deal with this secret subject beyond the text called "Secret-Assembly" the *Guhyasamaja* Tantra. Beyond that point higher matters were reserved for *tulkus* and yogis as well as the intellectually gifted. Moreover, he left the monastery as an adolescent, long before such teachings could even be approached. He recalled Gyalpo Rinpoche explaining to the young monks on their *Guhyasamaja* initiation why there were secret teachings at all. Something about not pouring milk into a river.

And then he wondered if Annie was asking about sexual practices. He had spent hours in those bookstores of Kathmandu with selections of used books in English. Many were common books about spiritual practices of Asia. Mostly popular inexpensive books. Not scholarly works, which were scarce and expensive. And in every such bookstore he noticed there was always a section marked "Tantra" in which a great many books, in both the Buddhist and Hindu traditions, were concerned with sexual matters. He had looked through them many times when he was younger but found little that meant very much to him. Except for the pause method used by adepts, the sustained cessation of movement en route to orgasm as an opportunity to glimpse the naked universal mind. That was useful. And actually, years later, listening to Macleod's afternoon talks, he gained a better historical understanding of the subject. Was there a way to explain that a Bodhisattva withholds semen?

"I really don't know what it is," he said. "We call it a mouth-to-ear tradition. You have to get the initiations and I never had them."

Third Night and Day

They packed gear and turned in for their final night. The initial configuration of left-facing spoons reached the stage of cuddling. The first night had been awkward, understandably. The second night had been when they ceased self-consciousness, and this third night became the night of friendship. They cuddled and enjoyed the sleep. She allowed him to cup her breast lightly one time, and in a passing moment of shallow wakening she felt his erection at her coccyx, smiled to herself, and returned to sleep.

His left arm was having a circulation problem. It had been half-pinned between their bodies. They needed to turn to the right. He started to roll and she moved in synchrony to change direction. An hour later when they turned back to the left again, he brought his right arm up, grazed her elbow with his thumb, paused, slid his arm forward so his hand rested lightly on her belly and they slept. Later he softly cupped her right breast again. Such an amazing warm and tender pleasure. It was truly amazing.

Dawn arrived and Pemba touched her shoulder and extricated himself to dress up. A blast of icy air came into the bag and she groaned. Half-hour later the tent and the vestibule were closed up snugly and the interior left in good order, with a note saying they had used food and fuel and had taken the spare rope. Then they shouldered their packs and worked over to the outermost ledge at the fork of the buttress forming the *Stimmgabel*'s handle. Pemba searched in the snow for the bolt and reinforced anchors he had put in four days earlier. It took some minutes of probing and digging before finding them. He was now all business, not just another climber.

They stopped what they were doing and turned to watch rosy fingers of auroral light become beautiful, and were compelled to pause in the icy air to see her approach. To the north, the grey face of Cho Oyu was turning pink, then red, then orange to yellow, and finally a brilliant white. A day like this held no terrors. They could probably reach the base area in less than an hour from their start, trusting the cold would keep ice-blocks from falling.

They could see both base camps down below. It was a rough granite pillar down most of the way until a rock littered slope skirted out to fourth class terrain. Pemba considered going for a single strand descent. It could save hours. Putting in a series of rappel anchors for a doubled rope would take time, mean exposure to spindrift and rockfall, and the fair risk of a rope getting snagged after it was pulled through an anchor loop. They had three ropes which knotted together would be just long enough to reach the fourth class talus field below. But it would mean taking the risk of coming out of the system twice to pass the fisherman's bends joining the rope ends which pass through the friction device. Could she do it safely?

"Sure," she said.

"Show me."

She gave him a look and showed him. But he was right to check. She had done single strand rappels on exercises and had taught it to novices at NOLS as they worked through "what if" scenarios. Always theoretical. Now this was for real. It was going to require more focus, but if done carefully meant a descent in thirty minutes. Or thirty seconds if she lost control.

Pemba knotted the three ropes into a single strand and knotted the free end securely to the anchor. Bomber. She judged his knot handling movements as beautiful and expressive, *presto ma legato*. They nodded at one another. He made another anchor and put in a sling to equalize, and went towards the furthest edge of the great buttress.

"I'll go now," he said. "After I heave it. Some of the rope will probably get entangled and I might need to traverse or pendulum to straighten it out. So give me time to reach the bottom and make the line nice and clean. You won't see me a lot of the time. But when I'm off I'll give three very sharp pulls. Look over the edge then and you should be able to see me. Ready?"

"Let's go."

"Be careful passing the knots."

"I know."

"Go slow" he said, "no rush, be smooth, enjoy the scenery, it's a beautiful day."

"I'm ready when you are." It made her slightly nervous and excited.

Pemba heaved the combined ropes outward where the breeze helped, and when the weight came on to the coils on the ledge they paid out smoothly until the full length seemed taut under its own weight. He tested it by pulling on it and nodded.

Annie was glad he was going first. Secured, she stood back from the anchor and watched him fix into his rappel system, lean back and test the anchor. Backing towards the edge he looked at Annie and opened an enormous smile. "I like you very much," he said, and lowered down out of her sight. She missed him immediately.

She sat on the snow for nearly half hour before standing and waiting for the rope signal. Pemba was hidden below in the rough features of the buttress. The three ropes would be heavy and taut, and she worried about not being able to notice the sharp pulls. But after some mild anxiety things came right. The three pulls were discernible though dampened by the rope's length, and she hauled in enough very heavy slack to get into her friction device and took a last look around. Time to leave the love nest. She leaned against the anchor and backed over the edge. She could see him waiting.

Pemba still had fifty feet of rope left when he reached the sloping ground which skirted the base of the buttress. From here it would be an hour's worth of unroped fourth class scrambling to reach the base-camp tents. He couldn't stop thinking of her. It was the first time in three days not in her presence. He stepped back so he could watch her descend. He knew they would hug one another when she touched firm ground.

Annie descended in balletic fashion, wide-spread feet triangulating against the slope, though at times the descent went free and over-hanging. At other moments she had to use her hands to climb around an outcropping to stay on the vertical line. After passing the first knot she gained confidence in the procedure and came down smoothly to repeat it past the second one. Over her shoulder she saw him waiting for her. And when she landed and undid herself from the rope Pemba came over and they hugged and held one another silently for a minute. The *Stimmgabel*, the tuning-fork, was behind them. They had shared the vibration, a unique event.

Au Revoir

They came down to the base area through a treacherous talus field where they laughed and held hands for balance on large wet boulders and then a scree filled gully. They could see Tashi watching them. Finally the mineral terrain yielded to a patch of alpine grass surrounding a small icy tarn, their tents on opposite sides. Tashi waved, shouted something which they couldn't hear, and turned to light the cook-stove.

They ate enormous portions of noodle and potato stew with chilies, followed by fried apple fritter for desert, and made the decision to continue heading down valley. The weather was clear, it was only mid morning and they felt refreshed and eager to have their bodies in motion after all the inactivity. Annie retrieved her sleeping bag and kit and Pemba collected his own gear from one of the Argentine tents and they started down energetically in the oxygen rich air. After leaving messages for the climbers still on the mountain they decided to attempt reaching Thame down-valley even if they needed headlamps to stay on the trail after dark.

So they went down the into the main Nangpa valley. To the old village of Thame and the first *Gompa* built in Nepal by the Sherpa people coming from Tibet over the Nangpa-La centuries earlier. They walked for almost nine hours. It was after dark when they reached Thame and they went straight to the first tea-lodge at hand. There was one small room available for four persons with two narrow double-decker bunk beds, but they could have it for themselves. No one else was expected at that hour. They took it on the spot, tossed their gear onto the lower bunks and ordered chips with chilies and yak cheese sandwiches.

They ate in the kitchen area, tired, stomachs full and staring vacantly into the small fire in the clay oven. Finally, over milk tea he asked the question. "So will you come back to work for Yeti this Fall?"

"I promised I would let Sonam know by the middle of the summer. I'd like to come back for a last time just to say goodbye to a lot of friends I've made. And see you again, too. But I have to see what happens over the summer. I'll email you when I know. I really hope you can come to America one day."

"I would like to come and see you; but it is difficult. You know."

They exchanged email addresses and headed for the bunk beds with the benefit of their headlamps. She intended to push off at first light and hoped to reach Phakding before dark, trusting for a flight from Lukla to Kathmandu the following day to deal with red tape, bathe in hot water, and eat fattening food before catching her flights home.

Pemba planned to take the trail's fork towards Phortse to rest there some days and visit cousins. Then to go over to Tengboche Monastery to pay respects to Gyalpo Rinpoche before leaving for Kathmandu and the airport security course at the police academy. He wrote out a mail address: c/o Dipankara Macleod, #34 Khora, Bodhnath, Kathmandu.

And it was bedtime again, this time to sleep alone. She watched Pemba splashing water on himself. He looked so handsome, such teeth, such eyes. Someone could develop a crush on someone like that. At the edge there was a deeper question. How could something like that possibly work, she asked herself. Someone, something, what does it mean?

They took the upper bunks, airier than the dark ones below. He used the blankets at the foot; she was in her own mummy bag. They lay on their backs holding hands in silence across the three foot gap between them. And then to sleep.

Annie woke earlier and packed and dressed in deliberate silence. Pemba was on his side, facing her, breathing softly through his nostrils. There was only one thing left. She leaned in close and placed a long soft kiss on the corner of his mouth and stroked his cheek with a finger. She felt the start of his smile as his eyes half-opened. She took his hand for a moment and whispered "got to go."

The light was dim, but he could see her features. He squeezed her hand. "I like you very, very, very much," he whispered.

"And I like you very, very, very much."

"Come back to Nepal."

"I'll try."

The Chinese Colonel

Though the old diplomats in Singapore and Delhi and the young climbers in Nepal were not yet linked directly, their degrees of separation were collapsing. A link In Tibet would connect them. There, almost 100 miles north of the *Stimmgabel*, across the frontier near a place called Tingri, a Colonel in the Chinese Border Forces named Thondup Gaomei, a tall thick-chested man with a slab-like face, close-cropped hair and a muscular body, looked out the window and tossed a cigarette into the gravel yard where the daffodils were emerging in the beds, a rare spot of color.

He looked out the window to scan the sky for its weather. His station near Tingri was a showcase of modernity and he hoped his successor would appreciate the improvements. In a fenced compound within a larger military station was a two story cube of cinder block painted dark green and topped with prominent antennas, satellite dishes, and a bank of solar panels. A bed of flowers surrounded three sides. There was a shaded car park for a few vehicles, a graveled helicopter pad and a rubbish pit in the corner of the two acre compound, all surrounded by a wire fence. A quarter of a mile away lay the main encampment of Thondup's own battalion-sized force on the central sector consisting of barracks, a mess, an armory, a vehicle repair facility, and a garage. He had moved all signal communications to his new building, a half mile back from the main road, the only road, between Lhasa and Kathmandu, near its mid-point. Staff maintained their workspace on the bottom floor while his own quarters and duty station were above.

He tapped the government-issue barometer on the wall and watched the needle move left. Falling pressure. Monsoon was creeping inland from the Bay of Bengal, moving softly over the foothills, and crawling up the valleys into the icy Himalayan Ranges. It would soon start snowing heavily up in the cold of the mountains, the roadless border crossings would cease for the season and he would return home to Lhasa, and then on to Beijing. And if all went well, a new stage in his career at year's end.

Thondup walked to his desk and turned on the computer, whose desktop image was a photograph of himself, his wife, and their daughter taken a year earlier. They were standing at the pebbled shore of Lake Namtso. Hsien, his ornithologist wife, like himself half-Tibetan and half-Han, was conducting a census of the nesting habitat of *Grus Negricola*, the national bird of Tibet, the great black-necked crane. She was looking up at something. His daughter was wearing the earpieces of an MP3 player. He himself looked stiff, with his hat set too square for the setting. In a week he would be joining them in Lhasa.

His current posting near Tingri was coming to a close for the season. By year's end he hoped and expected to have a new assignment. Exactly where and what was still not clear. With his impressive record there had been hints of a brigadier's star. Decisions would be made at the bi-annual Joint Staff Review in Beijing that summer. General Tu would be there, of course. Thondup knew the selection process was rigorous, but still, at his last promotion he had been the youngest colonel in the intelligence branch of the Border Forces. And while it was true his career path had been enhanced because of his father, he had proved himself meritorious more than once.

Perhaps there would be a posting abroad. Military attaché. Probably not. His skills were more specialized. More likely he would remain in China. After three years of operational command they would probably give him a staff assignment. A farewell to field operations. Beijing next year might even solve certain family difficulties; and allow him to see much more of Luo.

Thondup tapped the barometer again. Monsoon would be weak and brief this year; it was the type of legend he took as fact. The previous winter had covered the enormous Tibetan plateau with deep snow, whose vast whiteness meant a late melting of the bright surface. Dry winters meant dark areas of bare ground which Spring warming was said to heat a plateau-wide convective rise and pulled moist air from the Bay of Bengal over the mountains, depositing snow up high. Summer was the snowy season in the Himalayas.

A weak monsoon meant there would be a longer window of settled weather for roadless cross border trade in the Fall. And it meant more latitude in timing the yak caravan to the Khumbu district in the Fall for the *chungcxiao* cargo.

Crossing the snowy ranges of the international frontier once again for what was probably his last operation in the field. A promotion, a desk job and a mistress loomed in the distance. Enough of that. It was time to get to work.

Escapees

At hand was a matter which might raise eyebrows in Beijing. Two dead. Yet the laws were explicit. In the absence of a visa from another country, citizens of China were required to have documented exit permits. Failure to do so was in violation of a national law. His statistical unit's estimate for unauthorized crossings of China's frontier with Nepal was 1,500 annually. Thondup suspected the actual number to be twice greater.

By his own standing orders, escapees were to be detained, apprehended, and by other means prevented from leaving China without permission. In his mind, the use of "other means" included the discharge of weapons by border troops while executing their duties. The recent deaths of two escapees was unfortunate, but it served a purpose. It encouraged others not to follow such a course.

Patrolling frontiers was standard operating procedure and was proficiency training for mountain troops. He had noticed the pattern was changing. Individuals used to escape in small groups mixed in with traders and their yak teams. Most years the weather in the mountains permitted such cross border passages briefly in the Spring and Fall. But good policing by his troops put an end to such escape strategies and presently the few passes open to yaks were inspected by border control units in the season. This was Thondup's doing and no high passes remained as plausible escape routes. All others required technical mountaineering skills beyond the capability of most escapees.

There was a pass west of Kangchenjunga that belonged to the India section, as did the passes across from Ladakh. There was the easily controlled Nara-La, used mostly by pilgrims entering China on the way to Kailash. He had supervised the expansion of that border control point into a year-round station and persons wishing to cross in either direction needed to provide documentation. The Lajing-La near Annapurna and the Siyan-La opposite Mustang were difficult passes and relatively easy to patrol. Aside from the Nangpa-La, the others in the Khumbu demanded technical knowledge and equipment.

Last year it was discovered that escapees were moving undetected in large groups during the winter months when the weather was settled but extremely cold. They knew the saddle shaped Nangpa-La, at over 19,000 feet, was rarely patrolled in winter. They could reach the Dalai's people in India via Nepal. Thondup had walked across the pass in both directions several times over the years.

Late winter was a good season for such a crossing. The cold was cruel but the snow bridges were firm over dangerous crevasses. An experienced guide could show the safest route over the snow-covered *la*, which was little more than a rounded saddle of ground with the heads of two great long glaciers on either side. If the weather was favorable, a healthy and well-acclimated party, inured to extreme cold and walking without rest or other pause, could make the passage to a safe resting point on the Nepal side in a full day. As Thondup had instituted regular winter training exercises for troops, Lieutenant Li was assigned to commence regular high-altitude patrols when the weather was clear. And, needless to say, to do his duty to faithfully execute the laws of China. He had done so and two escapees were dead.

Lieutenant Li's report was thorough. The two dead boys were part of a group of nearly fifty. They were all making for the frontier's rounded top which was in sight ahead of them. Lieutenant Li was leading a squad of five candidate non-commissioned officers who were training in winter encampment techniques in addition to patrol duties. Early in the morning the squad detected the group of escapees approaching from below. Though outnumbered nearly ten to one, Lieutenant Li immediately ordered his men to form a line and display a threat of using force with ready arms. He believed this would deter the group's passage.

About half the escapees made a decision to turn around and descended by the way they came. For some others threats of force seemed to have no effect. They ignored shouted commands to turn around but instead they came on, trying to run at such heights. The squad members attempted to detain some escapees by physically overcoming them, but where one was being held down others ran through the line and passed beyond the unit.

Three escapees were physically wrestled to the ground while the remaining numbers were already moving off towards the top of the Nangpa-La as rapidly as was possible at such an altitude. As the squad was physically exhausted from their efforts at manually wrestling escapees, and as Lieutenant Li believed that the only means left to him to prevent their flight – he knew it would mean instant disgrace and forfeiture of rank if there were no casualties – was to fire upon the fugitives who had disobeyed loud orders to halt.

He drew his pistol and fired over their heads. They went faster. He ordered the two unengaged soldiers to fire above their heads. This failed to have any effect. He gave the order to fire once directly at a single individual. Two boys fell. One was killed instantly. The body was placed in a crevasse. The second was mortally wounded and took several hours to die and was placed in another crevasse lower down. Several escapees made it into Nepal.

Thondup wrote out Lieutenant Li's commendation. He decided to question the three fugitives himself, and waited in his office for them to arrive. They had been given hot food and a night's sleep and were being brought over under guard. Finishing his tea, he glanced at the day old newspapers, reports from Xinhua, the official news agency, fresh from Beijing. In India hundreds of rebels – hundreds! – had captured a passenger train in the Latehar District of Jharkand State.

It seemed clear that the struggle of peasants and landless laborers continued in India as well as in other countries. A second Naxal group of similar strength – almost battalion sized – also in India, attacked a government relief camp in Chhattisgarh State and set 20 houses on fire. These were large unit operations. Was this going to be a trend? There were recent battalion scale engagements by guerrillas in Nepal as well. He felt proud that China's no-nonsense policies prevented such developments at home. China had experienced such convulsions in the 1940's and 50's. This was the next century.

Prisoners

The three were brought in. Thondup sat at his desk. They stood before him, a guard behind each, and hung their heads to avoid his gaze. Having seen some of their companions killed, they were frightened and pitiful looking. Mere boys. Khampas, unmistakably by their dress and hair style. Nomadic herders rather than villagers. Two of them were brothers, age 16 and 14, and their friend was 12 years old. All their clothing was on their backs. Their only possessions were in over-the-shoulder cloth sacks: yak butter, milled roasted barley, hard cheese, a blanket, sleeping mats. Some charms wrapped in colored string. Some small idols.

Thondup spoke to them gently in colloquial Tibetan. He knew their dialect. Piece by piece he extracted their simple foolish story. They were from Amdo, hundreds of miles to the east. The younger children of two yak herding families. They decided, years earlier, while sitting on a high grassy hillside, that they wanted to be monks. Thondup believed this to be plausible. It was a move up in life for a nomad child. But many monasteries had closed, and the old practice of the parent's generation to offer younger sons to homosexual monastic life was over. The monasteries were no longer permitted to accept novices, leave alone recruit them. The old abuses, virtual slavery, the existence of *Dob-dobs*, serfdom, were all illegal.

The three had decided they would run away to India and ask the Dalai – unbelievable! – for his help and his blessing. They had been planning to escape for three years and finally received their family's blessings and took several months to make their way to Lhasa. There they slept in doorways until they found some labor and met others in their situation and worked for more than a year in the Barkhor market. Stall keepers hired them for pitiful sums to set up and take down, to sweep, to run errands. They worked as sweepers and as night kitchen servants in cheap hotels. When they had earned enough to pay for a guide, they joined the group Lieutenant Li had encountered.

The oldest one did most of the talking. It was not difficult to find a guide. They asked around until they found one they trusted. A monk in the Jhokhang temple vouched for his honesty. It would be a large party and three guides who worked together would show the way. They had to pay in advance. An early morning rendezvous was made at the western edge of Lhasa where a large truck took them and drive for two days. After rough side roads and they followed a dry river bed as far as the truck could go. After that they walked by moonlight and an occasional torch for more than a week, evading people, going higher and higher, staying out of sight of check-posts or patrols, eating *tsampa* and dried yak cheese.

The two brothers and their small friend said they scarcely knew the boys who had been killed. They only met them in Lhasa at the rendezvous. They were from another part of Tibet, from Golok. There were other young boys in their group, and at least a dozen girls. When they came to the line of soldiers ahead of them the three swore not to split up and thought they could make a run for it through the spaces between the soldiers. But a swift guard caught the little one and he in turn was set on by the two brothers. Two more guards ran to them and wrestled them all to the ground and held them at gunpoint as the remnant of their group ran on. The oldest one said that when the shooting started he prayed to the Dalai to kindly save them.

Save them from superstition, if anything, thought Thondup. He decided to save them himself. He knew with whom he was dealing. These were foolish children of limited background who were born to unfortunate lives. He scolded them harshly and told them they had broken the laws of China. As punishment he confined them to the base area with work in the non-commissioned officers barrack as servants, until discharged. This would be exactly what they would be doing if they could find some monastery to join. Thondup was convinced he could turn them into soldiers. They were tough enough to become border guards one day. He sent them off to be washed clean, doubtless their first bath in years, their clothes to be burned, with instructions to re-educate them and teach them basic discipline. They would be taught to read and they were to be brought back to him in six months.

A Fantasy of Luo

As the boys were taken away he mulled over how fortunate he had been in life. What was the meaning of human existence for three boys like that? Would they find a meaning or would they be so closely bound to the millstone of surviving that there was no room for meaning, for questions of meaning? A life beyond any meaning. He was beginning to sound like a philosophical Lama, he thought. All human beings wanted to improve their lot and make a just society. Don't be obsessed with yourself. That was all there was to it. It was the only way to peace of mind.

In the toilet he caught a glimpse of himself in the mirror. His hair was longer than it had been in years. A change from the standard military brush. But the October undertaking favored cultivating a civilian appearance and he would leave it uncut for the next few months, though it would generate comments by the unwitting. Identity was about appearance. Just not a military look.

He turned sideways and studied the reflected profile of his torso. More than acceptable for someone in his early fifties. Of course, staying sexually attractive gratified a man's self-image. Luo was sensitive to such things, unlike Hsien. The fact was, in his experience, sexual rewards which did not involve money or commitment were rare. And that was precisely the value of a woman who was also a sexual friend. Luo, the most understanding woman he had ever met.

He lit a cigarette and was annoyed at himself. It was the second one today. Then he stretched out on the sofa and started to read a military journal which seemed tiresome and uninteresting so he laid it face down on his chest and thought of Hsien and their daughter. Nearly a month since he had been in Lhasa. One more week. The girl would be off to a red pioneer camp two days after his return. Hsien and he would have the house to themselves for two weeks before he left for Beijing. Images of making love to her filled his head for a few moments. Perhaps he could get her drunk. Picturing her rounded breasts and the opening of her robe, excited him, but it passed. *Getting old.* Erections no longer stayed very long.

Did Hsien feel it too? He wondered. Perhaps that was why she had taken to making field trips with that photographer whom he didn't trust. The third time this year. Sharing a tent on bird photography expeditions. *"The Birds of Tibet"* *by Hsien Feng Gaomei and who?* When he made teasing allusions to tent sharing she treated his remarks as rude. But she was still sexually attractive. This was the modern world. Small pleasures need not destroy a family.

Thondup's desire to perform well as a lover led him to use traditional herbal supplements for male vigor. Like many who could afford it he used *chungcxiao* and ginseng and experimented with other traditional concoctions. They usually worked somehow but he could never be certain. He knew about the placebo effect and that traditional remedies involved wishful thinking and had variable effects, if any. Nevertheless, one did what one could. Insurance. A medical product was another matter. And now science was on the march. He had heard of the blue pill but had no idea how to obtain one. Were there even such pills in Tibet, or were they to be found only in the Capitol and Shanghai? It would be impossible to ask the staff doctors for the pill. Word would get out. He would be the subject of endless jokes. Still, he would like to try one. He would ask Luo in another month. She was sure to know a way.

It was pleasant to stretch out on the sofa and think about spending time with her when he reached Beijing. Their second summer since first meeting. A single long weekend was the most they had ever managed together, but the residues echoed in his mind all year. She was an administrator in the accounting department of the third army corps with the rank of captain. In a dull uniform by day, a gay party dress in the evening made her into another person. Unmarried, attractive, in her forties, witty, independent, and the grand-niece of one of the Party's most famous Marxist theoreticians, who was deceased but remembered and revered. In her network of relations, her *guanxi*, Luo was confidently above criticism.

They met at a social evening hosted by the Defense Ministry. A hospitality event for a Kazakh arms purchasing commission. Speeches. He was introduced as the conqueror of *Chomolungma*, the world's highest mountain. There was light applause except for a motionless woman looking at him in admiration. A long wide banquet table. The first dishes. Thondup's chair off to the left. He caught her looking at him again and she held his gaze for a moment longer than casual and turned to her food. Then some fleeting episodes of staring that ended smoothly; every occurrence unexpected. The air began to feel vibrated. When everyone moved to enter the exhibit hall they drifted toward one another. She touched his arm and they exchanged names and obtained an ignition so to speak.

95

After four consecutive evenings together they agreed, exceptional circumstances aside, to meet again the following summer at the Joint Staff conclave. There would be opportunities. She knew a lake resort where they could rent a cottage, not far from the Capitol. Their brief encounter thrilled them. They thought of one another during the long absence and exchanged holiday greetings that carried oblique meaning. During the second summer their one weekend together still felt new as they became sexually imaginative and thoughtful. They read aloud from China's great erotic classics, *The Golden Lotus, The Carnal Prayer Mat* and spoke abstractly about sexual heat and sexual desires, and the recollections of those conversations perfumed Thondup's night thoughts in the intervening year.

The approaching summer was full of promise. Could even lead to something serious, long-term. Ironically, given the operation at hand, he had been taking regular doses of *chungcxiao*. Two pinches every morning plus a spoonful of ginseng extract. It was supposed to build up slowly in the body. He thought of Hsien once again, trying to imagine her naked and panting in a tent with her photographer colleague, but the thought was unattractive. Her colleague looked like a scarecrow. Like one of the long legged birds they photographed. Not very sexual, Thondup thought. In any event, Hsien lacked a sincere interest in eroticism. This led ultimately to his organ diminishing. It was only when she was drunk, which was infrequent. He fantasized Luo and Hsien in sex play together, naked and inverted and found he was hardening. Why not ejaculate, he thought. Later he decided he would increase the doses to three pinches and two spoonfuls. The caterpillar fungus was a gift of heaven.

Plans for the Cargo

He called for a mess tray, had a wash and returned to the desk. Then made a note to review the file on the planned yak caravan over the Nangpa-La. He had arranged with the headman that at least eight of the yaks in the caravan were to be reserved for his own personal cargo. While it was usually understood that personal business was not to be involved in operational matters, in this case, ingeniously, personal business was actually the cover for the operation. Aside from General Tu's consignment of sneakers, Thondup had contracted for the annual down output of a goose farm in Szechwan and had a family of Muslim tailors in Chengdu make him forty sleeping bags and parkas. Exact copies of the ones in the internet catalogue pages. The web sites even permitted close-ups for showing the stitching details.

Then a broker in Hong Kong, with whom he communicated by e-mail, sent him faithful reproductions of brand labels and cleaning instructions. Good labels were the most expensive part of the whole business. Most tourists were not knowledgeable buyers, and the counterfeit labels sewn perfectly by skilled fingers made for a fine profit in Nepal's outdoor gear shops. Working in Nepal with his reliable counterparty who would receive his goods in Khumjung, Thondup had a profitable business which had taken years to develop. He planned to sell it at a fair price to his successor. It was still retail however. He was looking for something bigger, something wholesale.

Personal business aside however, he knew physically handling the *chungcxiao* delivery and making the counter-trade arrangements for a list of weapons and bomb-making material were serious matters. Matters which involved the name of Chairman Mao. The political implications could be unsettling so deniability was essential and the operation and circle of knowing persons had to be small and elite. The fact that the mission had been entrusted to him signified he had joined a sanctioned but covert intelligence unit in contact with the Nepalese communist military commanders, the 'maoists'; and he had been chosen as the channel for negotiations with them on future weapons arrangements. Details of an asynchronous and remote arms delivery would have to be clarified and deniability was to be foremost in their minds. An officer's career would be destroyed by so much as a hint of involvement in an undercover weapons trade with revolutionaries across the border.

It was sufficiently secret that he himself knew little of General Tu's circle which had always operated to ensure the autonomy of Border Command. Autonomy was the key to the business. In fact it wasn't clear to whom General Tu reported. It was he who master-minded communications with the guerrillas, he who designed the framework for masking the negotiations, and he who assigned Thondup to take personal charge of the matter. The sensitive discussions with the guerrillas were secret, unauthorized, deniable, and when useful – this part was General Tu's genius – were to be conducted in the guise of a shadow business operation for profit. The *chungcxiao* trade made for a solid cover story. The fact that it was profitable personally was beside the point. Thondup came to believed General Tu's network, his *guanxi*, was none other than the cartel that dominated the global trade in traditional Chinese herbal medicines.

The General, an old comrade of Thondup's grandfather, was one of a circle of officers who kept their eye out for the boy, son of a Tibetan martyr. A virtual godson, Thondup had risen to become the General's all purpose man for Tibet and it was made rewarding. He could start small and develop his own commercial networks. In addition to his sleeping bag business he expected a commission on the *chungcxiao* transaction itself. Even a small commission would be quite profitable considering the total value of the trade. And further he had the responsibility for negotiating the weapons manifest and delivery arrangement. His own share, though much smaller than General Tu's, would also allow some luxuries.

Over the coming summer General Tu would give him guidance for dealings with the Zone Commander in October. The *chungcxiao* would be ready and waiting in time for the caravan's arrival. The yaks were to be corralled, rested and fed in a fallow potato field in the Sherpa village of Khumjung. Thondup calculated that 500 kilos of *chungcxiao* would be worth several million dollars in Lhasa, if handled carefully. Considerably more in Chengdu and Xian. In the great metropolises of the coast, Hong Kong, Shanghai, Beijing, it could be closer to twenty million of herbal apothecary value. This was the largest consolidated quantity in years, as collection had been put under Maoist management by gun.

He intended to cross the frontier in October with the yak-trader caravan over the Nangpa-La, happy he was still fit enough to do it enjoyably. Disguised as one of the nomads he wouldn't be noticed at the checkpoint on the Nepal side of the pass. Without papers, his persona was merely a name and a count mark on the manifest. Once he reached Namche Bazaar he planned to change appearance, bring out his false documents and pass as a trekker.

He continued working at his desk. Reading, calculating yak loads, and writing reports until he enabled the encryption features of the small box cabled to his computer to send and receive the burst transmissions. There was a downloaded file from the satellite that required Thondup's personal security code to decrypt. He was known for pushing technology innovation down into his commands. His most recent medal was for his introduction of GPS global positioning systems into Border Force exercises.

This latest message from General Tu created an addition to the cargo list, which could mean a row with Paljor the headman, who would require more yaks. A rare product for the cartel's pharmaceutical inventory and marketing channels. The dried remains of two tiger carcasses from Nepal, shot illegally down in the *sunderbans*. The skins and paws had been taken instantly at a high price by an Indian dealer for a Russian client. But while the poachers were cleaning the remaining fresh carcasses for resale, a Maoist guerrilla squad came upon them and after an exchange of fire killed the poachers and seized the carcasses. General Tu wanted them even at an exorbitant price if they were carried with the *chungcxiao* in the handover. Left to Thondup to negotiate. He knew the headman would be nervous about the yaks behaving calmly if there was an unnatural cat odor on their backs. It would need special packaging.

But unboiled bones! The real thing and worth a fortune. Thondup planned to sequester a fragment or two. When dried, ground into powder and brewed into tea through a cloth it was famous. Even the dregs could be dried again and resold in pill form. The Hong Kong market for authentic tiger bone wine was richer than ever. It was illegal but authorities had a blind eye; Chinese were becoming rich which was glorious. In exchange Chandra had requested shoulder-fired Stingers and high-caliber sniper rifles with optics to take out microwave relay towers.

Thondup tried calculating the yak numbers again. More than a dozen if the guerrillas came up with more than five hundred kilos. Two loads per yak plus the packaging. There would be a yak for his personal gear. Another two yaks for his cargo of sleeping bags, and one for the load of sneakers that General Tu sent. The headman, Paljor, and his family would probably have at least ten more yaks for their personal trade. He made a final note to himself and closed the folder on the *chungcxiao* matter. Then he got out from behind his desk and did fifty push-ups on the floor.

Climbing Resumé

Thondup's sport mountaineering accomplishments had once been taken up by the national military newspaper. A color photograph of him on the summit of *Chomolungma* when he was still an adolescent made for popular recognition and led directly to his recruitment into the border guards and he was featured in the national press for a season. Women wrote letters to him and the border guards made much of him. As a boy he had taken any opportunity to go rock climbing and in his junior days in service he had turned down staff assignments because they would have put him behind a desk in a city. Now he was glad for a desk assignment in the Capitol.

Thondup knew that at his current age it was past time for long mountain forays. It was a young man's game, a time of estimable domestic first ascents. He had been an expedition leader in the Pamir and Kunlun ranges and commanded a military mapping mission in the Aksai Chin region along the Ladakh-Tibet cease-fire line. It was noted he enjoyed hardship assignments and was a natural leader who sought the front of the line. His personal and unsolicited report on undocumented trade across China's Kirghiz, Afghan, Kazakh, and Pakistan borders created a favorable impression in Beijing. Within a year and he was promoted to Major on the staff of Border Command in the Capitol. His was a new breed, hard, brave, and technologically adept. His relation with General Tu matured and gave him entry to a wider set of connections, developing his own *guanxi*. His father's legacy.

Accomplishments in his resumé showed he had set recruitment standards for mountain troops; standardized the training curriculum in survival, evasion and escape; improved the modernization of clothing and equipment for mountain conditions; and assigned the laying in of GPS waypoints in clandestine cross border infiltration exercises. Chinese troops would use science in any future war with India. And though he said "Chinese troops" to himself he was of mixed Tibetan-Han blood, which would not matter in a modernizing China. Would a Manchu or a Mongol doubt he was Chinese? No. He would think of himself as Chinese. A child of the Chin Emperor. Uighurs in Xinjiang and renegade Tibetans still resisted the historical integration. Especially the religious ones. But all of them, including himself, were Sons of the Yellow Emperor. He admired the ancient myth. Of course he was 'Chinese'. A Chinese citizen of Tibetan and Han extraction. There were many like him, more than ever.

There was still an unfinished task dealing with renegades. He was one of a few with combat experience against Muslim Uighurs, against Buddhist Khampas, against Christian American supporters of the Dalai's clique. He was the modern man who had learned to kill and was decorated for bravery. Not many Chinese officers could say that. Holding principal responsibility for the entire China-Nepal border he had kept things calm, in good form for turning command over to a successor at the end of the year. A productive negotiation with the Zone Commander in October would improve his ascension in rank.

On his own he hoped to convey to the Zone Commander that by calling themselves 'Maoists' the guerrillas were creating an ongoing international embarrassment. By misusing Chairman Mao's name they harmed the image of modern China's historic founder. The revolutionaries thought they were clever by reciting back Chairman Mao's own words in response. Annoying, to say the least.

Thondup's World View
He did more pushups and went back to the desk. His next item was a message from a former subordinate, presently a Captain in the Security Police based in Shigatse, 120 miles to the east. An increasing number of Americans were attempting to visit the great Sakya monastery in the long valley to the south.

They had ordinary tourist visas, and the numbers were increasing each season. There was a Lama somewhere in America whose disciples were intent on making pilgrimages to the ancient Sakya monastery. Did Thondup believe this could lead to mischief? Other than a few monks who were paid informers, there were no security organs in that valley. The Captain decided to create a checkpoint on the road leading there and was collecting detailed information from passports before permitting them down the road. Did the authorities wish to curtail foreign visitors?

Thondup was mildly amused. Tibet was in a new phase. Tourists brought hard currency. The fact that the Tibetan Autonomous Region was increasingly popular as a tourist destination was a marvelous thing. Who ever thought large numbers of people would want to see this place and spend so much money? He knew there had been several films in the west about Tibet. And of course, the weird mysterious attraction of the old religious superstitions. It was actually amazing that the land where the computer was invented which put men on the moon had so many followers of the ancient shaman nonsense of ignorant monks. Let them come. Let them spend on hired land-cruisers, trekking agencies, imitation bronzes, let them pay admission to the Potala, stay at hotels, raft the rivers, see the monasteries. Why not? China was advancing, and beyond prudent security matters had little to hide and much to share with the world.

He read the news bulletins. There was an item that Government officials in Nepal had closed the offices of the Dalai Lama and the welfare center it maintained for new escapees. That was a success for Chinese diplomacy. For years Tibetans had been stealing across the border into Nepal to blacken China's name. They called themselves refugees, he scoffed. They were merely splitters of the Dalai clique. There were fewer every year. When the Dalai dies, then the Panchen will speak for the Buddhists.

Nepalese governments had always been more than respectful of China's views and the Dalai's people were being kept firmly distanced from the Sherpa community. Several requests by the Dalai Lama himself to attend important ceremonies in Nepal had been refused. As far as the Nepalese government was concerned, the connection between Dharamsala in India, home base for the Tibetan Government-in-Exile, and the Buddhist Sherpa valleys of the Khumbu region was to be monitored and kept to a minimum.

Thondup was most familiar with the Tibetan version of Buddhism. It was the only branch of that religion he had observed at first hand. What he knew of the other branches he learned from Party literature, from encyclopedias and the internet, and discussions with colleagues. While it did not interest him particularly, he tried to imagine stages of development occurring in Buddhism since the time of its founder. A model figure. A proto–communist, as far as he was concerned. Selfless. He invented a Party of dedicated cadres they call the sangha. There had been a book recently in the Lhasa university bookstore espousing this interesting revisionist view. The Buddha as the first Communist! There had been a favorable book review in a key Party organ and no echo. No comments from on high. A possible sign of something. The once-great truly atheistic religion had been degraded. He saw the product in his boyhood. For whatever intellectual and ritual brilliance it once had at its early high point it had gone mad into idolatrous foolishness, filled with preposterous ceremonies, and in Tibet ended in feudal slavery, class tyranny and its ugly enforcers, the *Dob-dobs*. They gave him nightmares.

His earliest memory of the *Dob-dobs*, the military police of the monasteries, the huge enforcer monks who swaggered through the streets of Drepung, involved an outing with his grandmother when he was a very small boy. Three Dob-dob monks were escorting a young monk towards the main gate. They flanked him on three sides and continually gave him merciless blows and he howled as they passed in the lane. They had large iron keys at long ends of their rope belts which they used as whips. He remembered his grandmother and aunts telling him that he had to behave well or the *Dob-dobs*, who had a reputation of kidnapping boys for their monasteries, would attempt to snatch him and steal him away. Even now he could recall his fear. Their day was over. They would never terrify little boys again.

Great changes had taken place since the abolition of serfdom in Tibet half-century earlier when China renewed itself and defeated the separatists. Who could possibly challenge the facts? Once without any roads Tibet now had a highway network of thousands of miles with Lhasa at its center and was on its way to prosperity. There was the rail link, at such an altitude! Economic output was over 40 billion Yuan and for many years growing annually at more than 10 percent. Computers and mobile phones were equipped with input software in Tibetan script. And as for the yak herders, the per capita net income of nomads had been growing at a double-digit rate for six consecutive years. The economic report was on his desk.

What Thondup Saw

Thondup's mother was originally from Harbin on China's North Pacific coast where her father began a military career in the People's Liberation Army. His ultimate promotion to General coincided with an assignment to Tibet, where the family moved at the end of her adolescence. Her romance with Thondup's father, whose aristocratic ancestry was mentioned in the Blue Annals, was a major social event in Lhasa involving considerable self-congratulation on both sides. A rare moment when such things were conceivable.

Thondup had the dimmest memories of the arrival of Chinese troops in Lhasa. He wasn't sure if he really remembered the events, or whether he was imagining himself within them through old photographs he had seen. His father had him on his shoulder. Rank after rank of troops with red stars on their hats paraded with strict discipline. His father was so happy they had finally come into the city. The longed for revolution had come.

They were living in a house with many servants who were treated kindly. Not the way the other Lhasa aristocrats treated their servants. But his father was a modernizer. Supposedly, his father's father was the person who introduced the wearing of fedora hats among Lhasa's fashionable men of that day. They lived in a large house near the old medical college hill and had electric light bulbs though there wasn't much fuel for the generator. His father knew English and would sit with a dictionary as he listened to short wave radio broadcasts. There were very few radios in Lhasa in those days.

Their house was one of the places the rare foreigner would be urged to visit. No one would receive the German mountaineers, Harrer and Aufschnaider, until they had received his father's hospitality. And important Lamas would sometimes arrive. They would be received politely, but their attendants were required to remain in the street. Once a year a Rinpoche would arrive with rents for the use of potato and barley fields owned by Thondup's family.

His father looked down at the entire Tibetan clergy. He thought they were monstrous deceivers. He was fond of the metaphor of the opium of the masses. His father believed that in the future the Chinese revolution would be seen as one of the greatest events in human history. He was prepared from the first moment to turn all he owned to the service of the revolution. An act that was well appreciated by General Kojei, who had recently been assigned to Lhasa from a previous posting at Harbin.

When General Kojei's daughter, Thondup's mother, arrived to visit her father it was arranged she could visit the best of houses, which received her as an honored guest. Within months the possibility of Thondup's future existence was discussed and a marriage arranged. A Han mother and a Tibetan father, all children of the Yellow Empire. His parents adhered to the single child policy, and there was a succession of serving women who cared for him through early childhood. The household was bi-lingual although from the earliest age he heard and used English words and his father insisted on daily English practice through the late grades of elementary school. So he was fluent and articulate in Chinese and Tibetan without effort. And after English there was proficiency in the main Hindustani branches, including Nepali.

The *Dob-dobs*, kidnappers of boys, were his great fear. The Lhasa *Dob-dobs* usually came from the worker and serving monks who belonged to a special strong-arm fraternity which kept monastic discipline. They served as bodyguards to monastic officials, as traveling escorts. With a reputation for being quarrelsome, their worldly interests were in sports, especially long jumping, and young boys. Novices who were strong and who couldn't find a teacher or were bad at learning were recruited to join one of the cliques distinguished for their physical strength and courage into which the *Dob-dobs* organized themselves.

When he stayed at his grandmother's house just outside Lhasa as a child his window looked out on a field at one side of Drepung monastery. The *Dob-dobs* gathered there at first light, showering under buckets of cold water and running naked in the sand, or wrestling, or having contests of carrying and throwing heavy stones. Their most common exercise was long-jumping which always drew a crowd and there were jumping competitions with *Dob-dobs* of other monasteries. They were famous jumpers. He watched them take turns under the orders of a jumping master, who kept strict discipline and controlled their jumping exercises while carrying a stick with which he marked the distances. The whole business of jumping was taken very seriously.

Dob-dobs could be recognized by the special way they wore their robes which though longer than usual, were kept pleated and belted up higher than ordinary monks, which gave them a bulking look which they exaggerated by swaggering as they walked. Sometimes they blackened the skin around their eyes to look fierce and typically had a big key hanging from a belt. Once he watched a fight of the Drepung *Dob-dobs* with the *Dob-dobs* of Sera monastery, and laughed when he saw a monk's teeth knocked out of his mouth with a kitchen pestle.

Among their tasks at religious services was to keep time on the drums and play the oboes and long trumpet at ceremonies and to be in charge of monastery policing. The lay people of Lhasa preferred that monks should keep to themselves and not worry the city's womenfolk. So frequently the *Dob-dobs* had fights about favorite boys, a sort of behavior not looked on as especially bad. But what else could be expected in a community of only men and boys? Fights were part of the game.

Thondup and his friends feared them. It was a long-standing challenge to the *Dob-dobs* to try to carry off some boy of a good family from Lhasa and keep him in a monastery, beyond reach. Thondup's grandmother would constantly warn him of the threat. Years later he could recall the pleasure he experienced at pulling the lanyard when he shelled Drepung Monastery as a Red Guard during the cultural revolution. When he imagined the fear in the hearts of the *Dob-dobs*.

After the Dalai Lama fled Tibet for India things in Lhasa quieted down. His father was flown to Beijing for meetings, and when he returned – in an airplane! – he was dressed differently. The old brocaded gown with fur trimmings was gone. His father was dressed in a dark blue suit like the one Chairman Mao wore.

On several occasions he went with his father, who held an official Party position, in a big car with a driver to some distant monastery. Thondup would stand in the courtyard watching his father scold the head Lama in harsh tones. They were no longer permitted to have young boys join the monastery. There were labor shortages. Kidnappers of boys would be executed. Thondup watched the *Dob-dobs* carefully. They still made him nervous though he knew they were now harmless. Big and cruel looking. Scowling. They wore their robes in that peculiar way. Some with sticks in their belts and many with big iron keys on their belt thongs. His father spoke loudly to them. There was a count. The next time a new boy was found there would be harsh penalties. He felt proud of his father.

Thondup joined the Red Pioneers and was sent to a school in Lhasa which insisted that the Tibetan boys speak and study Chinese like the rest of their classmates. He was quite popular, and as he was a tall strong boy he was never bullied. The teachers taught Marxism-Leninism-Maoism as well as science and mathematics. It was so logical, historically inevitable. His generation would bring a new world into being and in the interim it was important to purge Tibetan society of the superstitious ways of the past. Ignorance was the anchor of the past. Dead hands holding on.

Thondup owned one of the first copies of Chairman Mao's little red book of sayings. They seemed profound then. His father gave him good natured quizzes. Finally he was old enough, or perhaps tall enough, to join the Red Guards. It was an exciting time. They went on field trips and were introduced to simple weapons. The first time he went into the high mountains it was with his Red Guard group. They taught him the first lessons about ropes and safety.

He participated in artillery exercises to practice targeting. Small Buddhist hermitages for solitary meditators were perched on remote cliffs. Supposedly abandoned, they were blasted to rubble with cheers and rallying cries and such practices grew in scale and frequency. Down with the old. Next there was shelling of monasteries. Life became very tense, as bad as the year when the Dalai fled Tibet. Labor battalions were undermanned. The crops were spoiling in the fields. Soldiers were being ambushed and Khampa horsemen were conducting guerrilla raids against Chinese outposts.

What Happened at Layul Monastery

One day his father invited Thondup and two classmates, all in their mid teens, to accompany him to a military compound, more than an hour beyond the city, where they were joined by a uniformed squad of soldiers under a Lieutenant. They had a staff car and the Lieutenant and squad followed in a canvas covered lorry trailing in the dust behind them. It was a two hour drive from the army compound to Layul monastery further east, that was refusing to surrender its potato crop. In general the monastery which belonged to the Nyingma sect of the Buddhist clergy had a bad reputation with the authorities.

Its head Lama had other monasteries in the wild lands further east and Layul was only one of several which belonged to him, a *tulku* named Yeshe Longdrul, Rinpoche, the current manifestation in a lineage of reincarnations. He was the eleventh *tulku* of an ancient shaman of the Kham region. The intelligence services had learned that the Rinpoche would be visiting Layul and it was decided to use the opportunity to confront him there with the new facts of his country's new life. They were not the monastery's potatoes, they were the nation's potatoes. Thondup's father was to inform them of that in harsh terms if necessary.

For half an hour there was no road at all. They engined up a dry river wash and then headed overland towards a certain cliff under which the fallowed fields and red walls of Layul monastery were found. They arrived in a cloud of dust and the trouble began almost immediately. At their approach they could see a number of monks struggling to close the massive wooden doors under an arch which formed a gated entrance to the monastery courtyard. Twice the height of a man, the gates might have weighed a thousand pounds on a side and were hinged on enormous iron dowels built into the five foot thick earthen walls. In ordinary times the gates were closed only one day a year, symbolically closing off relations with the outside world. But now the monks were urgently putting their shoulders to each door, which rolled on an iron wheel over an inset wooden track. The gate was barred from within with hardly a minute to spare as the vehicles arrived.

The noise of the motors ceased and the dust settled. There was scarcely a sound. Only cicadas somewhere. The squad hopped out of the lorry and formed up. Each carried a rifle, the Lieutenant had a holstered pistol. The officer walked to the great gate and pounded his fist on the wood beams. The door was so massive that it swallowed the sound. The puny noise of the striking fist was comic.

The Lieutenant approached the staff car to consult with Thondup's father. The three boys were told to stay within the vehicle. The Lieutenant explained that he could fire a few rifle rounds into the door, but that would not accomplish anything. There were more than 200 monks at Layul. They probably had enough food inside to stay closed off for months. There was a well too.

It became an important moment and well-known throughout Tibet. The monastery's considerable potato, barley, and buckwheat fields had been constitutionally declared the property of the Tibetan people. It was simply a question of labor. The coming harvest of the fields would require the labor force of the monastery. Failure to work would be punished. Thondup's father had clear instructions from Party superiors to personally inform the head Lama of this important decision. As a courtesy.

And now there was this matter of making an entrance. Credibility was very important. There was not a sign of movement or sound from within the walls. A thousand eyes were probably watching. The great gate under the arch was closed. They decided that a soldier was to take the staff car and drive quickly back to battalion regional command center with a request for reinforcements and a howitzer. Until they arrived the others would have a walkabout and wait in the shade of a lone tree. They had spicy rice and cold dumplings in lunch tins and thermoses of hot tea. They estimated reinforcements would arrive in less than four hours.

Led by the Lieutenant they walked around the quadrangular design of Layul monastery, the officer and Thondup's father examining the walls closely. They had been coated with red plaster many years earlier. In reasonably good condition he observed, which meant a labor force that did maintenance. Here and there were observation slits in the wall. Doubtless they were being watched but they could see no sign of it. On the side opposite the gate the rear wall was punctured with several oozing orifices which carried wastes away. These were largely of human excrement. Thondup's father said it was backward to recoil from excrement as unclean and not to collect the matter for productive use. In the rest of China it was well known. Progress must be total. There could be no turning back in the face of this kind of behavior, he told the boys. If Chairman Mao and the leading cadres were not firm in the face of difficulties the revolution would not succeed. A punishing shock must be applied if necessary. Authority must be established at the first instance.

The Lieutenant led them around the turn of the final side of their tour. Further down, a few more openings in the walls. Ashes. Egg shells. Pieces of bone. Sloshed with grey wastewater. The kitchens were on this side. Looking closely they could see chimney pots on the rampart.

It was approaching noon. Thondup's father decided they should picnic under a tree a few hundred yards away. They had the foresight to bring snacks, not desiring to eat monk's food which might conceivably have been offered if matters had gone well. As they waited Thondup's father provided the patriotic teen-agers with a dialectical explanation of what was happening. It was described most clearly by Chairman Mao. Destroy the old, bring in the new. The issue was labor. The government and Party, which represented all the people of China required the production of specific quantities of barley and potatoes. Buckwheat should be eliminated. This was calculated scientifically. It was about the greatest good for the greatest number. The Party's wisdom in this matter was beyond doubt.

Thondup's father understood that he was going to be judged by how he handled this forthcoming drama. This could be an important day in his career. Most of the monasteries he had dealt with previously were sadly humble and obedient in their attitude. Layul felt refractory, like resistance. It was a serious responsibility that he had been assigned and he was proud of it, to gather the labor of the monastery's 200 or more monks on behalf of the people, with orders straight from Beijing.

He determined on a direct approach. He had known other senior Lamas in Lhasa. They upheld non-violence. Not exactly revolutionaries, once they saw the force of a firm Party decision they came around. He decided to read aloud the text of an order from the Party immediately, without any preliminaries. No cups of tea. He would publicly instruct the head Lama, this Yeshe Longdrul Rinpoche, of the labor requirements; they were not to shirk this important duty, as in the past; the slavery of serfs was finished; the monastery was now a labor unit, not a nest of parasites; they were expected to reach production targets according to the guidelines specified in the five year plan. They would be provided with a food ration, but unlike last year's behavior, the entirety of the forthcoming crop would be turned over to the state. Nothing was to be withheld.

If they failed to do labor, or were found to be hoarding food supplies, then the monastery would simply be destroyed and its inhabitants gathered into labor battalions. Not today, of course. But soon. The important thing now, was to inform the head Lama of what was expected. If it went well it would be a brief meeting. They could agree or not. He would explain the consequences in a clear voice, speaking in their own language. Whose monastery was it? A King of England had once begged that question of a Pope.

When the reinforcements arrived he planned for them to blast down the gate and make their presence known dramatically, providing a taste of how resistance would be treated. The first thing would be to assign a squad to seize the bulk of the food stores from the immense sooty kitchens, whose location they had marked on their roundabout tour. That would put them all on a short leash.

The Diamantine Dagger of Emptiness

They lunched. Thondup and his friends threw pebbles and dutifully studied their little red books. His father worked on the planned speech. Finally the reinforcements arrived in the afternoon. Four lorries each with squads of sixteen soldiers. Officers in the cabs. Over sixty armed men. All Han recruits. Three lieutenants, a captain and a major. The Captain gave instructions on how to position. The last lorry towed a caisson with an artillery howitzer. It was detached and a team of six promptly chocked it and pointed the gun to face the great gate from a distance at which a strong arm might throw a stone.

The Major asked Thondup's father if any warning should be given before firing. He shook his head. There was no point in it. Fire when ready. Aim at the center, where a cross bar would lay. They fired and the shell's explosion destroyed whatever barred the doors with a sound of wood ripping. The gate's left side was mostly gone.

The Captain rapidly led half his force through the breach. The situation within was chaotic. Most of the monks had been napping or studying in their rooms. After the explosive shattering of the gates they all ran to the main courtyard in anxious confusion. Among the shaven heads were many long-haired Khampa tribals with red wool in their braids, who were also seen on the wooden galleries above them. The soldiers took up formation immediately with rifles held across their chests creating an impression of great discipline.

More than a hundred monks milled around toward the rear of the yard, where wide steps led up to the *gompa*, their temple with its large idols. The biggest monks, the guardian monks, the *Dob-dobs*, were to the front. They casually swung their iron keys at their sides. Several had sticks in their belts. The soldiers arrayed in a single line facing them. The Captain sent back a message saying the situation was under control, there were no signs of resistance. Shock and wide-eyed anger, but no resistance. The Captain barked an order in Chinese and then again in a pidgin Tibetan for the head Lama to appear and announced that a senior representative of the Party and government had come from Lhasa to say something to them. They were to be well-behaved and show respect. Any resistance would be met harshly.

Thondup's father and the Major led the way. The boys followed. They had put on fresh Young Pioneer scarves. The Major assumed his role as the senior military man. He strode close and intimidating, back and forth, along the crowd of angry monks who ranged from boys to old men. The Major's contempt for them was on display. He turned to face Thondup's father, to whom he made a slight formal bow. The Captain shouted again for the head Lama to emerge.

There was a movement to the rear of the crowd. In a moment there was a parting and two very muscular monks came to the center of the courtyard carrying a large chair painted with dragons, in brilliant colors. Two more of these imposing monks arrived behind them. One carried a pillow. The other only a glowing stick of incense. All four had long iron *phurbas*, three sided Tibetan ceremonial daggers, tucked in their belt robes. Likened to a scorpion and called the diamantine dagger of emptiness, the *phurba* was used to ward off demons.

After a moment Yeshe Longdrul Rinpoche, the head Lama arrived. The boys were astonished at his unforgettable appearance. Yeshe Longdrul Rinpoche was scarcely older than they. Perhaps sixteen or seventeen. He was treated by his followers with formal reverence and there was lots of bowing to him, to which he seemed entirely indifferent, and his appearance was exceptionally unorthodox by Lhasa standards. He was dressed in the style of Tibetan yogi hermits, particularly the old school Buddhists, who came to Tibet from India in the 8th century. A figure out of a dream. The Rinpoche looked like a wild man and but for the yellow tunic, he was dressed like just another Khampa nomad. A loop of heavy beads around his neck, and two long braids of hair laced with red woolen strings were formed into a careless knot on top of his head. He was small, well below average, with a prominent scar separating an eyebrow, a blaze of white in the middle of his dark hair, a bent nose and a heavy silver earring with a walnut sized turquoise hanging from a hole the size of a coin in an elongated ear lobe.

Yeshe Longdrul Rinpoche's eyes were dancing about. He almost looked as if he was sniffing the air through his bent nose. Thondup had never seen these rough countrymen in such numbers. Although he looked down on all monks as ignorant, backward, and superstitious, the high Lamas and dethroned Rinpoches he had seen in Lhasa and Drepung were tidy and dignified men, with clean robes and shaved heads. He had never seen a high Lama who looked like Yeshe Longdrul Rinpoche. The crowd of monks on either side started to hubbub and crowd in and draw closer in protective wings around their leader. The Lama gestured for them to be still as he sat down in the magnificent chair.

Thondup's father was momentarily confused. He did not expect to be addressing someone who was seated while he was standing. He felt he should have a chair himself, but it was too late for that and it would be a diversion. He then addressed them in colloquial and familiar Tibetan, looking at his notes, avoiding all formalities of phrasing and choice of words. Except for those formalities of phrasing and choice of words which were the standard impersonal political tropes of communist party expression. The monks were getting angry at the familiar style of speech. It was insulting to use such pronouns with a high person. Then he read his order of requisition to them. He told the Lama in a loud voice so that everyone could hear and in no uncertain terms that if they failed to deliver their crop production target at the next harvest, then Layul monastery, which had been there since the 13th century, would be shelled and reduced to rubble. There would be no further warnings.

Yeshe Longdrul rose from the chair and stood close before Thondup's tall father, who was not used to having anyone stand so close and staring up at him with wide-eyes. The diminutive Lama spoke very softly, hardly more than a whisper. It was a question of turning poison into nectar, he hissed, and he said communists did the opposite. He stared up at the party official, almost looking in his nostrils, and muttering something. Then he sat down again and appeared to be engaged in thought as he stroked the long but meager whiskers of his chin. It was not clear who would make the next move.

Thondup's father saw his son looking at him. He was being ignored by the Lama and felt he could not let the moment go by without some form of decisive action. He had a responsibility to do something. He had been visibly insulted by a feudal ignoramus *seated* in a chair! A Party representative must do something otherwise the entire event would be understood as a humiliating anti-climax. A cannon blast at the gates and then nothing? A Party representative must demonstrate a more productive and resolute outcome.

111

He decided to assess the state of their food supply and confiscate everything that was sacked. Thondup's father turned to the Major and spoke forcefully. Reinforce our presence. Bring the cannon into the archway and aim it at the temple, the *gompa*, at the top of the steps. Send an escorted squad to the kitchens and seize all unopened sacks – their accumulation of rice, barley, potatoes and cooking oils. Carry them out and load them on the lorries. Let this backward parasitic ignorant un-bathed superstitious lot understand the need for labor. The sacks would be re-distributed among more deserving social elements.

Meanwhile, the large crowd of muttering monks who were, only moments before, packed in a tight mass against the rear of the courtyard, slowly expanded as each created more elbow room. Others were descending from the galleries of the upper stories which caused them to swell in the space they occupied gradually so as to fill the entire courtyard now, bringing those in the forefront face-to-face with the line of soldiers. The Major was becoming nervous. Half his force was still outside the walls. And he had just ordered a lieutenant with six men and an escort to find sacks of food in the kitchens. The line of less than thirty green troopers faced a mass of several hundred monks who were slowly nearing them by inches. Aside from their brutal bullying of novices, monks were generally non-violent. But these were Nyingma bumpkins from Kham, and not very peaceful looking.

The Major turned to the Captain and gave him a command. Bring the cannon and all remaining soldiers except for five men stationed in the driver's seats of all the vehicles. The vehicles were to be faced away for rapid departure and the lorry towing the caisson should be positioned immediately outside the damaged gate. The engines should be started on hearing the cannon shot in preparation for a rapid departure. The cannon was to be positioned in the gateway and aimed at the dead center of the open-fronted *gompa* across the courtyard at the top of 27 wide stone steps. Aim at the statue in the back and be ready to fire on the order.

The Captain did as told and all the while Yeshe Longdrul sat on his pillowed chair, still staring into the ground at his feet, muttering something, and making strange faces. He appeared to be having a mild seizure. The crowd of monks ebbed around him and his four bodyguard attendants looked at him with mournful expressions on their faces. Thondup's father, arms crossed, could barely pace back and forth in the personal space around him. Waiting.

The howitzer and the other troopers arrived quickly. The Major filled in the line of soldiers. The three schoolmates were instructed to stand on the bed of the lorry at the arched entry so they could see over all the heads. A great pause where nothing seemed to change, and then Thondup's father nodded. The howitzer's blocks were wedged tightly and the angle sighted in. A shell was loaded in the firing chamber which locked with a sharp sound. A soldier held the triggering lanyard in his outstretched arm. The Captain turned, stood at attention, and saluted.

"Will you comply or not?" Thondup's father asked Yeshe Longdrul. The Lama ignored him, continuing to sit and search the ground near his feet while raising his volume with a unabated stream of incomprehensible religious imprecations.

Thondup's father gave the signal and the Major ordered the Captain to fire. The soldier snapped the lanyard to a flash and a roar and black smoke commenced pouring out of the front of the *gompa*. The blast made everyone's ears ring. In the *gompa*'s interior around the area where there had been a large statue of a protective Buddhist deity there was now a black smoldering space dotted with flickers of flame, and the explosion had caused a far corner of the temple ceiling to collapse, a bit of sky could be seen. The oil lamps were gutted out, and a shower of loose pages from oblong texts continued to float down in the smoke. Several monks were knocked over by the compression wave.

This was followed by a paralytic silence of great intensity except for the ringing in their ears. The monks were frozen by the shock of what had just happened. Thondup's father approached the Lama's chair. "Will you comply?" he asked sternly, once again.

Yeshe Longdrul Rinpoche stood up rather slowly and faced away to look over his shoulder at the desecration. Then, as he turned back to face his interlocutor, in one smooth gesture he took the long iron *phurba*, needle sharp, from an attendant's belt, and using two hands, in a violent bayoneting motion and with all his strength, thrust the triangular blade all the way to its skull-carved pommel upward through the center of Thondup's father's stomach.

Aftermath

Thondup had revisioned the scene of his father's death thousands of times over nearly forty years that had passed. He had nightmares for years. The image of the crazed Lama thrusting a sword into his father's belly was indelible. His martyred parent dropping slowly to his knees, wide-eyed and moaning as he fell over to his side, as the mad Lama violently ripped a string of prayer beads from his own neck and hurled them with great force at his dying father before vanishing into a milling crowd of monks. The Major instantly ordered the suffering and gasping victim to be carried quickly to the first lorry and emergency aid administered.

The throng of front line monks became aggressive and crowded the line of soldiers until they were nearly backed against the wall on the entry side and on the verge of being swarmed. The Major feared he lacked tactical depth and shouted an order to withdraw and form up outside the walls, which was only partially successful. A melee ensued. Nearly twenty soldiers including the Captain and a lieutenant, in addition to the unit sent to the kitchens, were swarmed and cut off from retreat.

The Major organized an evacuation and ordered troops to use warning fire at the gates to hold back the crowd of monks as they retreated. It was clear that his men were not capable of re-entering, leave alone holding the courtyard. The immediate tactical challenge was to control the blasted gate area under the entry arch, as the only way to gain time to rescue the howitzer and fix it for towing and to secure the welfare of the Party official and his son. The Major cursed his superiors for not allowing him a signals unit.

He put the remaining squads under the command of the sole lieutenant. No telling what had happened to the other officers. The entry gate was key. The more damaged wooden door, half off its fastening, was canted over a broken narrow passage and he ordered the squads to take to take firing positions behind the lorries and face the gate so as to keep the courtyard's occupants pinned within for several hours while the command car and the ambulance lorry raced to battalion headquarters for medical attention and reinforcements. The schoolboys were sent to the command car; the bleeding victim to the lorry with a single squad who attemped to stanch his blood as they raced to the clinic at their base. At best an hour. Young Thondup was in shock. One friend put an arm around his shoulder. His father lay on the bed of the lorry a hundred yards behind them, scarcely visible in the cloud of fine dust.

The communist martyr died of hemorrhages before the vehicles reached their destination. In due course a plane arrived and dropped a load of bombs but the pilot reported that the monastery showed no signs of life. There were numerous bodies visible in the courtyard and others outside the gate, he reported, but none moved. Two lorries were still smoldering from flame and there were dead all around. It appeared the troops assigned to the pinning down operation were overrun. Their bodies and the bodies of monks lay side by side.

The first units of a larger force arrived. Reinforcements weren't necessary. There was no resistance, just many dead and a few near it. Many monks had

114

been shot and died of blood loss, while the soldiers within the monastery had been crushed by the numbers and had their heads smashed or were strangled. Their weapons had been taken, kitchen knives distributed and a great offensive charge out of the gate had obviously succeeded.

More than half the surviving inhabitants of Layul monastery had escaped into the nearby hills. No sign of illumination in any direction that night. Later, a full army regiment arrived with an artillery unit and blasted the eight hundred year old monastery for several hours until it resembled only a colossal pile of red mud bricks. People came later searching the rubble for gold treasure they theorized was hidden there. The incident became well-known and the shelling of Buddhist hermitages, *chortens*, and monasteries by brigades of Red Guards continued unabated. Another case of the new replacing the old. They called it creative destruction. Nature at work.

Decades had passed since his father's dramatic death. The Major, Dongfeng Situ, who was promoted subsequently, returned Thondup to his family in Lhasa and became a hidden hand in Thondup's life while a grateful nation mourned his father, one of modern Tibet's first martyrs. There was a popular biography in print – "Selfless Hero" – and a large bust of his head in the reception area of Party headquarters.

The recurrent mental image of his father's death had its reciprocal. It was the recollection of pulling the firing lanyard as his own Red Guards group shelled Drepung Monastery and the pleasure it gave him to do so. Nothing was better than smashing idols. The idea of idol worshipping repelled him. Up from ape-hood, that's what it was. Yak herders performing ceremonial propitiations to avoid lightning strikes or hail. Crazy, and yet fashionable in the west he was told, and so it was spreading. Borne by the survivors of Layul monastery who had vanished into the hills and were never apprehended. It was assumed that they would merge into the resistance bands once supported by the CIA.

Thondup dedicated himself to taking up his life's work in the nation's service. With a reputation for mountaineering and a year at technical college, he volunteered for army duty with the Border Forces. The Major, now a Colonel, intended to look after him and became a lifelong mentor. He was sent quickly up from the ranks to officer training and given special courses in communications engineering; army experts taught him martial arts and he applied to mountain units and sought out intelligence assignments. After a while his masters decided to try the young officer in Dharamsala, the capitol of the Tibetan exiles.

Dharamsala

There were several Chinese espionage agencies in and around Dharamsala whose missions overlapped. Also a "Spider" not on any organizational chart. Obtaining reliable intelligence on the politics and personalities of the Dalai Lama's bureaucracy wasn't considered difficult. There had been agents in place for years providing an ongoing three dimensional picture of life in the exiled leader's entourage. Thondup's briefings were sufficiently thorough that when he went undercover to Dharamsala the first time—he had been there twice—it seemed familiar.

On the first occasion he came into India through Ladakh during the summer. It was early in his career. General Tu gave him the trial, sending him alone on a familiarization assignment to the Tibetan exiles home base. To test if he could pass unnoticed as a Tibetan refugee who grew up in India. Years later, just prior to his promotion to Colonel, he went under cover as a Mr. Liu Dzao, a businessman of Tibetan extraction with offices in Hong Kong, a dealer in traditional Chinese medicines and herbs. In fact it was through mastering this cover identity that Thondup first learned the basic economics of the *chungcxiao* trade as well as developing his personal habit. The mission was simply to become familiar with the station and receive control of two agents belonging to Border Command. One owned a small travel bureau, the other worked at the main bank. There was no way of knowing how many other government departments had agents in Dharamsala. As well as "spiders" who could simply come and go.

Of special interest to Border Command was the report of any activity, any scrap, however trivial, which could touch upon the Sherpa Buddhist community in Nepal, originally a Tibetan people, who lived on the borderland. Particular attention was paid to anyone traveling directly to the Khumbu region from Dharamsala. Any sign of intercourse between the Tibetan exile capitol and the Buddhists of the Sherpa heartland who lived on China's border was a matter of considerable interest.

Thondup liked to pull on a thread. It was a small item but it made him want to know more. His agent at the travel bureau reported the issuance of a Pathankot-New Delhi rail ticket with a connecting New Delhi-Kathmandu-Lukla air ticket to a Mr. Pasang Dorje for travel in October. Who was this person? He pushed on his people. The most they could learn of the traveler was that he was in the administration of the Dalai Lama's household secretariat; a civil servant in exile for a government in exile. He lived at one of the better hostels inside the very large gated compound where he was employed. They didn't have a photograph. There was a non-descript one-liner in their database on persons of interest *'Manuscript Librarian. Household Secretariat'*. Now this person was planning to travel directly to the Khumbu. Was there mischief here he asked himself? Somebody ought to take a look at the man. Good routine.

Fact was, he himself would be in the Khumbu with the yak caravan at roughly the same time as this Pasang Dorje. If the timing worked he could easily walk down to Lukla in a day or two. Also a good chance to have close-up photographs of the airport, and something to do before re-joining the caravan back to Tibet. The dates would work if there were no changes to the ticketed schedule. Have a look at him. A mysterious figure from the Dalai Lama's household in Dharamsala. Who would be meeting him? Where was he going? Why?

Summer Breaks

Annie studied the magazines in the economy seat pocket. Stories and pictures and advertisements of a world she had nearly forgotten. It was about fashion, elegant clothing, city life in Dubai, jewelry, beautiful people in Stockholm, perfumes, chefs in Palm Beach, and ads for electronic equipment which amplified every sort of productivity out of every moment; and on every other page beautiful and smart women and the handsome and powerful men portrayed with them. She felt an inadequate hick. How did people live in cities anyway? Too late for her she thought, to live like that. Likely the same for city people. Too late for them too. And then once again her brain defaulted to the memory of being in the sleeping bag with Pemba on the *Stimmgabel* with his arms around her. Her mind defaulted to him constantly. Go back to Nepal? What to do with the rest of her life? She had just danced a near two-step with death on the east rib.

As the miles passed below her on the flight home she felt troublesome uncertainty setting in upon her. She had paid her national service dues with the Peace Corps contract. She had had a year and a half of adventure, climbing and rafting and surfing with other volunteers and their friends. Now what was her next life about? Dude wrangling? Ski patroller? Most of the great climbers needed the money, used the fame to build a nest egg. She would come into the treasury bonds from her grandmother's trust next year and was sole heir to a valuable ranch. Was she going to live there one day and run it by herself? The Spring season just ended, leading treks for Yeti Travels netted her just over ten thousand dollars, gratuities not included, for nine weeks of work. Less than the interest income from the trust. She knew she could be independent, earn a living from mountain sports, but what was the point? She didn't really need the money. Before climbing with Urs, she had guided a young California girl up Island Peak and led two back-to-back sojourns to the slum city of soiled and broken ice called Everest Base Camp. The first with a breast cancer survivors team and the second time with one of the mixed ad-hoc groups who sign up on the website or just show up at Yeti Travels' warehouse office in Lukla on the right day.

Before meeting Pemba she thought of informing Sonam, Yeti's manager, not to count on her for the Fall season. But then she became unsure at the last moment and decided to leave all her mountaineering gear at the warehouse. That said something, didn't it? She might return. A lot depended on the situation at home. She wanted to meet the Mexican couple Dad had hired, Maria and Cruz, and wondered if Nepal might seem familiar to them.

Annie phoned the ranch from San Francisco airport as soon as she cleared immigration and customs. She would change planes in Denver and reach home by mid-afternoon, jet-lag and all. Mother kept saying uh-huh, uh-huh then wanted to talk about the cooking pans which had too much crud on them, which seemed slightly weird. Dad finally got on the phone. Did she mind if Hank Paulson picked her up in Rock Springs instead of Jackson? He was down there on an errand. The plane made a stop there before Jackson, he had checked.

Out the window flying over the Rockies she could see the ski runs carved out of the forested slopes. Mountain sports. Ranch work or mountain sports, the only things she knew how to do. How peculiar for human evolution to build whole economies based on sliding downhill, like otter and penguin chutes; or hanging out on vertical rock above shaky protection. Humans were peculiar at actually playing with fear. Like war, like war.

Hank picked her up at Rock Springs airport. He gave her a warm smile and a series of approving nods, but said nothing more than, "Howdy Annie." They drove in silence. He didn't ask her about Nepal or about anything. And no use asking him about anything either. Hank was the most taciturn man she had ever known, limiting himself most of the time to yup, nope, uh huh, and hmmm so there was no point in asking him about the wooden sign some eight miles north of town. A eight spoke wheel carved in relief and the neat lettering: Jamling Tibetan Buddhist Meditation Center. In Wyoming? What next? Just one of the many things reminding her of him every day, between morning's first thought to the last at night: Pemba.

They stopped in Pinedale to refuel the pickup and use the toilets, bought some cold apple cider and continued driving while listening to the country western station. Balls of russian thistle with five foot diameters blew across the highway. Pemba blowing through her thoughts. Was he an inducement to put in just one more season in Nepal? Instead of what? Living forever after in Wyoming by herself? Adult responsibility? Too bad she didn't have a brother or an energetic sister to share the ranch burden ahead.

She would inherit the ranch and it would support her decently if she managed it half well. It simply couldn't be sold without even a thought to what she might do with the money even if she did sell it. Pay the Feds' estate tax and buy another ranch, probably. Her folks were in their late 70s and Annie understood she was going to have to look after them in the years ahead. No one was planning to move.

The 2,700+ acre Wendover Ranch was operating presently as a cow-calf operation, Herefords at the moment. The main house was a stone and log beauty, the outbuildings – machinery shop, garage, hay barn, veterinary stalls – were sturdy and well maintained. It was blessed with a stream running through a park-like glade of large cottonwoods and willows and a mile-long chain of wide irrigated pastures. They hardly ever used the domestic well as the springs were so reliable. The land transitioned to native grass meadows running several miles up to the timbered portion bordering on the National Forest. They had a government grazing permit to access thousands of acres of lush seasonal grass in the summer. It seemed – in fact was – the far side of the planet from Nepal, this beautiful montane land almost entirely devoid of people. What would Pemba think?

She hadn't been home in two years and the sensation of re-entering the old familiarity was almost physical, cellular. What was the brain making of it? The main house had gotten a makeover since she had last seen it. Dad had put in a new gas furnace and replaced all the old sash windows with divided lights of double-glazed glass. The first things she saw on coming through the door were her mother's theosophy books all over the floor. The bookshelves in the passage were stripped empty. Mom was on her knees and giving her a puzzled look. "I'm helping them" she seemed to explain.

Dad had an unusual facial expression and felt stiff as they hugged one another. His movements seemed wooden and his hands had a slight tremor. She saw a carpeted wooden ramp going down from the kitchen to the dining room where there used to be a single step. "What's this?" she asked. "You never know," he said. His old well of quietness was there, but there was a fixed gaze to him that was new and his voice sounded hoarse. She loved her parents; they gave her everything. Two years apart had revealed their infirmities. Mom was having long and frequent 'senior moments'; Dad looked stiff and weak. Not tired, just weak.

Two days later she called Doctor Cleveland in Jackson and drove to see him. He had been intending to call her. An expert in wilderness medicine Doc Cleveland had been their family physician for as long as she could remember. One of the founders of emergency search and rescue programs in the Tetons, Annie trusted him.

"I'm giving it to you with both barrels, old gal. Your mom's in the early stages of Alzheimer's and your dad's got ALS, Amyotrophic Lateral Sclerosis, Lou Gehrig's Disease. They've both started medication. You ought to know that both conditions are idiopathic and degenerative, meaning their causes are obscure, and they decline at roughly equivalent rates."

"How long?"

"Could go on for quite a while, maybe a few years, and at some time require moving them to a special nursing facility. Otherwise, your mom's in good physical health at the moment. Your dad's problem is the reverse; his mind is as sharp as ever, but he's declining into muscular paralysis. Hank Paulson retires at year end, so I was relieved to hear you were coming home this summer. The folks were pretty anxious at the thought of you climbing in the Himalayas. They're going to need a fair amount of personal attention in the time ahead, leave alone managing the ranch."

"How much time do I have before I need to come home and be with them?"

"Six months at most, roughly. Maybe less."

It led to a heart-to-heart talk with her father that evening. He did most of the talking. "I didn't want to write. There's nothing urgent and not too much we can do so I thought we'd wait until you got here. It's only a month since we had the definitive diagnosis. Or diagnoses. We were at Mayo's by the way. So here we are. Everything's manageable right now. It's a year from now that I'm worried about. Hank will be gone, and that's the least of it. So I'm planning to sell off the stock and let the pastures come back strong and take time to figure out what to do with the place. Be a shame to sell it or let it go from disuse and I wasn't sure what you were thinking. So I hired Sullivan & Bar, that ranch management and consulting firm. They've got offices in Denver, Phoenix, and Salt Lake. Smart boys and progressive. I want you to read their report. It makes interesting reading."

She took it to bed with her and studied the seventy odd pages of text, charts and tables which made the case for the "highest and best use" of the property as well as the most desirable strategy for minimizing the punishing estate taxes. The outlook for grass-fed cattle in Wyoming and Montana was for declining revenue, higher costs, and ultimately for abandoned ranches. Reliable seasonal labor was lacking in remote areas and under recent court decisions the ranch even faced the possibility of losing some of its historic water rights owing to abandonment, or failure to use its full share. The underlying aquifer was a valuable asset but had never been used other than the domestic well. The fences were in excellent condition, as were the corrals and gates. Even without a positive cash flow she could see from the tables and the yield comparisons that the ranch was worth many millions though she couldn't contemplate the thought of selling it. What would she do with the money anyway?

The recommendations were bold and straightforward. There would be a large estate tax one day and it would have to be paid for by using the assets of the ranch in abatement. A sustainable future depended on intelligent usage of water rights and cropping decisions. In the current economy irrigated pastures in remote locations were not at a premium, and hay crops, even alfalfa, weren't worth the effort given the price of diesel fuel and the distance to markets. The several hundred acres of marshy meadow with beavers at the lower end of the ranch could be deeded over to the Nature Conservancy for preservation as a wildlife refuge. That and the reasonable financial offer from the Forest Service to acquire the timbered acreage, mostly Ponderosa Pine and Douglas Fir, would be acceptable provided that the ranch retained perpetual grazing rights to that section. That could deal with estate taxes. The remaining property would then consist of three land types. The wide meadows and pastures, with flood-irrigated stream flows and hay fields where ditches channeled water by opening and closing gates. Then there were the level pastures which could be irrigated easily by putting wells into the shallow aquifer. And finally the rolling native grass sections which could be allocated to a rangeland conservation easement.

In other words, the ranch had more water than it could use in its current configuration. Two appendices analyzed the possibility of a small spring-water bottling plant or the sale of a few hundred acre-feet of water rights to a distant purchaser. The main conclusion was stated in bold type. One and a half square miles of level land, 960 acres, would offer six quarter sections with circular center pivot irrigation systems to grow high value crops. Potatoes or barley would be ideal. Potatoes!

Potatoes

The proposition entered into Annie's awareness like a fish emerging from the depths. She could propose marriage to Pemba. He didn't have family to contend with and they could deal with the red tape of immigration and live together on the ranch and try the new potato cultivars released from the USDA experiment station. They could lead Search and Rescue. With his energy and strength they could design and work on installing the center pivot wells and pumps. He could go to the Jamling Tibetan center if he wanted; and the community college too; they could try hybridizing yaks and bison in the steel insemination pens; they could have children together and visit cousins in the Khumbu periodically and speak Nepali. He was perfect. If enlightenment could be instantaneous, why couldn't love? Why couldn't love square with smarts?

It circled in her mind for days. What were the negatives? Racism? No, that was over. The fact that they scarcely knew one another, though she believed they knew enough. She certainly knew Nepal's cultures. It would be a supportive outcome for both of them. She could see his handsome face, read his mind, and she felt a spiritual connection. It stood to fit their special situations and would bond and hold them level in a big and empty space. The feeling of his absence was all the confirmation she needed. She simply had to see him to lay the proposition out. To double check her instincts, and to propose marriage.

So she went to Pinedale to find a wi-fi hotspot and e-mailed Pemba to say she would definitely return but for only some weeks because of her parents' situation; and that she frequently thought about the time they shared together and missed him very much. She composed the whole message in transliterated Nepali and signed it 'Didi.'

Secretary to her father, they went through a backlog of paperwork and unpaid bills. His signature was becoming distorted and he wanted her to get a durable power-of-attorney. There were weeks of work ahead. Cruz took mother for a ride of several hours every morning. The oldest and calmest horses plodded patiently along a picturesque five mile loop. It was soothing to both riders. Mom was no trouble, mostly bemused and agreeable to be helped.

They had to finalize the pension distribution that had been set-up for Hank. Annie had to handle the cattle sales, to arrange for a signed and notarized five year contract for Maria and Cruz, to meet with the key people from the Forest Service and come to a final agreement on the timbered acreage, to meet with the lawyer from the Nature Conservancy about the wetland, and at her insistence, to install a satellite dish with a broadband digital link. On her own she visited several nursing facilities and had further consultations with Doc Cleveland. Mom couldn't understand why she had to give up her ride to see someone in Jackson and kept asking for explanations over again. Dad's weekly visits to a physiotherapist showed small incremental declines in muscle strength.

Pemba's email reply came from Kathmandu. He was in a police basic-training barrack and would go on to airport security training in a few weeks. Annie filled his thoughts, he said, and he was very happy he would see her in the Fall. It was signed 'your friend, Pemba.' She then wrote to Sonam at Yeti Travels explaining she could only work half a season as her family needed her. She would lead one or two big 'E' base camp treks, back-to-back, but that was it. Six weeks. No guiding on Island Peak. Sonam replied that he was very short-handed and her picture and biography had been on the Yeti website. Last year's clients had recommended her to their friends. At least mid-September through October, please. She agreed and copied Pemba. Then told Dad and Doc Cleveland of her plans. Six weeks and then home for the long haul by Halloween. She had a ranch to manage and had gone off the pill.

Ripp Goes to Washington

Although Ripp prided himself on falling to sleep easily, flying half-way round the globe took a toll on his body rhythm. Westbound was generally easier on the jet-lag, but eastbound, from Singapore to headquarters made for fewer hours in the air, and this time he routed through Los Angeles, crossing the dateline into yesterday. Despite a full length business-class bed, noise-canceling headphones, eyeshades, and three glasses of airline Bordeaux, he couldn't sleep. They were somewhere over the Pacific.

That morning he had furloughed the office staff on half-pay for the summer and told them he would be closing the shop and retiring to America at the end of the year. His expatriate life in Asia was coming to an end. It was time for hard planning about doing something new for the rest of his life, and ruminating on it was keeping him from sleep. Six months away from ending decades of employment with an all-powerful, all-protective, all-enveloping half-secret organization. Unattached, like Elsie's Buddhists. Free for a personal life.

The headphone pressed uncomfortably on his ear as he lay on one side. He tried the classical music channel and watched the toy map on the display. Elsie had introduced him to slow breathing and he tried it for a while. What other tricks did she know? He allowed his thoughts to billiard about in slow motion and lingered for a while on an image of the previous night, of Mei-Xie Chang on her back, her legs spread, knees up by her head, a mad look in her eyes and soft little grunts like a *shakuhachi* flute. He was going to miss living in Asia, a region where he had never experienced sexual boredom. Could he keep it going if he had a long term relationship with Elsie? Erotic monogamy? Ripp tried to recall the last time he had slept with a western woman. Two years ago. What was her name? A soft-fleshed French banker, at a conference in Seoul.

Coarse grained thoughts caromed slowly. Was it possible to think in whole chunks rather than words? In patterns rather than chunks? This was probably the next-to-last Singapore-Washington flight he would ever take. At least on government money. As he lived both his cover and his undercover he had served two serious professions faithfully. Unlike certain time-servers, he enjoyed both sides of his work, thought it progressive, exciting, even romantic. Goodbye to all that. Financially independent now, and fit in mind and body, he felt lucky to be alive and childless. A free man.

One thing was clear. Whatever happened, as of January his address would remain what it was for nearly the length of his service: P.O. Box 988, St. John, United States Virgin Islands, the address where he filed tax returns during his expatriate years. An address resulting from a hunch on a boozy holiday a decade earlier when on a gambler's impulse he made a lowball offer on an undeveloped two acre shorefront lot on the north side of the island, sheltered from the trade winds by a hook of land. At that time it was a remote piece of scrub jungle tilting gently down to the Caribbean. He had imagined a private dock. Now there was a paved road a hundred yards away providing access to utilities. For years he had planned to develop it, habitually sketching bungalow designs on the backs of napkins. So many women watching him do it.

Be decisive, he coached himself, don't change your mind. Cut the bloody cord. Stop reading newspapers, avoid the old crowd and keep them away. Get the house built and furnished. Take a year or more to clear the brain. No instructing at the Farm, no part time work, no Team B simulations, no call-up ready reserve, no red-team exercises, no memoir, no more articles to write, no more editorial deadlines, no more clients to consult, no more lectures, no more speeches, no more jungles. Finished. Hungry for the unfamiliar, he longed for something totally new. Someone to love.

As the plane approached California a cabin crew touched his shoulder and offered a hot towel. They would land in approximately forty minutes. Would he like some fresh orange juice? Back in the West. A western style breakfast?

European touches on the menu! A *jambon-fromage* crepe. A warm apple tart. Europe, Europe! Not much time there over the years. He barely knew it, he thought. The few big cities, the capitols. In and out. Airports. Taxis. Hotels. Meetings. Arms trade buyers and sellers. No time for rambling, for museums, jazz festivals, coffee shops, parks, bookstores, and points of interest. No time for Venice. Or Krakow, which his parents had described so often. To see the great plaza. The only Mediterranean he knew was a book by a French historian. He thought of chartering a ketch for a season. He had never been to Greece or to Rome. To live in Rome for a while, at leisure. To brush up on Latin. Walks in the Forum to decipher inscriptions and abbreviations. Refresher courses at Pontifical Gregorian University! Then Athens and Istanbul. Damascus. Finally the Holy Land. With a companion, even. Paradise enough. If only.

He arrived at Dulles airport in a mental haze and proceeded straight to the Cosmos Club and one of his favorite rooms. He fell asleep in the taxi and the Ethiopian driver was worried he was ill. He had slept on couches and cots at the Headquarters Building. On less demanding occasions he overnighted at motels in nearby Reston. But when affairs lacked urgency he declined to sleep in Virginia. Non-resident member Dr. Harry Ripp preferred the Cosmos, in the heart of the District. He loved the seedy atmosphere, far more congenial than any boutique hotel.

He slept for eleven hours and came to breakfast the following morning, jet-lagged with a molasses brain. It took about an hour to read the front page of The Washington Post. He would use the fitness facilities and then find a place to sit in the sun for the day. Perhaps the zoo or the mall.

Elsie's Situation

Elsie had been in Washington for more than two weeks. She didn't really mind the ritual of staying in furnished apartments on Connecticut Avenue, where the monthly rentals were a cut above the week-to-week kind. Sofas with crud under the pillows. Cigarette burns on table edges. India had made her indifferent to most material things and the two rooms were extremely high-class by standards of the sub-continent. Her mother would have had a fit to stay in a place with cigarette burns on the table edges. Well, this was the last summer of doing this kind of thing and living this way. She promised herself, the last time she would participate in a South Asia inter-agency operations review.

Despite all the benefits brochures for CIA employees, Elsie hadn't done a thing in the way of retirement planning. It never seemed urgent. She had a decent nest-egg for a single woman without dependents, with a respectable government pension in the offing and rental income from the property in Virginia her parents bequeathed. At times she thought of living in Georgetown. It wouldn't be difficult to find work on a part time basis. The Library of Congress would have her in a snap. But the glue factory of old operations officers working as instructors to new cadets was not for her. Not Washington. Not the city. Not the Agency. Something entirely different.

Cooking school was a perennial candidate. Years with cooks and servants meant she rarely saw kitchens. On stateside visits it was always restaurants. Cooking school. Why not? Six months intensive. A Cordon Bleu school in Nice or Lyon. Continental-Mediterranean. Enough of curry and its friends. Move to Florida perhaps. Virginia winters were too cold. She liked being out in the sun, perhaps she could visit Ripp on his island. He did have something in mind, didn't he, the fox. Thoughts had been stirred up at that dinner in Delhi when they hatched the *gumba* operation and she discovered she liked him more than she knew.

Beyond India her social circle was limited. There had been a marriage decades earlier, when she was a student. Where was he now? She hadn't a clue. Except for a few close friends from graduate school who lived in distant California or Boston or Santa Fe most of her friends were in India. Her several affairs over the years, duly reported, had been with educated upper class Indian men who did top management work of one kind or another and who always had sex on their minds. A few who were still single were eager to marry her and even proposed, if she would only make their home in India and submit to a Hindu ceremony. Sonia Gandhi did it, didn't she? Career obliged her to work in India, but Elsie couldn't give up America. As simple as that.

She decided to sell the big house and its acreage which had given her rental income ever since her parents died. Time to let it go. Unrealistic to live alone out in the country. The house was too big and falling apart slowly under make-do patches. And the interstate highway, which hadn't been there when she was a girl, was just near enough to produce an annoying motor hum in the distance. The county wouldn't permit a subdivision and the acreage required a farm manager or a crop-share arrangement. So sell. Some hedge fund manager could turn the place into a superb horse farm. It would sell. She thought of buying a condominium in Charlottesville, near the university. The library did have a superb Tibetan collection if she wanted to continue her work with de Groot. Perhaps to work on a translation of something choice. Or do something academically playful on her own. *Styles of Sexual Sadhana: Sublimations of Anger in Esoteric Eroticism* by Elsie Hornbein, PhD. She could probably finagle some sort of adjunct faculty angle. Office privileges, parking spaces, the university gym, bookstore, library. Pinko-grey pot bellied men would be all around and she would be one of many singles, heading for sixty. Divorcees, widows, and spinsters. Like fish need bicycles. Still. Ripp.

There was a message on her voice-mail from Berrigan's staffer. Ripp had arrived on Wednesday and was staying at the Cosmos. The review meetings would start as scheduled at 9:00 am the following Monday. The meeting would be in the Old Executive Office Building in the ornate conference room of the Vice-President's suite, crowded with Americana. The Veep was in Europe.

A Problem with the Weather

Ripp had to traverse bureaucratic hurdles before someone gave him her phone number and he called on a humid Saturday morning, two days before the operations review. Would she like to have dinner with him that night? Yes? Wonderful. Pick her up at seven? Excellent. Though they had spoken on the phone at various times he hadn't laid eyes on her since their dinner after the embassy meeting in New Delhi.

How should he look? Intending to court her he decided to reserve a table at the Casque d'Or, had his dark blue suit pressed and tested his University of Singapore necktie against a shirt. The afternoon ended with the arrival of a low pressure system over Washington which produced nearly two inches of rain through the next six hours. Under a club umbrella he managed to find a taxi and reached Elsie's rental apartment on Connecticut Avenue with soaked shoes and socks, trousers damp at the cuffs and ankles, and the dew of perspiration soaking his shirt. The rain didn't stop. It seemed worse than monsoon.

Her air-conditioned apartment breathed welcome and a cool perfume as soon as the door opened. She was in sweatpants and an oversized T-shirt and looked him up and down with the sweetest pity. "Oh you poor, poor dear. The Casque d'Or? I hadn't realized. I thought we could have a drink here and decide where to eat. How stupid of me. So listen my dear, let's eat here and healthy. You certainly don't want to go out again in that downpour. I've got a delicious poached wild salmon and a bottle of Chablis in the fridge. And I've got salad makings. Let's eat here, don't you think? We'll just call them and cancel. Take that tie off, why don't you; it makes me nervous." She laughed loudly and it was the first time he was focusing on her voice. It came from her diaphragm with the throat wide-open. It seemed so pleasant, almost a lilt in the middle register, smoothly up and down without a trace of a cackle as she laughed. Perhaps he could enjoy it for a lifetime. He undid his tie and removed his jacket. "Yes ma'am." He wanted to put his arms around her and hold her.

She brought him her largest T-shirt and a pair of fleece lined kick-off slippers so he took his shoes off, and his socks. Leaving the question of the trousers.

"That's alright I'll roll them up."

"Ridiculous, they won't dry that way."

"You want me to sit around in my underpants?"

"What do you think I am? Tasteless? I have just the thing, given that ninety percent of my clothes are in Delhi." She stepped into the bedroom and returned with handspun white cotton pyjamas bought on Chandni Chowk weeks earlier. Ripp was made comfortable quickly in the loose cotton clothes, and rejected the slippers in favor of bare feet.

"Come on," she said, "let's open the wine, and make the dressings while we talk. I'll do the one for the salmon and you do the one for the salad."

They opened the wine, found some soft jazz, and talked about their summer holiday plans. She was fixing up her old family place and putting it on the market. He was flying down to the Virgin Islands to start construction of his house. The one he had drawn on a napkin when they had dinner in Delhi, she remembered. They refilled their glasses, nibbled on olives and almonds and went on about their respective dealings with general contractors, securing against hurricane damage in his case, the question of broadband access in hers, the price of dry-wall and double glazed windows. By the time they emptied the bottle they got on to the business of the forthcoming recruitment attempts which would be an item at Monday's meeting on Nepal issues. Not quite up there in the Oval Office with nuclear proliferation or pandemics, but still, a small country with issues of concern to India. Getting near Chandra was nice, but he was small fry against the potential value of getting the Chinese Colonel in place. He would be a very big fish and they had joint ownership of him.

As they moved about the kitchen he thought she was quite shapely, given the inevitable ravages of age. He had never seen her in sweatpants and T-shirt. Well, years ago at the Farm. But most of the time when he visualized her she was dressed as a civil servant. How well she had crafted the southern belle's ability to hypnotize men. He was going for it and let the feelings happen as they would.

They bustled about. So much better than sitting on a satin *banquette* at a high-toned restaurant, don't you think? She laid out the Pottery Barn dinner service that came with the furnishings on the small table in the kitchenette, and they opened a second bottle, lit a candle and dimmed the lights. They clinked glasses, each wondering about the content of the other's thoughts, but somehow sharing a wordless understanding in the half-knowing looks exchanged. Recognition. Possibility. There was a flash of lightning and a thunderclap cracked over the pounding hiss of rain.

She looked him over steadily and wondered if they were unconsciously negotiating a future. He was solid. Well-known, liked, and trusted by the right people. She liked that he seemed to know what he wanted. Oblique perhaps, but he wasn't making a secret of it. Something far beyond sexual intimacy. He wanted a companion, a friend, a mate for the journey ahead. That's a maybe.

Getting Serious

They enjoyed the conversation over dinner and Elsie felt pleasantly tipsy as she scraped the dishes and racked them in the washer and put the corked remnant of the second bottle in the fridge. They moved back to the living room and had coffee at a low glass slab. He gestured with his chin toward a large table near the window which was piled with papers and a pair of books closed face down. "Work?" he asked.

"Hobby," she said. "Hobby scholarship. Got to keep my hand in if I ever want an academic position again. Some people do crosswords. I'm specializing in Buddhist texts, Tibetan and Sanskrit, that deal specifically with pleasure. Most Buddhist teachings, original Buddhist teachings especially, are all about suffering, dissatisfaction and impermanence. But after a thousand years go by there appear writings for the first time which deal interestingly with the phenomenon of pleasure. Or the problem of pleasure some people would say."

"What's the problem, exactly? To any particular end?"

"Oh, sure. You see, the rich kings hired philosophers to tell them whether pleasure can be used as a means, even as a technique, of obtaining a certain intrinsic awareness."

"Awareness of what?"

"Non-duality, technically speaking. Can it be accessed through pleasure as well as through austerity? And some said perhaps only in pleasure. So I collect Buddhist sexual metaphors. In certain circles I'm the Doctor Kinsey of Buddhist sexual metaphors." She said mock-seductively, "Come up and see me some time."

"I'll be damned. Must be a very hot area." He said deadpan.

"I have my collaborators. An Indo-Iranian philologist at Stanford, Fadoor Farvar; an historical anthropologist in Kathmandu named Dipankara Macleod; and a Jungian psychoanalyst, Andres de Groot, who works in Holland, at The Hague. Macleod introduced us and we've been collaborating for years for a book on sexual symbolism in Tibetan iconography. You've seen the *thangkas*. What does the weird painted strangeness tell us? We argue it's a technique for dealing with fear. The extended rituals and intentional visualizations displace and occupy the mind so thoroughly that they hold back anxiety from being dominant. You can see it physiologically with MRI. Andres thinks there's something universal to it, the idea of sacramental distraction. Have you noticed how calm Tibetans are? I think all high church stuff works that way. Sacramental distraction. Give the brain a little woo woo activity and keep it happy. Not everyone can do it the hard way, without support."

"What's with the other guy? The one in Kathmandu."

"Macleod? Ah, that's slightly different. It's awkward to talk about."

"Gimme a break."

"We've been tracing the lineage of an ancient sexual practice. There's some promising uncatalogued material at the Library of Congress."

"Come on."

"So help me. It's part of a bigger project on literary and shamanic connections between semen and bone marrow, but these days we're mostly searching for references to semen retention."

"By the mouth?" He sounded like an idiot, he realized as he said it.

"Idiot," she said. "Be half serious. You first see the idea in the oldest Taoist writings, and you see it in various cultures, *maithuna* for the Hindus. *Sahaj*, or *karezza*, or *coitus reservatus* for you Catholic boys. Not *interruptus*, but *reservatus*. Ever heard of it?"

"Heard of it? My dear Elsie, we even have patron saint of the practice, Saint Rocca. *Immissio membri virile in vaginae sine ejaculatio seminis.* Athletes and warriors refraining from emissions, et cetera. So is it an open secret?"

"Only if it gets fetishized by masses. Keep it close. The cultures all agree. Hush hush. Whispered tradition you see, just like at the office. Secrets and need to know." She winked at him.

"I'm a reductionist at heart. Show me the money."

"Do you realize," she said, becoming more serious, "you and I have been looking or deliberately not-looking at one another so many times for nearly twenty five years. I remembered it from the first days after induction. Ever heard of 'the male gaze?' I'd be getting it right and left, from you too, couldn't stand it. I never showed you the slightest interest for at least ten years. And then we had that drunken night of Buddhist philosophy in Bangkok about how everything was connected."

Ripp said "I remember a bus ride with our thighs pressing. I always liked to watch you. Used to think, 'Oh if I could only fall into her hands' she'd know what to do with me. I still think that."

"That's so sweet. But it's different after middle-age isn't it?"

"I'd like to know you better, Elsie. Tell me about Tibetan weirdness for a thousand and one nights. I'll explain the International Monetary Fund." He held her hand.

He decided not to attempt a physical advance. That was their deal. It seemed a good time to go. They had consumed most of the two bottles. And it had been an open and friendly evening. The convergence in the air was obvious to both of them. Obvious but unspoken. The rain had finally stopped. He dressed in his street clothes. As he laced his damp shoes and thanked her for the very satisfying evening he asked, "Got any plans tomorrow?"

"Not particularly. What are you thinking?"

"How about some of the museums? I've never been to the Holocaust Museum."

"I'd rather try the Sackler."

"What's there?"

"Greco-Bactrian sculptures found recently at Ghazni, in Afghanistan. Someone at the Sorbonne claims to see sexual messages in the features and gestures. Could be rather interesting."

"Monomania, I see. Okay, let's do the Sackler. And I'll take us out on Monday, after the big pow-wow. Not the Casque d'Or."

They walked to her rental apartment door. She offered a cheek. He kissed both of them, a bit slowly. And goodnight.

Operations Review

8:45 am. The Vice-President's ornate conference room. The early arrivals were drinking coffee in china cups and joked with much laughter about a recent sexual scandal of a well known Senator. Ripp was amongst sarcastic and skeptical chums. He winked at young Wurlitzer, and introduced him to a few of the old-timers. The principals sat around a long ovoid table. Elsie wore a featherweight cream colored suit made out of homespun cotton she had tailor-made in Delhi. Gandhi would be proud. Ripp thought she looked more attractive than in India. Nearly half the principals were women. There was an athletic looking Major from the Army's Defense Intelligence branch, the only uniformed woman in the room. The woman next to her was Assistant to the Deputy National Security Advisor. The third was the quiet Chief of Staff to the Chair of the Joint Congressional Committee on Intelligence, who was also chairing the meeting. Ripp and Berrigan represented the Agency. Hornbein and Wurlitzer, in theory representing the State Department Foreign Service. A few staffers against the walls.

Ripp knew they had as much as they needed *pro forma* to establish inter-agency knowledge of the operation, further down the agenda. Descending blood-sugar levels would make people irritable by then and accelerate decision making. Keep it crisp. The meeting started with a discussion for the Deputies Committee on the question of US policy towards Nepal. The item headline: "US Policy towards Nepal. Do we have a dog in that fight?" It took less than four minutes. Do everything we can to support and benefit India. That's our Nepal policy. Period.

The Marine Major briefed them on a special forces team providing training to Nepalese Royal Army Units. The impression was that the elite troops were physically strong and even brave in many cases, but that they lacked the inner drive of a guerrilla. Their small arms and mortars were entirely Chinese manufactured. She wanted authorization for a second special forces team, with the stipulation to the Deputies that the Indians be kept informed of the undertaking. Everyone nodded. She tried to draw them in and get them on the record firmly, but a variety of delaying tactics were employed by the bureaucratic infighters. Kick it over to the State Department. It wasn't necessary someone said, India's Defense Attaché knew what was going on and had even been on swamp maneuvers with the teams. So it went.

Ripp's item, next on the agenda, was his annual snapshot of the RIM, the revolutionary international movement. Few people in Washington took it seriously. They were treated as children pretending to be pirates, led by a pied piper professor of some kind hidden in a forest. Ripp flagged two issues. First were the mafia infiltrations of RIM networks. INTERPOL sources had evidence that Eritrean and Somali pirates actually applied to join the RIM, as did a bunch of Peruvian coke dealers taking over a local agricultural sector. In both cases it was obvious that gangs were using the cover of being leftist revolutionaries to give themselves a fig leaf of ideological fervor and purity.

A second thing had him worried. A cloud on the horizon no bigger than a man's hand. The evolving tango between the militant *jihadi*s and the revolutionary left. Red fascists. It went way back. The Baader-Meinhoff gang trained in Jordan with the Islamic Jihad faction of the PLO. Ilich Ramirerz Sanchez, aka 'Carlos the jackal', had urged all revolutionaries of the left to accept the leadership of jihadists like Bin Ladin. A member of Britain's parliament said a Left-Muslim alliance was vitally necessary. The enemy of my enemy approach, with a united front against Jews and capitalism. There were websites pushing this line. No one should be surprised if branches of Pakistani intelligence services start helping the Nepalese Maoists. He had seen it for himself in Bangladesh.

Then they came round to Chandra and Thondup, his two recruitment targets. Everyone had read the summaries. Ripp asked the first question, "So, why are we going after these two guys? One, because we're nosey, we like to know what's going on; two, because India's Home Ministry falls all over itself in gratitude, and will trade quality Iran information for anything we give them on the Naxalite-Maoist axis. And of course, we also gain some insight on the Chinese strategic approach to the situation."

Chandra's case was discussed first and it was stipulated that the idea of recruitment was almost entirely subjective and based largely on Ripp's instincts. His record in these matters carried weight and suggested it was worth a try, even though unlikely to yield much immediately. Ripp was convinced Chandra could be developed over time if handled carefully.

"We reach him after he quits. He'll actually be most productive then and the Indians will like that we're trying." He went into his familiar sentimental role of a lapsed Catholic. "*A propos* of understanding the Zone Commander's situation I call your attention to a phenomenon called 'ecclesiastical boredom'; related to, but not the same as 'burn-out.' I know something about this. My cousin is a priest and I myself attended St. Ignatius on Bernal Avenue in Chicago, where these matters are known."

"*Accidie.*" He pronounced it for them. "Ak-sid-ee. One of the Seven Deadly Sins. Not the same as depression. Not at all. And not just a lack of enthusiasm; but a pleasure dampening condition which leads to turning your back on things. St. Thomas, in the *Summa*, called it an 'inertia of the spirit' that causes a loss of energy."

"Hey, let's not get personal," said Berrigan, resting his clasped hands on the top of his head.

Ripp ignored him. "Old commies are just the same and I promise you Commander Chandra is suffering from *accidie*. I could smell it when I was with him. You can hear it in his voice." He felt a touch of irony as he said the words as he sensed it in himself sometimes.

"Why does this mean we can roll him?" asked the Assistant to the Deputy National Security Advisor. "What's in it for us?"

"If we can get him to talk to us the Indians will find something to trade. And he'll probably talk to us if we make it metaphysically attractive. We hear him say how much he admires the ancient *yoga* philosophers, so engage him intellectually and he'll talk to us. I saw it when I was with him. In a new environment and the sense that he's on his own he'll be happy to talk about his old life. Just let it ripen. Keep an eye on him. Less than a year I'd say. It's only that the questions have to be put to him intelligently. Let's get him to write a book or something."

"Okay. Work on the guy. He's small fry. What the hell. Big deal," said the Chief of Staff of the Congressional Committee on Intelligence.

Berrigan took his turn to recapitulate. He was now on home turf. "It was when General Tu's name emerged out of a Burma-Nepal arms deal that we heard the reference to an officer in Tibet. Then, because of Ripp's interest in Chandra, we also hear that there's a Colonel in Tibet doing a commodities trade with him. We look closely and learn it's the same guy. Good staff work, a bit of luck, and the pieces come together and reveal an arms deal involving people 1,000 miles apart. Ripp's discovery of the sex mushroom trade shows how the deal gets financed."

Berrigan paused and gazed at the ceiling. "Placebo aphrodisiacs," he offered. "Would you call them a soft drug?"

Ripp lifted his shoulders to say 'who knows?' and then remarked, "but generally recognized as safe."

Berrigan continued "This *gumba* commodity is a multimillion dollar deal and we know the players. Right? When you inquire of Tu Beijing people rub fingers together. So the Chinese Colonel must be a capo in Tu's border force mafia."

He gestured to Elsie with a sweep of his arm. "So now comes Madam Corleone bearing a superior product for erectile dysfunction and we ask: is the Colonel going to be a loyalist pushing traditional crap, or will he go for position at the top of wholesale distribution of counterfeit Viagra in western China? If he goes for it we own him; and he'll make General one of these days, believe me. As an agent in place he's priceless. So we've got one good shot at him and we need resources. He's coming to Nepal in October with a caravan of yaks to pickup the year's *gumba* cargo. Ripp will take it from here. It's wild."

Ripp told them about the tiger carcasses and showed the photos. In Singapore he had checked with local apothecaries and damned if they didn't carry tiger bone products, priced as a rarity and sold under several brands, all claiming to be the real thing with experts attesting to purity. It occurred to him that the aggregate demand for such compounds was so large and consistent that it had implications for human nature.

"I tell you all, the more I think about this stuff the more I see that there's something very weird and very big going on here. All these guys wanting to get a better erection. Take the Trojan War for instance. Wasn't it all about erectile dysfunction anxiety? What if it's 'make war, not love' because it avoids bedroom anxieties. You think I'm nuts?"

Then he handed out a sheaf of exhibits. On top was a chart from a private report by SMIC Shenzhen Matrix Information Consulting, a Chinese investment research firm. He had underlined the initials TCM, for Traditional Chinese Medicines. The chart showed the global market for TCM products had an estimated value of US $25 billion in 2004.

Next was a letter marked 'private' from the World Wildlife Fund, co-signed by the Fund's Chairperson and its Executive Director. It affirmed that competitively priced Viagra distribution in Asia would reduce demand substantially for several endangered animal species whose body parts were imagined to improve erectile function. Tigers, rhinoceros', seals, certain tortoises, and musk deer, for example, were hunted because millions of Asian men use their parts for supposed virility enhancements. Wildlife experts were positive that Viagra use in Asia would make large inroads into the market share of TCM products used for erectile dysfunction.

Elsie took over, "Well, what can I tell you? I have an old and dear friend, Dodi Kapoor, with whom I was romantically involved long ago and duly noted. Dodi is Chairman of the Board and majority owner of KKPharma Ltd. They make unlicensed Viagra, the sildenafil molecule, for the Asian under-the-counter market and their company is growing worldwide because of the internet. Ever had Viagra spam? Dodi holds a doctorate in chemistry from Stanford, his son is a software engineer with a green card at Hewlett-Packard married to a Jewish girl from Los Angeles, and the entire family loves America. So when I asked for a supply of pills he said we could have as much as we want without packaging. No charge. He says it's sales promotion and market development."

Berrigan remarked for the record, "We might need *pro forma* legal clearance if we use counterfeit products. We're all on notice, illegal copies violate the WTO treaty, hurt artists and writers, screw Microsoft, cheat Hollywood, rip off the music business and clothing brands." They all sighed. Yes, it was a pity. But they agreed that the Inspector General could not reasonably object to the Agency's use of counterfeit Viagra in a covert operation. Would he rather they send a purchase order to Pfizer?

They wanted more on the Colonel's personality. Elsie projected images of his house and car. There was a psychological profile put together by an Agency psychoanalyst. It argued that the fact that Thondup had grown up pampered in an aristocratic household full of servants had a lingering effect on his character. Mountaineering proved his indifference to hardship, but his current urban lifestyle suggested a hunger for status and accumulation. What jumped out was his father's decision to turn the family's lands and wealth over to the government when he was a boy. He was likely to unconsciously wish for its return. He imagines uses to which he could put it. Money, wrote the psychoanalyst, underlining the word, follow the money. In a horseback diagnosis, the analyst concluded, Thondup could be shopped. He was for sale. A good target; potentially an invaluable agent in place; a solid recruitment opportunity.

There was a subtle movement to be associated with the operation in some way. *Gumba*, what a word! Everyone wanted in. It was a hoot! A story for memoirs, one could dine out on the whispered version. Going over details in the next few hours was enjoyable. Opportunities for joking and raillery made it a very agreeable meeting.

The Plan

They went over the approach to Thondup with considerable care. They assumed he would arrive with the caravan. The meteorology people said the yak rendezvous with Chandra narrowed to a typical good weather window in early October, exact days being uncertain. Herding a caravan of thirty or more slow moving yaks from Tibet across the Nangpa-La and down to Khumjung in Nepal wouldn't happen on a schedule. Spotters would have to provide a few of days' notice. Likewise, local agents on the lookout would find it easy to detect hundreds of kilos of *gumba* being carried up to Khumjung at over 13,000 feet by a chain of porters.

The room grew cheerful as they discussed camera angles to document the transaction. Ripp projected images of the village and rendezvous location to a screen. There were photos of a fallow two acre potato field surrounded by waist-high stone walls where the traders would corral and rest the yaks. There were pictures of an adjacent two story stone house which was built above a wide stall open to the field. The likely work space for the *gumba* handover.

"Take a look at the stone walls," said Ripp. "Old glacier debris. Notice how the smooth rocks just pile up. No mortar. The rocks on average are the size of bread boxes. I need the tech shop to make us five or six camera and recording devices to fit into look-alike rocks. Invisible to the casual eye. Turn on and off wirelessly from a remote. Document the whole deal. Maybe even pick up voices. We've got a couple of months to fabricate them. Gives us time to put them in place in or on the wall. Elsie's got people who can position them accurately without getting noticed. Plenty of opportunities for that."

A staffer spoke up. "If we get pictures of the tiger carcasses being transferred it's enough to incriminate the Colonel for treaty violation." They could imagine the headlines: *Chinese Officer in Wildlife Scandal – Violates Treaty.* It would ruin the man's career. The hard part would be to persuade the wildlife people to keep the evidence secret if the officer was cooperative. The Colonel would know what was in store for him if he involved China in an international environmental scandal. They had a nasty stick and a very sweet carrot.

Wurlitzer urged the simplest cover for them, to appear as trekkers on holiday, staying at one of the lodges in Khumjung, the village above Namche Bazaar. With dozens of mountain-weathered foreign visitors from all parts of the world passing back and forth no one would single them out. In that way the Khumbu was ideal for an intelligence operation. They went over gear lists and communications equipment.

They finally got to when and how Ripp would make his approach. Only after the *gumba* and carcass handover was completed, it was agreed. How long would the Colonel stay around? The yaks would need to rest and feed for a few days before the caravan packed up and headed back to Tibet. Elsie raised the possibility, or even the likelihood, that having time available the Colonel might have other undertakings in the Khumbu. That would be interesting to know. Therefore, shouldn't the approach be made as late as possible, keeping an eye on him until he starts back to Tibet? Maybe there's something else he's up to.

It made sense and was agreed to unanimously. Ripp should contrive to stay near the Colonel and use his own judgment on the approach. "Ideally," said Ripp, "I'll find a way to warm us up socially, before showing him the stick and the carrot. After that it'll be yea or nay within a minute, and Elsie standing by if I need support on matters Tibetan."

It was approved. It was left to Elsie and Ripp to execute. All were pleased at being in on such a savory priapic operation and the claim of having been in on it at the outset. One for the archives, bars, and weekends if it worked. The meeting ended in cheerful conviviality and bursts of hilarity as people left the room imagining other possibilities along similar lines.

Margaritaville

That evening Elsie and Ripp decided for Tex-Mex and margaritas in Adams-Morgan instead of *haute cuisine* and *grand cru* in Georgetown. The Casa Alegre had a corner table where it was both pleasant and easy to talk with their heads close in true Washington style. There were trade-craft reasons for keeping their voices low and if it felt intimate that was a bonus. The review meeting had gone as expected. A bright green light. If it worked out it would be a delicious career finale. Everyone liked it, including the dour staffer from the Joint Intelligence Committee, who was skeptical of anything that sounded far-fetched. The World Wildlife angle put it over the top. It was unanimous. They had a budget and resources.

They were gossiping about the others at the meeting and half-way through their second margarita before he asked, "So how long are you here before heading back to Delhi?"

"Maybe six weeks. I'm taking some holiday with a cousin on the Maryland shore, and there's family stuff. I've got to visit an aunt in Richmond and manage the renovation of the old house before putting it on the market. And there's some desk work at Foggy Bottom. Also I'm giving a talk at the Library of Congress that needs preparation. How about you?"

"I'm around till September."

"Washington?"

"No, no. I'm down in the Virgin Islands for a few weeks. I'm starting construction on my lot and I've got meetings with my architect, surveyors, and a civil engineer. Plus my accountant, my lawyer, and my broker. And, of course, day-sailing, swimming, and snorkeling. It's going to be hotter than hell. Then

I'm going up to Annapolis for a two week refresher course on my boat handling skills. I want to get down with new electronics and navigational tools, and refresh on rules of the road."

"Sounds great. Is that the retirement angle? Buy a boat and cruise the world?"

"Nothing that ambitious. It's my winter refuge but I haven't figured out the rest of the year. I'd like to spend some time in Europe actually. Do an occasional charter in the Mediterranean. That might work for a year or two. How does it sound?"

"All by yourself?"

The words were out before the thought. They both fell into a momentary silence. Each recognized a pregnant question, and shared the taste in the field of their awareness.

He winked at her and held up crossed fingers, "I'm hoping to get lucky."

She winked back at him, "I hope you do."

"You know, Elsie, I really enjoyed being with you the other night and at the Sackler too," he paused, "and even though we don't know one another very well yet, I do think we'd get on with one another if we had a chance. Long term I mean, not just this op." There was something very kind and modest in the way he said it.

She replied, "I know, Ripp. All those years, those casual nods and handshakes. I don't think we ever did an exercise together even in training. Nearly twenty five years now. Amazing, isn't it?"

He went on, "I remember watching you once when my team was on an exercise downtown in the District in spotting and shaking a tail. I was on a backup team; you never knew our people were there. But I watched you take them into Woodward's department store on a Friday sale day and vanish before they had a clue."

She laughed. "My aunt, the one who lives in Richmond, used to work at Woodward's and it was the only place I knew well enough to outwit them. There was a two door toilet for employees and they stood out in ladies lingerie."

He signaled to the waiter and turned with raised eyebrows and his glass. "Another?"

"Absolutely. And let's order. I'm hungry."

They ordered the chicken *fajitas* and a bottle of Zinfandel and by the time they reached the *flan* had obtained a level of boozy frankness exchanging life and career highlights, shared gossip, discovered various people they both knew, told stories and consumed much wine. They bumped knees and flirted openly, enjoying themselves.

"So, no children, no ex-wives. And not even a pass from you. Are you gay?"

"Nope. Specializing in vaginas."

"Did I miss something?"

"A long engagement makes it hot. End of the year's not that far away. After that, I'm free, Elsie. What do you say?" He looked at her cleavage again. Pleasantly familiar now.

"You think about it a lot?"

"Are you kidding? Of course I think about it. It's quite erotic as a matter of fact. I'll think about it again tonight, with or without your permission."

"Naughty boy."

"That's me."

"And all those Chinese girls in Singapore."

"Mostly flat-chested. And all those *Kama Sutra* guys of yours." He wiggled his eyes like a Marx brother and mock-stared at her cleavage.

"Are you planning to stay Agency affiliated?"

"If there was a congressional declaration of war or national emergency. How about you?"

"I'm planning on a ten foot pole. I'm looking for the new thing."

"I might take that as an answer," he said.

She raised an eyebrow, "What was the proposal, exactly?"

"I'll do what you like, how's that?"

"You mean I'll end up in doing what you like."

"We can try it out. It won't be like that."

They bopped their knees under the table, stirred Kahlua in their coffee and continued the play.

"So tell me Ripp, do you use the stuff?"

"What stuff?"

"The blue pill. Viagra."

"You expect me to answer a question like that?"

"Why not?"

"Do you use lubricants?"

"Hey."

"Hay is for horses. You'll just have to wait for an answer." He looked into her eyes tenderly and smiled with confident affection.

"I'm just getting to know you," she said.

"I mean a jarful would take a long time to use up, don't you think."

"The quantity was figurative."

They found a taxi. It was logical to drop him at the Cosmos and head up Connecticut Avenue to her rental. As they pulled into the club driveway he ritually offered her a nightcap but she shook her head.

"It's been a lovely evening Ripp. The whole day's been great. Thanks for the dinner. It'll be fun working with you on this one. And about whatever comes next. I will think carefully. Of us. Give me some time."

"As much as you want. I'll be back here at the end of the month," he said. "Will you still be around?"

"Possibly. If not, I'll see you in Kathmandu, late September. Staff's already booked all of us into the Sheraton, out in Bodhnath. We can circumambulate the *stupa* together."

They kissed lips for just an instant, but it signified. Then he waited under the canopy as he watched the taxi carry Elsie away. It was beginning to drizzle. Maybe, he thought, just maybe.

Pemba Leaves for Kathmandu

Pemba was ready to leave for the Police Academy in Kathmandu with a minimal kit, suitable for summer in the city. He had stayed with a cousin in Phortse while inquiring around for a potato field which might be purchased, but nothing came of it. Word had it that the best land values weren't in the nGozumba drainage, but at Dingboche in the upper basin of the Imja, or over in the Nangpa valley, above Thame, on the caravan route which remained closed to tourists. That appealed to him as he liked being alone big empty spaces. Like the picture postcard from Annie dated weeks earlier from Wyo-Ming.

A final obligation before leaving for the city was to attend Gyalpo Rinpoche. He wanted to ask the Lama for three things: a blessing, advice, and a *mo*, a divination. He gave a farewell look at the potato fields of Phortse which had been taking up the summer rains. One day soon, he said to himself, he would plant potatoes. With a last look he set off descending the precipitous trail to the river which he crossed on the footbridge, and climbed the steep switchbacks on the opposite side of the narrow valley. Finally, some hours after starting, he gained the ridge-top and Tengboche monastery came into sight. He stopped to regain his breath and gazed over his boyhood home of those many years. A group of novices were playing the *Dob-dob* style long-jumping game in the big meadow in front of the main entrance. Pemba had excelled in jumping competitions and trained by running with boots full of sand. He was big. In Tibetan monasteries he could have been a *Dob-dob* candidate.

Annie had passed through this magical scene many times and had to have a conception of his boyhood. She could speak Nepali and knew the country so she understood who and what he was. And what he wasn't. He repeated her name to himself as if driving barbs into his heart. She seemed anchored to his brain and unable to vanish as spontaneously arising thoughts came to mind, intimate, loving and erotic. He felt helpless. Such strong emotions were entirely new to him. He was not in control of his mind. He was in passionate love. He would confess it all to the Rinpoche.

Then he was in the Lama's personal sitting room which was filled with old Tibetan rugs and *thangkas* on the walls. Pemba did three prostrations on entering and came forward in a bow with his head bent. Gyalpo Rinpoche gave him a hard bop on the head with his bead-wrapped knuckles and laughed once with pleasure. Come here. Up here with me, patting the platform beside him. It was a long visit. They talked about old times and the dead. Toward the end, it took Pemba some minutes to describe what had befallen him on descending the *Stimmgabel*. The American girl was now inhabiting all his thoughts and he feared being heartbroken more than any fear in the mountains.

The Rinpoche listened patiently, sympathetically. Did Pemba want to ward her off, purge her from his thoughts or did he want to achieve her? Oh, definitely, he wanted to achieve her. That was the problem, he had nothing to offer but his passion.

"Passion" said the Rinpoche, "gets turned by the wheel of time, Pemba-la. We are tied to this wheel by our emotions and we cannot avoid the experience of an inner life. Some of our strongest emotions are driven by sexual instinct. That instinct gave us our own births, is it not so? It is the fuel for an engine that turns the wheel. Desire, and then birth. Try to turn the wheel slowly by becoming mindful. You can gain penetrating insight down to the seed level, where there is no time. Whatever the speed, Pemba-la, if the motives are good it becomes a fortunate birth. That's all."

As for Pemba's three requests, the blessing was a formal act. The Lama wrapped his *mala* around his cupped fingers and rested them on Pemba's head while intoning a long-life prayer. As for advice, Gyalpo Rinpoche told him just to let things unfold spontaneously when the *khandro*, his 'sky dancer' arrives. Not to have plans. Only to be observant. As for the divination, the mo, what was the question? Pemba asked if the outlook for him with the American girl was favorable. Gyalpo Rinpoche closed his eyes and opened the loop of 108 beads and held them in a circle on his lap. What followed appeared as a computational exercise involving pushing so many beads one way and then another. It went on in permutations with barely audible mutterings for nearly a minute until the Lama opened his eyes wide, smiled, and told Pemba confidently that the outlook was favorable but only if he did his job. He wanted to ask more but Gyalpo Rinpoche rang a bell and an attendant came to escort Pemba out as the Lama nodded at him cheerfully and benevolently.

Constable Pemba

On arriving in Kathmandu Pemba had the immediate need to conclude a negotiation with Tsede Dolma concerning her offer to buy his father's mountaineering shop in Thamel, including the furnishings and inventory. Before father died he had hoped Pemba would join him in managing the shop. They were expanding the merchandise to include athletic equipment and there were two basketballs and a pair of ping pong rackets in the window now. But he was unfit to be a shopkeeper in Kathmandu and not cut out for city life.

They had been negotiating for months and were close to an arrangement. After the cremation she had stepped in to manage the business honestly during a weak tourist season and had a tight fisted idea of its value. One day mountain tourism would be back but there was no telling how long that might be. What was the business worth? She offered so much down at year end and the rest over five years and would pay the money in dollar bills. That, in addition to his years of savings, would be enough to buy a good-sized field so he decided to accept Tsede Dolma's offer.

He was ready to buy something. The constable salary would be more than enough to maintain him while searching for the right field. He had once supposed he would be ready at that time to find a wife and start a family. But since he had fallen passionately in love with Annie, he could not imagine marrying another woman.

Some years earlier the government had initiated an Aspirant Constable program to help in rural development. An international foreign aid program had insisted on it. The initial idea had been to provide the smallest villages with an un-armed man with a large shoulder patch and a *lathi* stick, whose principal job would be to prevent local quarrels, and half of whose salary would be paid by the village. Something like a muscular ombudsman. The shoulder patch was the key. It was undoubtedly the lowest ranking sub-deputy police position in Asia and was thought originally to be a way of reducing conflicts between castes. But with the onset of the People's War the position grew hazardous in most places and the program existed only on paper.

However, as the civil war hadn't come to the Khumbu, the *Panchayat* elders decided that Lukla could pay half-salary for a man with a shoulder patch to deal with unruliness and unpleasant peace disturbances by foreigners at the airport. Lukla's unique air terminal was the start and finish point for almost all expeditions and treks in the Everest region, and as they all celebrated or mourned one thing or another, mountain quarrels were revisited, and the oxygen of Lukla's lower altitude frequently combined too easily with alcohol to energize a drunken bellicosity as teams waited for their flights out. While arrivals were orderly and courteous; departures were hellish. The word 'security' was held to mean prevention of fights about boarding priority.

Someone remembered the big fellow from up-valley, from Phortse, name of Pemba Lodrup; very strong, who was giving up work as a climbing Sherpa. His English was excellent and he was familiar with westerners. Someone else remembered he had been a novice, a *genyen*, at Tengboche monastery when he was a boy. The *Panchayat* made him an offer and took him to the departure area and showed him what he would have to deal with:

"He's dead and all I know is you killed him by that shitty placement."

"Don't call me English, you turd, I'm Scot."

"The son of a bitch raised an ice-axe at me, can you believe it, and said he'd swing if I touched his line. And I wasn't even going near it so I told the asshole I'd see him in Lukla; he'll show up later today, I saw his porters."

"All I know is that I'm on that flight ahead of you so don't try to pull any shit."

"The fucker was dislodging rocks on us all day. I'm going to tell the slob what I think of his style."

At the Police Academy

When Pemba reached the cadet hostel at the training facility in Kathmandu he felt out of place. There would be no leave or internet for weeks and no chance of seeing Dipankara Macleod till then. He was disappointed to learn he would be confined to cadet barracks, canteen, and exercise fields for two weeks and required to wear a uniform. Higher powers had decreed that constable-aspirants seeking the shoulder patch must take the physical fitness and basic training course at the police academy. Calisthenics. Hand combat. Rules and regulations. Reporting and witnessing. Then he would be sent to the airport for further training and only then be free. Regular police recruits went on to take firearms training. Cadets were warned of danger from Maoist assaults in the city center if they left the base area in uniform.

Pemba excelled in the training course and finished at the top of most exercises. A certain Captain Shresta called him aside and attempted to recruit him to the regular police forces using a series of blandishments, to no avail. Throughout the training course recurring longings for Annie came to mind at the approximate frequency and intensity as daily rain showers. He had her email address and wrote he would be out of touch for a few weeks, but what else could he say? He was sick with desire. His great pleasure, which could not be taken away from him, was the past. He always had the memory of the days in the tent with her. Something had happened to him without knowing it at the time. Something sprouted in his mind like a tree from a coconut seed.

The international airport training curriculum was ludicrous in light of the departure situation at Lukla, which lacked technology, but he braved it through, actually found it interesting, and completed his qualifications for the shoulder patch. It was made for him and he had to go to a palatial building in the city center to receive it, a blue cup-shaped affair which was pinned over the left shoulder and fastened below the armpit with a tie. The word 'Lukla' in both Roman letters and Devanagri script was embroidered in gold thread. He was ready to leave for the Khumbu and commence a salary. It was finally time to visit Macleod.

He hadn't seen his old master in years and though he would be ancient by now, and probably more talkative than ever, his advice would be helpful. Macleod talked as knowingly about sex as he did about everything else and Pemba wanted his view on whether it would be better to curb his feelings and forget about Annie. Or to risk the likely outcome that he would be broken-hearted. His feelings of self-doubt were interrupted when he encountered several monks from Tengboche who were on a shopping excursion in Bodhnath. They all stopped on a street corner to catch up on things. The monastery was going to have its own satellite station? It seemed incredible but the monks assured him it was true; they were getting the funds from a supporter but it had to be kept secret in case China interfered. There was no point in asking for permission. Nepal's government scarcely existed at the moment.

Dipankara Macleod

When Pemba reached Bodhnath he took three turns around the great *stupa*, passing Macleod's doorway each time. The *chowkidar* recognized him and answered the main question. Yes, Dipankara was in good health but very frail. The best time to see him was in the morning. Tomorrow? Yes. He knew the master would be pleased; he had stopped receiving visitors two years earlier, but he would certainly welcome Pemba Lodrup. Tomorrow morning then, he would be expected.

It would be a relief to ask his advice. More than a half-century separated their ages but Pemba and Macleod had been frequently aligned in their attitudes towards practical matters. Pemba had known Macleod, whom he called *chacha*, uncle, since he was hired as his house boy when he first came to Kathmandu from the monastery. It was more interesting and more money than his father's shop. He knew it would give him pleasure to go up the flight of narrow stairs once again, where the eighth step squeaked, and come into the parlor whose large windows faced the enormous painted eyes above the *stupa's* dome.

The learned and eccentric academic dropout, 88 year old Andrew 'Dipankara' Macleod, started life as a grammar school boy from Glasgow who excelled at his A levels and followed it with a scholarship at Christ Church, Oxford where he discovered his gay sexual identity. He took a first in languages, ancient and modern, was a junior fellow at All Souls, where he completed his doctoral dissertation "A Comparison of Tocharian, Sogdian and Kharosthi", and subsequently became the youngest lecturer at the London School of Oriental Studies. For two years he shared a queen sized bed with Myron Ng, visiting from Hong Kong University, which was also an academic boon as Myron's Chinese and Japanese language skills saved Macleod years of work on his second book.

Macleod. Some people wondered if he even had a proper English prenom. On rare occasions elderly visitors from afar were heard to call him Andrew, but 'Dipankara,' as he was widely known, was the *dharma* name he took on the occasion of his formal induction into the Buddhist clergy decades earlier in Northern Thailand, at the Wat Pah Nanachat forest monastery. Shaven bald, given robes, a bowl, and beads, he was the only Westerner in his group's ordination as a *bhikku*, a proper monk. Subsequently, over the years, he had 'taken refuge' at other times in other Buddhist sects and had even acquired formal Japanese and Tibetan names. After several years at Sanskrit University in Varanasi, India, Dipankara Macleod as he became known, moved to Kathmandu where he lived for the latter half of his life. He once calculated that he had devoted more than 20,000 hours sitting in silent meditation; but for the most part he had given it up in his later and public years.

He lived in the rickety wooden three story house, one of the many forming a circle around the great *stupa* where clockwise circumambulators passed Macleod's door. He bought the property some 40 years earlier when motorized vehicles were rare and pilgrims arrived by foot or bicycle rickshaw. Macleod's house facing Bodhnath *stupa* became his lasting home. He lived there with a cook and a sweeper until the time he needed further help, when he hired a *chowkidar* to guard his door and Pemba to be his houseboy.

Actually, it was the house that acquired Macleod. What led to the purchase was the exceptional view directly through the parlor windows at the enormous pair of all-seeing eyes painted above the *stupa's* dome. The eyes stared down into the parlor with a concentrated intensity and the window's perpendicular face favored the heightened aspect of the room. Macleod decided in an instant that he had to live there and bought it using the funds of a depleting family trust of which he was the residual legatee. A five acre broken down piece of real-estate in Dundee which had been sold to a rich Pakistani grocer turned mall developer. After selling the house Macleod placed what remained of the trust proceeds in a life annuity offered by an Edinburgh bank and settled down to live the rest of his life in Buddhist Asia on the sums sent to him quarterly. In Nepal he could live contentedly with books, occasional friends, lovers, and interesting visitors who were transiting exotic lands. He himself loved Asia and had never wanted to return to Britain.

Once tall and slim, white hair in perpetual disarray, stooped now with sunken cheeks, Macleod was unsteady on his feet. As he aged he had developed a chronic imbalance and a painful hip and had started using a cane. One of Pemba's original jobs was to hold his arm as they went by the stairs and later supporting Macleod's three circumambulations of the *stupa* every afternoon.

He usually dressed in a long dark grey-blue robe. A wispy beard dangled to a point five inches below his chin. A vegetarian, he kept to a simple routine. Breathing exercises. Fruit and tea for breakfast. Several hours in a favorite chair reading in whatever interested him followed by a lengthy session of self-invented gymnastics. A shower. Dress. Yoghurt and tea. And years ago the front door open from 3:00 till dusk. Dinner alone or with an invitee, of which there was no shortage.

Academic specialization brought him to India in the late 1950s and he lived for several years at Sanskrit University. The *pandits* considered him a prodigious student, a polymath of Buddhist scholarship. He picked up street Hindi in a week. He could work in six scripts. He went from textual Pali to Hybrid-Sanskrit and then to Tibetan. He authored articles, still under the name Andrew Macleod, in learned journals and reviewed books on Asian Philosophy for *The Literary Supplement.*

Psychedelic Earthquake

A change in Macleod's life occurred one afternoon in Varanasi during the mid 1960s, when the Ganga was flowing high past the stepped tiers of the riverfront. Three hippies from California in saffron shawls printed with Devanagri *mantra*s engaged Macleod in conversation. He had come from a bookstore nearby when a sudden heat-breaking shower started and they all gathered for shelter under the awning of an umbrella seller's stall in the little plaza above the Dasashwamedh *ghat.* The four of them were examining carefully laid out *swastika* arrangements of umbrella displays without any intention of acquiring one and the proprietor grew sullen that they weren't buying and was threatening to roll up the protective awning. Macleod, garrulous at any opportunity, entertained everyone by relating an umbrella story about sectarian splits in nineteenth century Theravadin Buddhism over whether a monk should be allowed to own an umbrella. The rules of the order, the *vinaya*, were silent on this matter, but permitted *bhikkus* to own sandals, robes, needles, thread, and bowls. Nothing at all in the *pratimoksa* about umbrellas.

This crumb of information was sufficiently entertaining to the three sojourners to the East from California that they hoped to pick the brain of an 'old India hand.' Such lunatic enthusiasm for religion, thought middle-aged Macleod. Was he once like that? But they had rented a wooden houseboat just down the *ghat* and when the rain stopped they invited him to come for *chai* and a smoke.

The view of the distant shore of the Ganga was illuminated by a beautiful late afternoon sun. At their bare rental houseboat there was *chai* from a large thermos and a great deal of *charras*. Strong hashish, cheap and easily obtained which they bought from the *saddhus* at the Manikarnika *ghat* where bodies were burned night and day. His lodgings were a long bicycle ride away and it was dark. There was plenty of bedding and he was curious if any of them were gay.

The young sojourners resembled eager undergraduates, witty and consuming spirituality like hungry rats. They sent a boy from the *ghat* out for *alu paneer* and *chappatis* and lit a kerosene lamp as it grew dark. They once had a band in California but were now passionate about North Indian music. One of them strummed a *tamboura*, another played chords on a small harmonium and the third, who came to California from Brooklyn, chanted Vedic prayers. Macleod, cannabis intoxicated, stayed the night, curled up on a thin mattress on the wooden floor. It was like being with friendly puppies. The next day he provided them with a day-long seminar with questions and answers, explaining aspects of Indian religions that seemed elementary to him. When he informed them that all the ancient sources agreed that the Buddha was universally considered to be the ninth *avatar* of Vishnu, they laughed with delight. It was the best of all possible worlds. They could be Buddhists and Hindus at the same time. At the end of the day they passed around what they called sacramental communion and he consumed several hundred micrograms of LSD, which he took for the first and last time.

He experienced a transforming illusion of becoming illuminated and believed he knew everything. He had penetrated the last veil to the great heart of wisdom, to the jewel in the lotus. *Om Mani Padme Hung*. Everything was clear and greatly perfect. It took over a year for the illusion to leave. He had gone through a phase of drinking cow urine and was convinced that the legendary *soma* of the Rg Vedas was nothing more than urine from cows that had been fed psychedelic mushrooms. Moreover, and unfortunately for his career, during that time he had become unusually prolific and had written a number of highly peculiar articles full of incomprehensible thoughts and near gibberish, which led to his becoming an academic outcast. He had strayed too far off the reservation, and the great leap forward from scholarship to weirdness had permanently muddied his name in the world of peer review. At the end he had resorted to self-publishing short pieces on cheap paper, but this only made things worse. And then he stopped, grew quiet for a time, and re-emerged in a new form.

When he was roughly restored to his senses, nearly a year had passed and the broken ties with the establishment somehow worked in favor of his new independence. Good, it would allow him to be transgressive and find his own way. He wrote to the Dean of Sanskrit University informing him that he was retiring from academic life and was leaving India for Nepal, went about returning his vows and various robes to their appropriate sources, and moved to Kathmandu as a secular layman for the rest of his life. His only philosophy became light work without haste. Enough of haste. Time for new friends. More than a professor, he became a character. The learned scholar whose greatest pleasure appeared to lay in debunking religious humbug.

His modest financial independence allowed him to ease out of the closet of sexual correctness. He was gay. *Toujours gai.* He believed in love, kama. He believed in pleasure, *bhoga.* He believed in the unity underlying the polarity, *yoga.* He practiced *bhoga yoga.* Pleasure! Pleasure! Unconditional pleasure! Unconditional desireless pleasure! Every thought-form perceived as pleasure! Such unattainable secret pleasure!

Macleod had developed his salon when Elsie was posted in Kathmandu. The parlor was large and simple. The floors covered with overlapping rugs, a large rectangular table set under the windows fixed by the painted eyes. There was a steady turnover of visitors. If given the right question or lead Macleod would hasten to gloss spiritual teachings from the point of view of reductive science. And during those years of visitors from every corner of the planet, and during all their colloquies with Macleod on every sort of matter, the handsome adolescent Pemba Lodrup was serving tea, collecting cups, greeting visitors, pointing out where to sit, simply the friendly houseboy, listening and observing, until he went off to a year in agricultural college. For Pemba the experience of being Macleod's part-time houseboy for five years became a sophisticated education on one meaning of life: the brain's attempt to create pleasure in the mind.

A Reunion

When Pemba arrived the following morning Macleod's embrace was effusive. "Pemba my sweet boy," he said pinching his cheek, "how good, how very good to see you. Come, let's go down and have a bowl of curds and honey with our *chai* and we can talk the morning away. The sun will be just right for the herb-yard, we can sit there. Give me your arm." They went to the small room off the kitchen where a narrow glass-paned door opened on a miniscule herb-yard beneath a wall. Macleod barraged him with questions, what about this, what happened to that, where did they go, what was Switzerland like, how long was father ill, had he seen Gyalpo Rinpoche, who were the best climbers these days, why do some people fear death more than others?

Pemba got to the sale of his father's business to Tsede Dolma, and his objective of buying a potato field in the Khumbu with his savings. Potatoes? Did he say potatoes? Macleod was in talkative mode and took off on an octogenarian's tangent.

"That's a very particular crop you're thinking of, Pemba. Better know what you're doing. Because everything being connected and our knowledge limited, there are unintended consequences. I'll explain. People want starch, a complex form of sugar, a source of energy. Think of potato history. In colonial times educated people were usually learned in botany and many were great experimenters and collectors. So they encountered that plant from South America, the Andes, *solanum tuberosum* with round starchy root lumps the size of berries. A manna that humans started cultivating 7,000 years ago on lower mountain slopes. The Europeans came and took the easily stored cultivars home. The what? Some generations of breeding at Kew, and the India Company brought the potato to Calcutta. They tried plantings at many altitudes but the higher they went the more useful the plant became. It didn't have natural pests and it thrived."

"Well, wouldn't you know it, by the time General Younghusband arrived with his army a century later, in 1904, there were enough potatoes growing on the march to Lhasa to become a standard troop ration. Tibetans were quick to pick up on the new easily stored food which replanted from cuttings, and did better than barley or buckwheat and produced food in places where no other crop would work, where people couldn't live year round."

"So human settlement expanded. Net result? Pay attention! Extinction of the snow leopard! That's your bloody potato! The damn tuber invaded that shy cat's home ground and brought in humans. The potato is a colonist, no? Ha! And take those tens of thousands of *mani* stones everywhere in the Khumbu. It was potatoes that financed them. For the first time there was a surplus over and above subsistence and it was used to hire stone carvers in one generational explosion of religious labor. If you become a potato farmer in the Khumbu you'll be doing nothing more than feeding tourists who will shit it out. Is that what you want in life?"

"It feeds the hungry."

Yes, Pemba thought, feeding people was small, but still a good thing. He wasn't sure about the snow leopard. In a moment Pemba would tell him what he wanted in life, but decided to clear the ground first. He related the decision to sell the shop, of the promise to his father to stop mountain guiding, of the airport security job, the state of the Maoist cause, the instability of the government, the plight of Tibetan escapees, the comings and goings of various Lamas, several deaths, the decline of tourism, the rabid dogs near Pathan, the price of *ghee*, the quality of monsoon, his final climb on the *Stimmgabel* and when finally there was nothing else to divert him Pemba came around to Annie.

Three nights in the tent and now she inhabited his thoughts. What could he do? The situation was impossible. She was an educated foreigner of another class. Yet from the moment they parted he had never experienced such extended sexual longing before. How close they had come. Generally, if he and a girl liked one another they didn't wait. But they couldn't do it then and now she was coming to work part of the season in the Khumbu. How could he possibly have a future with her? He was nothing. But he was in love with her. Passionately. He was certain.

"Because I wore robes once she asks me questions. She asked what 'tantra' meant. What is it about *tantra* and sex?"

"Ah, I see. I see. Let me give you some advice Pemba. One of the central ideas of the *tantras* is to unite the polarities of energy and wisdom as if they were two genders. In that sense tantra is about sex. Now in the Hindu *tantras*, woman is the energy, *shakti*, and the man is the wisdom. But in the Buddhist *tantras* it's the other way round. Man is the energy principle, woman the wisdom bearer. Since you have grown up in a Buddhist tradition you have to realize your karma that way. And while woman is wisdom, Pemba, she is also an ascetic path. Use your energy to support her."

"I can see your situation. I tell you this from long personal experience, and my being an old queer has nothing to do with it, though I have been with women too. The fact is every human has or has had loving and sexual thoughts. Just try to remember that intense sexual pleasure provides a hint, a clue, to the nature of the universe. Even afterward as your central nervous system reorganizes itself. Wisdom is inside the nervous system. Try slow deep breathing and slow sex. Slow sex is a key to erotic monogamy. Sex is why there's a great wheel of time of births and deaths and why *tantra* is merely physics beyond comprehension. An infinite web of atoms and molecules in motion."

Pemba was sucking in the words, only half understanding, as Macleod continued.

"I can see you are in love. I'm reminded there once was a yogi who asked his woman what a yogi should know when he meets his own wisdom bearing woman? How best to show respect and honor her? She said that if he served her through love, it would give him power. You will see it yourself, she can bestow power instantly. She'll know if you fill her emptiness. Reach for her the moment you see her, don't waste a second. Go right to it. But not in a rush for heaven's sake, things will happen spontaneously. *Festina lente*. Make haste slowly. Don't you see? No? Well, good luck anyway Pemba-la. Go for it."

Pemba felt certain that Gyalpo Rinpoche and Macleod were telling him the same thing in their indirect way, but he wasn't sure he understood how to apply it.

Chandra's Plans

After Chandra attended the Party meeting in Kathmandu he grew more pessimistic about human nature. Increasingly, his comrades seemed shallow. He was beginning to dislike them and began questioning the motives of the leading cadres. Everywhere there were signs of self-interest beyond conscience or ideology. And they were going for decisive blows rather than use slower and less costly methods, and it was taking innocent lives. It was close to murder. They were arguing about the difference of a year or two, or three at most. Was war indeed the father of all things? Was humanity capable of harmonious change? He thought of the Peace Corps girl and the evening she explained the American constitution to him. But they once had a civil war.

The agenda of the meeting finally came to the *gumba* transaction. Discussion was perfunctory and the tiger carcasses were never mentioned. It was agreed that the Zone Commander and the Chinese Colonel would take a photo together and affix their thumbprints to a sheet of paper for a provisional list of weapons. Delivery to a village in Bangladesh, near the Indian border. Naxal comrades would bring them across the narrow chicken-neck of India into Nepal.

The trade made him nervous. The task of protecting the *gumba* from rough handling from start to finish was a constant source of distraction. It would affect the price. By late Summer the crop would be arriving at collection points in small lots. After weighing on a balance scale, layers of dried caterpillar-mushrooms were to be packed carefully into containers and arranged in bales. Great care was required to avoid breaking the unique intact shapes. The whole matter felt unclean. Bank robberies seemed more dignified

The last agenda item concerned opening a line of communication with the Dalai Lama's people. The confidential overture approved at an earlier meeting appeared productive. Comrade Chandra would meet with the Dharamsala representative, Pasang Dorje, in Tengboche monastery where each side would present its views and search for mutual ground. Several committee members spoke to the issue. Some said there would never be mutual ground. Chandra argued the Dharamsala link was improbable, but worth the attempt. The danger was in going too far and provoking a Chinese reaction. In any case, the fact of such discussions must be kept secret. The Chairman asked about the arrangements.

Chandra replied that Tengboche monastery was the venue for the proposed meeting, but the representative had expressed a desire to visit Thubten Choling in the lower valley to offer prayers for the murdered novices. He hoped to walk up to Tengboche over a few days if his health permitted. His strength came and went in cycles so he had a ticket from Kathmandu to Lukla in reserve in the event he felt weak. Someone asked, malaria? No, said Chandra, it was recurrent tuberculosis, which waxed and waned. The Chairman recommended that Pasang Dorje be encouraged to see life in the red zones for himself since the Indian press painted an ugly picture of the Maoist movement. He suggested providing the representative an escort if he decides to walk. A first hand experience might be helpful in gaining a desired statement from the Dalai Lama. Pasang Dorje should be escorted as far as Lukla, up until the army check-post. Finally, the chairman took the floor and delivered an encomium to Chandra's life and his commitment to the revolutionary cause. They knew he was on his way to retire. After a round of sincere applause the meeting of the Committee adjourned.

Chandra's disenchantment turned to constant melancholy. Once there had been an ideological framework where the meaning of things was beyond doubt. Was it battle fatigue from years of minor battles? Worn out. Weary. Too much responsibility for too many things gone wrong. For the first time he started to sharpen a plan for vanishing, for retiring, and began thinking through details. It was time to think through the exit plan.

If he shaved his short white beard and let his hair grow long and retrieved old identification papers and cash from a buried tin box he could disappear easily. Not many had seen the man called Chandra. They wouldn't search for him for very long. Increasingly, he sought a radical new direction and a decisive cut-off. Otherwise the Party would always be after him for some chore or other for an elder statesman.

Where would he go? Perhaps the *ashram* beneath the Arunachala hill. He had heard of it for years. What is the Self, the master kept asking. What was the Self after work was finished? Was a man ever allowed to rest? At times he wondered if could start by shaving his head instead of his beard and become a *sannyassin*, a renunciate. Take up the traditional ancient saffron path for a man finished with worldly life.

But not likely, he admitted. He was a secular communist and still too much in the world. Yet he fantasized being left alone, finally, to read books on the meaning of life, on finding the invisible absolute which breaks all suffering, and doing it while resting in the sun surrounded by marigolds. That was the picture. To study *vedanta*, get deeper into the *advaita*, and read the words of Shankaracarya. The old philosopher interested him in particular. Did he not teach withdrawal from life as the best thing for a man? But wasn't it escapism to renounce the world? A cowardice? He had never contemplated it. Gyalpo Rinpoche had been telling him he had done enough trying to change the world; that it was time for him to change his mind about the world.

He could make an honorable disappearance without leaving tasks unfinished. After the *gumba* transfer he had a few months to hand off his responsibilities. While the Party wanted the comfort of keeping him around, he didn't want them reaching out for him. The best thing would be to withdraw abruptly. His assignment to the RIM conference in Djakarta would provide the perfect opportunity. The move would be as simple as stepping out of a hotel, finding a barber and buying a ticket to Chennai. Comrades would wonder about his disappearance for years. But they would replace him and continue. After a while almost everyone would forget about him. Perhaps he could write something under another name. The American journalist had proposed a contract for his memoirs. Would they let him use a pseudonym? The thought of it stayed in his mind. He had the man's card. He might send him a note once he became settled.

Thondup in Beijing

Thondup entered the spacious anteroom well before the appointed hour. Most were in tropical uniform. General Tu, deep in an armchair, was surrounded by several other high ranking officers. The General caught his eye and gave a faint nod. Many colleagues had arrived, standing by the tall windows facing the inner courtyard or sitting on small sofas, drinking tea and smoking. Thondup was annoyed at how the tobacco habit had insinuated itself into his life. Hsien and her ornithological crowd were smoking a pack a day and he was smoking three or four cigarettes a day. He could feel it. They all smoked. Though not Luo, who didn't like it. She told him he smelled like an ashtray.

He walked about the room, bowing slightly and saluting the senior ranks. Within the week, or the following week at the latest, he would learn about promotion. If General Tu was as good as his word Thondup's name would be put forward on Friday. He glanced at the faces of the promotion board officers and the people from the Defense Ministry. Not a clue. A General's star would mean a change of assignment and the hope of developing the right *guanxi* with new relations. General Tu himself would retire one day and Border Command would have a new commanding general. Two stars. Possibly even three in a distant future.

At the appointed hour the large *curia* gathered and took seats in the main conference room. Principals at the large circular table with four staffers in two ranks seated behind. There was a microphone at each place, a pad of notepaper and pencil, and an empty glass inverted over the mouth of a small carafe. Thondup was one of four officers behind General Tu. It was the beginning of a week of meetings covering the globe.

Towards the end of the fourth day they came around to Nepal. The civilian from the Defense Ministry led off. He hinted at a context revealed only by one's understanding of elliptical phrasings. Nepal was economically trivial but valuable strategically to China. It was a foothold of an undefined nature on the far side of the Himalayas – should it ever be needed. China welcomed the inevitable arrival of a communist dominated government under a new constitution. China would be an energetic friend of Nepal in such a circumstance. A successful communist revolution in Nepal would also have long term implications for India which had been engaged in protracted warfare with guerrilla elements of its own for more than forty years. They were urged to be mindful of this as they proceeded in their discussions.

It did not take long before the issue of Nepal's guerrilla war took center stage. They all shared the view that the monarchy would fall within two or three years at most. The question of China's clandestine support of rebel weapons procurement was never mentioned, a tactical matter not for this meeting. Instead, the guerrilla's use of the word 'Maoist' was considered worthy of special discussion and two other individuals in civilian clothes from the Foreign Affairs Ministry sat in to give them guidance.

One of them pointed out that China's Ambassador to Nepal had remarked publicly that the rebels were misusing the name of Chairman Mao by associating the name 'Maoist' with torture, summary executions and the killing of innocent civilians, all of which harmed the image of China's great leader. It was undesirable to have Chairman Mao's name associated with these things. There had been more than 12,000 civilian deaths in Nepal in the last few years, victims of crossfire and reprisals. The world had to learn that China did not and could not control the Nepalese revolutionaries. And unlike India, which shared a porous border with Nepal, China had nothing to fear from armed people's movements.

A senior general with a salad of ribbons on his chest, asked the civilian if he was suggesting that the Chairman's words and teaching concerning armed and protracted struggle were for a bygone age? Or was he suggesting merely that Nepal was a special case. The civilian was thankful for the opportunity of clarifying. Of course, Nepal was a special case. The meaning of this exchange was simultaneously clear and unclear. There was a banquet filled with congratulatory toasts. The atmosphere was convivial. China was on the rise. There were retirements and promotions in the air. The branch chiefs would meet on the fifth day to select candidates for change of rank and assignment.

The next morning was the bureaucratic conclusion, reserved for formal action approvals, sign-off's, and new report forms to master, paper work. Intelligence branches and covert operations held separate meetings in secure rooms. Pending foreign intelligence operations were docketed for final approval. The joint counter-intelligence teams concerned with Tibetan exile groups and the activities of the Dalai Lama's office were assigned a large and comfortable sunlit room where they sat around a long oval table. The several branches of the security services, half of them in civilian clothes, were permanently hungry for information on Tibetan factions around the famous Lama. It was still difficult to penetrate the clergy who were suspected of criminal communication between Dharamsala and the remaining monasteries of Tibet, Qinghai and Szechwan. One had to be on guard.

China Policy

The attitude in the meeting room was unanimous. It would be over before long. A few years were nothing compared to what was at stake. Chinese diplomacy, that is protracted war by other means, had been effective in its patience and was coming to a simple end-point. The Dalai Lama was going to die. The old exiles were going to die. Enterprising young Tibetans in India and elsewhere were finding better things to do than waste time on ancient revanchist politics and idolatry. Nevertheless, eternal vigilance was the watchword. There were hints that Dharamsala was attempting to stir up anti-China politics among the Sherpa people.

Ho Zhang, the National Security Advisor, was finally coming to a point. Several agents, within days of one another, reported a rumor that a representative of the Dalai Lama would be holding talks with the Nepalese revolutionaries. Could this possibly be true? If so it would be a shocking surprise. And if this rumor was also being heard in both Kathmandu and in Dharamsala it would then certainly be heard in New Delhi and in Washington. And at this moment it was now being heard in Beijing. What could be the meaning of such an action? This is a matter of considerable interest to the Presidium. Was someone from Dharamsala intending to meet with the guerrilla leadership? Where? Was the Dalai clique sticking its nose into Nepal's Buddhist community to make anti-China mischief? They would deny it, of course.

Thondup whispered something to General Tu who nodded and he spoke up for the first time. His unit had some information. Intelligence fragments hinted that a representative called Pasang Dorje was planning a direct journey Dharamsala-Kathmandu-Lukla in October. Little was known of the person, only that he was part of the so-called 'household administration.' Two reliable agents in Dharamsala had their own informants but found nothing. The name yielded a nearly blank file in their watch list of 'persons of interest' in the bureaucracy of Tibetan exiles. They had a brief physical description but little more. *Short man, always in dark western suit, white shirt no necktie. Subject seen monthly at bank. Subject lives in Dalai Lama's large compound. Administrative duty: Librarian. Rarely seen in Dharamsala town.* With a name search they found the man's routing and dates after scanning the Indian rail and air reservation systems. Ticketed in early October. General Tu suggested learning what the man was up to after arriving at Lukla.

The security advisor agreed immediately and urged that it be followed up. He wanted to know more, definitely. It could have major implications. General Tu added that Colonel Thondup was his most well-informed officer on the Khumbu region and had informants there. The security advisor said in that case Colonel Thondup should go and have a first hand look at this Pasang Dorje fellow. General Tu said it would be done. He exchanged a glance with Thondup. They had authorization and a positive reason to go. It was an order. And it solved an annoying headache.

After they adjourned the security advisor shook his hand and said it was a pleasure to meet him. How would he reach the Khumbu? With one of the nomad yak caravans over the frontier at the Nangpa-La. He then intended to purchase clothes and a backpack and walk down to Lukla so as to be there under cover, timed for the man's arrival at the airport. Was someone meeting him? And if so, who?

Thondup was optimistic he would find answers and intended to use the cover which had served on prior occasions. Once out of his yak herder's robes he would become, once again, Mr. Liu Dzao, from Hong Kong, a wholesale dealer in traditional Chinese medicines, whose customers were chains of western health food stores. A man taking his long dreamed-of trekking holiday. They had all the old cover paperwork. His Chinese passport still bore a more youthful photo. Born in Xian, attended middle school in Shanghai, pharmaceutical certificate, head of trading operation in Shenzhen, then relocated to Hong Kong headquarters. A bulletproof cover.

The long summer weekend with Luo lay ahead. Thondup went off to the officer's hostel, showered, changed into civilian clothes and telephoned her. He would stop by the apartment for a hasty moment on the way to General Tu's for dinner. He wouldn't be able reach the rented bungalow until well after dark.

An hour later. Her apartment, a family inheritance, filled with fine Chinese art. "Chiang never knew about these pieces or they would be in Taiwan today," she said casually, waving her hand around. "Will you have a whiskey?"

He declined but came up close and kissed her. They had made love there once before, on the day he arrived in Beijing a week earlier; their months apart made him more fond than ever of his dear friend. She still felt new and he held her close. What might come of their relationship, he wondered.

"I have to be at General Tu's for dinner, but I wanted to kiss you. I can't wait to be with you at the lake tonight and listen to the crickets. My driver has all the directions on how to find it and it really looks like the weather might give us a beautiful weekend."

He held her at arms length and gave a military salute. There were traces of grey in her hair and fine wrinkles around the corners of her mouth. And the pores near her nose were noticeable. Nevertheless. A beautiful woman, filled with sexual energy. Exactly what he needed. Could they keep it going for years?

Dinner with General Tu

General Tu kept a tasteful suite of rooms in one of the thousand surviving buildings off the outer courtyard of the Forbidden City, the old imperial capitol. The walls dated from the 15th century and there could have been over 20,000 rooms at the time of the Ming dynasty. The General used it on week nights, as weekends found him in the country with his wife. There were ornate porcelain spittoons on trays located throughout the residence as the General spat tobacco juice frequently in addition to exhaling cigarette smoke.

Wearing a brocaded silk jacket, the General waited at the open door of the reception room, while a uniformed aide ushered Thondup to his presence. The General embraced Thondup and held him at arm's length. A year had passed since they had been alone with one another and the General looked him up and down, then linked his arm, and spoke softly as he led him out of the entry and into an upholstered parlor. A ceiling fan turned slowly and stirred the air which bore a faint scent of pine, as if from an earlier incense offering.

"My dear godson. I am very happy to see you again. You will forgive me if I kept distant from public displays of affection. It is only in your own interest. The ways things always are, if I am seen to favor you certain persons could draw unhelpful conclusions. In my generation we treated the name of Confucius with great respect since he understood the importance of correct behavior between a benefactor and his favorite at the imperial court, such as we are. But tonight we can dine together, just the two of us and discuss other matters. This is an auspicious time for you. Your father would be proud."

Thondup felt a burst of pleasure as he heard these words. He could smell the promotion, it could not be far away. A star. General Thondup. The reference to Confucius was the General Tu's way of praising him for using the Dharamsala visitor to deflect any hint of the weapons-for-*chungcxiao* trade. It was assumed the revolutionaries had various sources for weapons and the means of paying for them, but it never descended from the level of tactical abstraction to the daily heartlessness of any armed struggle. The caterpillar-mushroom transaction was off the official radar.

They shared a Scotch whiskey while the General questioned him closely on the details of handling the *chungcxiao* cargo. There was no telling how careless these mountain people could be. Although there was no scientific reason to think broken fragments were less powerful there was a substantial premium for intact mushrooms. That was clearly the superstition of ignorant people. And why? Just because the fungus frequently looked like a little penis. Who wants to ingest a broken penis? However, the marketplace was speaking clearly. There was that premium and so careful attention to packaging was important. Thondup assured him that the requested method of packaging had been reviewed and agreed to by the Zone Commander and it would ensure that most pieces arrive intact.

They dined on 'beggar's' chicken and pickled cabbage and talked about the demand for such virility products. The conversation led to the General's ruminations on women, sex, aging, ginseng, and the traditional Chine medicine business. "It's been a good year for that kind of product. We now have those tigers, and Admiral Ma of our circle just acquired fourteen tons of dried seahorses from an African syndicate harvesting the waters off Angola."

Thondup spoke directly for the second time. "About the armaments list for the counter-trade? They will want a proper manifest. They want night-vision goggles."

"No problem," said the General. "We had their wish list months ago and we used 500 kilos as a benchmark and showed them what we could provide, subject to market conditions later in the year. There was some negotiation. I had to give a little on one or two items which they want in particular, not in the Burmese inventory. I agreed to help our partners out a bit for those items – he gave a warning look – *that stays in this room forever*. As anyone can see, the Burmese are proof of the value of being a middleman. A wholesaler providing assurances to both sides. And don't bother weighing more than a few samples. We will make all the adjustments when we take delivery at our own scales. On the whole I'm inclined to be generous. They're fighting for something glorious aren't they? Oh, and one more thing. The sneakers. You've arranged the yaks? Good. A man will come to collect them the moment you reach Khumjung."

After dinner they returned to the parlor where General Tu spoke at length, without interruption. He rose from his seat occasionally and walked about gesturing in the air to accent his words while he smoked a cigarette. Once he missed the spittoon entirely and spat on the tray. There were glasses of sweet plum wine on a low table and the parlor was illuminated by a single lamp with a decorative shade modeled after a Sung dynasty scroll painting. He spoke softly.

"I want to create a picture for you of where things stood before we received this bombshell story of our Nepalese friends opening a dialogue with the Dalai's clique. It's hard to believe, but you can't exclude anything these days. You can imagine the ripples created on our side. Such an attempt at triangulation would have profound strategic consequences. So it raises the usual question. What is to be done?"

"Recall that before we learned about this rumor our syndicate had a slight problem. There were grumblers in other departments who questioned the importance of learning about porters strikes and labor unrest in Nepal, whether that was sufficient to warrant an officer of your rank personally undertaking a foreign intelligence operation. There were Embassy staff for that kind of thing. There were challenges. So why exactly was Colonel Thondup going to Nepal, I was being asked. No one understood you were going to do our *chungcxiao* business!"

"Well, as of today, owing to your wits, you received an order from the security advisor to go there. And in fact we need the kind of intelligence requested, namely what the hell is going on between the communist movement and the Dalai's people? And as that's the official focus it sidestepped the entire question of how we - or should I say you - happen to be in contact with Chandra in the first place. So our business still remains our own private matter. As of now you are instructed to go find this Pasang Dorje and your after-action report should write it up that way. As an order to go. Our business has finally perfected its cover story. The enemies of Border Command have been nipped in the bud."

"But do understand, until we heard this rumor, unfriendly questions were being asked at the inter-agency level. The 'spider' influence was around, if you know what I mean. One of the doubters said you just sought any excuse to go up into the mountains, even if it was just walking across the Nangpa-La. But you were smooth in the way you handled things. Very commendable. Others are making provocations, but we continue to outflank them." He paused for a moment and then spoke emphatically, "Border Forces must remain an autonomous command, like the Coast Guard."

"Now to other things for a moment. I have put your name forward for promotion to Brigadier. As I know one or two members of the promotion board I have reason to think the results will please you. However, the dragon's advocate had a list of negatives and I think you should pay close attention to what some people are saying about you as they look at your record, and particularly your own words in after action reports. Do not misunderstand. The promotion is in order. Everyone was quite complimentary on the whole. You are the son of a martyr who has risen on merit, and not merely on the affirmative action that Tibetan minorities enjoy. You are a national icon in the world of mountain climbing. You and your wife are persons of influence in Lhasa social circles. And your youth was never a handicap to prior promotions, and it's not now. So what is the problem which is marked out in your record?"

"Impulsiveness. Reflexive hotheadedness. Your own words over the years reveal a self-reported partiality to shooting first and asking questions afterwards. As a result, you were turned down for defense attaché at an embassy as your next posting. Someone who is actually a friend of ours off-handedly suggested that you could be seconded over to the Ministry of Defense since the Border Forces liaison position becomes vacant at year's end. It's better than military attaché and actually requires someone with the rank of Brigadier. Our friend, a far-sighted man, said that staff work at the defense ministry would encourage prudence and a bit more caution in you, once you gained a more panoramic view of things. So, if all goes according to the latest plan, and it will be definite next week, you are going to be working here in Beijing for the next two years. Staff will help you find suitable quarters for your family." Thondup experienced a fright at the thought of Hsien and Luo meeting one another. The General went on. Things were approaching conclusion.

"So, let us be frank. Your posting here in Beijing means our circle has a vacancy in Tibet. I am not clear about your successor, he is yours to appoint. But we must be absolutely certain that whoever it is will understand his duty to you. He will not find that duty in an organizational diagram. There are years of profitable opportunity ahead if we choose the right man. I cannot make that decision from here in the capitol. Unless you want to spend a few more years in Lhasa yourself. Who do you have?"

Thondup cleared his throat. "Lakpa Chodren, a Major in my command. In his late forties. He'll be reliable. I've known him for years. Wants to get up in the world. Sharp on opportunity. I know how he thinks. I've made him the sectional procurement officer and he's been on roving duty up and down the border for the last two years. Originally from a nomad family up north. Very steady temperament and the men respect him. I've been on climbing expeditions with him too and can tell you he's fairly bold. Unmarried. Since the time he enlisted as a kid he's used the army self-improvement curriculum: reading, writing, calculating and now has a school equivalency certificate. Speaks all the border languages better than me, including some obscure dialects. Ambitious, and my counter-intelligence people who have listened in on him more than he realizes, say he's a model of loyalty on both a personal and professional level. But he's one hundred percent Tibetan blood, if that's of concern."

"Need not be if he's the right man. Send him to me for a little talk when the weather cools down a bit. If he can work with us these next few years it might be promising. You never know what opportunities will come up and you have to understand how sensitive these matters can be. He has to pass that test too. Nothing given away and that's exactly how it should be. We're not the only ones active in business. General Hsu, who was sitting next to me, the army's top computer man, owns a factory making computer disks with perfect copies of the expensive stuff. It costs pennies and he does it on the army's budget. So who is the officer who refers to such a matter, however indirectly, however innocently, however unconsciously, however well intentioned, at a senior staff meeting? That will never be the right man."

Thondup was escorted to his car by General Tu who shook his hand again and clapped him on the shoulder and saw him off. The car headed west towards the lake district and after a while Thondup could smell fresh odors which were new to his nostrils and became a memory in his brain. How rare to see the moon reflected on still water, surrounded by forest and the docks of occasional cottages. For an instant he felt irritated that he didn't know how to swim. But these people didn't know about mountains either.

163

The Bungalow

Thoughts filled his mind as the car wound its way. His thoughts tumbled. If General Tu was correct he might be in Beijing for at least two years. Once in the Capitol a lake house for the summers might be affordable. Hsien would lose her main social circle in Lhasa. Perhaps she would prefer a divorce.

The roadside cottages appeared prosperous. New bungalows had been built on the scalloped lake edge along a kilometer of forest reaching the water's edge. Theirs was in an advantageous location. Luo made the arrangements. An able woman he thought, and the way she stimulated him, the variety of her fantasies amazed and aroused him.

He arrived at the cottage near midnight. The number of the driveway was conspicuous from the road and they went through the woods for a few hundred yards to stop at the illuminated entrance. Thondup told the driver to be off duty for the weekend and to take his ease but to keep his phone on in the event he was needed. The man saluted and Thondup took his valise and walked up the wooden steps to the door which was left ajar. There were long grasses sticking up between the stairs.

"Am I too late?"

"No, never too late. I knew you had reasons. Come in, take off your jacket and shoes and have a drink. I'm not tired in the least and we can sleep as long as we like in the morning. I'll put on some music." Her voice sounded sweet and sincere but her eyes were full of irony.

Forty five minutes later they were naked in bed, panting hard. When their breathing rate returned to normal she propped herself up on an elbow and gave him a sly look. "My stallion," she said as she rose to find a towel and bring two partially drained glasses of Xinjiang brandy to the night table. Her buttocks were smooth and only slightly dimpled.

"Well," he said, "it all depends on the mare." They laughed and relaxed, gossiped about people they knew, former lovers, his family situation, life in Lhasa, her sister's breast cancer, his future assignment in Beijing. She turned to look at him.

"Thondup, my dear, don't you think there will be problems if your wife comes here with you?"

"I don't think she will want to come. We will get a divorce I think. We both will want it that way. Our daughter will start university in September."

164

"Then what will come of us?"

"We should be partners."

She squeezed his hand and they shared a long and enjoyable silence, their bodies uncovered, he on his back with his arms wide at ease with himself on a summer night, Luo facing toward him, her head cradled above the pit of his arm. He played endlessly, gently, with a strand of her hair. She rubbed his knee with small light strokes. They felt peace. Thondup made the most minimal sound of a laugh.

"What?" she asked.

"It's just the complete contrast to what we do all day. It's funny, isn't it?"

She laughed, tossed the towel at him, and went to make herself a hot bath as Thondup showered in the adjacent stall. There were scented oils above the washbasins and he decided to offer her a back rub when she emerged. He left the door to the bath ever so slightly ajar which gave the room a glow after their lamp was out, and he carried a flask of oil to the night stand on his side.

She lay on her stomach and he began massaging her back. After a minute or two he straddled above her, working her neck and shoulder muscles just like the masseurs at the senior officers club. She moaned softly from time to time. He worked down to the lumbar and sacral parts of her back. The warm oil oozed smoothly beneath his fingers. The cleavage of her buttocks became powerfully appealing as he worked on her thighs, causing her legs to spread slightly more to a wider angle. And then, as he could not resist, he moved his oiled fingers to her anus and below. She moaned irresistibly as he entered her.

But after perhaps ten seconds, in a blow to his manhood, his erection subsided. He felt it slacken. No climax, no premature ejaculation, just a softening noodle. He didn't want it to happen but it was happening. It happened.

She turned, made a sympathetic sound and stroked his cheek. "Let's get some rest," she said. "It's been a long day."

"Your gelding," he said. "The horse gets tired. The horse is old."

"Don't be foolish." She turned on her side and pulled him in to nestle behind her, putting his hand on her breast and she fell to sleep. After ten minutes of motionless silence he shook her shoulder ever so gently.

"What?" she said.

"Do you know about the blue pill?"

"Viagra? My brothers use it. We make jokes all the time. For sure. Why? You want some? You don't need it."

"Just to try."

"I'll bring you one in the city. My brother has a container of them. They sell for 150 yuan a pill. Twenty dollars."

He gestured to his wallet on the night table.

"Don't be ridiculous. I'd like to see what it does for you."

FALL

The airport's single short runway proceeds directly up a slope that near its top actually cuts through the main street of Lukla. A siren blast gives warning that a gate-arm will come down to block pedestrian or bovine passage until the plane turns onto a small apron. The passenger shed, the nearby lodges, and food establishments form a ragged holding area for air travelers to and from the region. Keeping the peace on airport property and immediate surroundings was Pemba's principal responsibility as the new security officer. It was generally agreed on the basis of his first few weeks that he was a success.

For an arriving passenger, the first building one saw on emerging from the ramshackle terminal was the windowless Yeti Travels warehouse across the street. Painted dark green, it had a cartoon picture of a grinning Yeti stenciled above the company's name. The warehouse contained a large stock of camping, trekking and climbing gear, most of it used, though quite serviceable, and some of it new. Off to one side was an attached shack with a window facing the street and over the door the word "Bookings" was lettered neatly.

Yeti Travels Ltd. offered brochures and a website promising to spare mountain travelers the need to fly enormous amounts of mountaineering gear half way across the globe. While many Himalayan sojourners arrive fully equipped, or even over equipped, others arrived to find that they needed to rent extra layers of protection against the cold, or that a tent was lost and they needed another for hire. Under the headline "Save on overweight charges – Rent from us," Yeti Travels displayed entrepreneurial talents. In addition to gear supply, a menu of specialized services was offered: expedition support, yak rentals, guide services, porters, cooks, and *sirdars*; custom and self-assembling treks, Everest base camp tours, and so forth. And though there were other companies claiming to offer similar services, Yeti Travels had a long history, an experienced staff, a prime location, and had been associated with several famous expeditions. There were always clients who started as strangers and ended as bonded friends.

Sonam Chime had been the Yeti warehouse manager for nearly two decades and was a part owner of the enterprise. A short stocky man with a cheerful outlook on life, he had rented Pemba a small unused outbuilding behind the fenced rear courtyard of the warehouse, beyond a laundry shed where a goat was penned. Pemba could have it for next to nothing for as long as he liked as Sonam was glad to see it tended. In the weeks since returning from Kathmandu Pemba had worked diligently to make the little dwelling presentable.

Which it was. He had scrubbed the neglected interior to a spartan geometry of clean horizontal surfaces. His possessions were minimal: personal clothing and toiletries, a few agronomy textbooks, and his unused climbing gear, which Sonam had offered to buy from him, filled a corner in a neat arrangement. There was a simple kitchen area, a cast iron stove, and a wide sleeping platform with a dun colored duvet over the mattress, cotton quilting over four inch foam. The only decorative element was a little altar beneath a small scroll painting of a naked red-bodied goddess dancing on a prostrate dwarf. Annie's arrival was now days away, which made his prayers to the red *dakini* heart-felt.

Geography Lesson

Fresh off the flight from Singapore, Ripp half-stretched on the sofa in Wurlitzer's apartment. He sipped a whiskey and opened several buttons of his shirt. Wurlitzer, an enthusiastic former special forces veteran and CIA case officer, had informants and agents throughout Nepal's government departments, his usual territory. The word came down from headquarters: provide full assistance to Elsie and Ripp for the drama ahead in Khumjung.

Wurlitzer handed him a thin folder. It had a list of telephone numbers and code words, a stamped trekking-permit from the Government of Nepal with a small black and white photo of Ripp stapled to the pink form and receipt for a fee, to be shown at the entrance of *Sagarmatha* National Park, the World Heritage Site where one enters the upper Khumbu region. And a tourist map.

"That's all the cover we need," said Wurlitzer. "We're all just a bunch of average foreign trekkers on holiday. I've got plenty of gear for you. The trick is not to get altitude sick so we need to give ourselves some extra days. We'll hire porters at Lukla, take a few days staying at lodges, and walk slowly up to Khumjung with enough time to acclimatize. Tech support is already up there and they're just nursing our equipment. They'll give us a case of beer if we can spot the cameras or the mikes."

Ripp sipped his drink. "Meeting the Zone Commander will be easy. I met him last Spring. It's the Chinese Colonel I want to meet without him suspecting anything so I can stay close till the last moment. Elsie could be right and he might have other business too. He's got a few days on his hands before the yaks get loaded and head back to China. Once we document the handover, it's Katy-bar-the-door. He'll know immediately whom I work for. Nothing to hide once I reveal the proposition. We're both foreign nationals meeting in a third country, so it's secure for him. And with the blue pills to sweeten the deal it'll be pay-or-play on the spot. I'm not giving him time to think about it."

"Well, we're good to go," said Wurlitzer. "Hornbein's up in Namche Bazaar. She's got the Defense Attaché's helicopter for the ride and has some radios for us."

At the Embassy the next morning Ripp faced an enormous wall-mounted display revealing the photo imagery of the region. Wurlitzer used the controller to rotate and tilt the picture to reveal the contours and used a laser pointer to show the trail alongside the milky river, the Dudh Khosi, the sum of the Khumbu's tributaries. He circled the laser dot on Lukla village, perched on a prominence above the river gorge. On the trail below the village a Royal Army Post marked a de facto line of control. Above lay a spectacular and peaceful world of government supported tourism. Below, an impoverished rural world under harsh Maoist control all the way down, far down, to the paved road, and further to the Indian border. The red point danced here and there.

Wurlitzer remarked, "Tourism could be taken out with a few hand grenades if someone wanted to. In theory the Maoists could take the entire region up to the Chinese border. Life would just go on without tourists. There's a party faction wanting to use a few well-placed grenades to shut the trade down. Expedition cancellations after those monks were killed. The party line is that a labor action by porters would have a stronger effect than hand grenades. As for the porters, as we know, they'll follow the lead of our secondary target, the Zone Commander. They've known him for a long time. There's no one else they'll trust as much."

Wurlitzer zoomed the image in on the army post and followed his description with a red dot. "You can see the trench of the landline that goes up to a major telecoms facility located in the airport's control tower building. That's the Khumbu's main communications hub. Have a look, the trail comes up from the river, then after the army checkpoint, you can see over here," the pointer showed the place, "the trail tops out at the low corner end of the airport runway, walks alongside the runway until the main street of the village. On the other side of the village the trail goes above the tree line to Namche Bazaar and Khumjung. One or two days of walking. Tengboche's still another day further and higher. "

Ripp made a face. "Let's take our time. I need to acclimatize. I'm from sea-level. Help me with the geography again."

Wurlitzer let the laser pointer do the work. "Here's the border with Tibet. Runs right through the summit of Everest and a range of the world's highest mountains. Here you can see three enormous glaciers flowing south into Nepal from Tibet, separated by two short interior ranges. On the west the Nangpa glacier begins at the only usable pass called the Nangpa-La. That's where our caravan enters Nepal. It's very high, around 19,000 feet but can be traversed a couple of weeks a year. They treat it as a legal entry/exit point for holders of special-permits, like the yak wranglers. Both countries have seasonal border police check-posts below the pass on both sides."

"The middle glacier, the longest of the three, is the nGozumba. It's fun pronouncing it. And to the east is the Khumbu glacier which comes down off the southwest face of Everest itself."

He brought up a series of high resolution images. "This one is of Khumjung. Stone houses, potato fields, stone walls. We'll be half acclimatized by the time we get there. We'll go slowly. Some people more sensitive than others."

"How cold is it going to be?"

"Water bottles freeze solid, even in the lodges, unless they're in your sleeping bag."

"Oh, shit."

Gumba Shipment

Chandra's team of 14 porters were ferrying the *gumba* bales to Khumjung. Harish, the oldest porter, had been in the profession, if it could be called that, for nine years. A gaunt dark skinned man without a sign of fat between loose skin and taut muscles. Legend had it that a porter, like a bicycle rickshaw *wallah* in the city, would be dead within seven years of the day he started that kind of work. One's frame became so debilitated that the slightest illness carried one off. Harish was coughing and Chandra didn't like it. He had known the man for years and had used him to organize.

"Jai Ram," said Harish when the column paused for a break by sitting on their thick T shaped crutches and half-resting loads on small rock ledges so they wouldn't require un-shouldering.

"Harish *bhai*," said Chandra, calling him brother, "do you need water?"

"*Nahi*, only rest a moment before bridge. Who is using so much *gumba?*"

"China people."

"What for?"

"Softness. Needing to make stronger."

"For what?"

"Women."

"*Achaa.*" Yes. He shook his head, sorrowfully, and grimaced.

Chandra took the gesture to mean it was beneath dignity. He felt this way himself, that there was something almost dishonorable involved, as if he was drug dealing. Women! Robbing banks was one thing but somehow this felt unclean. He considered how many years it had been since he had sexual relations with a woman and wondered if this was the source of his dissatisfaction, if the sacrifices he had made for the revolution, had rendered him celibate like a *brahmacharin*. He could not remember, or even imagine sexual pleasure.

Circumambulation

Elsie and Ripp ambled amongst the thin afternoon crowd circulating clockwise around the great Bodhnath *stupa* in Kathmandu. They were talking about security leaks at headquarters that could affect changes in how policy got made. How to share knowledge and keep it secret. As they passed a particular doorway Elsie pointed to the rickety house above.

"The guy who used to live there, Dipankara Macleod, could have been a great MI-6 asset if the Brits hadn't been so up tight about gay men. He knew more than anything in our records. He had me figured out on the spot. We had barely met when I was new in Kathmandu, when he looked me up and down and asked me if I had ever compared tantric secrecy with the secrecy of intelligence work. He had a psychological analysis of initiations and security clearances, all concerned with protecting secrets. The need-to-know business. You couldn't tell whether he was talking about our outfit or about Tibetans. I've never been able to get it out of my head."

"Half the time," said Ripp, "it's covering your ass against screwing up publicly. But tell me, after you drill down in that yoga stuff what do you find? What the hell is so secret?"

"Other than the integrity of oral transmissions, there's lots of theories and dissertations about so-called secret teachings. The Masons, the Great White Lodge, the secret of the mummies, that sort of thing. Magic diagrams. I just read a paper about a rare Tibetan manuscript at auction about a secret to understanding bird speech. It went for seven figures. Another one claims to teach how to stop breathing. And even loonier claims, like making yourself invisible, or flying, but the Lamas don't talk about it at all because it easily brings disrespect, like the fake yeti skulls a few years back. Like a magician's trick, secrets have no power if everyone knows them. Most yogi secret methods are mundane. I think they're about fending off anxiety, mind calming techniques at the core."

Ripp speculated "It's just left over stone-age shamanism, isn't it? Psychophysical techniques to create altered states of consciousness. Maybe trying to observe your own mind working is more evolved. But there's so much horseshit around. How do you tell a good secret from a piece of junk? Does it survive confrontation with modernity?"

"The shamanic stuff is what 90% of Tibetans practice. Propitiating deities, pacifying dangerous ones. Pleasing, bribing, and paying ransom to spirits. It's mostly about mundane goals, crops, easy childbirth, avoiding hail, love spells, and so on. Only a small minority pay attention to meditation, or enlightenment, or higher consciousness."

"And what do they get to know?"

"Depends what they want."

"You're going to have to explain things better." And before she could say anything he stopped walking and turned to face her. The circulating crowd flowed around them.

"Would you like to go hiking with me next summer?" he asked, "in the Carpathians?"

"Pardon?"

"Would you like to go hiking with me in the Carpathian forests next summer? I've got cousins in Zakopane, not far from Krakow. I'm told the blueberry crop is amazing."

She gave him a long look under raised eyebrows. "Wow. Maybe."

Crossing the Nangpa-La

On the Tibet side of the border, near Tingri, Thondup stood before a full length mirror under the light of a single overhead bulb and inspected his costume of soiled black robes, like a pastoralist from the outer edges of human habitation. Major Wang, his adjutant, standing by, commented that his hair was still too well-cut and they improvised a head covering of braided yak hair under a felt cone and a chin cord. At the police check-point on the Nepal side of the Nangpa-La he would look like one of the illiterate yak-herding nomads of the caravan. Only a head-count and a thumb print required.

He doused the light and lay down in his robes for a nap, terminated when Major Wang knocked precisely at 0100 as ordered, and carried Thondup's black canvas bags holding his personal gear into the off-road staff car. There was a thermos of tea and some cold buns and they started immediately on the long drive to the rendezvous. The final few hours required four-wheel drive, a continuous grinding of gears, and close attention by Major Wang who was driving.

Finally, just at dawn they reached a meadow where the headman was waiting. The staff car had been heard from afar and the yaks were fully loaded and standing restlessly at their tethers. Thondup could see daubs of blue paint on the horns of those carrying General Tu's fake Nike sneakers and his own counterfeit down bags and parkas with the North Face labels. He shook hands with Wang who wished him good luck.

It was the start of several long days of slow walking alongside cargo-laden animals. Plenty of time for wandering thoughts as he enjoyed the outing, very likely the last time he would be in field conditions on his own. He would miss it. In good weather there was nothing as fine as walking slowly into Nepal across the wide Nangpa-La and enjoying the stupendous views on all sides.

General Tu had been as good as his word. It was official. The promotion ceremony had been scheduled for late November in Beijing. Brigadier General Thondup Gaomei, Border Forces Liaison, Ministry of Defense. He said it to himself again several times. He was very pleased with the new assignment. Camouflage. He had been asked to develop a unified plan for concealing China's military facilities in border regions against detection by satellite photography. He could envision it all. An amicable divorce from Hsien. Moving his personal effects to Beijing. Desk work. He would have a staff. A car. Crisp formal uniforms. Luo. A new social life.

As the caravan inclined toward the top of the pass Thondup could see a pennant cloud streaming off Everest's summit, still so much higher. On his left and bulking over the Nangpa-La was Cho Oyu, one of the border giants above 8,000 meters. His gaze followed its main ridge to where the base camps would locate and he mentally traced the standard route to the summit on which he had once succeeded. He turned to look back from where they had come and tried to imagine Lieutenant Li's situation earlier in the year when escapees were shot and killed. Of course Li had done the right thing. He reminded himself to inquire of the three captured boys when he returned to his base, and thought of looking into the possibility of a erecting a remote camera near the pass to observe and record movement on a year-round basis.

The caravan paused for a windy half hour at the top of the *la*. It was midday, bitterly cold and the herders were preparing wind-flags and adding stones to a cairn while the yaks kept their backs to the wind and huddled together. A string of old bleached and ragged prayer flags stretched from cairn to cairn and bellowed in the wind amid the several small and whitewashed – at this altitude! – *chortens* containing every kind of superstitious talisman, bones, pills made from feces and other such mad relics of some dead shaman. He despaired of his countrymen.

There were seventeen of them, clad in thick woolen robes of layered felt covered with yak skin capes. Each carried only a cloth purse over a shoulder; all other weight was on the animals, more than fifty sure footed beasts – larger than the Nepali varieties – loaded with salt and other cargo for a Saturday market session in Namche Bazaar.

Once in Nepal the caravan rested at the check-post at the first narrow place below the pass. As nomads did not carry papers and the commodities were alike each year the old Sherpa official who manned the post made a head count and waved them past. His fingers were too old to undo iron-like knots on pack loads. And the big Tibetan yaks looked nasty, not like the smaller ones and the half-breds used in the Khumbu.

Once past the check-post Thondup shouldered one of his personal bags, and began walking rapidly ahead of the others. They would catch up in a few days in Khumjung where Chandra was waiting with cargo and carcasses. The yaks would be rested and fed there, and the traders allowed time for their own commerce. It would be a week or more before the loaded caravan started back to China. Adequate time for him to have a close look at this Pasang Dorje from Dharamsala. Even time for shopping.

He reached Khumjung a day ahead of the caravan. When he entered the village, which he had not seen before, he looked for the stone and plaster house

173

as sketched on a map diagram and located it at the upper end of the village. The lower story enclosed a wide animal stall with a gate open to a tilled potato field surrounded by waist-high stone walls. The field, ready to receive a bounty of fertilizing yak dung as rent, was prepared with piles of hay and half-drums filled with water. As Thondup approached the house its door opened and a small dark skinned man with cropped grey hair and beard was waiting for him.

Documentation

Wurlitzer had a watcher who relayed news of the caravan's arrival at Lungare, the tiny highest settlement in the Nangpa drainage. Steep grassy sides pinched in close to the melt water at the start of the tributary river. It would take a few days for the yaks to reach Khumjung, where Ripp and Elsie's team waited at Lucky Lodge, a former Sherpa dwelling. They all shared a triple-bunked room on the upper floor with with cameras and electronics enjoying an unimpeded line of sight to the potato field a hundred or more yards away. Ripp, still slow on acclimatization, felt lethargic, shivered with a headache, and kept to his sleeping bag. Elsie touched his brow and brought hot noodle soup. The others let him doze until he sensed he might recover. Upright and taking nourishment, he felt improved the second day.

The wall of glacial stones surrounding the potato field suited their purpose. Cameras, transmitters and batteries were packaged in fabricated shells of dull brindled plastic, indistinguishable from other bread-box sized glacial rocks on the wall. Their technician could power the remote camera units and mini microphones with a wireless signal from a single hand unit. The displays showed clear live pictures from several angles framing the interior of the stall and its contents. They revealed tiers of bales and two wrapped oblong bundles near an improvised table. Unoccupied by humans at the moment. All they had to do was wait to document the transfer.

The caravan arrived, unloaded, and the yaks fed and rested inside the stone walls of the potato field and a man came for the sneakers and sleeping bags. Chandra urged Thondup to select any of the bales to examine the packaging. Thondup demurred; it wasn't really necessary, they were trusting comrades; and in any case commercial inspection would be made in Tibet. Then they discovered a screw-up. No one had calculated the weight of the packaging, though in fact there were 610 kilos of *chungcxiao*. Net. Free On Board. But in fact, with the addition of the packaging, the gross weight of the bales approached a thousand kilos which led to an embarrassing negotiation. Chandra made it clear: they had delivered the *gumba* and if Thondup insisted they would remove the packaging, which had been painstaking and done in good faith. Thondup acknowledged that the problem was the headman. They needed more animals to handle the unplanned weight. It was a clumsy oversight, and at the end, Thondup laid out money to buy four new Nepalese yaks.

Chandra and Thondup then went through agreed procedurals. Thumbprints were inked to lists, photographs taken, a hand shaken, and the *gumba*, now referred to as *chungcxiao*, officially belonged to General Tu's syndicate. And while reviewing details of the weapons list they discovered a last minute snag concerning missing manuals, which Thondup resolved by arranging a full set to be delivered separately to Kathmandu. Then they agreed on the procedure for the incoming weapons transfer at the Burma-Bangladesh border, some 500 miles to the southeast. Finally they came to the tiger carcasses.

While it was true that such animal parts were prized in China, even if they agreed on what a weapons barter might be worth, the tiger carcasses weren't part of the original arrangement. Whatever new weapons they agreed on would have to be handled in a separate shipment. A few rounds of haggling still couldn't reach a value. Chandra wanted Stingers, six at least. At an apparent standstill, after a toilet break, Thondup changed the subject and asked casually if there was anything to the rumor of a porters strike. There would be no strike, said Chandra, with an unexpected certitude that arose spontaneously in his mind.

And then Thondup, even more off-handedly, "and what of that representative from the Dalai coming to Tengboche, a man named Pasang Dorje?"

Chandra held him in a long cool gaze and chose his riposte, "Never heard of him."

"We think he is a friend of the Dalai Lama."

"I have no idea."

"He's a member of his household."

"You sound like you would like to meet him."

Thondup was nonplussed at that disarming idea for a moment, and shifted his approach. He spoke coldly, "I would like a look at him. Our people think the goal of exiles under the Dalai is to split China and undermine the modernization and social stability of Tibet under the cloak of an idolatrous religion. What do you think?"

"I think those exiles are harmless even if there are a few conspirators among them, like boys pretending they command armies. But what does that have to do with some man coming to Tengboche? Do you think he is on a provocation?"

"He's coming from Dharamsala. Some people are suspicious he will plant poisonous seeds amongst the Sherpa people to grow ill-will against China."

"Does Buddhism generate ill-will to China?"

"It does when it's nationalistic. But forget about Buddhism. China is following its plan to modernize and develop the Tibetan region, and obviously that will benefit Nepal in trade, transit, tourism, culture and otherwise. When your victory comes in a year or two both our peoples will join hands so we don't need any ill-will between us. That's why I must ask you directly, as I am bound to inquire once again, is the revolution entering into some sort of discussion with the exiles in Dharamsala?"

Chandra feigned disinterest. "I don't know of any discussion underway or what the future might hold. It would be original, to say the least. But if there were talks they would take place in India, not in the Khumbu, don't you think? And as for what is in the mind of some religious visitor to a monastery it is something you can ask face-to-face when you say the man arrives. Why don't you meet him for yourself?"

This was a diversion from an outright denial and Thondup recoiled at the idea. The implications of having contact with an emissary from Dharamsala were beyond his calculation. It would be overstepping his brief by far and rather different than acting as a clandestine observer under cover; though it was growing interesting. The sidestepping was evident. Fortunately, he had time to track the emissary for a few days; to take photos of the man and put some detail in the file on persons of interest. What was the visitor's game? Was it merely a religious visit to the Rinpoche or was it a political visit to the Zone Commander? He was confident he would find out.

Chandra found much to dislike in his counter-party and wanted to end their business as soon as possible. He had the documented agreement. Observing ironically it was signed and sealed by a corrupt officer, of a government which had betrayed its own revolution, socialist in name and capitalist in fact. The dishonorable example of military men engaging in under the table black market weapons business! Mao shook up the old order but Deng, his successor, sold the revolution to the dogs. Marxism was dead and buried in China. The business of China remained business. Still, the barter for the tiger carcasses was the last item.

"I'll get you the Stingers," said Thondup, "just help China help you. Stay away from that exile crowd."

"Six."

"Four."

"Five and night-vision goggles."

Then it was done, they shook hands and Chandra's bodyguards took it as a signal to prepare for leave-taking. As a farewell gift of official friendship Thondup presented an automatic pistol to Chandra, who showed surprise and pleasure and gave it to one of his bodyguards to conceal. They shook hands again, and the guerrilla unit started down on the braided trails to Namche Bazaar, the village below. Before the first dip Chandra turned and saw Thondup standing with the headman at the half-gate; they waved. In another part of the village three trekkers were at the window of their lodge. One of them was looking at the potato field through binoculars.

The Next Things

"Well, we got something," said Elsie. They replayed the revealing episodes a few times and copied the most telling parts to a memory chip in Ripp's camera. There was a picture of two tiger skeletons held together by dried muscles, jaws tied open and the carnivorous fangs exposed. Alongside Ripp's photos, months earlier, of ants and beetles reducing the carcasses at Chandra's camp, and General Tu's words recorded earlier in the year, the evidence was more than credible. It was time for the next stage. They arranged their radio contacts. Ripp would track the Colonel. Wurlitzer to follow Chandra. Elsie to hold position in Namche, a thousand feet lower and keep the link to Washington.

In Ripp's experience recruitments were of two types. There were the recruitments that took place in a single step, rather quickly. Certain irresistible inducements and blackmails were of this type. And there were recruitments that were multi-stepped, recruitments where somebody has to think something through. Thondup was the first type, he thought, Chandra the second. It would be days before his target returned to China. Every hour spent observing him would sharpen Ripp's intuitions. The *gumba* transaction being concluded., what would the Colonel be up to before rejoining the yaks? Elsie thought he wouldn't be sitting on his hands. Likely he had other business. No choice but to wait and watch, said the old pro Ripp, be patient.

Finally Thondup moved. Ripp saw him emerge from the stone house with a small brown shoulder bag and converse with the headman. They were both gesturing to the tiger bodies. Thondup clapped the headman reassuringly on the shoulder, made a dismissive gesture and started down the trail towards Namche Bazaar. Ripp radioed Elsie that Thondup was starting down her way. And then shouldered his backpack to follow him. She would see them arrive in less than an hour. Ripp pulled on his hood, tightened his cuffs, put on his gloves, and under dark lowering clouds and an icy-whipped wind focused his thoughts on how nice it was going to be in his beloved tropics, warmth, beaches, blue water; the sea, the sea.

Palpitations

Elsie sat at the window in the rented room of the Khumbu Lodge which looked over the street. She suddenly felt panicked by an unexpected feeling of palpitations and arrhythmias in her chest. Unrelated to anything she could understand, it had occurred unpredictably at times over the course of the last year, and she tried to analyze it. She had stopped taking menopausal hormones years ago. The last routine physical, blood work-up, EKG and all, made out she was healthy, body-mass index a little above the desired value; she worked out and ate intelligently. What could it be? Genetic? Unlikely. Mother died of a toxic jelly-fish sting in Antigua, while father had expired of a pancreatic tumor; these palpitations were cardiovascular. Her pulse was racing madly while she sat still looking out the window. She couldn't stop thinking about heart illness, which skipped a beat every once too often. Why while otherwise in a fair mood, relaxed, and thinking of her future, was she suddenly worried she was going to have a heart attack? Life was short. What was going on? Would Ripp lose interest in her? Should she tell him?

The radio vibrated and of course it was him, talking fast and sounding pleased. "He's on the move. I'm behind him."

"Okay. How are you feeling?"

"Shitty but functioning. Headaches and nausea. This mountain stuff doesn't agree with me. How about you?"

"Fine. Well, actually I'm having heart palpitations at the moment. Can't figure what the hell is going on."

"Serious?"

178

"It's happened a few times this year. My pulse is racing like mad and I'm not doing anything. The last few times it woke me in the middle of the night, and today I'm just sitting here looking out the window. Scary."

"Intimations of mortality, said the poet. I wouldn't worry about it, you look great. Why don't we go for a check-up at Walter Reed around the end of the year. Me too. Mountains aren't for me."

"Aren't the Carpathians mountains?"

"They're only little bitty things, like the Appalachians. Is that a yes?"

"I wouldn't want to saddle you with a cardiac victim."

"In for a penny, in for a pound. I'm a committed gentleman."

"Well, let's see what Walter Reed has to say."

"You're on."

"What else?"

"Nada. I'll talk to you later if you're still alive. I'm in the Khumbu Lodge."

"Bye, plunge on."

Thondup's Plan

As he walked in a cold drizzle down the trail to Namche Bazaar, the business with the Zone Commander concluded, Thondup reviewed matters. He had given clear instructions to the headman, who had his own family's goods to manage. The yaks needed some days of rest and a good feed of hay and potato peelings. The bales of *chungcxiao* were to be fastened securely to the yak frames so as to prevent jostling, and were never to be opened or handled roughly. But the headman continued to create difficulties about the carcasses, insisting his yaks were made nervous by the odor. Not a problem insisted Thondup, just get an old and calm one and walk it separately from the others. He walked the headman over to the skeletal carcasses and described the contract which required the tiger remains be dry, brush-coated with shellac and paraffin, covered with aromatic leaves, and wrapped with muslin strips. They kneeled to sniff at the bodies. Thondup clapped him on the back reassuringly.

He told them that he would probably meet the caravan on its way back to the Nangpa-La and Tibet. They would be slow but he moved rapidly so there was no need to wait for him. But there was a possibility he would be delayed. In that case they were to go ahead and deliver the cargo as arranged. Major Wang would be waiting at the meadow with a small lorry where he would provide payment for their teamster services. The likeliest reason for missing the caravan was that the shadowy figure from Dharamsala might lead to something of significant intelligence value. He could always fly home as Liu Dzao from Hong Kong, with perfect passport, credit cards and an open ticket. Fly Lukla to Kathmandu and the routine non-stop to Lhasa.

The next task was to walk down to Lukla and get there before Pasang Dorje's arrival later in the week. He assumed he would detect the man the instant he debarked. Who would be meeting him? Would he start walking to Tengboche immediately? In any case, there was no point lingering in Khumjung. The baled *chungcxiao* was safe and sheltered with the herders. He had sufficient time to go shopping in Namche Bazaar. Examine the mountain sports gear in the shops and buy a few choice items of hardware, and clothing more in keeping with his cover as a trekker.

Trekkers

From the window Elsie watched Thondup arrive in Namche Bazaar followed minutes later by Ripp. In the light rain the footing down from Khumjung must have been slippery and the going slow. They each wore flimsy short-use plastic ponchos. She watched Thondup examine the colorfully worded hostelry signs along the cobbled main street of Namche and choose Taweche Lodge, diagonally across the street from her position. Ripp headed straight for their room at the Khumbu Lodge. They could watch the street from a dry space and stay out of sight.

Across the narrow street, inside a plywood cubicle at the Taweche Lodge, Thondup emptied his shoulder bag and tested the mattress. His automatic pistol, ammunition clips, batteries, digital camera, satellite phone and global positioning unit formed small craters in the bed-foam. The load-carrying situation cried out for improvement, and he planned to buy a full sized pack. It was time to go shopping, time to update his gear rack. Aside from his own good boots and crampons this was a perfect chance to sample the Western mountaineering wares pictured in their climbing magazines, old copies of which were passed around at his club on occasion. There were interesting stories about the new underwear from New Zealand. China could learn something there; it had plenty of sheep too. Lhasa might be a very good place to have an underwear factory to compete.

Eager to use the credit card he examined the few mountaineering shops in the village and went through them a second time. Most of the wares had been used, but one of the shops had a nook at the rear where new gear could be bought. Promising a large purchase Thondup negotiated a discount and bought himself a yellow 65 liter backpack, 60 meters of climbing rope with an artistic sheath, a heavy fleece mid-layer, waterproof overpants, a green insulated and hooded parka, heavy mittens, and a fleece hat. On the hardware side he bought himself a new ice axe, a modular ice tool, titanium ice screws, a friction device and a clutch of carabiners. It would be the envy of climbing friends and all the sweeter as the price was earned by the fruit of his own enterprise. He had invested in the fabric and the imitation labels; he bought the down from the goose farm; he hired the Muslim tailors in Chengdu; why shouldn't he buy some clothes and toys for his own account?

It had stopped raining. They went down to the street and saw Thondup pay with a credit card, then visit another shop where he bought a stack of CDs of rock and roll music for his daughter, recommended by the westernized Sherpa boy at the counter. When Thondup returned to his lodge Elsie went immediately for the vendor's credit-card slips and within minutes had charmed a glimpse at the copy from the shop owners. A Master Card on a Hong Kong bank. The name, Liu Dzao. And with a mnemonic practice learned from an Agency psychologist she focused and memorized the card's string of numbers.

Ten minutes later, back up in her room overlooking the street, they relayed the name and numbers to Washington.

"He's a gear freak," she said while gazing out the window. "Men's toys."

"Is he going climbing?" asked Ripp.

"I think he's going to take the stuff home with the yaks and show it to Chinese designers. Or maybe just keep it in a closet to look at from time to time, recalling youthful epics. Or maybe to show off. Hey, wait, I think he's moving out," she said it in a loud whisper. They could see him standing in the entrance paying the bill to the lodge owner. He was dressed more like a typical mountain trekker.

Her phone vibrated. It was Washington. "The card was used forty-six minutes ago," a voice said, "but not previously in years, though it's been renewed annually."

"Lousy tradecraft," mumbled Ripp as he shouldered his gear. They looked out the window. Thondup was moving. "I gotta go, he's going somewhere and I'm following him. Call you later."

Elsie stayed in Namche while the erstwhile Mr. Liu Dzao, now just an average international trekker with a stuffed yellow backpack strode down valley with Ripp not too far behind him. There was only a single trail descending and Lukla the only plausible destination below Namche Bazaar and it a day and a half getting there. Why was Thondup going there? Was he planning to fly out? to Kathmandu? Was there another mission in Nepal? No point in asking. Just stay near him. Perhaps Colonel Thondup had never intended to walk back over the Nangpa-La with the caravan.

Meanwhile, striding happily down the trail, Thondup felt energized by the oxygen rich air and was genuinely eager to see Lukla at first hand. As he descended toward the river and crossed the swinging foot-bridge over the gorge he felt a pleased with his work. Nothing amiss. A close-up view of the airport was a little bonus to the mission. He planned take archival photos and put in GPS waypoints. One never knew, the day might come when Chinese special forces might want to seize the place.

He came down into a rich rhododendron forest zone intending to go as far as he could before finding a lodge and moving on again at first light the next day. He estimated reaching Lukla the following morning. More than a full day before the Dharamsala emissary arrived. It had been checked weekly and now daily. The reservation was confirmed on Royal Nepal Air flight #307. Weather would be the main variable, but Thondup was hopeful as the sky looked promising. He decided to reward himself with a cigarette when he found a lodging.

Down in Lukla Constable Pemba had convinced the airlines to post standby and wait-list rankings on a large board. The new approach was tried and everyone was pleased with the reduction of shouting at the clerks. He was especially lighthearted as Annie would be arriving the following day. He could hardly endure the sweet unprecedented pain of waiting for her. And there was the chance of weather. Arrivals were sketchy and given the vagaries cancellations or diversions were frequent. On occasion the entire day's roster of flights would be compressed into a fifty minute visual window, one rapid turnaround after another. But next day's weather actually looked promising.

At the end of that day's flights Pemba went to the main street to buy candles when he encountered three young monks from Tengboche who had been in the *genyen* dormitory with him long ago. They greeted one another and stopped for a round of salt tea at the Snow Lion Lodge where they shared a room. Gyalpo Rinpoche had sent them to Lukla to escort an important visitor arriving the following day who was to meet them at the Snow Lion. They showed Pemba the fine quality white silk *khata*s for the visitor as they sat at a table facing the only street of the village.

He knew Annie's trekking group would be holding their get-acquainted meeting at the lodge – 'Happiness Lodge' – across the muddy street. Every time Pemba's thoughts gravitated to Annie he tried to imagine himself obeying Gyalpo Rinpoche's advice to let things unfold by themselves, spontaneously, and only to be observant. And Macleod's strange advice to make haste slowly. They wouldn't have much time together before she departed with her trekkers.

As Thondup entered the outskirts of Lukla the tradecraft issue came to the fore. Beijing rules insisted on the perfection of cover down to the smallest detail and he wasn't going to fight them about it. The masters had determined he appear as trekker Liu Dzao, and upon arriving in Lukla he was to join whatever prospective trek the mountaineering outfitter Yeti Travels had on offer. The perfection of cover. He stopped at the clean looking Happiness Lodge and booked a narrow room.

After a cigarette while stretched on the bed, he padlocked his door and headed for the booking office of Yeti Travels opposite the airport shed. There was a chalkboard outside listing treks that were still open. It amused him considerably to enroll himself for the Everest base-camp trek, a risible footnote to his own dear *Chomolungma*. The operational order was clear. If Thondup determined the man from Dharamsala was not a person of interest he was to continue the cover but leave the trekker group and head up the Nangpa valley to rejoin the caravan.

However, in the event he felt it desirable to follow the man as far as Tengboche he was free to choose his operational methods, but was to use his sat-phone to inform communications center by code words that he would not be returning with the caravan. In that case he was to leave Nepal by air via Kathmandu. So he followed good practice, booked the base camp trek, rented a sleeping bag and foam pad, and was pleased to learn his fellow trekkers would assemble at the Happiness Lodge in two days. Enough time for him to have a good look at the visitor and make a determination.

Ripp had little difficulty pursuing his quarry as the yellow backpack could be seen at a fair distance. When they neared Lukla Ripp raised his pace and saw Thondup examining the hostelry signage and enter Happiness Lodge. Five

183

minutes later Ripp booked himself in the same accommodation, deposited his pack, and sat in the common room facing the street sipping a cup of tea and scanning a tourist guide-book while he waited for whatever came next.

An hour later Thondup came down the stairs without his pack, nodded courteously to the stranger, and went out. It was simple for Ripp to wander the street and appear to be inspecting the wares of various shops as he observed Thondup make a determined walk to a green warehouse opposite the airport shed and enter the door marked "Bookings." What the hell was going on?

A Braid

At about this time, as Annie was handing her boarding pass to the gate agent at the Jackson, Wyoming airport she was seized suddenly with a spasm of uncertainty. Had she gone mad? Three nights in a sleeping bag with a nice Sherpa and now thinking of marrying him? But she understood if she didn't go to him at this very moment, on this very flight, it would start to fade. The uncertainty persisted during the short flight to Denver as she worried about the clarity of her memory. She could still envision his handsome face, but did she know the quality and nature of his character, his soul? An empty canvas on which she was projecting dreams? However, by the time she took her seat on the flight to Munich she told herself that she was a sensible person, of good judgment, and not given to madcap folly. The proposition made sense from the point of cool logic combined with a deep intuition that it could work. It didn't feel like a momentary infatuation, without sex no less, but more like a recognition that a spark of love could grow. Why wouldn't he agree?

When she had said, "I hope you come to America one day," he did answer affirmatively, and when she kissed him on the corner of his mouth on leaving the lodge in Thame in May, he whispered, "I like you very, very, very, much." He said "very" three times. She remembered that. That was good.

She tried sleeping on the thick carpet of the transit lounge at Munich Airport but the exciting thoughts of her undertaking kept her awake. What did she know about him? Not very much. That he took care of her on the mountain; that he was brave; that he was strong; that he was spiritual; that he was handsome and had beautiful teeth; that he was calm and steady and cheerful and that his eyes twinkled with sexual promise; and that he wanted to grow potatoes. Was that enough for marriage? Yes, she decided. It was enough, far more than a Wyoming red-neck or mail-order husband could provide. They could work the ranch together and once again she trusted her intuition. Her folks would like him.

But what if he said no?

Wurlitzer was on the radio to Ripp.

"Well, I followed Chandra but he didn't head for the monastery like we thought. He and his guys just walked down valley. At first I thought they were going to rest in Namche but they went right on through and kept walking all the way down to Jorsale, which is where I am."

"Where's that?"

"It's the first little hamlet with a couple of lodges on the river when you enter the National Park."

"He's skipping Tengboche?"

"Looks like it."

"Shit, I can't do both of them at the same time. And he's a guy I need at rest so I can talk to him. If he starts in the morning he'll be here in Lukla by mid-day."

"Well, I'll stick near him and give a shout in the morning."

Ripp tried to digest this information. Why wasn't Chandra going to the Rinpoche? Had there been a falling out with the Lama? Unlikely. An emergency in the red zone? There was no way of knowing. A typical operation. Ignorance reigns.

Chandra tried to organize his thoughts as he descended from Khumjung, glad to be finished with that unattractive business. Aside from the proceeds from his one-time bank robbery the consideration for most weapons trades was left to others in the leadership, and they had assigned the *gumba* traffic to him only because the Nangpa-La was in Zone 3. So be it. It was over.

He turned his thoughts to the task immediately ahead. The date was firm and representatives from all the porter castes would be waiting for him in Monjo. Members of the *panchayat* would also be there expecting his political statement concerning the decision for the potential labor action, the *bandh*. He had decided firmly against a strike during the current season. It needed better coordination with labor actions in Kathmandu. The following Spring would be more suitable.

He would have to explain his decision to the hard men, and the hot heads would be disappointed, but much could happen over the winter to justify a delay. It was also going to be his last time amongst the porter leadership and promised to become a sentimental occasion.

Then he would have to return back up valley to Tengboche and make his farewells to Gyalpo Rinpoche, who would be very pleased that he had decided to retire from political life. And if his meeting with Pasang Dorje at the monastery turned out to be fruitful according to the detailed proposal of the Central Committee, Chandra thought that at least he would have ended his revolutionary career by building a bridge to reconciliation.

Beyond that, it would be a great pleasure to see once again the old friend he had nursed to life in Dibla in Assam so many years ago. He was very pleased that Pasang Dorje felt his health was strong enough to allow him to walk with escorts and see the Zone's progressive villages for himself. So much better than flying to Lukla and starting from there, and by now he was merely a day away and on schedule according to his aides.

"And so," said Ripp to Elsie over the radio, "after I followed him down, and got a room at the same lodge, guess what he does? Under a phony name he books himself on a trek to Everest base-camp! The guy's climbed Everest, no less. It's screwball and I can't figure out what's going on."

"I told everyone he could be up to something other than the *gumba* business."

"Yes you did, dearest, and that's why I've now also booked myself on the base camp trek. We're going to be trek-mates."

"And Commander Chandra?"

"Wurlitzer's on him."

"You have a plan?"

"I'm going to take a nap."

The Airport

The following morning Thondup inquired about passenger names on RNA Flight #307 and was told that passenger information wasn't available in Lukla, only in Kathmandu. But as attention to detail was part of the practice, and against the chance that Pasang Dorje might have moved to an earlier flight he planned to be near the shed for every arrival, and in the intervals between flights to check the various lodges to inquire of him and take some photos. The Sherpa airport constable noticed him lingering about and asked if he could help. No, thanks very much. Not sure which flight a friend was on, that's all.

Persistence paid-off. Yes, the Snow Lion Lodge was in fact expecting a Mr. Pasang Dorje late that day. Some monks were waiting for him said the owner, gesturing to three robed figures in the common room. This was reassuring. Thondup relaxed and found a place where he could drink a Coca Cola and have a cigarette while waiting for the flight. Thondup was now enjoying the afternoon. The next flight was over an hour away, and the last one after that was RNA#307, two hours later.

He went back to his room for a closer look at his new gear. Now that he had a sleeping bag and foam pad he needed a duffel bag or two from one of the shops. The climbing hardware, meaningless for trekkers, was awkward to stow, and as he hefted the new ice-axe he wondered if he had chosen the right length. The 75cm shaft seemed too short. Still unused, he thought of exchanging it for a longer one. He would test it for balance; the new alloys had a different feel to them.

He strolled along the sloping street parallel to the runway and paused to regard the impressive angle of its slope. The runway ended in mid-air as the shoulder of land fell away steeply to the gorge of the Dudh Khosi far below. Some painted stripes and a pole with an orange windsock marked the edge. A low turret at the runway's corner was where the main trail arrived from below and he could see a police checkpost down at the switchback. Beneath the runway lay a bracing stone wall ten feet high and then a series of small garden terraces stepping down at high angles. Cabbages, onions, radishes, and mustard. He switched at weeds with the ice-axe and strolled across the topmost garden patch to the parallel street on the far corner and completed a rectangular circuit. It was a pleasant walk and the view was beautiful and strange in the late afternoon light. There was still more than half an hour and he walked the circuit several times again. If this Pasang Dorje was a nobody, well at least he had good photos of the airport and tower.

Lukla was small enough that Ripp could take it all in. He watched Thondup's coming and going and grasped that he wasn't planning a departure but simply waiting for someone to arrive. This was interesting in itself and not the best time to make an approach; the target appeared distracted. And who was he expecting? Would a new Chinese intelligence agent be revealed? That would be a scoop. He called Elsie to ask if she could get passenger lists of the day's departures from Kathmandu to Lukla.

He decided to try Wurlitzer. "What's up?"

"Chandra's saying goodbye to a bunch of people right now. We're in a market village just outside the National Park. It seems he came here with his guys for this meeting. Maybe forty people, mostly porters I think. Outside on a lawn under a shade canopy. Nobody seems to be paying me much attention. They're hugging him and patting him on the back.

"I can hardly hear you."

"I'm talking through my collar mike. Need to be quick, it looks like I'm talking to myself. He just gave a talk about the strike action, a *bandh*. No *bandh* this year. Crowd seemed relieved. Said the Politburo thought it needed better collaboration with events in the capitol. More preparation required. Decided to postpone strike possibility to next Spring. Then he gives a little pep talk and finishes saying he's getting new responsibilities at the end of the year and this is his last visit with them. Right now he's still shaking hands."

"And then what?"

"Heading up to Tengboche to say goodbye to the Abbot."

RNA #307

Annie arrived in Lukla as scheduled on the day's last plane from Kathmandu, RNA #307. The sky was clouded for much of the flight, but there had been a special moment when Annie had a glimpse of a distant mountain she thought was Gaurishankar. The Tetons were such little outcroppings by comparison. Finally, the small plane descended below the cloud deck into the gorge of the Dudh Khosi and Lukla's short sloped runway could be seen in the distance through the pilot's nose-down window. The plane touched at the slope's low end, barely clearing the edge in a perfectly executed and beautiful maneuver. It lost momentum quickly and required power to continue upslope until the pilot gunned the port engine, turned the plane onto a small apron and cut the throttle. The propellers spun down to silence and the co-pilot opened the door hatch. Through the window across the aisle Annie could see Pemba, in a neat blue shirt with a shoulder flash, standing near the bottom step.

She felt happy through a fog of fatigue and jet-lag as the passengers forward of her in the narrow fuselage waited turns to debark. Her eyes were on him through the window port. He looked handsome and dignified. Against this, Annie was convinced she looked particularly ugly at the moment. The continuous economy class journey went 180 degrees around the globe on five consecutive flights, Jackson to Denver to Munich to Delhi to Kathmandu to Lukla, and had reduced her to a sponge. She was nervous it was all a stupid dream. When it was her turn to debark she shouldered her small day bag and stepped out. Pemba, waiting, had a *khata*, the white scarf, in his hands. She reached the bottom step and came close to him with her palms pressed together in greeting. "*Namaste*," she said.

"*Namaste*," he replied and put the *khata* around her neck. "Welcome" he whispered and led her a few steps away from other passengers. He turned to face her again. Neither said anything but simply held one another by the shoulders and pressed their foreheads together. "I missed you" she whispered, her eyebrows gathered poignantly. "I missed you too" he replied. Trite and true they knew. It seemed like a great wave was forming beneath their feet. They were simply speechless.

Her baggage was minimal since most of her gear was stored at the Yeti warehouse but it took some minutes to offload. They stood still, leaning quietly against one another as they waited for her bag. Her eyes were half open; jet-lag and fatigue were mixed in with a haze of happiness. Pemba shouldered the bag and put his arm around her shoulder. "Come. You need to rest." They walked in silence, smiling and nervous.

The neat austerity of Pemba's makeshift home comforted her as she stepped through the door and took it all in. It lay off a quiet courtyard where he pointed out a toilet and a pouring hose at the far end of the yard, near a goat pen. It was very nice by Peace Corps standards. There was a small wood-burning stove in the center of the room with a chimney pipe through the low ceiling and a thin curtain on the single window. Shelves with some folded clothes and things, some books on agronomy, his devotional altar, and the foam bed on a platform.

He pointed to it. "Take some rest. I'll make tea. Tell me about the journey if you feel like it."

She took off her shoes and got as far as describing the transit lounge at Munich before her eyes closed involuntarily and she stopped talking. When he brought the cup of sweet milk tea to her and spoke her name softly she jumped up, startled. "Oh, Pemba. Give me a minute," she said, "I need a quick refresh." She went hastily to her bag and removed a toilet sack. "Back in a bit." Moments later she took off her T shirt and jeans and stood under a garden hose tied to a nail. The hillside above the village sported a hundred rivulets and there wasn't a cut-off valve or a means of temperature control. Just a strong jet of icy water 24/365. She stood naked and let it run on her head and neck until it became painful. She spread her arms and spread her legs and turned her face to the splashing sky. Yippee yahoo! And she rushed bare footed and nearly naked across the yard to where he held a towel.

Awakened now, glowing, wrapped in a towel, Annie sat at the edge of the platform bed with wet hair and sipped the still hot tea. She finished telling him about the trip, talking with effusive speed. They exchanged clumsy and groping words to describe instances of how they had missed one another. Spontaneously Pemba took her cup, put it on the floor, sat down next to her and they embraced tenderly, lightly. Their cheeks nuzzled and they began to kiss delicately with dry lips that sensed the flowing air of breaths. They lowered themselves slowly and her damp towel slid off as they moved to the center of the platform bed. Wet mouths began to open hungrily and they became overwhelmed at the erotic intensity of the approaching intimacy which promised untainted fulfillment. They understood perfectly the impermanence of it all. Which made the pleasure and beauty all the more poignant. Without haste he removed his clothes. She feasted on his nakedness. And they came close, with eyes open, faces inches apart, their hands cupping one another's cheeks as they kissed, their tongues moved in a slow dance of foretaste.

Pasang Dorje Arrives

Believing he had the stamina, Pasang Dorje had taken the bus from Kathmandu to Jiri where a young monk on a motorcycle waited to drive him and his heavy pack over a wide trail to the Thubten Choling monastery, a daughter monastery to Tengboche. He stayed there for several refreshing days and made offerings to the victims of the recent violence. Then, by arrangement, three young men sent by Chandra came for him. They were extremely solicitous of his health and carried his heavy backpack and small briefcase and saw to it that he was never tired on the trail; that he ate and slept well on the slow walk to Lukla for his rendezvous for which he was exactly on schedule. Pasang Dorje thought the walking had been healthy for him and he enjoyed the company of his youthful escorts, despite their differences in world-view. Finally they separated as they neared the Army check-post below Lukla which signified the *de facto* end of the red zone and the beginning of the Sherpa high country, nominally under government control. His escort helped him put on the weighty backpack for the short carry uphill to the village. It made him stagger for a moment. He hadn't opened it since departing Dharamsala, merely living out of the briefcase.

So he bade his escorts farewell, and under the top-heavy load started up the short path to the village, ascending quite slowly, stopping frequently after a few steps, and clearly burdened under the weight. There wasn't far to go and the young monks from Tengboche would carry things over the next several days. In the dying light of dusk he could see an orange windsock at what had to be the lower corner of the runway. In another minute or two and he should be in the village.

Half an hour earlier, Thondup had waited as Flight #307 debarked the 19 passengers. There was a Korean woman's hiking club, an Australian expedition to Baruntse, a group of European trekkers, students by their looks. A few others, but none plausible. He saw the Sherpa constable with the odd shoulder patch and a young western woman embrace one another and then the plane was empty and ready for re-boarding. There was no sign of anyone waiting other than himself. No unclaimed baggage. He spent an hour quizzing the clerks at the carrier's desk. No. No such person arrived. They didn't have a record of no-shows, only the printouts of the passengers. No such name. No Pasang Dorje.

Thondup was confused, the man was expected at the Snow Lion Lodge. Something must have happened. He felt disturbed and made himself take a slow walk to calm his thoughts. He whacked at the weeds in irritation as he went. This would have implications in Beijing. As there was interest in the emissary from Dharamsala it had become the pretext for his own presence in the Khumbu. An investigation might lead to compromising himself and General Tu. This was grave. They had checked and re-checked the reservation many times.

How would he explain this, Thondup asked himself, was he so self-assured that he lost the person he was looking for? Furious at himself, he continued to reflect carefully on the eventualities as he walked in the approaching dusk with just enough light to have another turn around the runway. There was a place where he could sit at the lower end and think it out carefully while the sun's last sigh made a glint in the distance on the river flowing down toward the Ganga.

At the corner of the runway where the main path came up Thondup watched a small man in dark city clothes bearing a backpack and briefcase coming up the path slowly with considerable effort and hesitating to rest after every few steps. Thondup thought to lend him a hand but merely paused to observe him approach. The man had his head down, watching his own steps and was breathing heavily. He came nearer and nearer and as he approached the top of the footpath he paused as he realized someone was standing in front of him a step or two away and he looked up, surprised.

Thondup looked down at the small man's unmistakable features, the big scar separating his eyebrow, the bent nose, the blaze of white in the middle of his hair, and the elongated earlobe with a large vacant hole. Thondup's instant recognition of the Lama who had killed his father, and what followed, displayed a situational awareness prized in combat. He grasped that at this instant in the darkening dusk the two of them had to be totally unobserved, and without any intervening thought he swung the pick of his ice axe with all his strength into the top center of Pasang Dorje's head, who went down with a single soft groan.

It was in the basic training curriculum for mountain troops: where to strike to kill someone with an ice axe. Without a moment's hesitation Thondup pulled the twitching body up the last step and laid the dying man out on his back. There was no doubt in his mind who it was. He felt cool and without hesitation kneeled and went through the contents of the shuddering man's emptied pockets and stuffed the lot in his jacket. As he stood he wrenched the ice axe out of his victim's head in a forceful way that caused a faint noise of bone cracking, and the body went still. There had hardly been a sound to bring attention to what had just happened and scarcely thirty seconds had passed from beginning till end.

Moving quickly and smoothly Thondup shouldered his victim's backpack which surprised him by its weight, tucked the briefcase under an arm and continued his passage through the cabbage patch, as before. He stopped once to clean the ice axe of blood and gore in the water of the small irrigation ditch. Act calm, be calm, he told himself. The approaching darkness covered him as he stepped into the lane on the far side of the runway, and from there one lane over into the village. Only then made a right turn up the hill and another turn into the lamp-lit main street at the busy hour, where he merged with trekkers and shoppers, until arriving at the lodge and his room. He hadn't seen a person until reaching the main street and he thought there was a realistic likelihood of having been unnoticed. If the next few hours passed in silence the most perilous moments would have passed. The body might not be found until morning light.

The New Situation

What he had just done presented Thondup with an entirely new situation. Perspiring and breathing heavily, he padlocked his plywood door and lay on

192

his back to focus on his feelings. He knew he had to bring them under control and get a cool head. He was in a dangerous situation and the first thing was to calm himself so he could think clearly. He could recall an aged man in robes and skullcap who had been brought in to address their officer class at staff college. An ancient master of Taoist practices they said, long wispy beard and all, who spoke for an hour about breath control in the wild melee of combat. The image of that old man occasionally came to him in the stress of firefights and he thought of him again now, but this was unique. He had just killed his father's killer. A sudden killing for a sudden killing. He deliberately halted the painful excitement he was feeling and tried to think clearly again.

First, there was his present situation; and if he got out of it, then the ramifications in Beijing. He remembered Gen Tu's accusations of hotheadedness, impulsiveness. No, he decided, it should be presented as a bold martial act. Pasang Dorje and Yeshe Longdrul Rinpoche were the same person, a leader of bandits and the assassin of his father, and still a fugitive from China's justice. Now that Thondup had calmed himself it seemed almost literary, almost like the cinemas when he was in the young pioneers. Vengeance and justice satisfied; the father's killer avenged by the son's hand. Beijing could not help but approve, even commend his action. He gave a passing thought about the report he would have to write. He had clearly ended the man's mission, whatever it was. The story itself would probably stay in the classified archives for a long time he thought, but one day schoolchildren would have a song about his exploit. But first he had to return to China.

Minutes passed without a knock on the door or unfamiliar sounds in the street and he became calm enough to appreciate the self-regarding idiocy of having worried about Beijing's reaction before working out his own predicament. But soon he became cooler-headed and sat up and stretched and did some push-ups. Escape wasn't going to be simple and he realized he had every reason to be grateful for the tradecraft which gave him cover as an innocent trekker from Hong Kong. The masters were correct again.

Though hungry he intended to keep to the room until the following morning, which now gave him time to examine his victim's effects. Thondup had previously removed the man's pocket contents to his own fleece jacket and now emptied them out on the bed. Some coins, a few hundred Indian and Nepalese rupees, a string of prayer beads, a small pocket knife, a comb, a pen, a pencil, and a few keys. And a breast-pocket wallet. In it were Indian rupees in higher denominations, a single British £100 banknote, a folded newspaper page about a new peace *stupa* near Dehra Dun in India, a few faded and cracked photographs of old Lamas in elaborate headdress, and an Indian passport with a photograph for one Pasang Dorje and separate identification of this Pasang Dorje as a member of the household of the Dalai Lama in Dharamsala. He would take the wallet and congratulated himself for having had the presence of mind to have emptied the man's pockets. At first impression the matter would be seen as the product of a local robbery gone amiss. How could anyone suspect a long hand from China? If he got rid of the incriminating debris he would feel safe.

He turned to the small briefcase. A cheap affair actually made of painted cardboard with small reinforced corners of tin. The snap-lock opened at a touch and revealed contents of little interest. And diminutive photograph of the Dalai Lama and a small bronze Buddha. He would have to rid himself of these incriminating things. Last of all, he lifted the man's pack onto the bed and again was surprised at its weight. He pressed the sides and felt some sort of paper packaging. The top flap of the pack was cinched down tight and the grommets were bunched by a cheap three digit combination lock. Using the tip of his ice axe as a lever he popped the lock easily and undid the cord holding the puckered mouth. The pack's entire contents were in a black plastic bag slip-knotted at the neck by a string.

He undid it and studied what he had in disbelieving silence. Fist-sized bundles of folded currency tied in twine. A bag full of money, a great deal of money, a fortune in fact. He guessed there were at least twenty bundles of cash. Dollars. Euros. Yen. Sterling. Apparently all in higher denominations. His heart was pounding at the sight of so much money. And there was something else down there, even heavier than the paper notes. His fingers had to hold it tight to extract it from the jumble of currency bundles. It felt like ten pounds of something. Something hard wrapped in padding and sewn tight in a cotton cover. About the same weight as his automatic. Was it a pistol?

He pulled it out and examined the package. Someone with a felt tip marker had written the word 'Dorje-Ling' in Tibetan characters on the cotton and he used his pocket knife to cut it open and found the object itself covered in layers of Indian newspaper held by rubber bands at crossed angles. Unwrapped, he beheld a Buddhist statue whose lustre and weight suggested it was made of solid gold. Ten pounds or thereabouts of gold was a fortune within a fortune. The treasure as a whole had a powerful magnetic effect on Thondup's brain. The possibilities exploded in a wheel of directions, and even more. He looked closely at the statue. If it was some sort of national historical treasure he might have to turn it over to the State. Unless he melted it. It was solid gold, without a doubt.

Thondup sat at the edge of the bed and tried to steady and organize his thought. He was still breathing hard and forced himself to slow down. The implications of the situation ran in too many directions to comprehend. Managing a return, an escape to China without incriminating evidence linking him to the death was one thing, but it was now supercharged by feverish thoughts of taking this weighty treasure with him. Not so simple. It would require particular care but could change his life forever. He determined to find a way. By early the following morning at the latest someone would surely find the body.

For a moment he considered hiding the fortune in cache somewhere and retrieving it at a future date. But treasure, by law of natural magnetism, creates attachment. It makes its holder reluctant to leave it even briefly or safely. For the moment it was under his control and he certainly wanted to have it with him when he returned to China, otherwise it might never be seen again.

He had turned his victim's pockets inside out. It would look like a brutal robbery and while an alarm would soon be raised, in the absence of a witness he was an unlikely suspect. The immediate problem would be disposing of incriminating debris. His own pack was already heavy: a sat-phone, pistol, ammunition, batteries, toiletries, digital camera and lenses, clothes, the ice screws and carabiners, a climbing rope, the ice tools and other heavy gear. He attempted adding the cash into his new backpack but there wasn't enough room. He was going to need duffel bags to hold everything. Buying them in the morning would equip him like an average trekker. And then he would be forced to engage in a charade as a base-camp trekker until he solved the problem of how to escape to China with his treasure in hand. This time it was he who was the escapee.

They would be looking for the perpetrator and someone out there would be missing a great deal of money. He focused on reframing his persona so as to become Liu Dzao the innocent trekker. At 5 o'clock the next day he would join the get acquainted meeting of the trekking group. He looked at the brochure he took at the Yeti bookings office. It described the route they would take to base camp and there was a small photo and a two line biography of the trek-leader. She looked like the woman from RNA#307 embracing the Sherpa constable at the airport.

He turned to the briefcase which was flimsy enough so that well placed blows from his ice-axe chopped it into palm-sized fragments which he rolled up in the dead man's shirts together with other small items and stuffed them all into the man's pack, *him*. He had to get rid of it and reasoned that several small lots of debris could be moved surreptitiously from a duffel to his backpack and then to the outhouse latrines along their trekking route, disposed easily over a couple of days. If he spread the currency and the statue in one of the duffels together with his sleeping bag and clothes the weight wouldn't be as noticeable. A trekker's locked personal baggage was untouchable by others.

A few days incognito would give him time to think and let the trail go cold. Flying to Kathmandu was out of the question. Lukla airport would be screened and baggage searched. There was already a constable there. Alternatively, once the body was found they might assume the perpetrator had gone down valley into the red zones, and consider it a pre-meditated guerrilla crime, like one of their bank robberies or bomb incidents. Or, just as likely they might think of the wild men, the yak traders who had come from Tibet. There would be a missing man. Him.

News of a missing fortune as well as a death would drive them to zeal. Police units would be summoned and an alarm raised. Someone would post a reward. Bags would be opened and examined. The caravan going back over the Nangpa-La in three days would be among the first suspects and the herders and the cargo would be searched closely. He winced. The loss of a premium. He had an image of the delicate *chungcxiao* pieces breaking as bales were opened and examined. The Nepalese frontier post would certainly be reinforced. Returning over the Nangpa-La with the traders and the fortune was out of the question. At best he might go back in disguise as a yak man if he wanted to leave everything behind. It just wouldn't do. He was boxed in so long as he held the fortune. It was like the monkey trap; putting a hand through a tight hole to grab a big nut and unable to withdraw the hand without dropping the nut. He knew very it would be a public relations disaster for China and a mortal disaster for himself if he failed and the facts came out.

Almost fifteen pounds of banknotes and a heavy gold statue wouldn't be easy to hide. He needed time. If he kept his head down, he could move safely under his cover. To walk from Lukla up to Everest base camp and then return would involve close to three weeks. Time to think of something. Improvise, his incessant message to junior officers – take initiative, confront problems. Goal: a safe return to China. A possibility had to emerge. The case would grow cold in a week or so and he had only to keep a low profile. Masquerading as Liu Dzao from Hong Kong was the safest course for the time being. Finally, after recycling these thoughts and attempting to digest the problem further he fell to sleep in his clothes.

Alarm

Well before dawn Annie and Pemba were in profound sleep together when two Rai porters tapped softly on the front door, waited, and tapped again. On their third attempt a bleary eyed Pemba came to the door. The porters had come to tell him that a man's body had been found near the lower end of the runway. Astonished, and rubbing sleep from his eyes Pemba shone the torch on them. They scarcely came up to his shoulders and looked familiar. They knew him. Two lads from down the valley, carrying a load of plate glass windows for a new lodge in Namche Bazaar, too young to be Maoist organizers. They had been sleeping under a vacant lean-to in a mustard patch below the end of the runway. Intending an early start they went to make their toilet close by, and they found a man's body.

Pemba kept the torch lit and dressed rapidly as Annie remained sleeping soundly. He leaned over and kissed her softly near her ear and whispered her name. When she didn't stir he found a sheet of paper and left a note saying an unexpected and urgent police duty called him, but that he would see her later that day at her group's meeting; and that he was in love with her. He underlined the word. The young porters, in deteriorated Chinese tennis shoes and wrapped in thin blankets, waited patiently. Pemba laced his boots, found his digital camera, moved his prayer beads to his pocket from under the pillow, and clasped his hands to bow hastily to a soot darkened thangka on the wall, of the wrathful goddess who dances on ignorance. Adjusting a small photograph of the Dalai Lama tucked in a mirror frame he went out into the pre-dawn where the porters led the way. His first weeks as seasonal constable at Lukla airport where, just his luck, a corpse was found on the premises.

A white frost covered the stiff body in the dim grey light. Pemba wanted to move it out of sight as soon as possible and started taking close-up photographs almost immediately. The unusual facial features of the dead man seemed intact and there was rather little blood from the lacerated and punctured brain, and tissue matter had been levered out from the upper rear of the skull and formed fragments of what looked like a stiff grey pudding. He had dealt with corpses before in climbing disasters but this was a murder victim. When he knelt close he could just make out a row of serrated tooth marks scraped along the scalp's flesh, as from the underside of the pick, and he guessed the weapon could be an ice-axe, which horrified him. Scarcely twenty minutes earlier he had been pressing warm and naked to the sweet flesh of his beloved girl.

The victim's pockets had been turned out. A robbery gone wrong? Some rough yak herder? He took more photographs before touching anything and then realized that decisions about the corpse belonged to him. To whom did the corpse belong previously? Should it be cremated? Buried? He forestalled matters and used an old bivouac sack from the nearby Yeti Travels warehouse which lay moments away. With the aid of the two adolescents they carried the stiff corpse and rested it on a stack of plywood boards under a tin sheet in the yard behind the bookings shack. It was still dark and not a person in sight.

He thanked the Rai teen-agers, and gave them each twenty rupees, a plastic water bottle, two bags of Yeti's special trail mix, two blankets and some shoelaces from the Yeti inventory. Solemnly he swore them to avoid speaking of what they had seen. It could interfere with an investigation. Too young to be cynical they took this with grave seriousness. After he sent them off he sat alone next to the body for a minute or two and recited the hundred syllable *mantra* of purification nine times. He couldn't separate his thoughts from shuttling between the two human bodies he had touched within the hour. It reminded him of the first time young Siddhartha saw a corpse, after coming from a paramour's bed.

He tried to think about whom to inform. As he had a key to the dark and empty airport control tower, he went to the lower floor with the phone and called Salleri, the district capitol. The duty officer told him the District Commissioner and the Deputy DC were 'away;' many government functions had ceased in the district. For want of a better idea he called the Captain who led the summer school in Kathmandu, a Gurkha named Shresta. The Captain could hardly believe him, accusing him of a prank. Pemba said it would be on his head then but he needed someone to tell him how to proceed. Murder hadn't been covered in the summer course and he didn't know whom else to call. The Captain said he would try to get someone to fly there but that a disturbed situation in Kathmandu required all hands. Until learning more Pemba should look for clues but not talk about it. Try to identify the victim. Bringing in the local council might only confuse matters and end up hurting tourism. Keep the matter quiet at all costs.

Pemba then called the Army control post below Lukla and their headquarters post above Namche Bazaar and spoke to the senior rank in each location describing what had occurred. He was concerned that the culprit might be among the yak traders and asked that the check-post below the Nangpa-La be reinforced and personal possessions searched thoroughly. The army was in immediate agreement and a squad was dispatched to proceed directly up the Nangpa Glacier to take a position below the pass.

Finally, it was near mid-day, and for the first time since before dawn the other part of his life came into the foreground. He raced to his abode and found her note on the same sheet of paper. "I missed you and I love you too dear Pemba. I'll be at Happiness Lodge or the Yeti warehouse all day. Come to me. A." Overjoyed with relief and happiness, he had a wash, changed into a clean shirt, and went to find her.

On the way he encountered the three monks from Tengboche. They were disturbed that Gyalpo Rinpoche's visitor never arrived yesterday. He was supposedly walking up from Thubten Choling but missed their rendezvous. What to do? Pemba asked for the visitor's name but they only had a simple physical description. A small man with a white blaze in his hair. Pemba had the images in his camera. It meant that Gyalpo Rinpoche could identify the victim.

Pemba confided to his friends that the visitor had been murdered and robbed during the night. He urged them to race to inform Rinpoche. He himself would come up to Tengboche the following day to learn the visitor's identity and more. There was the question of the corpse, which lay wrapped behind the warehouse. He needed Rinpoche's instructions. The monks were in shock, but left at once at their strongest pace.

Escape Plan

The solution to Thondup's predicament came to him that night in a half-sleep, causing him to sit upright with excitement. He suddenly realized he could ascend the nGozumba Glacier for a technical climb over the Nup-La into Tibet and then cross home easily on the low-angle West Rongbuk Glacier. He had crossed the pass in the other direction many years earlier with companions. He usually assigned it every few years in cross-border infiltration practice. The dangerous part was avoiding crevasses on the glacier and solo climbing the double icefalls on the Nepal side.

But the pinnacle of excitement was in realizing that Major Wang had led a penetration exercise over the Nup-La and put in GPS waypoints through the icefalls down to the end of the snow line, the *firn*, where the old hard ice glacier was exposed. He himself had issued the order to make the laying-in waypoints standard procedure in all infiltration exercises. Glaciologists in Lanzhou had suggested the idea. It meant that they were presently stored on his own GPS device! An incredible advantage in route-finding. Weight would be an issue and the weather would have to be good, but he started to think it was plausible, even with a very heavy pack.

He had done so much time in the mountains that the techniques of travel over glacial terrain felt straightforward. He was long experienced, felt strong and even had suitable gear. Most of the risk would be under his control. Three days of settled weather and some help from the waxing moon and he could travel by night some of the time. The load would slow him, easily by twenty percent, though there were more than a few things he could jettison. His daughter could spare the CDs. The main thing would be the weather window.

The decision was simple. Staying with the Yeti Travels group to base camp would give him time. He thought through equipment issues and went over essentials. Food was needed but he could sequester nourishment at the lodges. Cheeses, cooked potatoes, *chapattis*, dried fruit and nuts, sweets.

The idea began to please him. It could become famous in intelligence circles. "Summit Conqueror Goes On Trek;" it would make a fine part of his career story. "Thondup Gaomei's final bold challenge in the Himalayas." A first solo ascent of the Nup-La and a fair proposition at his skill and fitness level. That it should mean escape with a fortune in hand favored his odds. Enhanced commitment did count. He could only think of five or six occasions when the Nup-La had ever been climbed. Shipton back in the 1930s; Hillary in 1952; the illegal crossing by the Sayre group in 1962; his own command's infiltration exercises from the other side, including Wang's penetration.

Sunrise came and he waited impatiently for the shops to open. Buying duffels was the first order of business. He padlocked the flimsy door, and rushed through a breakfast pancake and tea in the common room. Outside, on the street the village showed the first commerce of morning. Diagonally across the way the westerner sat on a narrow bench writing postal cards. He looked up and smiled. A fellow base camp trekker? Thondup moved smoothly into the role of Liu Dzao from Hong Kong. The cover unimpeachable. Nothing more to do but act the part of a man on holiday and he bought two large duffel bags when the shops opened, one red, one blue, with small locks so as to package his trekking gear suitably for the porters.

Returning to the Lodge, he saw the westerner had moved to the common room and was studying a guide book. Back in his own cubicle again, Thondup reviewed the effort to clean it of anything which might link him to the killing. For the moment he felt safe. He stuffed the dead man's possessions and other debris into the original dark pack and put it in the blue duffel along with his daughter's CDs, all of his technical climbing gear, and his insulated outer parka, and then locked it. He turned to the red duffel into which he put the banknotes, gold statue, pistol and ammunition, satellite phone, GPS unit, and wrapped them in his sleeping bag and foam pad. The porter carrying these bags would be instructed to stay in sight.

His own yellow backpack would serve as an over-large day pack which he would use to ferry fragments of incriminating evidence to their fate. It would take some innocuous juggling but it could be done. The group would make relief stops at local outhouses where items could be dropped conveniently in the toilet holes. By the time they reached Namche in two days, the incriminating evidence would vanish into piles of excrement. The only thing remaining would be to go along with the trekker charade and join the get-acquainted meeting of his group that evening. The schedule was for a dawn start the next day, to leave Lukla, where nothing pointed at him, or at China. So far, so good. Everything depended on the sky conditions.

Ripp, having observed Thondup's coming and going, was confused and intrigued. What began as watchful waiting to make an approach was turning into something else and very odd. He didn't have a clue. To all appearances the Colonel had walked down to Lukla, signed in for a base camp trek with Yeti Travels, spent the entire next day apparently waiting for someone at the airport who never arrived, and then shopped for some items of gear the following morning. What now? In a few hours the entire trekking group would meet in the common room. So let it play, he thought, it was a useful opportunity of getting close to his man.

Ripp called Elsie and described the situation. He and Thondup would be introduced to one another formally in a few hours at a get-together.

"I'm about to be his tent mate on our way up – we're the two single males. I'm telling you, something weird is going on and I can't figure it out. Why is he acting through this trekker performance if he's planning to rejoin his caravan. I don't get it."

"He could be frightened of something and diving into his cover. Or maybe he's going to meet someone else."

"Under cover as a trekker with a phony name? Why would he do that?" said Ripp.

"Or maybe he's studying Sherpa tourism. A recon."

"Way too thin. Anyway, you'll spot us as we walk through Namche."

"Well, hang in there. If he wants to come out with us I can have a bird up here in no time."

"Listen, I'm thinking about you a lot these days."

"You're sweet."

"I just wanted you to know."

"I do know."

"Later, then."

Love in the Afternoon

Annie's closet-sized room at Happiness Lodge was typical of most lodges. A narrow double bunk with bare foam mattresses, a candle in a glass, clothes hooks of bent nails, a light fixture lacking a switch, and walls framed by single sheets of plywood. Annie's gear filled the floor as she and Pemba lay hugging one another on the narrow bunk, fully clothed against the cold. Happiness filled that room of the Lodge. They stared into one another's eyes at great length and stroked their cheeks, and murmured over again how much they had longed for one another during the summer.

"I want you to come to America with me" she whispered in his ear.

"Okay."

There was a very long silence as they meditated on what had just been transacted. Somehow, the length of the silence underscored an appreciation of the life-altering properties of the words. For Pemba, the happiness he was experiencing had erased the day's horror.

He told her about it, of course, that he had made photographs of the scene and moved the corpse which would freeze tonight.

"Life is *so* fragile" she said.

"Impermanent. Like all things."

"Who do you think did it?" she asked.

"A demon. Someone very strong."

"Why?"

"Maybe a robbery. They say it is someone Rinpoche can identify. I need to go to Tengboche tomorrow to talk with him about what to do with the body. I'll come across your group on my way back down. I called the District Commissioner's office but they are all away, and I spoke with a police Captain in Kathmandu. We shouldn't talk about this with anyone."

"Never."

"Thank you."

They took off their boots, stripped off their bottom layers, and preserving their down jackets above the waist, worked their lower selves into Annie's sleeping bag and made love to one another eagerly, laughing at their luck. Then they dozed for a while and finally got up to attend the five o'clock meeting.

As they were getting dressed she asked "what about non-attachment? Isn't that what we're doing right now, attaching?"

"This is just our good *karma*. How can you be attached in emptiness?"

"I don't know" she said, then heard the sound of people gathering in the common room below. "We should go down."

"You go first. I'll come and just stand in the doorway."

Getting Acquainted

The last of Annie's trekkers had arrived in Lukla earlier that day and all were gathering for the first time. The arrangement was to have an introductory meeting of tea followed by dinner in the common room of the Lodge before shoving off early the following morning.

The last to join was the American, Harry Ripp, who sat next to the big Chinese fellow. The group formed a U shape of benches and tables and Annie stood facing them with her backside near an iron stove, wherein several hours of dry yak turds had morphed to slow burning embers. It was said that potatoes didn't taste as good if they were roasted in wood charcoal.

Pemba looked on from the passage to the kitchen and studied the group as Annie brought the room to order. There were ten of them aside from the staff. Pemba knew her crew as they were all from Phortse and he admired Annie's self-assurance as she began talking to her charges.

"I'm very happy to see you all here right on schedule. We have a lot of traveling to do together in the days ahead. And I gather that this is the first time in the Khumbu for all of you, and the first time in really big mountains at high altitude for most of you. So it's important that everybody stay strong and healthy. We can go through all the do's and don'ts later, but as we have about an hour or so until we eat, let's start by introducing ourselves."

"I'm the Annie Wendover described in Yeti's brochure, which you all have. That's Dawa over there, raise your hand Dawa, he's our *sirdar,* the captain of our crew. The four boys, Norbu, Rinchen, Lakpa and Kunzang, their English is only fair, will do the heavy lifting; carrying our gear other than your daypacks, putting up tents, cooking and serving. Normally Sherpas don't act as porters, at least not below 15,000 feet, but they're all friends of Dawa. I think Rinchen is Dawa's nephew and Norbu is some kind of cousin. They're on school holiday and volunteered to make some rupees. They're shy but fun loving. Dawa wants to see if they're strong enough to get into the mountain game. That's where these guys can make some real money. First and foremost would be their ability to carry loads at a good pace. Okay, let's all introduce ourselves." She turned to her left. "Why don't you start?"

There sat a foursome from Toronto – one of them a dentist everyone was happy to learn. Fit and good natured Canadians. Friends to all. Two middle-aged couples. Schoolmates and neighbors for most of their lives and married in the same year, who play bridge together. A twentieth wedding anniversary trek. If they liked it, then New Zealand next year. One of the women did most of the talking for them while the others nodded cheerfully.

Next they looked to Ripp, who sat nursing a hot lemon drink; his throat scratched. He sat up straight and spoke softly. "I'm Harry Ripp. Originally from Chicago, but I live and work in Singapore doing consulting work for banks. The highest I've ever been before was in Mexico City but this is something that I've always wanted to do." He laughed at himself as he said this. There was nothing he less wanted to do. Why was it so cold the last few days?

The pair of newlyweds from Switzerland, Freddie and Frederica Irchel, gave their names and their hometown, Eglisau. They had climbed in the Alps but nothing on this scale. They had walked up from Jiri; six days. After this they were planning to go on a houseboat in Kashmir.

Thondup, 'the Chinese fellow' was next. "My name is Liu Dzao," exaggerating the name in a joking way by using inimitable tonal inflections but continued in accented English. "Call me Lew. I'm from Hong Kong and I have always wanted to see the great Himalayas, and Mt. Everest up close. So this my holiday. Thank you." He bowed slightly in several directions.

Annie gestured to the next couple. An unlikely pair. He looked north European and she was a Nepali Hindu with a small red *tilak* in the middle of her brow. The woman began by holding her palms together. "*Namaste*, everybody." She spoke in pleasantly accented English. "I am Sugata Saraswati; I am a nurse at Kathmandu General Hospital and this is my husband Sergei" she reported, and gestured to him with hands like a dancer's.

Sergei gave a broad smile showing a tooth crowned in steel. A thick handsome man whose sweater had epaulet holes at the shoulders. "Hallo. I'm Sergei. Sergei Kaptsov. I am flying helicopters. Russian "Kazan" helicopters, big ones. I am man in middle seat. Engineer, radioman, mechanic. Many times flying to Khumbu but I never walk. And now Sugata makes me do it. She says I will stop smoking if I can walk to base camp. So we shall see. You all will help me. Today, not one smoke." Thondup smiled to himself.

A hot meal was served and Ripp managed to stay seated next to Thondup and a thin but pleasant friendliness commenced between the two of them. Ripp shuddered from the cold and told him of the house that was being built in the Virgin Islands after he retired. They spent minutes on the geography of the Caribbean and the climate as Ripp went on about sailing and scuba diving. Thondup seemed interested in hearing about it and in fact did find it interesting. One day he would like to visit that part of the world. After he learned how to swim, he laughed.

Thondup was able to dodge the oblique inquiries about himself. He had only been in Hong Kong for a year, he said, his firm was based in Xian, and so it went. He enjoyed inventing himself on the fly and telling good stories about cooking and about the birds of China. Over the following days they became a natural pair on the trail, Thondup waiting for the right moment before making off for the Nup-La; Ripp waiting for the right moment for his recruitment pass.

At Tengboche

The Zone Commander approached the end of the trail and passed under a great arch surmounted with a bas-relief of a spoked wheel supported by recumbent deer. Said to be the emblem of Nalanda University a thousand years earlier. It marked the beginning of a stone path to the treeless ridge which exposed an awesome panorama. On one's right, the large *stupa*, and two small lodges beyond it. On one's left, the large bulk of the monastery and the monk's housing compound behind it. Fifty four stone steps led up to the porch of a colorfully decorated temple. And directly ahead lay a great broad meadow, tilted and open to a vista of mountain giants, the great Nuptse – Lhotse wall with the peak of Everest behind it, and close to the right the exquisite Ama Dablam, its twin rock arms embracing the ancient monastic settlement which had become an international tourist destination by the twenty-first century.

Chandra had three principal reasons to be in the upper Khumbu. Two of them, the transfer of the *gumba* and the labor strike meeting at Monjo, had been concluded. Only his farewell visit to the Abbot remained. At the monastery he was shown to a room he could use for rest, provided a toilet, given a bowl of warm water and a towel, and finally escorted to where Gyalpo Rinpoche was waiting for him. It was a different room than the previous visits and the Rinpoche gestured for him to sit near on some cushions. Chandra bowed slightly and immediately apologized again in a grave voice for the tragedy of the monks killed by a grenade last Spring. The Rinpoche nodded slowly without speaking until the matter came to an end.

After a long silence they resumed speaking in a relaxed and friendly way about their health, the Sherpa economy, the postponed porters strike, the situation in the *terrai*, and the situation in Kathmandu. Chandra said he was looking forward to the arrival of Pasang Dorje, and Gyalpo Rinpoche remarked they were once novices at the ancient Dorje-Ling monastery in Tibet. Perhaps something could be worked out to the mutual benefit of *dharma* and Maoism. It could be an interesting, if unlikely, attempt.

Finally, Chandra came round to himself. He was finished. The time had come to retire. He intended to go south at year end, and today was probably the last time he would be with Rinpoche. He wanted to express the gratitude of the Party for the progressive influence of the Lama. The Party would adhere to their understandings crafted over the years. He had to say he was personally grateful for what he learned about the working of his mind during the years they passed together. Learning to understand the mind from within was a suitable goal for a man. It might be done by science, he thought. The Lama agreed, it was conceivable – the mind was constructed, wasn't it?

Chandra said he decided against Kerala. There were too many communist pacifist intellectuals down there, talkative fence-sitters. No, he decided to visit the Shankaracharya *math* in Karnataka to ask for directions in finding a place. His savings could last a few years if he lived simply, and no one would know him down there. He was confident he would find something, a non-theistic ashram possibly, for the weeks or months he needed to clear his mind of politics. After that, something would happen as life's random collisions took over. Something always happened. Always. And he was ready for something new.

As they were talking about this there was a commotion at the door and Gyalpo Rinpoche's senior attendant came into the room with an agitated look on his face and apologized for intruding, but he needed to say something important to Rinpoche. Three young monks with grave faces who had just come from Lukla stood just back of the doorway looking into the room.

The senior attendant came over and whispered into Gyalpo Rinpoche's ear. The Lama swooned and nearly fell over, catching himself on his elbow. He sat upright, very pale with a look of horror on his face and turned to Chandra.

"Our friend has been murdered in Lukla."

"What!!"

Pemba Arrives

It was nearly dusk when Pemba finally came up the last switchback of the hill to the monastery. It had been a very long day. Tourists not used to the altitude usually required three days of walking to reach the monastery but he had done it in one. He couldn't stop thinking of the pleasure of making love with Annie the night before, which was even better than their first occasion and she had kept him quietly within her for a long time. They had somehow developed enormous confidence in each other, and he had never experienced such trusting feelings before, without a doubt. Perhaps his parents, but that was in a special category of love. They planned to steal some minutes when they crossed paths the next day. Her group would be coming up, he would be descending. After that it would be two or more weeks before they would see one another. There was so much to say. What would their future be? Come to America, she said, but how?

When Pemba arrived at the monastery he was shown directly to Rinpoche and his dark-skinned visitor. The three monks had already broken the news. Pemba did a quick prostration and apologized for intruding but he had been ordered to obtain positive identification of the victim, and he showed Gyalpo Rinpoche a few close-up digital photos on the camera display.

Yes, that was him said the Lama in a tremulous whisper, that was Yeshe Longdrul Rinpoche, a reincarnated *tulku*, whom he had known since boyhood. He lived as a lay person in Dharamsala and worked as the manuscript librarian in the Dalai Lama's household and was carrying a large donation of cash and something else very valuable. If they were not found with the body it meant they had been stolen. And then it came out. He had killed an important man once long ago in Tibet and he had returned his robes and declined to use his lineage name. He barely survived his escape to India where Chandra had nursed him to health, and had spent his subsequent life rescuing and restoring old manuscripts. He was not at all political, he was just a librarian. Gyalpo Rinpoche urged Pemba to return to Lukla immediately and ordered eight of the younger monks to bring the body up to Tengboche for the *bardo* ceremonies which would take a few days. Then a ritual cremation of the remains.

So Pemba descended to Lukla early the following morning. The Lama cancelled all audiences and retreated for two days of mourning and asked Chandra, whom he felt still needed guidance, to stay with him. It was becoming too much for Chandra. After the monks were killed, Chandra's letter to Dharamsala caused this *tulku*, having taken birth in a child named Pasang Dorje, to arrive in the Khumbu to be murdered.

One of the attributes that once made him a successful guerrilla leader was the ability to face death coldly; whether his own, of comrades or innocent unfortunate bystanders. But finally, the death of two monks from a stupid grenade attack had cracked his emotional armor and now the murder of his old friend had mauled the crack wide. Who would do such a thing? He was suffering battle fatigue, whatever. A replacement as Zone Commander would be required before the end of a current cease-fire. Chandra asked the Rinpoche if the perpetrator was evil or merely ignorant. Demons had to be propitiated ritually, said Gyalpo Rinpoche. When they were aroused in their wrathful forms the energies become so strong that they even extinguished thoughts of suffering or attachment but simply filled all of space beyond questions.

The Trek

Over the next several days Annie's group ascended the long trail towards Mount Everest. The trekkers strung out over a few hundred yards as they walked and mixed, becoming acquainted with one another, testing their capacities for humor or irony or knowledge, and gravitating to their favorites. After several outhouse stops, Thondup finally rid himself of all the incriminating debris, which buoyed his spirits. Ripp commenced bonding with him as they both played with their ostensible identities.

Thondup took Ripp at face value, as an economic journalist about to leave Asia for someplace in the Caribbean Sea. Ripp, witting, had the advantage in getting to know his man. As they walked they discussed whatever non-personal matters caught their interest. Ripp talked about tropical butterflies and micro-lending. Thondup contributed bootleg knowledge of Chinese bird species gleaned from Hsien, the wife who would want part of the fortune much of which he would hide. Put it under military control, he thought.

The group stayed in Monjo that night, sharing cubicles of narrow bunk beds. In the morning they walked along the river until they approached the confluence of two powerful branches of the Dudh Khosi. It forced the trail to ascend steeply to a swaying cable footbridge which spanned a thundering gorge.

208

The uphill side had a natural rest area and Annie could see Pemba sitting on a boulder watching her group approach the airy bridge.

The others paused to catch their breaths. Annie hugged Pemba when she crossed over and spoke with him in Nepali, asking what he had learned. He told her what he knew. A friend of Gyalpo Rinpoche was robbed of a fortune. He had to rush to Lukla to send the identification to the Captain in Kathmandu and resume work at the airport. They would notice his absence. The last time they had spoken Nepali was on the *Stimmgabel*, and it gave them renewed pleasure to be bilingual. Annie had been thinking of it throughout the summer. He told her it would be painful to be without her over the next weeks.

"I am going to think of you every day" he said.

"I'll think of you all the time I'm walking. We have plenty of time, Pemba-la. We can have all the time in the world." She thought how wonderful it sounded in Nepali. It had more poetry.

Ripp and Thondup, standing nearby, were professionally curious to listen in but couldn't follow the words.

"Speak it?" asked Thondup.

"*Namaste*," said Ripp.

Tent Mates

Walking alone with his thoughts in a peripatetic musing, Ripp felt as if something was going to be revealed. That a veil would soon be lifted and he would grasp what Thondup was up to. He was close and available for an approach at any moment. But the fact that Thondup's behavior made little sense only increased Ripp's determination to get to the bottom of the puzzle. Where was Thondup going? Elsie said there could be something else. Did it have to do with a failed rendezvous at the airport?

Meanwhile, Thondup kept rehearsing the plan in his mind. He could still change everything, find a secure cache for the fortune and bluff his way out of Nepal over the Nangpa-La. They could search him at the border station and find nothing. But it would mean leaving the prize behind for a pick-up in the future, and he just couldn't do it. He wanted it with him and it solidified his intention to cross the frontier by a climb over the Nup-La. He resolved to stay with the trekkers as they moved up to the high country and to keep a close eye on the weather. The promise of three clear days was all he needed.

It usually takes nine or ten days to walk roughly thirty miles from Lukla at 9300 feet to the 17,700 feet at the mountain's base camp, gaining more than 8,000 feet in altitude. Annie, solicitous of the group's health, used the old practitioner's rule of thumb for acclimatization: a thousand feet of altitude gain a day, with a rest day every fourth day. With nights in tents or lodges.

Near Namche Ripp remarked "You said you were in the traditional Chinese medicine business."

"True. Bulk and wholesale end of the business. Mostly buying, selling and trading for clients."

"Herbal products?"

"Yes, mostly herbal, you know, nutritional supplements; but some mineral, like *shilajeet*, even some animal, snake and turtle parts."

"So you do *Ayurvedic* stuff for the Indian market?"

"Oh no, not so much. It's different. We actually buy from India. Ayurveda and Chinese medicine theories are similar, but we have different climates, different illnesses, different plants. How about you? Work in Singapore, you say."

"Credit analysis and economic journalism, dry stuff. Mostly the world under fluorescent lights. One bonus of this trip is an article on third world tourism." They both sidestepped once again. Not yet.

As the the Yeti trekkers came into Namche Bazaar Ripp spotted Elsie and Wurlitzer in a coffee shop pretending to study a map. Annie's group would be staying at the Taweche lodge for the night but it wasn't long before the three Americans conferred in the room they used days earlier.

"There's something fucking peculiar going on and I just can't figure it" said Ripp as he described Thondup's behavior in Lukla. "He's up to something but I don't have a clue. He's climbed Everest, so why is he pretending to be on a commercial trek?"

"Maybe he's scouting the Tibetan tourist industry of the future" said Wurlitzer, "or making an alibi for himself; or he's covering his tracks."

"What tracks?"

"Got me. But I'll tell you this, the yakkies up at Khumjung are shoving off tomorrow back for the Nangpa-La. So is our boy going to join them?"

"Not before I own him."

"And the Zone Commander too?"

"Both of them."

At that moment Thondup was standing at the uppermost part of the village where the satellite link would be clearer. He disliked using the brick-sized phone as he knew all conversations would be sucked into unknown databases, but he made the ordained call as requested. Coded words and terms were used and the messaging was brief. He would not be returning with the traders and did not mention the man from Dharamsala. Only that Major Wang was to collect the cargo at the meadow.

He looked at the sky. High horsetail shaped clouds were moving in. The weather wasn't promising.

Pasang Dorje's Cremation

A day later when the Yeti group passed under the arch to Tengboche monastery Annie congratulated them for having come this far. At 12,800 feet they were about halfway in the altitude gain between Lukla and base camp. Many hikers stopped at the beautiful location and went no further. Dawa, the *sirdar*, had the boys arrange their tents high on the far side of the big meadow under a grey sky. The first night they would stay in tents, not lodges.

Tengboche's great meadow area was nearly deserted but from the rear of the monastery buildings there were sounds of deep horns, thumping drums and cymbal clashes accompanied with the low bass tones of men chanting in somber rhythms, hinting at infinite depth in the universe. Annie talked with a local woodcutter in Nepali and had the story. A cremation ceremony was underway behind the monastery, near the shrines of the protector deities, and smoke could be seen rising from the burning cedar, whose unique offering aroma filled the air, even at distance. It was old friend of Rinpoche, the woodcutter said, a *tulku* who had returned his robes.

"Let's stow our gear and have a look," said Annie to the group. Exotic were rituals on display.

Thondup believed a cremation, whoever it was, foretold something unpleasant and he decided to decline the excursion. Nevertheless, aside from the escape predicament, he was gratified to see the upper Khumbu from ground level, and

211

curious about the famous monastery with the sights and sounds of his boyhood. It even smelled like Tibet. He had time. This was not a day for the Nup-La. But if he was being left alone it would be an opportunity to prepare his gear in the tent he and Ripp were to share.

Ripp was cold continuously and bearing an altitude headache. The high northern geological drama of rock and ice was not his idea of fun. He was too old for this sort of thing. Compared to bone-fishing in the Bahamas it went in the wrong direction; Greek islands, the Yucatan, Hawaii, Florida, the Virgins, warmth, abundant photosynthesis, that's what a man needs. Working through the possible outcomes he assessed the chances of Chandra's recruitment at 50% and that today was the best time to cultivate the seed planted months earlier. Chandra would decline of course but the seed would grow in his mind whether he liked it or not. Today for a little bit of fertilizer and observing the tell-tale. It was an odd thing. Ripp's magician's probe. He had learned to read a piece of body language. At a key point he would offer a business card. The arm and finger movements of the recipient was telling and hinted at mental dynamics.

Leaving only Thondup behind the others went to have a look at the funerary spectacle, the sound of which had come down to a single drum. Annie led the way, no photographs please, and the group arrived to see a great pile of red embers stirred by a monk with a long pole and eighty or more persons standing watch in a semi-circle. The Yeshe Longdrul incarnation once embodied in a nomad child named Pasang Dorje was turning to ash and made free. The last embers were shoveled into a large pot with two iron rings so as to be carried by a pole.

At the center of the half circle of watchers stood Gyalpo Rinpoche, who was scattering rice in four directions. Chandra, who stood toward the rear, suddenly found himself looking across at two familiar faces in a group of tourists. The American journalist, and the girl, so familiar looking, yes, she was the Peace Corps girl. How very strange, what were they doing together? The journalist saw him looking, nodded, and touched his hand to his forehead in a gesture of recognition. The small clearing which had been filled for hours with a ritual sound which expressed the cacophony of the planet, ended suddenly with a loud bang by the biggest drum and the air became dramatically silent. Ripp sensed this was his moment for Chandra.

A procession formed, led by Gyalpo Rinpoche and followed by carriers of the slung pot of ashes with a robed monk on either side. The company was led to the great meadow in front of the monastery where it began a clockwise circumambulation as the ashes were scattered by the flanking pair of monks.

Chandra stayed behind and approached the trekkers, addressing himself to Ripp and Annie.

"How unexpected to see you two here, together, how comes this?"

"I'm leading a team of trekkers," she gestured to Ripp and the others. "He's one of them. I told you I was going to work for Yeti Travels after I finished my Volunteer contract."

"That's right. I remember." And turning to Ripp, he said, "And you? Your name slipped my mind."

"Harry Ripp."

"Of course."

They shook hands. Ripp went on. "Well, I'm writing a piece on third world eco-tourism with a section on mountain regions. I think we talked about it, you might recall. It fits well with micro-lending. I'm trying to discuss the morality of resort development when governments become the main investors, that kind of thing. And how are you?"

Ripp stalled for time and estimated that if he kept Chandra engaged in conversation that Annie would go off with her charges and leave them by themselves for a while. Which was exactly what she did, saying she would come back to visit Chandra in about an hour. And so it began as Ripp refrained from asking of the *gumba* or the tigers, but went straight for the goal.

"Look, sir, I would like to ask you something. I've been thinking about it since our interview in Aruna last Spring, five months ago. You saw what I wrote. I really think there's a book here. From your youth to your retirement. A memoir looking back. There aren't any meaningful secrets and you should be free to say whatever's in your mind, or whatever was in your mind at the time. If you don't want to write it you could dictate it. Or do it through a series of interviews. Add some black and white photographs of your own choosing. A good editor could turn it into an international success, I promise you."

"Who are you really Mr. Ripp?"

"Just a high class journalist. And I know a publishing opportunity when I see one. Give me a commission and I'll find you a contract and an advance. I'm near retiring and it could be a nice project to work on. With a good editor might be an international success. I know the publishing world."

"How much if I just disappear? How much is that worth?"

"Hardly anything. A charitable contribution?"

"Well," said Chandra, "if you think of it, make your contribution to the Maha Bodhi Society of Calcutta, they could use some support. Otherwise Mr. Ripp, I will have to disappoint you. I may change my line of work but it doesn't lead in your direction."

"Well, take my card, at least. Please." He handed it over in a slightly raised way and Chandra lifted his arm palm up to receive it after a slight hesitation. "In all sincerity, it could be an international success. Royalties for a few years. Think about it. No harm in that. In fact, it could even help many people. I'm serious. It's the real thing."

"Well, nice seeing you again Mr. Ripp." Chandra smiled benevolently and put the card in his shirt pocket. "Thank you for the offer but I think I'll catch up with the young lady now. *Namaste*."

Ripp judged Chandra when he took the card. A 75% chance thought Ripp, the odds are improved. It was hard for people to resist talking about themselves, especially for money and Ripp took it for granted that Chandra would keep returning to the idea in his head. A memoir.

Chandra located Annie amongst the trekker tents and they elected to take a turn around the meadow. "Tell me your name again" he asked.

"Annie Wendover."

"Of course, of course. My memory for names is going."

"So robbed any banks lately?" It made him laugh as he improvised a cover for himself.

"No, no. That's for the younger fellows these days. I'm just a labor organizer for the porters protective organization now. We're trying to work up an insurance scheme so now I'm only a fellow traveler. And because of you I like America more. It's been how long, two years since I saw you?"

"After Peace Corps I went climbing a lot last year and hanging out in Kathmandu. Then I went to work for Yeti Travels last Spring and again now, and then back home in another few weeks."

"You like Nepal."

"I really do. And I made a very special friend. He's the constable at Lukla airport. If you see him please say hello for me."

"I know him. He came here to see Gyalpo Rinpoche two days ago. Nepal is in turmoil."

"It is. Even more than when we had our motorcycle trip to Biratnagar. That was quite a trip, I'll never forget it. You guys seemed so well-planned."

"Not really. Sita has never come back you know. It was a condition of her release."

"I do know that. When I returned to my latrine project I didn't know there was a mob waiting for me at the border. The Embassy had a fit and ordered me to Kathmandu; pulled me away from my best project. There's a Miss Hornbein who took charge of Sita when she got handed over. She called her smart and brave."

"That's also my opinion of you, 'smart and brave.' I will always remember you reading the Declaration of Independence out loud to me and explaining the Constitution." They both laughed.

"Let me ask," said Chandra, "who was that gentlemen with you?"

"One of my trekkers. A journalist and a professor of some kind. From Singapore."

"A tourist?"

"What else?"

Who Killed Pasang Dorje?

The thought had been flitting in Chandra's mind as he headed down valley to the home red zones. He wondered if the murder of Pasang Dorje was an act by Chinese provocateurs to sever his own overture to the Tibetan exiles. There were rumors to that effect and Chinese agents were capable of it. Could it possibly be that unpleasant Chinese Colonel who received the *gumba*? Who warned him to avoid the exiles. The porter Harish in Monjo had mentioned he had seen the "China man" walking down to Lukla. The man had the inclination and an opportunity. He argued against it in his mind, perhaps he was exaggerating a passing intuition. But the thought recurred, and by the time Chandra and his guards reached Lukla, he had half convinced himself. What should he do? He had no proof. What could he possibly do? And these were his thoughts as he crossed the pedestrian path at the top of the tilted runway and saw him, the Wendover girl's "special friend", the airport constable with the shoulder patch, the one who had come to Tengboche with the photographs of the body.

Pemba saw the older man approaching and recognized him. They came within speaking distance and Pemba said, "You were with Rinpoche when I came yesterday."

"Yes. And I also met your friend there and she said to greet you when I pass through Lukla. She is a very good person and you are a lucky boy."

"Thank you."

"I need to tell you something." He tried to let the words sink in. "The murder of that man was not by our revolution. Someone from China I think. Maybe with the yak caravan. Get to the check-post below the Nangpa-La before the traders arrive. Search their bags. You might find what was stolen."

"Are you sure?"

"No. I'm not sure. But it's what I can imagine."

Recruitment

That evening in the tent at the edge of Tengboche's meadow Ripp sensed a change in Thondup's mood. They had been tent mates through circumstance, and as neither snored and, to the contrary, were considerate and well-mannered, the two of them had solidified a rapport of the trail. But that evening at Tengboche Thondup was withdrawn. He was frustrated and eager to head for the Nup-La. But the mountain weather was unpromising and a glance at his wrist altimeter confirmed a low pressure trough crossing the region. Even the yak route on the Nangpa glacier's upper passage would be dangerous, and the Nup-La in such conditions was out of the question. It would need two or three days before conditions improved, just about when they would reach Lobuche, a day before base-camp. From there he could cut across the inner range on the west over a pass and come down onto the nGozumba. By the time he reached the foot of the Nup-La there would be a near full moon and a night ascent of the icefalls could be ideal.

In the pre-dawn Ripp woke with the conviction there was little point in holding back on his approach. Moreover he feared he would be altitude sick if he went much higher than Tengboche. An unpleasant night in the tent gave him the idea and he began to exaggerate his symptoms for Thondup's benefit. He moaned about a headache aspirin couldn't fix and a growing nausea. Thondup, in the sleeping bag next to him, inquired if Ripp felt like throwing up and received a universal hand gesture, so-so. Thondup commiserated.

At the first grey hint of light Ripp came upright and felt the top of his head brush the tent fabric. It was now or never. Thondup stirred half-awake and got up on one elbow and then upright, rubbing his eyes. In the cramped space their faces were scarcely more than a foot or so apart. Ripp moved his pawn and asked, "Isn't there Chinese medicine for this altitude sickness?"

Thondup said, "Yes, certainly, several actually." He flexed his arms and stretched his shoulders as he became more fully awake.

Ripp developed the opening. "How about *yartsa gumba*, or *chungcxiao* whatever you call it in China?"

Thondup gave him a very slow querulous look. *What was this?* "Yes, that would definitely help, especially if taken continuously before ascending."

"Know where I might find some?" asked Ripp. Thondup's eyebrows revealed his thought. *This was interesting.*

Then, to put him in check, Ripp said, "Let me show you something" and took out his digital camera and displayed the time-lapsed photos of the transactions days earlier at Khumjung. The *gumba* bales and the tiger carcasses were unmistakable. As was the picture of an automatic pistol being presented to Chandra. Thondup sat poker-faced, internally bewildered, as Ripp scrolled through the dozen odd frames. "I'll explain this in a moment, if you allow me."

Thondup could scarcely believe what was happening and froze into expressionless silence as he examined Ripp, slightly wide-eyed.

"The zoomed ones with the tiger carcasses are pretty sharp, aren't they? Tigers, tsk, tsk. You look pretty good too. I guess you know trading them is prohibited by the World Wildlife Convention. Some people think treaty violation is a big deal, don't you know? It might mean something unpleasant for a violator." Ripp let the words sink in. "Trading endangered wildlife for weapons for the Maoists. Embarrassing for China, don't you think? Do the top people know you're doing this?"

By now Thondup grasped that he was probably dealing with an American intelligence agent. It was like a curtain going up in a theatre and miraculously, truly a miracle, the American's next words mirrored his very own thoughts.

"Look, Lew, your cover name, it's just the two of us and we're both in a foreign country. I know your name, Colonel Thondup Gaomei, soon to be General, unless..." Ripp let it go by wiggling his fingers. "Okay, my affiliation is less important but what is important is to acknowledge that our governments have developed relations and that you and I are meeting innocently in a third country. So there's no harm, only benefit if we are open and frank with one another. Am I correct?" He left the question hanging in the air. Thondup's face remained blank, an eyebrow raised slightly in curiosity, remaining silent.

"I assure you nothing that we propose is harmful to China. We, my employer that is, have been interested in you for some time and believe you are someone with whom we would like to do business. We know of your association with General Tu and our interests are commercial just as well. We would like to have friends in the Chinese army. For example, next year an American company, the Boeing Corporation, is competing with Aerospatiale of France for a very large helicopter contract. Boeing's superior load lifting capability with better fuel consumption at high altitudes could make the difference, you might imagine. Unfortunately, your General Staff in Beijing and the Naval establishment, which thinks in terms of sea-level, both overlook the strategic significance of performance at high altitude in our opinion. It needs someone from Tibet, someone at your level, perhaps someone in the Border Command, to emphasize this and make the case for us. That kind of thing. You see the picture." There was a long silence.

Thondup felt a thrill of excitement but revealed nothing. He was not only being approached by an American intelligence agent but it had nothing at all to do with the incident at Lukla! Nevertheless, his career was at stake.

"Something else?" inquired Thondup softly, speaking for the first time, and appreciating that his career might be ruined.

"Oh yes. In exchange for being our friend on commercial transactions and such things in your sphere of influence, and being someone we can talk to once in a while, about matters of mutual interest – such as the future of Nepal – we are prepared to compensate you with a distributorship. We learned you were the counterparty for the funny mushrooms, so we thought to conserve delicate soils and save endangered species by giving you a profitable opportunity to share the good deed." Ripp reached into his pack and extracted the translucent half-liter flask and held it close to their faces, rattling it. Then he unscrewed the top to show that it was filled with blue diamond shaped pills.

"It's called Operation Scheherazade. A thousand and one nights of pleasure courtesy of Western chemistry. We had them counted. Made in India. *Sildenafil citrate*. Send it to a lab. Try it yourself. You'll see."

Thondup's thought of Boeing's helicopters was overwhelmed at the thought of having so many blue pills in his hands, which almost made him laugh, this on top of the treasure in his yellow pack.

"Are you asking me to sell them?" He pointed to the flask with his chin.

"Retail? God, no. We just hope you and General Tu could move a few hundred thousand annually. It comes in bulk so we'd leave the packaging and pricing to you. You see, the thing is, those pills now come to China on the Pacific coast and are very scarce in China's west and interior. So we think Tibet is a back door to a very large inland market near term. We're thinking you could develop distribution channels in western China, still an untouched market. Could be huge. Same market as your mushrooms."

"And what do you want from me? Just to talk to me? I know how the game gets played. You'll just reel me in until I'm put before a firing squad."

"No, no, no, nothing like that. Just the big think stuff. The strategic world view. Nothing operational. The action with India, Nepal, and all the 'Stans. Plus Iran. We'll make it easy. Just don't double on us. Otherwise my boss will cook you and China for the dirty treaty violation business, in the UN, in the media, even in Hollywood. The basic idea is you get rewarded for good predictions which we can use. Think of us as clients."

"Let me think for a moment." So they sat facing one another in complete silence for several minutes, heads nearly touching in the cramped space of the tent. The main fact in Thondup's mind was that Ripp was ignorant of the incident at Lukla or that there was a fortune in the yellow pack inches away from where he was sitting. The Americans were idiots he concluded. To think that an embarrassing pinprick like the tigers affected anything, as if it would "cook" him. To the contrary, he would be seen as the reliable man. Scarcely anyone in China would ever hear of it. And of course he would double back on them. However. The proposition of the blue pills was another matter and that was definitely worth entertaining. He certainly wanted the ones in the flask.

"I accept," he said. "How do we proceed?"

"We'll manage to get in touch with you in Beijing later this year after you're settled in the new post to set up all the protocols. It won't be hard to find you. Congratulations on the promotion, by the way." Ripp extended his hand.

"That keeps it simple," replied Thondup, and shook it.

"Let me ask you something else. Why the hell are you on this trek?"

"To tell the truth, we wanted to see what mountain tourism looks like here so China can develop its own regions intelligently. We've got a mess on the Rongbuk side of the mountain and we had to build sanitary facilities and a morgue."

"But aren't you going back with the caravan?"

"Oh, no. I'm planning to fly out from Kathmandu." It was weak, but there was nothing else he could think of. "I'll just go up to base camp, take some pictures, write a report. What about you?"

"Well, after shaking your hand I'm finished here and can't wait to head down. I'll probably start after breakfast. I'm feeling better already. A pleasure meeting you by the way, you're in great shape."

Making a Date

"We have a deal and a half," said Ripp to Elsie on the radio. "I recorded the whole episode."

"He'll double on us, I promise."

"I think he'll look for himself first. We'll ruin him and he knows it. Remember, I lived with him for four nights. We're not asking for anything operational, just eyes and ears and payoffs for making useful predictions."

"And what about the half deal?"

"Chandra's leaving the business and heading south to retire in meditation. He's got a book proposal in his pocket. With no income and meager savings he'll go for it. Give it six months. The Indians will be very grateful for him."

"And what's the Colonel up to?"

"Scouting mountain tourism, he says."

"How are you holding up?"

"I'm sick as a puppy and leaving in an hour or so. They're finding a porter to accompany me down to Lukla. Will I see you?"

"It breaks my heart, dearest, but they want the chopper back in Kathmandu."

"How about flying down to Singapore for a long weekend?"

"That actually sounds nice. It's a deal."

"When?"

"Say the first week in December?"

"See you then. I'll count the days."

Clues

Pemba and Annie each felt the pain of separation from their lover and could only distract themselves with work. In addition to his airport duties, Pemba continued searching his memory for clues, and on two occasions went down to the corner of the runway where the body had been found and tried to re-imagine how the killing had taken place. The Zone Commander's suspicion stayed in his mind. How would a robber know that Pasang Dorje was coming up the trail with a fortune? There was no sign of struggle and the death must have been near instantaneous. Was the robber waiting for him? He walked to the Snow Lion Lodge where he had tea with three monks. The proprietor, a strongly built Sherpa matron, remembered them clearly. The monks had been troubled that their visitor never arrived even well after dark. Was anyone else waiting for the visitor? Who else knew he was coming? She had no idea, but come to think of it someone had come by to inquire, yes she could remember it clearly now, a Japanese man came to ask about his arrival.

A Japanese man with an ice-axe. Pemba had two clues.

Base Camp

The hamlet of Lobuche, hardly more than a few lodges and outhouses, sits above the edge of the lateral moraine on the western side of the Khumbu Glacier, a massive tongue of ice coming off the southwest face of Everest. Shortly before reaching the place, while leading her trekkers and alone with her thoughts, Annie wondered if she might be pregnant. The timing was plausible, if unplanned. Something ever so subtle inside her torso, an ever so slightly different tone in her breasts and nipples and the fact her period was due but didn't feel like it was going to come. Perhaps she was imagining it. Wish fulfillment? A bit clearer in a few days.

She had gathered her group in the food tent to prepare for the final day of ascent and stepped outside the lodge to gather her thoughts. The gibbous moon came over the ridges of Nuptse and overcame the stars with its bright clarity. Annie wondered if she would ever be in a place like this again. Had it all been worth it? And as opposed to what?

At the evening meal Annie encouraged them to get a full belly and a good night's rest before the long day ahead, with a thousand feet of gain over four miles on the hard glacier. They planned to start at dawn, reach the base camp area at the foot of the great icefall around mid-day, have a long rest and return to Lobuche before dark. The weather promised to be clear and they all did as she suggested except for Liu Dzao who feigned a splitting headache and nausea, as he prepared the context for remaining behind.

At dawn she looked into the tent and found him in his bag. It surprised her as he was usually ready and eager to get moving. But as she believed Ripp was intelligent to have descended the day before, she acknowledged that altitude distress could come on suddenly. Acute mountain sickness isn't fun and

Thondup knew exactly how to fake the symptoms. He hadn't been able to sleep, he told her, and was suffering from an extremely painful headache despite the aspirins he had taken and he thought he might vomit.

Annie told him she would leave Lakpa behind to look after him, and if he did not feel better within an hour or two, he was to start walking down to lower altitude immediately. He would probably feel much better once he did so. Lakpa would stay with him and carry his packs as far down as the rescue station at Pheriche and they could wait at one of the lodges down there until the team returned by that route two days later.

First a sick Ripp, she thought, now the second one. It wasn't unusual for some first timers in a high altitude trekking party to drop out or descend. Some people got seasick. She had vomited the first time she went sailing in Alaskan waters. It was hard to predict which newcomers to the mountains would be afflicted but she wouldn't have guessed that Lew would come down with it. The remaining eight members of the Yeti Treks group started early, and were strung out in a ragged line as they moved from cairn to cairn on the rubble strewn glacier surface. The fatigued Canadian couple had decided to stop at a small shelter at Gorak Shep and wait for their return. Hours later, less than a mile from the goal, Annie, walking backwards for a moment, observed her six remaining trekkers.

The two Swiss looked fine but Annie noticed Sergei gesticulating and speaking earnestly over his shoulder to his wife. They all shuffled slowly, their eyes more frequently on the steps before them than on the great mountains on all sides. No one was wise-cracking. It was now just a matter of walking slowly from cairn to cairn and steering clear of the obvious crevasses. In another half hour they would reach this decade's base camp area, the totemic El Dorado of their mountain touring. They could see the multicolored tent colony and short stone walls of the climbers and the great Khumbu ice fall tumbling down on their right.

A stretched rope with dozens of prayer flags divided the trekkers from the permitted mountaineers. Annie steered the group to a lunch spot where they could spread a tarpaulin and sit in the brilliant sun, the clear sky an unnaturally dark blue. Base Camp, at last. Cameras and binoculars were put to work. One of the Sherpa boys pumped up the kerosene stove and put water on the boil. Biscuits, cheese, and trail mix were handed out. Bowls of Rara noodles were minutes away. After the feed everyone became quiet and drifted off to some kind of vegetative state, stretching out in the sun. As if Annie had led them towards a semi-conscious doze.

In Full Flight

At Lobuche it was Thondup's time to go. He felt the chill of dampness around the back of his neck, there when preparing a hazardous undertaking. That first hint of perspiration signaled the opening of an energy reserve, creatively packaged over the years. He considered throwing away the western cigarettes but rationalized keeping them. Ideal gifts for the squad that would be coming up to meet him on the West Rongbuk in Tibet. At least he had called the weather and the moon correctly. Chances looked good overall for the two crucial nights ahead.

The rest of the trekkers and crew had departed at first light, leaving only Lakpa and himself which permitted Thondup to luxuriate in his sleeping bag until the sun was up. Finally he roused himself and called out to Lakpa, asking him to fix a big breakfast, as he was feeling much better and was hungry. Half hour later he dispatched the obedient boy to inform Annie that he had fully recovered, but would rest at Lobuche by himself until they returned and was very comfortable.

Finally alone, he examined the gear he for any oversights, laced his boots, shouldered the heavy loaded yellow pack, and laid a false trail by writing a note saying he had gone down to the medical station at Pheriche. In 36 hours, if all went well, he should be across the international frontier and within reach of a patrol coming up from Rongbuk monastery. He planned to inform the Border Command communication node once he was on the glacier and closer to the pass. Once over the Nup-La around dawn he would be less than fifteen miles from the climbers base camp area on Everest's north side, with a jeep track. From there he could be back in his own bed at Tingri late that night with an incredible fortune in hand and a major business opportunity ahead. He thought of making General Tu his advisor.

He set off, well-adapted to the altitude, feeling strong, adventurous, and highly motivated. The weather was excellent, the moon would offer valuable light, and the GPS coordinates would show the way. After a short descent on the main trail, he made a sharp turn to the right and entered a drainage, five miles long, ascending northwest for the little pass over to the nGozumba drainage.

His absence wouldn't be discovered until late afternoon. What would they do? They would read the note and assume he went down to Pheriche to get medical attention. Why should they doubt it? They would be going down to Pheriche themselves the following day. Instead, he intended to cross the interior range over the low pass called the Cho-La to reach the tiny lodge at Dragnag on the east side of the nGozumba before dark. It would be a long day, and the following day even longer, but he was confident the task was within his ability. There was no alternative.

After some hours the load began to bear and the shoulder straps were probably affecting the circulation in his upper limbs. He mentally weighed the yellow pack again, for the fifth time. It was slowing him. Certainly near seventy pounds or more. The dense contents weighed   heavily and uncomfortably. It was stuffed as tightly as he could and obviously overloaded. He regretted not having chosen a 75 liter model. He went through the contents he could remember. Bundles of paper currency and the gold statue were the heaviest items and not dispensable. There was a headlamp, batteries, binocular, weapon, ammunition, water flask, camera, satellite phone, 60 meters of rope, ice axe, ice tool, crampons, other hardware, mittens, underwear, clothes, and what else? The half-liter flask filled with the blue pills. Toiletries. Yak cheese. Potato slices. Heavy plastic bags for emergency waterproofing. Sweets for his daughter. CDs.

Exposed

Annie felt the light taps on her shoulder though she was tempted to ignore them. It was so delicious to be stretched on her mat in the sun. But that wouldn't do, clearly. Somebody wanted her attention. She opened her eyes, shaded under the hat and sat up. It was Sergei.

"I need to speak to you," he said.

"Sure. What is it?"

"Please, let go over someplace there. I need to speak with you. Private."

Privat, he said in his thick Russian accent. What was this about? She slipped into her unlaced boots and followed him a stone's throw away where he gestured for them to sit. They leaned against the boulders.

"What's going on?"

"I explain," he answered. "You know I am cigarette smoker. Yes, I come here because I want to walk what I seeing from helicopter, but also to try stop smoking. From Lukla till Pheriche, six days, six full days, I don't smoke. Nothing. Very nice. Sugata is very happy. After Pheriche dinner I go to make shit in little house. China man, Lew, is sitting inside smoking cigarette. So he gives me cigarette. And I like, of course. Next day we do walk to Lobuche. After eating supper I watch Lew. He opens his big yellow bag and takes out pack cigarettes and sees me watching. He smiles and gives me cigarette again. We walk behind the little house for yaks and smoke cigarettes."

"I can't take his tobacco away from him."

"No, no. Listen. This morning, after breakfast, I am hoping to catch him again. Maybe he gives me another cigarette. But I'm ashamed to ask."

"Does Sugata know you're smoking?"

"Yes, she smells it and is angry. But listen, Annie, this something else. So this morning I watch Lew goes to make shit. And I know he keeps cigarettes in top of pack. And pack is in front of his tent, right next to mine."

"You're not going to tell me you're stealing cigarettes."

"Annie, listen. I open top of pack. You know why pack is so heavy? Inside pack is pistol, sat-phone, and money, so much money, in bundles. So much," he gestured, holding his hands a foot apart. "Big money. American dollars, Euros, and papers with Chinese writing. *Chinese!*" He paused to share the drama. "What you think? I think not my business, but Sugata making me to tell you."

Annie sat motionless for a moment, experiencing a clarifying calm center within a tornado of thought. If Lew was the murderer and faking altitude sickness down at Lobuche, he was probably on the run at this moment. But boxed in unless he was heading for the border over the mountains. She saw it clearly. She saw the whole thing. What to do? She absolutely had to reach Pemba.

"I'll be back in half hour," she said hastily with a wave of her hand and jumped the rope over to the mountaineer's tent colony, where various teams had staked out their respective base camp territories. A garden of colored tents in various sizes was dwarfed by a larger geodesic dome tent with a sign reading: "World's Highest Internet Café". Inside was an Espresso machine and pastries brought up daily from the Swiss bakery at Khumjung and three well-used desktop computers on a planked table. Tariff for the satellite telephone was charged at 600 rupees a minute and credit cards were accepted.

But there was a queue and a sign-up sheet, with nothing available till late in the afternoon. Then she remembered that Urs had said last Spring he'd be leading a route on Nuptse with a team under strong sponsorship. They had to have a sat-phone. It took five minutes to locate the German team's four tents. Hildegard Zipf, a blond, tanned, 32 year old, medical doctor and base camp manager. Emergency? "A friend of Urs? Of course. Know your name. Use the phone. I'll make some tea." In all the world Annie knew only a single Nepalese telephone number, the Yeti warehouse. If Sonam was in the office he might track down Pemba.

At that moment Pemba was in the polygonal control tower, two stories plus a basement just off the highest corner of the runway where Lukla's main street crossed. A roof festooned with antennas and sky-facing dishes. In addition to aviation functions, the tower served as the Khumbu's communications hub. Standing by the large windows, Pemba was speaking to the Captain in Kathmandu. He said nothing about a treasure, but he had a suspect in mind.

As he looked out the window he saw Sonam standing in the street and gesturing repeatedly with two hands to come down, and then holding one hand to his ear to mimic a handset and drawing an imaginary bosom with the other. It could only be Annie! Pemba ended his call and raced down the wide spiral of stairs and out the steel door to the street.

"Pemba-la," said Sonam, "Annie calling me from base camp with sat-phone just few minutes ago. Says to give you message that person you are looking for who did that thing is her Chinese trekker. He left Lobuche maybe five or six hours ago and she thinks he might be going to the Nangpa-La. And that he had a pistol. And that she will be very happy when she sees you."

Pemba reacted instantly. "I have to go now," he said. So it was exactly as Rinpoche's friend had suggested; a Chinese spy who had done the vile deed, not some Japanese. He ran to his small dwelling and started moving rapidly through his climbing gear, unused since the *Stimmgabel* in the Spring. First to retrieve everything he would need to stay warm, he filled the pockets of his red parka, and took crampons for his boots. There was no firearm but it didn't matter. He wrote a note to the airport manager explaining his absence.

As he walked steadily from Lukla up toward the base of the Nangpa-La Pemba kept asking himself what he would do in the spy's place. He tried to guess his opponent's mind and reconstruct him, to picture him. He recalled the man lingering around the airport that day who was taking pictures. And the Hong Kong trekker that first night at Happiness Lodge. The same person. He could barely reconstruct the face, flat like a wooden slab.

Pemba reached Thame and stayed the night. On the next day he went further up the Nangpa valley until reaching a hamlet called Lungare, about five kilometers below the glacier's snout. He sat on a boulder and tried to think it through again. If the spy was experienced on mountain terrain and racing for the Nangpa-La from Lobuche he could travel the straightest line by crossing two interior ranges and traversing the nGozumba glacier between them. If one had sufficient skill it would be shorter than the semi circle of conventional trails.

But there was something wrong. Escape would not be possible over the Nangpa-La. An army unit was at the checkpost. The killer had to know there was no exit possible that way, nor through Lukla. The areas would be heavily guarded. What could the man do? Hide? If it was himself and he was Chinese and desperate he might try the Nup-La though likely to die, benighted, lost searching a route in the icefall, exhausted, and without supplies. But it gnawed at him.

He realized there was little point racing to the Nangpa-La police check post, which was by now reinforced. He let his thoughts fly and started calculating distances. There was a pass on each of the two interior ranges. The Renjo-La was a half-day from where he sat. With a track leading down to Gokyo on the west side of the nGozumba glacier. Someone coming from Lobuche could cross the Cho-La on the east side and follow the glacier up to the ice fall.

The idea of the Nup-La seemed absurd. No one ever crossed the frontier at the Nup-La. He couldn't think of anyone who had ever done it. An out-of-the-way and dangerous place with a double icefall on the Nepal side and never considered a worthy climbing objective. But it bothered him, a trapped desperate man experienced in mountaineering might try for it. There were no guards.

Could he overtake him?

Dragnag to the Icefall

Beyond the highest yak pastures, Thondup could see the permanent snowfield at the bottom of the Cho-La, the pass on the ridge between the Cholatse and Taweche peaks. Once across he would be in the nGozumba valley and in a few hours could descend to the hard glacier and the tiny hamlet of Dragnag beside its edge. Despite the heavy load his progress was steady and crossing the pass was relatively simple, a short technical passage of fifty odd feet at the very top, where the snowfield calved off the rock, forcing the route into the fissure, the bergschrund, which then exited by a steep ice ledge to the top.

There Thondup gazed across Nepal's longest glacier, at this point a half-mile wide, and the expansiveness of it all made him think about the future again. What would he do with the money? It would be the first time he had real capital. He would have to avoid any awkwardness with General Tu and planned to search Confucius on this matter. He would enjoy spreading some of it around to seed goodwill, make a generous contribution to the officers club, that kind of thing, and could afford a fine residence for himself in the Capitol.

He reached Dragnag after dark with the aid of his headlamp. There was a single small lodge on a wide gravel bench just above the main lateral moraine on the east side of the glacier. The owner served him a bowl of meat *momos* in broth with fried potatoes and hot chilies. Then he took a cigarette and allowed himself a six hour rest.

At dawn he had a large bowl of noodles and tea, and paid his bill. As he started heading north, alongside the glacier, the Sherpa lodge keeper ran out the door and shouted that he was going the wrong way. There was nothing in that direction. The track to Gokyo, he pointed and shouted, was on the glacier's far side to the west. There would be cairns. Thondup ignored him and kept walking. It didn't really matter what the lodge keeper thought.

From here on the route would be slow going. Initially there was a faint track on the moraine but it soon vanished in the glacial debris. It meant picking an unmarked way through the geological chaos. There was much loose footing, with passages requiring him to run up collapsing slopes of wet mud mixed with the grit-stuff of grinding rock. It was tiring though still early in the morning, and the weight was wearing him with the Nup-La still fifteen miles on. He planned to bivouac at the base of the icefall by the time it was dark and to start climbing when the full moon appeared over the ridges. He would need all his strength.

After a while he was forced out onto the hard glacier and proceeded towards its middle to avoid a dangerous maze of crevasses on his right where a smaller glacier joined the flow in a great smash-up. And later, in the afternoon, when the snow bridges would be at their weakest he knew his weight was becoming an objective hazard and there was little for it except to make the burden lighter. The moment had arrived.

He sat resting on a boulder and ate half a *chapatti* and drank water from the rivulets. The load slowed him and was tiring, hazardous in the circumstance. Time had come to jettison weight, to make a cache and hide it in the debris. He put in a GPS waypoint and added a descriptive note. He could have a training exercise retrieve it the Spring. Opening the yellow pack he began sorting the gear inside while keeping the ice axe and modular tool lashed to the outside webbing.

Small items in the undecided pile. The ten millimeter rope he bought in Namche, in its original coil, with such a beautiful design on the sheath. Seventy yards, at least eight or nine pounds. A pity. He cut and saved about twenty feet, enough to tether his pack if he had to jump a crevasse without weight on his back. The rest went into a black plastic bag for his cache. To take the binoculars or not? Take them he decided, scanning crevasse fields from a distance was valuable. And of course, there was the irreducible weight of the paper currencies, at least twenty pounds and the golden statue, ten pounds or more. And the irreducible weight of 1,001 blue pills.

He retrieved the heavy automatic pistol and holster and four full ammunition magazines. It was over ten pounds he calculated and thought it through carefully. He disliked being unarmed. It was a small standard issue cannon, replaceable, and he couldn't imagine needing it between now and the location of his own troops down on the West Rongbuk glacier. He could reasonably abandon the weapons and a box of American batteries. The ones in his headlamp would do for a night. Another pound or two lost. What else? An inch or more of paperwork, the official receipt of the mushrooms, thoughts on camouflage, budgets, a party journal, a book on birds for Hsien. He decided to keep the small steel wrench for his ice tool, and to change the adze to a hammer. He dug deeper into the bag. Wind goggles. Featherweight. Keep them. A flimsy bag with CDs of western music for his daughter and a Sony video player. Goodbye. A bag of sweets for his pocket. And his Japanese camera with photos of bridges and the airport. And arousing photos of Luo, out of place at the moment. It could all be retrieved in the Spring. Everything else was light, like the titanium ice screws he could plan on using. He had reduced the weight by close to half without including the heavy satellite phone needed to make a final call into the communications node before abandoning it as well. His message would be brief; he would be descending from the Nup-La the following morning and requested a squad to be sent up the glacier to meet him.

He knotted the large plastic bag and cached the stowed weight under an arch of boulders, closed the space with a third and positioned a slate slab on top. He laid the waypoint carefully into his GPS unit and re-shouldered the pack again, now weighing less than forty pounds by his estimate. He continued ascending the hard glacier for several hours until forced back onto the moraine. He had been moving at a forced pace since dawn when he left the lodge at Dragnag. Traveling at this speed was for younger men. After the strenuous passages back on the moraine, racing up little walls of avalanching sand and scree, mantling up onto rock shelves, working through ice chimneys, it had been exhausting. It was those cursed cigarettes. He hadn't felt this way in a long time, relieved that he would be in China soon. He would be a hero then. Slow down, he told himself. He thought of his family. He thought of his promotion in rank. He thought of the pills and Luo and the arrangements with General Tu. Perhaps General Tu could find the right buyer for the statue if he didn't melt it down. And again, he contemplated all the things he might do with the money. It would allow him to make investments. A woolen underwear factory in Lhasa. He knew where to buy New Zealand labels.

The glacier's eastern side presented complex obstacles of narrow steep-sided ridges of unstable debris, very different from the smooth gravel bench on the western side of the glacier where a near horizontal track allowed walkers to reach a viewpoint at Fifth Lake. There were few attractions to venturing on the glacier's east side, and he was still well below Major Wang's lowest waypoint. The lightweight GPS unit, key to route-finding, lay warm in his inside breast pocket. The footing was miserable, and at times he had to crawl over boulders while wearing the pack. Finally, he found a rising ridge of the moraine where he made good time and found an excellent viewpoint.

At eye level a crevasse field is difficult to analyze. While visible crevasses were navigable, hidden ones and detours were to be expected. From his elevated viewpoint he studied the crevasse pattern ahead where the main body of the glacier branched to the right. Through the binocular he tried to memorize the general layout. He turned to scan the great face of Cho-Oyu. And then turned again to study the route he had taken thus far.

He could see where he had dislodged a small avalanche of yellow sand which had spilled out onto the ice and marked it clearly. On the far side of the glacier he could make out the individual lodges in the hamlet of Gokyo, seven miles distant. As he rotated the view, about to put the glasses back in his pocket he thought he saw a glimpse of a moving speck and tried to find it again. Was it a raven? No, much larger. And then he saw him. About two miles away. A dark red color. A madman crossing the glacier. Who?

Immediately he regretted jettisoning the pistol. Was someone following him? The red clothing wasn't the army or the border police. It could be a monk. Was there a shrine this way? Why cross the glacier here? Some mad monk trying to reach Tibet, over the Nup-La? It made no sense. Or did it? He felt cold. Perhaps the Dalai's clique had somehow learned of his violent act and were sending an enforcer monk, a *Dob-dob*, to catch him and he recalled his boyhood fear. That was impossible, surely. At any rate the important thing was not to be detained. He studied the small human speck again. No sign of a rifle. It was crossing the great glacier just below where its two main branches joined. The madman must have gone to Fifth Lake and was now crossing over to the east side. It made no sense. While Thondup felt he had nothing to fear, he was a master of martial art, he regretted jettisoning the pistol.

He turned his attention back to the route, where he lost time occasionally at dead-ends where he had chosen a wrong direction. One either works around or over a crevasse, visible or implied. It was always a judgment call. A quarter of a mile walk might gain only twenty feet of forward progress. Should he take fifteen minutes to work around the end of a crevasse or do an instant leap across a three foot space without an apparent bottom?

Finally, he reached the *firn* line, where snow, the *nevé*, starts covering the hard ice and marks the low tide of the accumulation zone. Now he was on stiff snow and before long arrived at the lowest of Major Wang's GPS waypoints. He could see a small test ahead. A long two foot wide crevasse. The weight of the pack was unnerving. From then on he kept the rope's short remnant slip-knotted to his wrist with the far end to the pack's haul loop. Jumping crevasses was a desperate game and he had never liked it. Still, sometimes it was the smart thing to do correctly. Putting down the weight, tamping down snow for a running start and while holding his ice ax in self-arrest position leaping to the far side, anchoring himself and hauling the yellow pack across.

Some hours later the crevasses turned in a new direction, paralleling his line of travel for a while and took him up past where the glacier forked. Major Wang's GPS waypoints were becoming invaluable. The nGozumba's right hand branch now curved sharply to the east and there for the first time, above an ice curtained wall, the low-point of the skyline ridge between two peaks revealed the pass itself. The Nup-La 19,631feet. Immediately below it were the steep masses of the double icefall, bathed in a pink dramatic alpenglow in the last light. The fluted icy columns and broken blocks fell directly from the lip of the pass itself. From its top the West Rongbuk Glacier went off to the other side in a wide and gentle slope. He imagined alternate wordings of his account as he moved upward.

An hour later, in the growing darkness he pushed on by the light of his headlamp, pausing only to refill his water flask with a rivulet of ice-melt and to urinate. The base of the icefall was still more than a mile ahead on the hard snow covered the ground which now felt like frozen foam under the bite of the crampon points. The weather remained perfect, stars filled the sky before moonrise and it became colder and calm.

Another hour and he found a large slab of rock flat on the rubble. Close enough to the foot of the icefall and the start of high angle climbing. There was some time for a rest and food, with hours before a full moon rose above the surrounding peaks. The view about him on this clear night was so beautiful that it made him thoughtful, in a philosophical vein, about his deed in Lukla and the meaning of a human life. It was unusual for him to have such thoughts. In his military career he had taken a fair number of lives. What did one more matter? Only history mattered. The imperative of duty. He wondered how he could make a unifying connection between the extreme beauty of his surroundings and the recollection of his ice-axe penetrating the man's skull. Perhaps nothing was connected at all. And then his philosophical thoughts were interrupted by the recollection of the red dot moving on the ice and his boyhood apprehension of *Dob-dobs*. There was no reason not to feel safe. But the childhood fright echoed. Was that what it was?

He wondered if he still had a follower and searched for a moving object but didn't see anyone. Was he imagining the whole thing? There was a feeling of being pursued, but by whom? It was a strange presentiment and he couldn't recognize it; unknown, but with a promised familiarity, in the strangest of landscapes, as surrealistic as the supernatural wall paintings in the old monasteries. It didn't matter, how could a *Dob-dob* possibly climb the icefall?

Pemba's Gamble

Pemba had realized he would have to make a decision immediately. If the killer tried for the Nup-La could he overtake him? There was little point in going to the police post below the Nangpa-La, which was now reinforced, on alert, and with clear instructions. But that the murderer might try escaping by way of the Nup-La was just conceivable for an experienced mountaineer. Which meant that Pemba was in the wrong valley. He decided to make the move at once and started up a track that crossed the range and led down to Gokyo and the nGozumba valley. If he could locate the killer he would chase him, try to outpace him. And what then? Throw rocks? Tackle him physically? Though he lacked a firearm, his determination remained. Something would work. It had to.

Pemba crossed the range at the Renjo-La and came down towards Gokyo on the western side of the long glacier. Half-way down he paused at the panorama of the nGozumba, a half-mile wide, where above and beyond the intervening ridges was the southwest face of the mother goddess herself. Sagarmatha, Mt. Everest. He made a place to sit where he could rest his elbows on his knees, and searched the far side with his binocular. The light was behind him and he could see the lodge at Dragnag across the glacier.

The distant moraine was pinched in between cliffs of conglomerate rock and boulder filled shelves and in places the glacier came up against a rock wall to force a traveler out onto the ice to make a way through a crevasse field until regaining better footing. It would be slow going, full of small impasses, each requiring a work-around. If the killer had come from Lobuche and was heading for the Nup-La he would be making his way over that complex terrain. Pemba recalled poking up that way as a boy in Phortse when looking for lost yaks.

It took nearly half an hour of scanning before Pemba spotted him on the far side more than two miles further north. A tiny figure of a man coming out on the hard glacier, using his ice-axe as a cane, bearing a large yellow pack and moved slowly and deliberately. In another minute he descended into a trench and disappeared from sight. Pemba, having spotted his quarry, saw the possibility of overtaking him before the border, catching him in Nepal. He knew the terrain and this was his native valley. Glaciers were his familiars.

The moraine on the western side was more like a wide and long beach, with an easy near horizontal trail as far as the fifth lake beneath the south face of Cho Oyu. Years earlier he had worked as a cook-boy for a Swiss expedition there and now saw that he would make good time and could cross the glacier higher up with the wind at his back. And hours later he did cross it just below where two colossal branches joined, and the only difficult passage involved the central ridge where two ice streams fused into a main feature. Beyond lay the Nup-La.

In the fading light of dusk Pemba finally saw the Chinese spy's track for the first time and judged that he was within mile of him. The light was going but he could see that the ice crystals around the deep pits made by crampon teeth were still well-formed. Small steps, as if by a man carrying a load. Without any need to repeat his quarry's false starts, Pemba had the advantage and knew he would gain on him if he kept moving all night. And at length, hours later, as he neared the base of the icefalls he caught a glimpse of the killer's headlamp. Less than a half mile separated them.

The Icefall

Thondup stirred in his bivouac and looked at his watch-altimeter. He was at close to 18,000 feet, it was past midnight and he hadn't really slept, but hadn't been conscious either - only a suspended mind, awareness banked down. About three hours had passed since he had adjusted his body to minimal discomfort on the slab. He forced down the last of the potatoes and cheese and most of his daughter's sweets, and tried to rest in preparation for the day ahead, the icefalls, the crux of the enterprise.

He had judged it correctly. The full moon finally came above the surrounding peaks and flooded the challenge before him in a pale fire of sharp contrasts. It was time to move in the coldest and most stable hours, navigating with the technology of the GPS miracle. What a wonder that human beings could achieve this! China had more scientists than any nation!

He recalled the map. The contour lines showed the icefalls originating from a lake of ice. Above it a short cliff whose rim formed the edge of an undulating snow-covered plateau sloping gently toward the West Rongbuk Glacier. Shaped like a gingko leaf at its head it gathers its branches and flows down Tibet to join the Tsangpo, which the Hindus called Brahmaputra. Somewhere past the lip of the snowy plateau was a theoretical drainage divide forming the legal international frontier on a map.

The weather was holding and Thondup envisioned his descent on the Rongbuk. He would have to work over to the right hand side. Somewhere along the way his squad would meet him and would have hot liquids and would carry the load. It would work. It was so near. He could envision two stars on his collar one day.

Thondup was massaging his calves when he looked up and saw the pinpoint light of a headlamp below him on the glacier. A white dot of an LED bulb appeared and disappeared as it moved past rock and ice features. Was he seeing things? A reflection of moon on ice? But there it was again. A headlamp and unmistakable motion, and coming closer. His pursuer still! The old *Dob-dobs* fear came to mind again for an instant. Whoever was following him had to be strongly motivated. Perhaps he had underestimated the number of the Dalai's spies, sneaking into Tibet this way. The thought surprised him. Monk mountaineers? Was such a thing possible? He would have to assign this question to one of his officers. The man would be entering China illegally, and Thondup decided to order his squad to arrest him.

It was time to move. The moon had just topped the ridges and the air remained still. He shouldered the pack, which made him top heavy but there was nothing for it, and he switched on the GPS. The display showed the waypoint for the start over to the extreme left. He looked up and could see snow cornices, each resting on its own *serac*, and flutes of hanging icicles, like a giant pipe organ made of frozen water. He knew the hazards: going solo, overconfidence, bad judgment, bad route finding, slips on ice or rock, falling blocks, and fate.

There were really two ice falls, with an awkward little basin to cross, but the GPS waypoints were saving hours of probing and guessing. And so it went for a time, until the first serious problem consumed over an hour without much to show for it. A *serac* the size of a house had fallen during the intervening season and had obliterated a waypoint indicating a snow bridge. The passage looked dangerously unstable but had to be traversed. On Thondup's fourth attempt he found a route which gave him a sense of progress. It cost more than an hour of repeated trials to avoid the dead-ends and he knew his pursuer would have the successful way marked out for him by examining the crampon tracks.

He had been enfolded by this puzzle of the icefall like an insect that can't find the exit from a maze. Finally, there was a less than obvious twenty foot high chimney of ice on the far side of a crevasse which seemed the key to a clear patch. But first he had to work down. The width was ideal and crampons bit firmly to the sides as he descended and stepped onto a bulge extending from the far side and with both his tools pulled himself over a shelf which emerged on the top of an old looking bloc.

He was back on route and the next waypoint lay straight ahead. There he came to a snow bridge which crossed a terrible looking gap, but which formed part of the route. After traversing it he thought of chopping at it, weakening it to deter his follower, but training taught him it might not work and to harvest time and continue moving. It was hard to believe that the mad monk was gaining on him and might even reach him since the man didn't have a load and didn't have to encounter dead-ends.

And there it was again, the light of the headlamp, much closer now. Close enough, in the moonlight which washed colors, to see the red clothing. It was maddening. A *Dob-dob*, he laughed to himself. It didn't matter. They would both be in China before very long and somehow that would change everything. He had a squad coming up to meet him and they would arrest the fellow. No time to waste. A mist was coming in and the first grey tones of impending daylight softened the sharp contrasts of the moon's light.

The going became strenuous. He had traversed the basin which was strewn with talus half-covered with snow which involved treacherous footing. It took nearly an hour to traverse a hundred yards, and he was breathing hard, resolving once more never to smoke again. He suffered a false start between two waypoints. One section had him cutting steps where a giant slab had tilted. Another time, near the very top, he put in an ice screw and stood on it to gain the passage. He paused for several bitter seconds as he considered taking the time to unscrew it, but decided to race for the top, he could see the exit moves and knew he was approaching the plateau. If he had to confront his pursuer he would do it in China. On home ground what could he fear?

As he moved on he heard the sound of an ice tool, and once again saw the headlamp. In the emerging grey light could see the bulky scarlet shape less than a hundred yards below him. He could see the man's face, Tibetan looking and familiar, and he was gaining. Thondup wondered if he was hallucinating. There were such stories in the mountains. Who could it be? Some mad monk from that dead Lama's monastery? A *Dob-dob* with an ice-tool on a mission of revenge? Despite his considerable self-confidence the thought gave him a chill.

The upper fall had been more difficult at the start, but near the top it began to level off and emerged into a gully cutting across the highest cornice. As he neared it he could see where the lay of the pass started to flatten and a thin mist lingered on the far side from where the sun would come shortly. It took ten more minutes of careful straddling moves while using his tools for balance before his head emerged above the cornice. With a single move Thondup mantled one final time and stood on the top of the Nup-La and saw the rising sun's yellow disk rise through the mist as it came up above a far horizon. Under the weight of the pack and the lack of oxygen the effort had nearly defeated him and his breathing was labored, but he had surmounted the icefalls.

An undulating plateau of hard snow, riven by small crevasses, now lay before him and sloped gently to form the head of the West Rongbuk Glacier. In theory, he knew, there was an international boundary somewhere on this vaguely horizontal surface, the joke of a legal line in unmarked space. He rested a moment to catch his breath. It was completely calm as the rising sun was turning the grey mist into a magical golden haze. The seam between sky and land wasn't visible and all features beyond a hundred yards were obscured. Thondup could just make out a long canoe shaped crevasse ahead of him at the edge of visibility which sliced across his line of passage. There was no wind and a great silence. The Nup-La.

Crevasse

Pemba was amazed at Thondup's route-finding skill. It seemed incredible that he had proceeded so unerringly to find the stable route through the complexity of the icefall. All he had to do was follow the killer's unambiguous track. Finally, he saw the man surmount the topmost ice block and disappear into what seemed an exit gully. Pemba still had no idea of what he would do if he closed on him. A minute or two later Pemba emerged over the lip of the cornice and beheld the undulating plateau. He could see the killer moving skillfully amongst the cracks, with hardly a hundred yards between them.

Thondup concentrated on threading his way through the crevasse field, picking his route carefully and looking nervously to his rear as he worked around the corners of the cracks. There was no time for GPS consulting and another minute passed before he turned to see the mad monk in red emerge and start running toward him, barely a hundred yards separating them. He could hear loud breaths above his own gasps. They each tried running but were forced to stop to catch some thin air, their distance reducing inexorably by Thondup's age and heavy load. Then they both stopped and stood staring at one another, each with terrible looking ice-tools in hand, in a golden haze at over 23,000 feet.

Thondup could see his pursuer, a Tibetan face. Confirmation a *Dob-dob* was pursuing him. It seemed unreal, and he wondered again if he was hallucinating. There were more than a few such tales in extreme mountaineering. And then he watched Pemba do a running leap across a small crevasse instead of following Thondup's tracks which went around the end. *He had just gained a minute and was closing rapidly.* Thondup was now convinced at what he had just seen, the famous *Dob-dob* jump! If the *Dob-dob* came much closer something dramatic was imminent. There was no sign of a firearm and Thondup wondered if there was going to be a physical struggle in this strange place. Yet he felt very confident of his martial arts skills.

The *Dob-dob* was coming rapidly and shouting something and waving his ice-axe. Stay ahead of him, Thondup thought. It was almost like a boys' race to cross the nearly horizontal surface at this altitude towards where the slope began tilting down to the east, into China. What could this mad monk do to him? Another few hundred feet, at most. He would be home!

In the middle of the area ahead lay the larger crevasse, shaped like a giant war canoe. It revealed the pulling strain on the icy surface from the lay of ground below. As if the ice-crack itself marked the legal tear between Nepal and China. Thondup came to it near its middle where it cut acutely across the flat ground of hard ice and he estimated the gap at about a yard and some inches, the far lip somewhat lower above a vertical face. The canoe shape was at least fifty or sixty yards long and he could barely see the ends in the mist.

To stop here and wait for the *Dob-dob*? Would they have a duel with ice-axes? It seemed so. He took off the heavy pack and put it down. Now he could fight more effectively and confidently, and he was almost eager for a confrontation.

He had been an instructor in combat skills. The mad monk was coming closer and he could hear his heavy breathing and the crunching sound of crampons on hard snow. They were not many seconds away from a clash and Thondup reflexively took up a defensive fighting position, with both axe and ice-tool at the ready. And then he felt a sudden stab of anxiety as he realized that one end of the haul-line was tied to his wrist in a slipknot and the other end to the pack's haul-loop. His fighting agility was compromised but abandoning the pack was out of the question. There was only one thing to do. His body felt light and there was plenty of slack.

He turned and without hesitating prepared to jump. He had jumped hundreds of crevasses. This one, about a yard, was not so threatening even with the fatigue of altitude. No way to guess its depth, only a fearful blue edging to darkness below. Simple. An easy jump without the weight and only the haul-line to bring the treasure across. He had done this maneuver more than a few times on the glacier. The *Dob-dob* was shouting at him, an English word "Stop! Stop!" There was just time to do it. He stamped the surface to make a firm patch for launching his leap and looked at his pursuer for an instant, backed up some steps, held his ice axe in the cross chest self-arrest position and took a running leap.

Thondup saw a thin grey line on the far lip while in mid-air and saw his fate unfolding as his right leg sheared the edge and his front crampon points scraped the wall and flipped him backwards. He heard the sound of ice brushing his clothes. There were extraordinary flashes of light at the back of his eyes and the clicking sound of bones breaking, an instant of extreme pain and then darkness. Shock. Moments later he recovered enough to become puzzled at how shallow his breaths were. It was hard to draw a breath. He could taste blood running into his mouth and his nose.

Pemba stopped in his tracks as he saw the far lip of the crevasse shear and break off under the crash of the killer's leading foot. The front points of his crampon catching for an instant, scraping the ice and spinning him back upside-down. In an instant the man vanished into the crevasse pulling the yellow pack in behind him. There was a thump, a cry, and a moan and then silence.

Good Technique

Minutes later, in the brightening daylight, Pemba lay on his chest and crawled to the edge. He went through the protocols of a rescue situation and set up a solid anchor so that he could inspect the scene. He peered into the crevasse and thought he heard the rumble of water from a *moulin* far below in the darkness. Twelve feet down was a sight he would never forget. The man was moaning, his upper body firmly wedged into a narrow V shaped portion of the crevasse, torso inverted, legs askew, one crampon missing, one dislodged and hanging by a strap. The man's head was turned unnaturally to one side and folded to his chest improbably close to his waist, his spine and neck probably broken in several places. The ice axe leashed on the right hand was pinned by the torso against the wall. The man's left hand, the lowest part of his body, hung in free space where the crevasse widened and a rope from the wrist went straight down to a yellow pack twenty feet below. It swung slowly above a dark immeasurable depth.

Thondup knew he was going to die shortly. It was cold. His hat was gone. There were flakes of ice in his ear. Hypothermia was coming. Wedged so tightly he could not move or breathe or even locate his limbs. He felt amazed at what had happened and blacked out again and came to, and heard noises in his head, what he thought were crashing Tibetan monastery sounds of horns and cymbals and oboes and drums. Then there was a ringing in his ears, a hiss of water below, the glacier sounds, creaks, groans, rumbles, snaps, tinkles. It was a Tibetan orchestra, he was certain he could hear horns. Was it his funeral? Too bad about wife and daughter. General Tu would be annoyed. Something important was hanging from his hand somewhere but he couldn't feel anything and didn't know where his hand was. A ridiculous fate. Every part of him was numb. He could barely breathe and felt panic.

Pemba went to work quickly and reinforced his back-up anchor and was glad for the rope he had carried by default. He chopped a tear shaped bollard into the hard snow surface, hammered a snow picket into either side and equalized the resistance into a firm anchor from which he could rappel into the crevasse. He wrapped three prussik friction knots onto the rope and lowered himself over the edge until he drew even and locked off his descent. He saw immediately that the man was mortally injured, his face deep grey with dark blue lips and streaks of blood trickling from his nose and mouth. The eyes were half open and one pupil was noticeably dilated. Pemba managed awkwardly to place his ear next to the man's face. There were irregular shallow jerking breaths and very soft high pitched moans. Pemba spoke to him in Tibetan and tapped his cheek.

At first unresponsive, Thondup came into a dim awareness but he was seeing everything double and was confused and disoriented with a roaring sound of cymbals and drums once again in his head. He tried but could not remember what had happened. Where was he? There was a terrible pain in his neck and when he opened his eyes he saw a split image of the *Dob-dob's* face, lips opening and closing, staring at him. But he couldn't hear what he was saying. Was it a curse? The *Dob-dobs* had come for him and he had never felt such fear. The deep blue icy walls were beginning to spin, and he had a vision of the paintings of wrathful-protector deities on the walls of monasteries all over Tibet.

Pemba understood immediately there was nothing he could do. The murderer, the Chinese spy, would be dead in moments. He felt he should stay with him until it was over. Though the *bardo* story comforted the human desire for heavenly justice, reincarnation was not something Pemba took seriously as it made no sense to him. He tried to recall Dipankara Macleod's talks on *phowa*, the act of sending the spirit of a person at death's door to a purer land. He wasn't sure he remembered exactly how it worked to transfer consciousness from the mundane world of existence to the miraculous world of unborn existence. It almost seemed funny; it was really marvelous, attaining the unborn state through birth!

So he rested in his harness, hanging between the walls of ice and softly chanted the hundred syllable *Dorje Sempa mantra* of purification which he remembered from his boyhood. *"Om benzar satto samaya, manupalaya..."* and tried to imagine the spy-murderer's passage into the *bardo* state, the intermediate transitional state prior to re-embodiments caused by the past. Only part of him felt obliged to wish for the man's good karma in the cycle of existence-forms to come.

The man was dead. Pemba loosened the lock-off knot and lowered himself further into the crevasse to where he could take the rope holding the heavy yellow pack hanging from the hand. He felt the weight as he hauled it up slowly and swung it over one shoulder. He then untied the rope on the dead man's wrist and began the slow strenuous task of pushing the friction knots up the rope. As he came level again with the spy's body he paused to examine his pockets, and could only find the GPS unit in his breast pocket, which he took. It required close to half an hour to work the knots up the rope far enough to gain the few remaining feet to the surface.

It was over and Pemba realized he could return to another life. He thought of Annie immediately and wanted to be with her more than anything in the world, more than anything he could think of. Only to be in her embrace again.

Two Days Later at Tengboche

Two long days after taking his leave of Thondup, exhausted, unshaven, pounds lighter, and following his porter, Ripp half staggered down a long passage of stone steps to arrive at Namche's main street. Elsie and Wurlitzer were sitting on the curb at the entrance to the Khumbu Lodge. Embraces and congratulations all around. She had informed Washington. But it appeared Washington also had other matters on its mind.

"Someone was robbed and murdered in Lukla just before you all left for basecamp. Victim a friend of the Rinpoche. Name of Pasang Dorje."

"I know. We actually witnessed the cremation."

"Headquarters wants details on the victim and likely motive. Who done it? The Tibetan exiles are freaking out, which is freaking out the Indians. There's a Head of State visit up ahead so the Director wants us to be very clear on this one. It's a big deal if Chinese intelligence agencies are doing hit jobs on Tibetans in exile. If it's only a robbery gone bad it's just a police matter. So which is it? Uncle Sam wants to know."

"The Abbot would know the victim, right?"

"He might even guess the killer. Let me give you the news. We're flying there. Tengboche. The Defense Attaché's chopper is picking us up on the grass strip up that hill."

Ripp groaned, "I just came from there. Two days."

"It's a ten minute ride. There's nothing more here in Namche. They've reinforced the Nangpa-La and have security people at the airports. And nobody can find the constable."

"And my gear?"

"Bob's taking everything you're not carrying back to Kathmandu. We can have the chopper on two hours notice to fly us there." She tilted her head to look at him. "By the way, a beard looks good on you."

They heard the woof-woof sound and watched the clear bubble of the tiny helicopter approach and set down gently on the hill above the village. Ripp squeezed into the third seat while the marine pilot kept the rotors turning. He said the monastery's altitude was near the craft's operational limit. Minutes later they put down in the middle of Tengboche's big meadow to the fascination of a small crowd of trekkers and monks. After debarking its passengers in a downdraft the little air machine rose and dove into the gorge, vanishing quickly. The two visitors were shown promptly to Gyalpo Rinpoche and held their palms together, bowing slightly as they entered the reception room in stockinged feet. Cushions on the rug floor. The Rinpoche looking at them curiously and nodded faintly at Ripp who was at the cremation. It was such a sudden request for a visit.

Elsie started in colloquial Tibetan which clearly surprised the Lama and pleased him. She promptly offered her diplomatic identification card for inspection, which the Lama studied carefully, curious about the hologram. She and her colleague worked for the American Government she explained, whose diplomatic service employed many *dharma* protectors, and she extended her *bona fides* by naming several of her former teachers with whom she had taken refuge, and the several studies and translations she had produced. Would it be agreeable if they inquired of his knowledge of the murder victim?

After a pause, a sigh and a deep breath, Gyalpo Rinpoche replied in a slow and deliberate manner which Elsie translated for Ripp's benefit after an interval.

"He says he and the Yeshe Longdrul *tulku*, called Pasang Dorje, were boyhood novices at their root monastery in Tibet and shared years of friendship. Then, when Yeshe Longdrul was only seventeen he visited one of their other monasteries, where a Communist official defiled and seriously damaged the *gompa* in his presence. Yeshe Longdrul then killed the official without thought to what he was doing. As a direct result many people had died, monks and soldiers. He says after that Yeshe Longdrul gave away his robes and beads and fled to India, and came to Dharamsala using his birth name Pasang Dorje. He became a manuscript librarian in the Dalai Lama's household. Frequently in poor health, but over the years he did some scholarly work and made a concordance of Tibetan Buddhist technical terms." She turned to Ripp and added "I have it on my bookshelf. Never connected the name."

"Ask who would want to kill him? Who would do such a thing? Was he very political?"

"No, no," answered the Rinpoche, "he was just a scholar."

Ripp again. "Ask the Rinpoche how did he get so much money?"

Elsie and the Lama talked back and forth for several minutes. Then she gave Ripp a short version.

"Fascinating. Over the years Yeshe Longdrul became expert in buying and selling rare and ancient manuscripts. Some of them of a type called *terma* - buried wisdom treasures. At the outset to help other Lamas who fled with such possessions, but then started for himself. He was in a good position to know values. Some universities and libraries paid a great deal for certain items, so over many years he accumulated a lot of money. The Rinpoche says that when Yeshe

Longdrul was murdered he was on his way to bring his years of savings as a gift to Tengboche monastery. He had a cancer and no family. They were planning to build a Sherpa satellite facility and link it to the monastery website. The Rinpoche has letters and engineering drawings to that effect, many signed with the name Pasang Dorje. And get this, also he was coming to have a meeting with the Zone Commander. He says Chandra once saved Yeshe Longdrul's life decades earlier, when he was escaping."

"Ask him if he knows the purpose of that meeting?" Ripp urged. And there was another round of back and forths over a minute or two before Elsie continued translating.

"They were going to meet to talk about the future of Buddhism in Nepal under a communist government. Two monks were killed by a grenade near Thubten Choling, and the Lama says those cruel deaths awakened the Zone Commander's regret, his *bodhicitta*, his seed of compassion, and that caused him to write to the man he only knew as Pasang Dorje, who replied by suggesting they meet at Tengboche and exchange ideas. Rinpoche says he hadn't seen him in more than thirty years and was looking forward to the visit. But only his body came and his ashes now encircle the big meadow."

"I was there," affirmed Ripp.

Just at that moment there was a commotion of a man hurriedly taking his boots off outside the reception room. Then an exhausted Pemba, like a wild apparition, still in his parka, came in breathless and carrying a yellow backpack. He put it down and went to his knees quickly to perform three short prostrations before coming upright.

"The Chinese murderer and spy is dead," he blurted out. "He went into a crevasse on the Nup-La. And here is Rinpoche's money," and he thrust the pack in front of him, overturned it and emptied the contents directly at the Lama's feet. There were gasps, and while all eyes were fixated momentarily on the heap of foreign currency, Elsie came over without missing a beat and deftly appropriated the GPS unit which she held to her breast and said softly, "Pemba, America owes you for this. I won't forget." And she put it away.

Bravo, said Ripp to himself. The Rinpoche continued to look at the pile of treasure with his eyebrows knitted up and with the long nail on the little finger of his left hand he scratched his head and pointed to the half-liter flask of blue pills. What was that?

"That's also mine," said Elsie in Tibetan. "Woman's stuff." The Lama nodded and was distracted by the gold statue. He gestured to it, and Pemba proffered it with two hands. The Rinpoche took it, hefted it, examined both sides and grunted. It belonged to the lineage. Elsie asked to photograph it with her pocket camera. And as she did so she thought Pemba would treasure a photograph of himself with the Lama but was too shy to ask, so she suggested it herself. She had them sit cross-legged, next to one another, the Lama staring through the camera, Pemba composing his uncertainty.

Afterwards Elsie, Ripp, and Pemba came down the steps of the monastery and stood at the edge of the meadow as they went over the description of the chase in detail. He must be exhausted. Yes, he said, very tired but also excited so it was hard to rest. What were his plans? He would wait here until Annie's trekking group arrived, which could be later this day. After that he wasn't sure. Elsie and Ripp assured him that he had done a very brave thing and it would not be forgotten. Then she called in for the chopper.

Pemba went to the shrine room and sat quietly for an hour, filled with gratitude. He went to the kitchens, took some food, and emerged to sit on the monastery's stone steps and think how beautiful the world seemed, how extraordinary life was. Then he saw trekkers emerging from the rhododendron grove at the low corner of the meadow.

It was her.

Annie, in front of her group, saw Pemba loping down the slope towards her. They embraced with enormous happiness and he took her pack and held his arm around her as they walked up the meadow. She was alarmed and forestalled at his physical appearance. Are you ill? He told her of all that happened since her telephone call from base camp to Sonam.

Hours later, she had everyone in her group squared away. Finally, it was just the two of them stretched out in her tent, where they lay fully clothed and hugged and kissed and she told him straight out.

"Pemba-la, I'm pregnant." She paused, studying his face intently for the slightest change of expression and went on. "Will you marry me and live with me?"

Pemba then experienced something utterly new to him, not something he could ever have imagined: spontaneous weeping of joy. All he could do was nod his head and contain himself from laughing and weeping at the same time. He hugged her and kissed her ear. "I am so happy," he whispered, "you have made me so happy."

They heard the sound of a helicopter approaching and went out to make their farewells to Ripp and Elsie who were waiting.

Annie took the older woman aside.

"You probably remember me."

"Could I forget you?"

"I've got to attend my group so I don't have time to explain very much."

Elsie interjected, "Before you say anything I must tell you that I learned it was your phone message to Pemba that saved the situation."

"Just lucky that Sonam was in the Yeti office and could find him. Look, the reason I wanted to talk with you is that I'm pregnant, and Pemba over there is the father and I'm really in love and we both want the baby so I need to get my man home with me. Can you help? Can we get married at the Embassy and get all the paperwork done? I know two Wyoming senators who'll vouch for me."

"I love it! Of course we can help." She gave Annie a huge hug. "As soon as you reach Kathmandu come see me. I'll have everything arranged."

Pemba came over as Elsie was about to board the chopper.

"Miss Hornbein, I have something to tell you."

"Call me Elsie, please."

"I know you for a long time. From long ago."

"You do?"

"I was houseboy for Dipankara Macleod and you were coming many times. Long time ago."

"You! Yes, yes. Fifteen or more years ago when I worked here. You were always around, serving tea and listening to us talking. How you've grown! I'm so happy it's you. We owe you for what you did. I'll help, I promise."

"And we can visit Nepal many times?"

"Of course. I know you will be good for one another. Good for America too. I'm really so happy for both of you. When did you last see Macleod?"

"This summer. He's very weak and old."

"He showed us the way."

One week later Pemba Lodrup and Annie Wendover were married and witnessed at the American Embassy in Kathmandu. Elsie was matron of honor. Ripp stood up for Pemba, for whom a special visa was arranged at short notice. Is there an alternate universe where lives that might have been get played out? Or is there only our own, where there is no alternative?

Chandra's Fate

Chandra could remember the moment he knew he would quit the revolution. The report that two monks had been killed had turned him around. To Chandra it represented an insane loss of control for which he felt accountable. Monks! Enough. It pained him that Pasang Dorje's death was on his head, and would not have happened but for his letter. The revolution's tide of blood had gone too far. His day was over, it was time to vanish, to cut the rope to Marx and Mao.

Vanishing wasn't difficult. They saw him off, but instead of proceeding into the city, when he arrived at Jakarta's airport for the RIM meeting he went directly to the Garuda ticket counter and found a flight to Chennai. With his modest savings and Indian passport he went by rail to Karnataka and to the original Shankaracharya temple where the great apophatic guru preached the doctrine of withdrawal from the world. Was such a thing possible? He was determined to test it for himself.

He found lodging nearby and sat at the temple's *ashram* during the day and meditated, meditated on the self and on the non-self. At the end of three weeks he found it unbearable and decided he couldn't take it any longer. It did not seem possible to separate cause from effect, and no conclusion could be drawn. One thing appearing, another thing arising, that was all. And what to show for it? One valuable thing. That he was sick and tired of being iron-willed. As for becoming a recluse, retreating from the world, his stupid experiment, a mere three weeks long, one which he had idealized for so long, proved to him that he was incapable of it. Too old and too set. But it was a swift outcome, understanding he was permanently habituated to the restlessness of his own un-tethered mind. Just take the middle path he said to himself, be in the world, not of it.

Yet at the end of ideology, what to do? Just carry on. Attitude, he thought, make yourself a good attitude. He felt youthful, shaved his beard, allowed his hair to grow out and gained a few pounds. He felt the need to invest his energy in something. This impelled him to go to Bangalore, a proper city, where he found lodgings near the university and located a good bookstore. It had a kiosk selling India's English language newspapers, *The Hindu, The Times of India, The Statesman*. He felt like a young student. Free.

Without any intention in mind and mainly for amusement he started reading the classified matrimonial advertisements and began wondering if it was humanly progressive to advertise for a mate. The thought of a life partner began to grow in his mind. Something he had never experienced. Before long he defined his requirements and after an interview with Sri Lal Gupta he turned the proposition over to the man's well-known spousal search agency. Following some weeks they had a candidate. Her name was Devi Venkatesh, a dark-skinned widow of 52 like himself with two happily married daughters. She had a hawk-like nose and two naturally arched eyebrows. Slim. A cultured lady with no interest in politics whose late husband was a teacher of the sitar while she herself had once been a student of *bharatanatyam* dance and was presently studying vocal carnatic music, with no interest in politics whatsoever. She had recently sold the old family home and was living in a sunny modern apartment in one of the new tower blocks. The lady's family own several pastry shops and she is warm to his idea of a commercial partnership combined with marriage. To become a mature bourgeois couple.

They met and Chandra sketched out his business idea and showed her what he meant. There was an unused warehouse midway between the university and the new technology research park. If most of the painted brick wall in front was removed and replaced with large glass windows the spacious high ceilinged interior would become filled with light. They could put in pastry ovens and high capacity espresso machines toward the rear, arrange newspapers and periodicals for sale from all over the world on both sides, and fill the place with tables and chairs, even offering a few chess sets. A cash register and floor safe near the front and a pair of colorful finches in a decorative cage at the window so that a passersby would pause to look and see a beckoning interior and a clientele at ease. It wouldn't be difficult to manage and would throw off a steady income for years. Communism was dead and buried. Died without a crisis. Just died.

Chandra and Devi married in a modest Hindu ceremony. Once they became physically intimate she danced for him unclothed by candle light once or twice a month. It was always arousing and he thought of all the poor men in China who lacked a woman but used the *gumba*. It could make one crazy. He and Devi lived in the tower block. Their recently opened cafe was a quick success and became an "in" place. Devi went to her music teacher every day and kept saying to Chandra "why don't you write something?" He thought he could, in fact, write about a veteran soldier's change of perspective. He still had the man's card in his wallet. A memoir. There was no rush but he e-mailed him. The man was on holiday but his business partner replied. There was definite interest, possibly even an advance of some kind. Chandra promised he would think about it, there was no rush. Under Devi's influence he had become untroubled. Indeed he felt sane. It was a new feeling. He had never been so untroubled before. Was this there all the time? Devi's granddaughter was showing him how to use a computer keyboard. He had never been happier. A bourgeois man. After all those years.

Singapore

By early December Elsie had transitioned out of her Embassy responsibilities and was routing home to America by way of the planned stop-over with Ripp in Singapore for a long weekend. She felt open-minded about what was going to happen. A few revealing days, *a priori*, of nakedness, intimacy and exposure in order to see what was foretold in such a condition. They had meshed smoothly enough in the Khumbu operation, professional despite all the allusions. Now it was going to get very personal. It has to be B+ or better she said to herself.

Ripp met her with flowers at the arrivals exit and had his driver holding the car door for them as they settled on their seats.

"Would you like a bit of a tour?" he asked.

"I'm in your hands."

"In that case I'll take you home."

Elsie was impressed by the elegance of his accommodations. He demurred, it was government property after all, and he showed her to a handsome guest room with wide windows and an ample bath area.

"Why don't I leave you to unpack and freshen up? I'll be in the library in an hour or so and we can have a drink before dinner. Cook has left us crispy duck."

She came down in sandals and a loose cotton shift, he was in jeans and a white T-shirt, and he opened a bottle of champagne.

One thing led to another and before very long they had launched themselves to their first intimate taste of erotic love – filled with pig-like grunts and soprano moans. Filthy sounding by Singapore standards he thought. At one pause in their evening, as she drained a glass, Elsie became girlishly cheerful and clad in a thin sheet went barefooted to the guest room to retrieve something and returned to come alongside him. He lay on his back, feeling gratitude for what had occurred. Half-sitting Elsie held the flask of blue pills behind her back, and giggled.

"Guess what?" she said, rattling the flask at her rear.

"I surrender."

"What do we do about these?" she asked, and held it out.

"Oh God," he said, "I actually saw you take them when Pemba emptied the pack at Tengboche, but I figured you returned them to KK Pharma. Unbelievable! A thousand and one nights, I told the Colonel."

"Roughly ten years of Saturday night fun."

"I'll get a refill."

"You won't get bored?"

"I'm too old to get bored, sweet Elsie. It's amazing just to be alive and in one piece."

"You really want to do this thing?"

"I do."

"It looks so sensible. Okay. Let's get checked out at Walter Reed and see if we can pass our colonoscopies. Learn what the *haruspex* says."

"Come again?"

"*Haruspex*, a fortune-teller who makes predictions by examining entrails, guts. My PhD is technically in anthropology."

"Fly me to the moon. You're going to be fun to live with. I do love it. And I love you too Elsie." He meant it.

She leaned over and licked him softly at the corner of his mouth and let the sheet drop away.

Washington

Ripp came home. He had closed the office and turned the building over to the Agency security people in charge of facilities. He was leaving a fortune in Asian art which had provided pleasure over the years but he left the pieces without regret or desire. They belonged to the US government with the profits of his cover identity and would probably end up in an Embassy or the White House. There was also about twenty thousand Singapore dollars in the petty cash box which he emptied and had remitted to the Maha Bodhi Society of Calcutta. He arranged printed notices in Indian newspapers and *yoga* journals thanking Dr. Ripp for his gift to the Society. A gift which Chandra requested, and a justified expense. Someone else could take over the account. Give it a few more months.

At Walter Reed, after the colonoscopy he emerged from the dissipating anesthesia and didn't know where he was until he saw Elsie waiting for him to have a mandatory ten minutes in a recovery wheelchair. She had experienced the indignity hours earlier. No polyps or malformations found on either of them. They were good to go.

As year end approached, there was a Reuters report that a long term truce had been arranged between the Maoist guerrillas and government forces, and that there would be a national vote to end the monarchy and craft a new constitution. It was an upbeat ending. Elsie and Ripp sent congratulatory notes to various people they knew, with an underscored parenthesis warning that full integration of the militaries would be the key to stability.

A few days later at the small Christmas party at Berrigan's house the host clinked his glass with a spoon and stood on a stool by the Christmas tree from which he proposed they all drink "a toast to the forthcoming nuptials of two great people" which was greeted with a huzzah. Berrigan went on in his high-pitched Boston accent.

"I still have a few years to go before I retire and I look forward to the change of perspective it brings. I know that Elsie and Ripp weren't lured by consultancies or part time work so I'm sure they're going to have a new perspective on life. That's it, a new perspective. I'm sure you all can identify the person who said this. Quote: 'You know, I've come to see that violence doesn't really solve anything. You have to win hearts and minds to bring about lasting change.' Anyone know who said that?"

"Genghis Khan writing from retirement," a woman's voice called out.

"Buy that lady a drink. Just so."

On the following day a drawn-down cohort of Agency veterans was mustering out on their twenty-fifth anniversary of service. There was a reception which the Vice President attended. Elsie and Ripp were presented with citations along with a dozen or more of their cadet class. In a special ceremony they were given merit bonuses for one of the most valuable intelligence hauls of the year, the product of the Chinese Colonel's GPS device retrieved by Pemba. The software on the unit, though useful, was minor compared to where it led.

Using the coordinates on the GPS display Wurlitzer had taken a small crew of Sherpas to locate the waypoint on the nGozumba glacier with the Chinese character for "cache". After some hours of careful searching they found the three rocks that covered and framed a black plastic bag. The retrieved paperwork and satellite phone contents were exceptionally rich. By using the data coded on the phone the National Security Agency was able to penetrate a Chinese communications node which allowed them to peek at a gigantic data stream. Thondup's paperwork was equally valuable, as he had kept elaborate notes about Chinese plans for camouflaging military facilities in border regions. There was also the duplicate receipt for the mushrooms. And some astounding photographs of a naked Chinese woman wearing an officer's hat.

Beijing

General Tu's aide passed on the connection. Major Wang was calling from Lhasa. The *chungcxiao* cargo had arrived intact and was in a house not far from the airport. Communication control had relayed a satellite phone message that the Colonel would not be returning with the caravan, followed by a second message a week later that he would be exiting Nepal over the Nup-La and had requested he be met on the Rongbuk Glacier.

However, over a week went by without a word from or about him. A squad had been sent to meet him and operations staff tried to recreate his movements. Additional search parties were dispatched and failed to discover any sign. Crossing into Nepal and searching the icefall was too desperate and fruitless as monsoon had arrived and filled the crevasses with new snow and ice. Finally an official notice and lengthy obituary were released together with a posthumous decoration. The circumstances of the Colonel's death were confined to a single sentence, that he perished in a mountaineering accident while on assignment.

The Kathmandu newspapers had a report which raised eyebrows at several intelligence agencies, and was picked up by the wire services, that an insane tourist from Hong Kong had killed a Tibetan scholar in Lukla and had fled into hiding and was reported lost in the mountains. Rumors emerged from other circles in Beijing. An operation of some kind had gone wrong. Something about Border Command. Inquiries were reaching General Tu. Even Luo Ma, over at the financial department, had stood from her lunch table as he was leaving the officer's mess and was bold to inquire of Thondup. He threw up his hands. He knew nothing. At least they had the *chungcxiao* but the other omens didn't feel right.

A few days later the arrogant young Ke Zheng, the modernizing Chief of Staff to the Defense Minister, summoned him in writing and asked him to appear in person at eight o'clock the following morning. General Tu arrived in his best uniform and was ushered into an ultra-modern office where Ke Zheng was waiting, ready to pour tea for them at a low table between two soft chairs.

"It is so good to see you, General Tu. Our visit is long overdue and there are several matters that are worthy of our joint attention, and it will be good to get all this behind us. Recent events certainly catalyzed some important changes in the way the Minister intends to manage all of us in the future."

"Border Command will be solid in support."

"Ye-es," he drawled it slowly, "that's one of the things we should talk about. You see, we did put two and two together and grasped that your Colonel Thondup Gaomei, operating under his cover identity, stands accused of killing an emissary of the Dalai in Nepal. They failed to mention that in the obituary. It's a serious matter, don't you think?"

"He was a brave officer. One day we'll find an explanation for what he did."

"I'll give you the explanation right now. Our Spider teams have found all the evidence we need. This so-called emissary of the Tibetan exiles was none other than the mad Lama who killed the Colonel's father thirty odd years ago. Can you believe it?"

"So!"

"Exactly. What we're going to do is make him a national hero martyr. His elevation to Brigadier is being made retroactive, and his family will receive a generous pension. His name will be written in golden characters in the secret archives."

"I was honored to be his superior."

"Ye-es," drawled the Chief of Staff. "You know, the failure of independent intelligence operations to connect the identities of Pasang Dorje and the Lama Yeshe Longdrul, even though the data were actually in your files, almost in plain sight, was another failure to connect the dots. You see, there was another major operation that was taking place under your nose, from another department about which you know nothing, that went badly because their clandestine intelligence unit was operating with too much autonomy. Too much autonomy," he repeated.

"Please continue. I am eager to hear of this." But General Tu felt unsure where this was leading.

"For some years now it has been the task of a particular branch of the State Security Bureau, unknown to the Defense Ministry I might add, to run a clandestine anti-monarchy campaign in Nepal. The unit, a Spider unit, was tasked to take every conceivable opportunity to blacken the royals and their cousins, and it promoted the younger generation to misbehave in every way so as to ensure their unpopularity. They were encouraged to gamble and whore around and drink and use drugs and drive recklessly and to show themselves lordly as the monarchy's privilege."

"Not much encouragement needed," averred General Tu, cautiously.

"Precisely. Well, several operatives working as a team had befriended the young princeling with sex and cocaine over the course of a year. One day they had him take a pill of LSD and let him smoke a bowl of hashish laced with some other powerful mind-altering substance and then gave him a submachine pistol with an extended magazine and drove him to the palace gate. As we all know, he did the rest on his own, including himself."

"No loss to anyone, I think."

"Ye-es. Unless these things get out of hand as a result of organizational ineffectiveness. In this case the Spider unit had gone so far as to find the most extreme royalist faction, and convinced them, as a matter of high strategy, that driving a wedge between the Buddhists and the Maoists would work to the advantage of the monarchy. It wasn't long before one of the whipped-up bad-boy cousins in the guerrilla's Zone 3 caught the fever and conned a poor idiot into throwing a grenade at some monks in a tea house in exchange for a pocketful of rupees. Successful work by our own *agents-provocateurs* I regret to say." He let this sink in and continued.

"I hasten to add that such a provocation should have and could have been prevented. The point is that Border Command detected nothing of this though it has watchers throughout Nepal. A real failure on the intelligence side I would say. The failure to understand what was taking place resulted in the Spider unit's unsupervised manipulations. The Minister has decided there must be consequences and as a result we are going to implement the long-discussed re-organization of the services. The order has been given from the top and it would be affirmed at the next People's Congress. Border Command will no longer be a stand-alone autonomous force but will be integrated into Army General Command. Customs and immigration matters will be integrated with the appropriate civilian agencies."

Ke Zheng walked with him down the corridor to the elevators and they shook hands. Ke said he would call in a few days. For General Tu the meaning was clear: honorable retirement or a meaningless assignment to a dismal locale. Actually, there was nothing wrong with an honorable retirement from the People's Army, he felt assured. More freighted with loss of power was the required parallel retirement, on a point of honorable custom, from his position as a grand factotum of the syndicate. So be it. That was life. He and Madam would enjoy their golden years and travel a bit. More golf.

He had to get the *chungcxiao* and the tiger carcasses to Chengdu but the arrangements were simple and that was about it. There was this Major Lakpa Chodren coming to see him about being their man in Tibet, but the interview was for his successor now. He decided to go to his country house and inform his wife. She would be pleased by now that his career was over. Honorable retirement sounded sweet. They decided to celebrate at a famous sea-food restaurant. Several days later there was a call from a young woman with a lovely voice. She was an assistant to Ke Zheng and he had asked her to convey his understanding.

It was a lengthy and one-sided telephone call. General Tu made a long series of guttural grunts signifying comprehension. "Uh," he uttered repeatedly and once or twice grunted an iambic "uh huh" to signify assent.

Retirement. He thought of what it might mean. In military terms it was a campaign of holding out against attrition. He would take up *tai chi* and give up eating pork. Old soldiers never die, someone said, they just fade away. Too bad about the younger ones like Thondup.

Going, Going

During a rare Kathmandu ice-storm and the sound of a penetrating wind Dipankara Macleod went all the way beyond. The root cause was birth, the proximate cause was pneumonia. During the last weeks of his life the weather had been cold and clear and he had his bed brought to the place where the refectory table had once stood beneath the windows. For hours he lay propped on the cushions with life leaking out of him as he and the painted eyes above the *stupa* stared compassionately at one another.

It was a blood cancer they said. Not much in the way of pain, but incredible fatigue. And recently coughing and it being hard to breathe. The opium pills helped him sleep, but his mind felt clear when awake. There was nurturing help on call for a helpless condition. He had arranged it so. He could see himself going, the flesh, the body, sublimating into the beyond. An ecstasy of decay. The promise of liberation at hand. He felt he was at last being rewarded for a long and difficult life. Finally, the opportunity to slip off into the safety of nothingness. The brain clears. Pure white space. What an awakening!

Wyoming

Annie and Pemba went to live in Wyoming and made plans to install circular center-pivot irrigation units and experiment with potato varieties. Sometimes at night as his arm encircled her swelling belly they would remember how they met on the *Stimmgabel*. She recalled that the only reason she had been free to go climbing with Urs was that her clients for Island Peak cancelled because of a grenade attack on two monks. Nepal was becoming too violent they said. Pemba said he too had been on the mountain unexpectedly. A guide booked by the Argentines came down with appendicitis and Yeti travels arranged for Pemba to substitute. It was amazing beyond understanding. Random collisions and frozen accidents. To the extent they could intuit the boundless connections involved in all the things that always had to happen, their imaginations gave them vertigo.

Yet they stood on earth and loved the isolation of the ranch. With the help of Cruz and Maria, they mindfully tended to an old woman who didn't know who she was but was physically strong, and carefully tended to an old man who knew exactly what was happening but couldn't move. After a cycle of several seasons they were brought to a nursing home near Jackson, with a view of the Tetons.

Annie and Pemba installed a satellite dish for an internet connection and used Skype to talk with his cousins in Phortse. They enjoyed the physical labor required by the irrigation project and were planning to start a 'yakalo' experiment. On the whole they practiced slow organic food, slow sex, slow breathing, slow thinking and generally felt very peaceful and calm. Sometimes at night, naked, in the radiant warmth of logs burning in the stone fireplace, on a thick bison rug, they sat naked face-to-face holding one another lightly at the waist, his legs folded under her, Annie's spread upon him, practicing motionless pleasure. There was a way to go.

They named their first daughter Jetsun. Twenty months later she was followed by her sister Thinley. Annie was filled by motherhood. Pemba enjoyed becoming an agricultural entrepreneur. Far in the future Jetsun became a cell biologist at Columbia University in New York City. Thinley starred in an all-girl rock band called "City Life". But for the death of two monks these girls could not have come into existence.

Of what use can we make of this observation? Can it give us peace?

A Visitor at St. John

At the beginning of the year Louise Carol "Elsie" Hornbein and Harald Jan Ripp were married in a civil ceremony and life's next chapter commenced. Childless pensioners with savings, they bought a two-bedroom condominium, still under construction, within walking distance of the University of Virginia, in Charlottesville. After the closing they planned to spend the rest of the winter on St. John enjoying the fun of furnishing the new hurricane-proof beach dwelling, now their legal tax-paying residence. They were planning to visit Sicily in late April and intended to travel to Poland and north Europe over the Summer and the Mediterranean in the early Fall. And then return to Virginia to furnish the condo.

One afternoon in mid-February on their small beach on St. John, Elsie, in a cotton sarong, pencil in her hair, sat under a table umbrella's shade while proofing a translation she had completed recently. Ripp, in tattered shorts and barefooted, was belly down on the reclining beach chair, half-dozing over drawings for a wooden dock and a pair of moorings and they were considering a swim when the phone rang. Elsie took it as Ripp opened one eye. It was Berrigan calling.

"The National Security Advisor is holidaying in another part of St. John for a few days and would appreciate a visit with you about the RIM/Jihadi connection and another matter. He's a Presidential favorite you know, big on asymmetric warfare and what he calls 'banana peel' strategies; a big crook taking down financial markets, that kind of thing. Black swans. He wants to know if atheistic communist revolutionaries could agree on a war strategy with the Al Qaeda franchise. So he's coming to see you."

"When?"

"In about forty five minutes after I get off the phone. Will that work?"

She paused, took a breath, "sure."

"Adios. Have fun."

They had a quick swim, showered, cleaned up the remains of lunch and were filling the ice bucket when they saw the whaler approaching. The outboard motor cut and retracted as it nosed onto the beach. The National Security Advisor, originally a famous Russian specialist, had arrived with his protection, as foretold. He wore a floral shirt, an ancient panama hat and his linen pants were rolled up at his knobby knees. He held his sandals as he stepped ashore.

They had met before a few times over the years. Ripp liked him. He had endorsed and confirmed Ripp's authority to stop a special forces raid to rescue the Peace Corps Volunteer in Biratnagar. Great to see you again and so forth. Hoped he wasn't intruding. No. Nice to have a visitor. "Would you like some lobster salad?"

"Nope. Have a drink though. My guys there will start squirming in a while."

They made a round of rum and tonics and went into a serious discussion of a RIM-*Jihadi*st axis. The Advisor thought there were precedents for that kind of thing, the Mufti and the Nazis. A decision would have to be made in a few weeks. Did they think it was worth an assignment for someone, a full portfolio with a line item? How to search for such a connection? What kind of staffing? They talked around it for an hour, exhausting the possibilities, and twice refilled their glasses. The Security Advisor was enjoying himself and stayed for a final drink and his attention turned to sharing several inside stories in the end of the afternoon's sun. At one point he lifted his glass to them in salute for the capture of the GPS unit and the intelligence haul to which it led.

"Too bad that guy's recruitment went nowhere, but don't underestimate the power of a good idea. I'll tell you a story about Wurlitzer before I shove off. He's working in the 'Stans just now. Your operation in Nepal last October got us thinking about the use of that kind of incentive to gain support in rough places, like clan and tribal areas, where masculinity appears to be in crisis and, incidentally, women oppressed. Your buddy lit a fire under us."

"There was this Pashtun chieftain, a clan leader in his 60s, a patriarch with three younger wives. He knows every mule track in the area, and his village controls important passages through the hills. The guy is stand-offish with us, doesn't oppose us, but doesn't really cooperate."

"Wurlitzer is working with a NATO psych-war team visiting the village and asks about the man's big family, the traditional opening, and it leads to Wurlitzer giving him three blue pills, one for each wife. 'Try one of these,' he says, 'you'll like it.' God bless America."

"It works. Wurlitzer returns a couple of weeks later to a warm reception and gets fantastic information about Taliban supply routes and movements. Of course the guy wants more pills and starts to get real cooperative. So we figure we've got a couple of years until there's an actual market in the boondocks."

"Anyway, Wurlitzer and his team-mates start looking at the idea of using sex pills as behavior changers among tribal elites. Pharmaceutical enhancements for aging warrior chiefs with slumping libidos, you know it's a very interesting approach to making friends and influencing people like religious fanatics and opium lords. But they have the same needs so you find what motivates people anywhere. Flashy gifts lay one open to being an informant, which can get somebody killed, but handing out a few blue pills for home use turns out to be real currency. Particularly where the guy's got a few wives."

"Meanwhile our wise men who think about these things say that the hang-up which fundamentalist *jihadi*s have about sex and gender creates a dangerous masculinity crisis in Arab societies and the condition of women there is probably one of the explanations for the backwardness and overcompensated aggressiveness. A regular feature in the Arab press is a story about the Mossad putting something in the drinking water or in soft drinks."

A member of the security detail appeared around the patio's edge and pointed to his watch and the sky. It would be dark soon. The advisor held up a hand with fingers extended. Five minutes. He continued to his hosts.

"So now you'll appreciate that story because nearly a year ago, about 7:30 in the morning, I'm with the President in the Oval Office and he's looking over the summaries while listening to the daily intelligence brief. So he gives a single short cackle, which for him is what passes for a belly laugh and the briefer stops and we look at the President. He's fascinated by the footnote describing the plan to recruit a Chinese field-grade officer with a counterfeit Viagra concession. 'That's imaginative thinking,' he says. We should look into using that stuff."

"So the idea becomes hot, the briefer goes back to headquarters, half a dozen spooks hear about the President's remark, and one of them is about to shove off to Afghanistan and brings a bunch of blue pills at Wurlitzer's request. Well, I just told you the story of what happened. The next thing you know the Director gets RAND to do a study on the use of erectile enhancers in psych-ops; the National Science Foundation awards a grant to a brilliant investigator in the anthropology department of Stanford on 'Adaptive Response in Three Cultures: Ego Fragility and the Male Erection'; and the Census Bureau in Commerce is tasked to analyze the demographics of violence in societies where access to females is limited by culture or by skewed ratios of adult males to females."

"Then, months later, around the end of the year, the President gets to read your after-action report. Your recruitment idea nearly worked of course; too bad the target got himself killed. But it set the President thinking maybe there's something big that we're missing. He'd think about it at Camp David where he kept his books on evolutionary biology and got into it more and more. They both have advanced degrees, you know, and he loves outside-the-box thinking. Right now he's freaked by the ratio of men to women in China which he thinks promises major troubles. The First Lady even put together an informal women's group in the White House residence one day and decided they should push for social-science funding on the theme of erectile dysfunction – or should one say misfunction – and misogynistic societies."

"So by now there's an informal group which doesn't have a name and isn't on any organization chart – it could be too embarrassing. Almost twenty of us. Top brains. Anthropologists, statisticians, psychiatrists, demographers, a guy from the Chiefs, me, and your old pal, Berrigan. The subject is 'Erectile Dysfunction and its Relation to Military Violence,' I kid you not. The President wants to know if we can legally subsidize free distribution of erectile enhancers in a few backward international hotspots to see what it does. He wants to know if it will empower women, like in that Greek play. And he wants the Attorney-General to tell him if it violates any treaty on chemical warfare. You know, sort of like H.G. Wells' 'peace gas.' I just thought you'd like to know what you two characters unleashed."

There was a pause. Ripp sucked loudly through his straw. Elsie spoke up. "Where exactly are you planning on testing the idea?"

"Well we're thinking of Gaza. The gang at NSA tell us the place originates one of the world's higher hit rates linking to pornographic web-sites; they can even tie it to time of day; traffic peaks a little after 9:00 pm in case you're interested. So our guys think Arab society is a good milieu for this sort of experiment. Apparently while *sharia* is silent on the subject of erectile enhancers it does oblige a man to get his organ up for his wives. At the moment there's no telling how permissive their jurists are going to be. We need to find the Arab Bob Dole. Any chance the two of you might want to run a cultural operation? One year contract?"

"In Gaza?"

"In Cairo actually."

"Well, it could be a behavior changer," said Ripp. "Give them a new perspective and all. Make love not war." He bowed slightly, ironically, his palms together. "But we're retired."

"Just thought I'd ask."

Elsie and Ripp exchanged glances. She pursed her lips and blew a kiss to him. Saturday night was directly ahead. The Advisor stood to leave, staggered to balance for an instant as Ripp caught his elbow. He thanked them for the visit on short notice. Elsie held up her glass. "To any peace that passes understanding."

And they automatically said, "Amen."

Late that night he whispered, "You remember telling me in Bangkok about how everything's connected?"

"Uh huh."

"Must be true. The insubstantiality of it all."

"Feels good," she said, "loving kindness."

"Fills the void, I guess," he remarked after a minute's silence.

"Now you got it."

"Amen."

"Ah men."

The End

A portion of the proceeds of this title are donated to The Himalayan Rescue Association of Nepal. The HRA is a non-profit, non-governmental organization formed in 1973 to prevent and treat high altitude mountain sickness and related health problems in the Himalayas. It is supported by the sales of souvenirs and modest donations from individuals and organizations.

Himalayan Rescue Association
http://www.himalayanrescue.org
Dhobichaur, Lazimpat
P.O. Box No. 4944,
Kathmandu, Nepal
Phone: +977-1-4440292 / 4440293
Fax: +977-1-4411956
E-mail : hra@mail.com.np

Donations by bank transfer to:
Himalayan Rescue Association Nepal
A/C No. 11983 40
Nepal Investment Bank Ltd.
Durbar Marg, Kathmandu, Nepal
Swift Code Number: NIBLNPKT

CPSIA information can be obtained at www.ICGtesting.com
Printed in the USA
LVOW06s0513010813

345577LV00005B/12/P